THE PARIS REVIEW BOOK

for Planes, Trains, Elevators,

Also available from Picador

The Paris Review Book of
Heartbreak, Madness, Sex, Love, Betrayal,
Outsiders, Intoxication, War, Whimsy, Horrors, God,
Death, Dinner, Baseball, Travels, The Art of Writing,
and Everything Else in the World Since 1953

THE PARIS REVIEW BOOK

for Planes, Trains, Elevators,

and Waiting Rooms

⌖

By the Editors of The Paris Review

WITH AN INTRODUCTION

BY RICHARD POWERS

PICADOR • NEW YORK

www.picadorusa.com

Library of Congress Cataloging-in-Publication Data

The Paris review book for planes, trains, elevators, and waiting rooms / the Paris Review.—1st ed.
    p. cm.
  ISBN 0-312-42240-7
  EAN 978-0312-42240-0
  1. Literature—Collections. I. Paris review.

PN6014.P233 2004
808.8—dc22

                                                          2004044461

First Edition: July 2004

10 9 8 7 6 5 4 3 2 1

Contents

✣

ELEVATORS

WAITING ROOMS

Introduction

❧

We are living in the middle of an epidemic, one of those viruses
that we've spread everywhere, almost without noticing. Yet
we've adapted so well, it seems to have been with us forever. We live in
and around it, hardly even feeling its symptoms anymore. Like so many
plagues, this one is iatrogenic, medicine-induced. Our cleanest instruments have produced an illness worse than the one they treat, infecting
us with the contagion of *real time*.

In real time, each day's every transaction is listed on the global exchange. Strangers with whom we are inextricably linked buy and sell
futures on everything we do or fail to do. In real time, we are forever
losing massive fortunes' worth of squandered opportunity.

In real time, every second counts. Every minute must be maximized.
Since we cannot stop the escaping moments, we have our machines
give us the next best thing: two moments, crammed into one. Split
screen. Multitasking. Mobile wireless voicemail message forwarding.
RSS feeds. Picture-in-a-picture. We need miss nothing. In fact, we
can't.

In real time, every pleasure and pain plays out in public. Our most
intimate fears are blogged and annotated with real-time communal
comments a thousand times a day, retrievable anytime from anywhere,
at least for the time being. Everything we put our hand to is collectively
evaluated, its Amazon-user Stars continuously updated, in real time.
We are kept in every loop, current on every development: film of the

year, record of the month, personality of the day, scandal of the minute.

Real time guarantees that we're always reachable, always up to date, always immersed in the unfolding world image, never alone, never outside the surging current of data intent on moving us ever farther downstream. In real time, we live in two minds, three tenses, and four continents at once, and buy back the bits lost in transit with frequent-flier miles.

In short, we have grown so good at mastering time that nanoseconds now weigh heavy on our hands. And still, time stays, and we go.

Roberto Calasso: "Is this the prelude to extinction? Only to the superficial observer. For in the meantime all the powers of the cult of the gods have migrated into a single, immobile and solitary act: that of reading . . ."

Reading may be the last secretive behavior that is neither pathological or prosecutable. It is certainly the last refuge from the real-time epidemic. For the stream of a narrative overflows the banks of the real. Story strips its reader, holding her in a place time can't reach. A book's power lies in its ability to erase us, to expand or contract without limit, to circle inside itself without beginning or end, to defy our imaginary timetables and lay us bare to a more basic ticking. The pages we read are a nowhen, unfolding far outside the public arena. As long as we remain in them, *now* reveals itself to be the baldest of inventions.

How fast does real time flow? Clearly, one second per second. What is the rate of time of a book? Figuring that is like buying rupees on the black market: name your rate of exchange.

T. E. Lawrence: "I'm re-reading it with a slow deliberate carelessness."

How long does a story last? I know a story where a game of cards lasts longer than a life prison sentence. I know a story where the Hundred Years' War wraps itself up before the salad course.

Inside a book, we remember what we were born knowing: time exists not to use but to refuse, not to leverage but to lay waste to.

How long is an elevator ride? That all depends. What will you be reading on the way up?

So how would you like your stories ordered? Surely not by use, not by relevance, not by currency, not by net present value. Stories arranged by how long you have to read them: does that seem gratuitous? Consider the Koran, its chapters arranged in descending length, from those that last hundreds of verses to prayers of two or three lines: "To every prophecy is a set time, and in the end ye shall know."

So why not stories arranged by the length of available time? The length you might steal from the flow, and still get away with?

Proust: "But let a noise or a scent, once heard or once smelt, be heard or smelt again in the present and at the same time in the past, real without being actual, ideal without being abstract, and immediately the permanent and habitually concealed essence of things is liberated and our true self which seemed—had perhaps for long years seemed—to be dead but was not altogether dead, is awakened and reanimated."

We read to escape—if only briefly—the trap of real time, and then to return and recognize—if only briefly—the times we are trapped in. And for an instant, at least, time does not flow but is. You hit that last sentence, and look up: Humbert Humbert in the train seat in front of you. Charles Bovary beside you in the hospital waiting room. La Belle Dame Sans Merci checking you out as the doors slide open and you step off at your floor.

—Richard Powers

PLANES

Denis Johnson

❊

Beverly Home

Sometimes I went during my lunch break into a big nursery across
the street, a glass building full of plants and wet earth and feeling of cool dead sex. During this hour the same woman always watered the dark beds with a hose. Once I talked with her, mostly about
myself and about, stupidly, my problems. I asked her for her number. She said she had no phone, and I got the feeling she was pur-
posefully hiding her left hand, maybe because she wore a wedding
ring. She wanted me to come by and see her again sometime. But I
left knowing I wouldn't go back. She seemed much too grown-up
for me.

And sometimes a dust storm would stand off in the desert, towering so
high it was like another city—a terrifying new era approaching, blur-
ring our dreams.

I was a whimpering dog inside, nothing more than that. I looked for
work because people seemed to believe I should look for work, and
when I found a job, I believed I was happy about it because these same
people—counselors and Narcotics Anonymous members and such—
seemed to think a job was a happy thing.

· · ·

Maybe, when you hear the name "Beverly," you think of Beverly Hills—people wandering the streets with their heads shot off by money.

As for me, I don't remember ever knowing anybody named Beverly. But it's a beautiful, a sonorous name. I worked in an O-shaped, turquoise blue hospital for the aged bearing it.

Not all the people living at Beverly Home were old and helpless. Some were young but paralyzed. Some weren't past middle age but were already demented. Others were fine, except that they couldn't be allowed out on the street with their impossible deformities. They made God look like a senseless maniac. One man had a congenital bone ailment that had turned him into a seven-foot-tall monster. His name was Robert. Each day Robert dressed himself in a fine suit, or a blazer-and-trousers combination. His hands were eighteen inches long. His head was like a fifty-pound Brazil nut with a face. You and I don't know about these diseases until we get them, in which case we also will be put out of sight.

This was part-time work. I was responsible for the facility's newsletter, just a few mimeographed pages issued twice a month. Also it was part of my job to touch people. The patients had nothing to do but stumble or wheel themselves through the wide halls in a herd. Traffic flowed in one direction only, those were the rules. I walked against the tide, according to my instructions, greeting everybody and grasping their hands or squeezing their shoulders, because they needed to be touched, and they didn't get much of that. I always said hello to a gray-haired man in his early forties, vigorous and muscular, but completely senile. He'd take me by the shirt front and say things like, "There's a price to be paid for dreaming." I covered his fingers with my own. Nearby was a woman nearly falling out of her wheelchair and hollering, "Lord? Lord?" Her feet pointed left, her head looked to the right, and her arms twisted around her like ribbons around a maypole. I put my hands in her hair. Meanwhile around us ambled all these people whose eyes made me think of clouds and whose bodies made me think of pillows. And there were others out of whom all the meat appeared to have been sucked by the strange machines they kept in the closets around here—hygienic things. Most of these people were far enough gone that they couldn't bathe themselves. They had to be given their baths by professionals using shiny hoses with sophisticated nozzles.

There was a guy with multiple sclerosis or something like that. A perpetual spasm forced him to perch sideways on his wheelchair and peer down along his nose at his knotted fingers. This condition had descended on him suddenly. He got no visitors. His wife was divorcing him. He was only thirty-three, I believe he said, but it was hard to guess what he told about himself because he really couldn't talk anymore, beyond clamping his lips repeatedly around his protruding tongue while groaning.

No more pretending for him! He was completely and openly a mess. Meanwhile the rest of us go on trying to fool each other.

I always looked in on a man named Frank, amputated above both knees, who greeted me with a magisterial sadness and a nod at his empty pajama pants legs. All day long he watched television from his bed. It wasn't his physical condition that kept him here, but his sadness.

The home lay in a cul-de-sac in east Phoenix, with a view into the desert surrounding the city. This was in the spring of that year, the season when some varieties of cactus produced tiny blossoms out of their thorns. To catch the bus home each day I walked through a vacant lot, and sometimes I'd run right up on one—one small orange flower that looked like it had fallen down here from Andromeda, surrounded by a part of the world cast mainly in eleven hundred shades of brown, under a sky whose blueness seemed to get lost in its own distances. Dizzy, enchanted—I'd have felt the same if I'd been walking along and run into an elf out here sitting in a little chair. The desert days were already burning, but nothing could stifle these flowers.

One day, too, when I'd passed through the lot and was walking along behind a row of town houses on the way to the bus stop, I heard the sound of a woman singing in her shower. I thought of mermaids: the blurry music of falling water, the soft song from the wet chamber. The dusk was down, and the heat came off the hovering buildings. It was rush hour, but the desert sky has a way of absorbing the sounds of traffic and making them seem idle and small. Her voice was the clearest thing coming to my ears.

She sang with the unconsciousness, the obliviousness, of a castaway. She must not have understood that somebody might be able to hear her. It sounded like an Irish hymn.

I thought I might be tall enough to peek inside her window, and it didn't look like anybody would catch me at it.

These town houses went in for that desert landscaping—gravel and cactus instead of a lawn. I had to walk softly so as not to crunch—not that anybody would have heard my steps. But I didn't want to hear them myself.

Under the window I was camouflaged by a trellis and a vine of morning glories. The traffic went by as always; nobody noticed me. It was one of those small, high bathroom windows. I had to stand on tiptoe and grip the windowsill to keep my chin above it. She'd already stepped from the shower, a woman as soft and young as her voice, but not a girl. Her physique was on the chunky side. She had light hair falling straight and wet almost to the small of her back. She faced away. Mist covered her mirror, and also the window, just a bit; otherwise she might have seen my eyes reflected there from behind her. I felt weightless. I had no trouble clinging to the windowsill. I knew that if I let go I wouldn't have the gall to raise my face back up again—by then she might have turned toward the window, might give a yell.

She toweled off quickly, briskly, never touching herself in any indulgent or particularly sensual way. That was disappointing. But it was virginal and exciting, too. I had thoughts of breaking through the glass and raping her. But I would have been ashamed to have her see me. I thought I might be able to do something like that if I were wearing a mask.

My bus went by. Bus Twenty-four, it didn't even slow down. Just a glimpse, but I could see how tired everybody inside it must have been, simply by the way they held themselves, pitching to and fro. Many of them I vaguely recognized. Usually we all rode together back and forth, work and home, home and work, but not tonight.

It wasn't all that dark yet. The cars, however, were fewer now; most of the commuters were already in their living rooms watching TV. But not her husband. He drove up while I was there by his bathroom window trying to peek at his wife. I had a feeling, a terrible touch against my neck, and ducked beside a cactus just before his car turned into the drive, at which point his eyes would have swept the wall where I was standing. The car turned into the driveway, out of sight around the building's other side, and I heard the engine die and its last sounds echo out over the evening.

His wife had finished her bath. The door was just shutting behind her. There seemed to be nothing left in that bathroom then but the flatness of that door.

Now that she'd left the bathroom she was lost to me. I wouldn't be able to peek at her because the other windows lay around the building's corner and were visible, full on, from the street.

I got out of there and waited forty-five minutes for the next bus, the last one on the schedule. By then it was pretty well dark. On the bus I sat in the strange, artificial light with my notebook in my lap, working on my newsletter. "We've got a new crafts hour, too—" I wrote in a bumpy scrawl, "Mondays at 2:00 P.M. Our last project was making animals out of dough. Grace Wright made a dandy Snoopy dog and Clarence Lovell made a gunboat. Others made miniature ponds, turtles, frogs, ladybugs and more." The first woman I actually dated during this era was somebody I met at a "Sober Dance," a social event for recovering drunkards and dope addicts, people like me. She didn't have such problems herself, but her husband had, and he'd run off somewhere long ago. Now she put in time here and there as a volunteer for charity, though she worked a full-time job and was raising a little daughter. We started dating regularly, every Saturday night, and we slept together, too, at her apartment, though I never stayed all the way through to breakfast.

This woman was quite short, well under five feet, closer, in fact, to four and a half feet tall. Her arms weren't proportional to her body, or at least not to her torso, although they matched her legs, which were also exceptionally abbreviated. Medically speaking, she was a dwarf. But that wasn't the first thing you noticed about her. She had large, Mediterranean eyes, full of a certain amount of smoke and mystery and bad luck. She'd learned how to dress so you didn't observe right away that she was a dwarf. When we made love, we were the same size, because her torso was ordinary. It was only her arms and legs that had come out too short. We made love on the floor in her TV room after she got her little daughter down for the night. Between our jobs and her routines with the little girl, we were kept to a kind of schedule. The same shows were always playing when we made love. They were stupid shows, Saturday-night shows. But I was afraid to make love to her without the conversations and laughter from that false universe playing in our ears, because I didn't want to get to know her very well and didn't want to be bridging any silences with our eyes.

Usually before that we'd have gone to dinner at one of the Mexican places—the posh ones, with the adobe walls and the velvet paintings that would have been cheap in anybody's home—and we'd have filled each other in on the week's happenings. I told her all about my job at Beverly Home. I was taking a new approach to life. I was trying to fit in at work. I wasn't stealing. I was trying to see each task through to the end. That kind of thing. She, for her part, worked at an airline ticket counter and I suppose she stood on a box to accomplish her transactions. She had an understanding soul. I had no trouble presenting myself to her pretty much as I actually was, except when it came to one thing.

The spring was on, and the days were getting longer. I missed my bus often, waiting to spy on the wife in the town-house apartment.

How could I do it, how could a person go that low? And I understand your question, to which I reply: Are you kidding? That's nothing. I'd been much lower than that. And I expected to see myself do worse.

Stopping there and watching while she showered, watching her step out naked, dry off and leave the bathroom, and then listening to the sounds her husband made coming home in his car and walking through the front door, all of this became a regular part of my routine. They did the same thing every day. On the weekends I don't know, be-

cause I didn't work then. I don't think the buses ran on the same schedule then anyway.

Sometimes I saw her and sometimes I didn't. She never did anything she might have been embarrassed about, and I didn't learn any of
her secrets, though I wanted to, especially because she didn't know me.
She probably couldn't even have imagined me.

Usually her husband came home before I left, but he didn't cross my
line of sight. One day I went to their house later than usual, went to the
front, instead of around to the back. This time I walked past the house
just as her husband was getting out of his car. There wasn't much to
see, just a man coming home to his supper like anybody else. I'd been
curious, and now that I'd had a look at him I could be sure I didn't like
him. His head was bald on top. His suit was baggy, wrinkled, comical.
He wore a beard, but he shaved his upper lip.

I didn't think he belonged with his wife. He was middle-aged or better. She was young. I was young. I imagined running away with her.
Cruel giants, mermaids, captivating spells, a hunger for such things
seemed to want to play itself out within the desert springtime and its
ambushes, its perfumes.

I watched him go inside, then I waited up at my bus stop till it was
night. I didn't care about the bus. I was waiting for darkness, when I
could stand out in front of their house, without being seen, and look
right into their living room.

Through the front window I watched them eat supper. She was
dressed in a long skirt and wore a white cloth over the crown of her
head, something like a skullcap. Before they ate, they dipped their
faces and prayed for three or four full minutes.

It had struck me that the husband looked very somber, very old-
fashioned, with his dark suit and big shoes, his Lincoln beard and shiny
head. Now that I saw the wife in the same kind of getup, I understood:
They were Amish, or more likely Mennonites. I knew the Mennonites
did missionary work overseas, works of lonely charity in strange worlds
where nobody spoke their language. But I wouldn't have expected to
find a couple of them all alone in Phoenix, living in an apartment, because these sects normally kept to the rural areas. There was a Bible
college nearby; they must have come to take some courses there.

I was excited. I wanted to watch them fucking. I wondered how I could manage to be here when that was happening. If I came back one night late, after dark, I'd be able to stand by the bedroom window without being seen from the street. The idea made me dizzy. I was sick of myself and full of joy. Just watching for a glimpse of her as she stepped from the shower didn't seem enough anymore, and I left and went back and waited to get on bus Twenty-four. But it was too late, because the last bus had already gone by.

On Thursdays at Beverly Home the oldest patients were rounded up and placed in chairs in the cafeteria before paper cups of milk and given paper plates with cookies on them. They played a game called I Remember—a thing to keep them involved with the details of their lives before they slipped away into senility beyond anybody's reach. Each one would talk about what had happened that morning, what had happened last week, what had happened in the past few minutes.

Once in a while they had a little party, with cupcakes, honoring yet one more year in somebody's life. I had a list of dates, and kept everybody informed: "And on the 10th, Isaac Christopherson turned a whopping 97! Many happy returns! There'll be six birthday people next month. Watch for April's 'Beverly Home News' to find out who they are!"

The rooms were set off a hallway that curved until it circled back on itself completely, and you found the room you'd first looked in on. Sometimes it seemed to curve back around in a narrowing spiral, shrinking toward the heart of it all, which was the room you'd begun with—any of the rooms, the room with the man who kept his stumps cuddled like pets under the comforter or the room with the woman who cried, "Lord! Lord!" or the room with the man with blue skin or the room with the man and wife who no longer remembered each others' names.

I didn't spend a lot of time here—ten, twelve hours a week, something like that. There were other things to do. I looked for a real job, I went to a therapy group for heroin addicts, I reported regularly to the Local Alcoholic Reception Center, I took walks in the desert springtime. But I felt about the circular hallway of Beverly Home as about the place where, between our lives on this earth, we go back to mingle with other souls waiting to be born.

Thursday nights I usually went to an AA meeting in an Episcopal church's basement. We sat around collapsible tables looking very much like people stuck in a swamp—slapping at invisible things, shifting, squirming, scratching, rubbing the flesh of our arms and our necks.

"I used to walk around in the night," one guy said, a guy named Chris—kind of a friend, we'd been in detox together—"all alone, all screwed-up. Did you ever walk around like that past the houses with their curtains in the windows, and you feel like you're dragging a cart of sins behind you, and did you ever think: behind those windows, behind those curtains, people are leading normal, happy lives?" This was just rhetorical, just part of what he said when it was his turn to say something.

But I got up and left the room and stood around outside the church, smoking lousy low-tar cigarettes, my guts jumping with unintelligible words, until the meeting broke up and I could beg a lift back to my neighborhood.

As for the Mennonite couple, you could almost say that our schedules were coordinated now. I spent a lot of time outside their building, after sundown, in the rapidly cooling dark. Any window suited me by this time. I just wanted to see them at home together.

She always wore a long skirt, flat-heeled walking shoes or sneakers, delicate white socks. She kept her hair pinned up and covered with a white skullcap. Her hair, when it wasn't wet, was quite blond.

I got so I enjoyed seeing them sitting there in their living room talking, almost not talking at all, reading the Bible, saying grace, eating their supper in the kitchen alcove, as much as I liked watching her naked in the shower.

If I wanted to wait till it was dark enough, I could stand by the bedroom window without being seen from the street. Several nights I stayed there until they fell asleep. But they never made love. They lay there and never even touched each other, as far as I knew. My guess was that in that kind of religious community they were kept to a schedule or something. How often were they allowed to have each other? Once a month? Or a year? Or for the purpose, only, of getting children? I started to wonder if maybe the morning wasn't their time, if maybe I should come in the morning. But then it would be too light. I was anxious to catch them at it soon, because nowadays they slept with the windows open and the curtains slightly parted. Before much longer it would be too hot for that; they'd turn on the central cooling and shut themselves away.

After a month, or very nearly, the particular night came when I heard her crying out. They'd left the living room just minutes before. It hardly seemed they'd had time to get undressed. They'd put away the things they were reading a little while before that and had been talking quietly, he lying back on the couch and she sitting in the easy chair perpendicular to it. There'd been nothing of the lover about him right then. He hadn't seemed inflamed, but maybe a little nervous, touching the edge of the coffee table with an idle hand and rocking it while they talked.

Now they weren't talking, though. It was almost as if she were singing, as I'd heard her do many times when she thought she was by herself. I hurried around from the living room window to the bedroom.

They'd closed the bedroom window, and the curtains, too. I couldn't hear what they were saying, but I heard the bed springs, I was sure of that, and her lovely cries. And soon he was shouting also, like a preacher on the stump. Meanwhile I was lurking there in the dark, trembling, really, from the pit of my stomach out to my fingertips. Two inches of crack at the curtain's edge, that's all I could have, all I could have, it seemed, in the whole world. I could have one corner of the bed, and shadows moving in a thin band of light from the living room. I felt wronged—it wasn't that hot tonight, other people had their windows open, I heard voices, music, messages from their televisions, and their cars going by and their sprinklers hissing. But of the Mennonites, almost nothing. I felt abandoned, cast out of the fold. I was ready to break the glass with a rock.

But already their cries were over. I tried the window's other end, where the curtains were drawn more snugly, and though the view was narrower, the angle was better. From this side I could see shadows moving in the light from the living room. In fact they'd never made it to the bed. They were standing upright. Not passionately twining. More likely they were fighting. The bedroom lamp came on. Then a hand drew the curtain aside. Just like that I was staring into her face.

I thought to run, but it was such a nauseating jolt that suddenly I didn't know how to move. But after all it didn't matter. My face wasn't two feet from hers, but it was dark out and she could only have been looking at her own reflection, not at me. She was alone in the bedroom. She still had all her clothes on. I had the same flutter in my heart that I got when I happened to stroll past a car parked off by itself some-where, with a guitar or a suede jacket on the front seat, and I'd think: but anybody could steal this.

I stood on the dark side of her and actually couldn't see very well, but I got the impression she was upset. I thought I heard her weeping. I could have touched a teardrop, I stood that close. I was pretty sure that, shadowed as I was, she wouldn't notice me now, unless perhaps I made a movement, so I stayed very still while absently she put her hand to her head and removed the little bonnet, the skullcap. I peered at her dark face until I was sure she was grieving—chewing her lower lip, star-ing and letting the tears fall across her cheeks.

In just a minute or so, her husband came back. He took several steps into the room and paused like somebody, a boxer or a football player maybe, trying to walk with an injury. They'd been arguing, and he was sorry, it was plain in the way he stood there with his jaw stuck on a word and kind of holding his apology in his hands. But his wife wouldn't turn around.

He put an end to the argument by getting down before her and washing her feet.

First he left the room once more, and after a while he returned with a basin, a yellow plastic thing for washing the dishes, carrying it in a careful way that made it obvious there was water sloshing inside it. He had a kitchen towel draped over one shoulder. He put the basin on the floor and went down on one knee, head bowed, as if he were proposing to her. She didn't move for a while, not perhaps for a full minute, which seemed like a very long time to me outside in the dark with a great loneliness and the terror of a whole life not yet lived, and the TVs and garden sprinklers making the noises of a thousand lives never to be lived, and the cars going by with the sound of passage, movement, untouchable, uncatchable. Then she turned toward him, slipped her tennis shoes from her feet, reached backward to each lifted ankle one after the other, and peeled the small white socks off. She dipped the toe of her right foot into the water, then the whole foot, lowering it down out of sight into the yellow basin. He took the cloth from his shoulder, never once looking up at her, and started the washing.

By this time I wasn't dating the Mediterranean beauty anymore; I was seeing another woman, who was of normal size, but happened to be crippled.

As a small child she'd had encephalitis, sleeping sickness. It had cut her down the middle, like a stroke. Her left arm was almost useless. She could walk, but she dragged her left leg, swinging it around from behind her with every step. When she was excited, which was especially the case when she made love, the paralyzed arm would start to quiver and then rise up, float upward, in a miraculous salute. She'd begin to swear like a sailor, cursing out of the side of her mouth, the side that wasn't thick with paralysis.

I stayed at her studio apartment once or twice a week, all the way through to morning. I almost always woke up before she did. Usually I worked on the newsletter for Beverly Home, while outside, in the desert clarity, people splashed in the apartment complex's tiny swimming pool. I sat at her dining table with pen and paper and consulted my notes, writing, "Special announcement! On Saturday, April 25th, at 6:30 P.M., a group from the Southern Baptist Church in Tollson will be putting on a Bible pageant for Beverly Home residents. It should be inspiring—don't miss it!"

She'd lie in bed awhile, trying to stay asleep, clinging to that other world. But soon she'd get up, galumphing toward the bathroom with the sheet half wrapped around her and trailing her wildly orbiting leg. For the first few minutes after she got up in the morning her paralysis was quite a bit worse. It was unwholesome, and very erotic.

Once she was up we'd drink coffee, instant coffee with low-fat milk, and she'd tell me about all the boyfriends she'd had. She'd had more boyfriends than anybody I'd ever heard of. Most of them had been given short lives.

I liked the time we spent in her kitchen those mornings. She liked it, too. Usually we were naked. Her eyes shed a certain brightness while she talked. And then we made love.

Her sofa bed was two steps from the kitchen. We'd take those steps and lie down. Ghosts and sunshine hovered around us. Memories, loved ones, everyone was watching. She'd had one boyfriend who was killed by a train—stalled on the tracks and thinking he could get his motor firing before the engine caught him, but he was wrong. Another fell through a thousand evergreen boughs in the North Arizona mountains, a tree surgeon or someone along those lines, and crushed his head. Two died in the Marines, one in Vietnam and the other, a younger boy, in an unexplained one-car accident just after basic training. Two black men: One died of too many drugs and another was shanked in prison—that means stabbed with a weapon from the woodworking shop. Most of these people, by the time they were dead, had long since left her to travel down their lonely paths. People just like us, but unluckier. I was full of a sweet pity for them as we lay in the sunny little room, sad that they would never live again, drunk with sadness, I couldn't get enough of it.

During my regular hours at Beverly Home, the full-time employees had their shift change, and a lot of them congregated, coming and going, in the kitchen, where the time clock was. I often went in there and flirted with some of the beautiful nurses. I was just learning to live sober and in fact I was often confused, especially because some Antabuse I was taking was having a very uncharacteristic effect on me. Sometimes I heard voices muttering in my head, and a lot of the time the world seemed to smolder around its edges. But I was in a little better physical shape every day, I was getting my looks back, and my spirits were rising, and this was all in all a happy time for me.

All these weirdos, and me getting a little better every day right in the midst of them. I had never known, never even imagined for a heartbeat, that there might be a place for people like us.

Issue 124, 1992

Junot Díaz

✠

Edison, New Jersey

The first time we try to deliver the Gold Crown the lights are on in the house but no one lets us in. I bang on the front door and Wayne hits the back and I can hear our double drum shaking the windows like bass. Right then I have this feeling that someone is inside, laughing at us.

This guy better have a good excuse, Wayne says, lumbering around the newly planted rose hips. This is bullshit.

You're telling me, I say but Wayne's the one who takes this job too seriously; he pounds some more on the door, his face jiggling. A couple of times he raps carefully on the windows, tries squinting through the curtains. I take a more philosophical approach: I walk over to the ditch that has been cut next to the road and sit down. A drainage pipe half-filled with water. I smoke and watch a mama duck and her three ducklings scavenge the grassy bank and then float downstream like they're on the same string. Beautiful, I say but Wayne doesn't hear. He's banging on the door with the staple gun.

At nine Wayne picks me up at the showroom and by then I have our route planned out. The order forms tell me everything I need to know about the customers we'll be dealing with that day. If someone is just getting a 52" card table delivered then you know they aren't going to be too much hassle but they also aren't going to tip. Those are your Spotswood, Sayreville and Perth Amboy deliveries. The pool tables though go north to the rich suburbs, to Livingston, Ridgewood, Bedminster. And lots go out to Long Island.

You should see our customers. Doctors, diplomats, surgeons, presidents of universities, people who dress in slacks and silk tops, who sport thin watches you could trade in for a car, who wear comfortable leather shoes. Most of them prepare for us by laying down a path of yesterday's *Washington Post* from the front door to the game room. I make them pick it all up. I say: Carajo, what if we slip? Do you know what two hundred pounds of slate could do to a floor? The threat of property damage puts the chop-chop in their step. The best customers bring us water and leave us alone until the bill has to be signed. Few have offered us more, though a dentist from Ghana once gave us a six-pack of Heineken while we worked.

Sometimes the customer has to jet to the store for cat food or for a newspaper while we're in the middle of a job. I'm sure you'll be all right, they say. They never sound too sure. Of course, I say. Just show us where the silver's at. The customers ha-ha and we ha-ha and then they agonize over leaving, linger by the front door, trying to memorize everything they own, as if they don't know where to find us, whom we work for.

Once they're gone, I don't have to worry about anyone bothering me. I put down the ratchet, crack my knuckles and explore, usually when Wayne is smoothing out the felt and I can't help. I take cookies from the kitchen, razors from the bathroom cabinets. Some of these houses have twenty, thirty rooms. I often count and on the ride back figure out how much loot it would take to fill all that space up with cherrywood tables, Federal blue carpets and ottomans. I've been caught roaming around plenty of times but you'd be surprised how quickly someone believes you're looking for the bathroom if you don't jump when you're discovered, if you just say, Howdy.

After the paperwork's been signed, I have a decision to make. If the customer has been good and tipped well, we call it even and leave. If the customer has been an ass—maybe they yelled at us, maybe they let their kids throw golf balls at us—I ask for the bathroom. Wayne will pretend that he hasn't seen this before; he'll count the drill bits while the customer (or their maid) guides the vacuum over the floor. Excuse me, I say. I let them show me to the bathroom (usually I already know) and once the door is shut I cram bubble bath drops into my pockets and throw fist-sized wads of toilet paper into the toilet. I take a dump if I can and leave that for them.

Most of the time Wayne and I work well together. He's the driver and the money man and I do the lifting and handle the assholes. Today we're on our way to Lawrenceville and he wants to talk to me about Charlene, one of the showroom girls, the one with the blow-job lips. I haven't wanted to talk about women in months, not since the girlfriend.

I really want to pile her, he tells me. Maybe on one of the Madisons.

Man, I say, cutting my eyes towards him. Don't you have a wife or something?

He gets quiet. I'd still like to pile her, he says defensively.

And what will that do?

Why does it have to *do* anything?

Twice this year Wayne's cheated on his wife and I've heard it all, the before and the after. The last time his wife nearly tossed his ass out to the dogs. Neither of the women seemed worth it to me. One of them was even younger than Charlene. Wayne can be a moody guy and to-night is one of those nights; he slouches in the driver's seat and swerves through traffic, riding other people's bumpers like I've told him not to do. I don't need a collision or a four-hour silent treatment so I try to forget that I think his wife is good people and ask him if Charlene's given him any signals.

He slows the truck down. Signals like you wouldn't believe, he says.

On the days we have no deliveries the boss has us working at the show-room, selling cards and poker chips and Mankala boards. Wayne spends his time skeezing on the salesgirls and dusting shelves. He's a big goofy guy—I don't understand why the girls dig his shit. The boss keeps me in the front of the store, away from the pool tables. He knows I'll talk to the customers, tell them not to buy the cheap models. I'll say shit like, Stay away from those Bristols. Wait until you can get some-thing real. Only when he needs my Spanish will he let me help on a sale. Since I'm no good at cleaning or selling slot machines I slouch behind the front register and steal. I don't ring anything up and pocket what comes in. I don't tell Wayne. He's too busy running his fingers through his beard, keeping the waves on his nappy head in order. A hundred-buck haul's not unusual for me and back in the day, when the girlfriend used to pick me up, I'd buy her anything she wanted, dresses, silver rings, lingerie. Sometimes I blew it all on her. She didn't like the stealing but hell, we weren't made out of loot and I liked going into a place and saying, Jeva, pick out anything, it's yours. This was the closest I've come to feeling rich.

Nowadays I take the bus home and the cash stays with me. I sit next to this three-hundred-pound rock-and-roll chick who washes dishes at the Friendly's. She tells me about the roaches she kills with her water nozzle. Boils the wings right off them. On Thursday I buy myself lottery tickets—ten Quick Picks and a couple of Pick-Fours. I don't bother with the little stuff.

The second time we bring the Gold Crown the heavy curtain next to the door swings up like a Spanish fan. A woman stares at me and Wayne's too busy knocking to see. Muñeca, I say. She's black and unsmiling and then the curtain drops between us, a whisper on the glass. She had on a T-shirt that said NO PROBLEM and didn't look like she owned the place. She looked more like the help and couldn't have been older than twenty and from the thinness of her face I pictured the rest of her skinny. We stared at each other for a second at the most, not enough for me to notice the shape of her ears or if her lips were chapped. I've fallen in love on less.

Later in the truck, on the way back to the showroom Wayne mutters, This guy is dead. I mean it.

The girlfriend calls sometimes but not often. She has found herself a new boyfriend, some zángano who works at a record store. *Dan* is his name and the way she says it, so painfully gringo, makes the corners of my eyes close. The clothes that I'm sure this guy tears from her when they both get home from work—the chokers, the rayon skirts from the Warehouse, the lingerie—I bought with stolen money and I'm glad that none of it was earned straining my back against hundreds of pounds of raw rock. I'm glad for that.

The last time I saw her in person was in Hoboken; she was with *Dan* and hadn't yet told me about him and hurried across the street in her high clogs to avoid me and my boys, all of whom could sense me turning, turning into the motherfucker who'll put a fist through anything. She flung one hand in the air but didn't stop. Before that, before the zángano, I went to her house and her parents asked me how business was, as if I balanced the books or something. Business is outstanding, I said.

That's really wonderful to hear, the father said.

You betcha.

He asks me to help him mow his lawn and while we're dribbling clear gas into the tank he offers me a job. Utilities, he says, is nothing to be ashamed of.

Later the parents go to the den to watch the Giants lose and she takes me into her bathroom. She puts on her makeup because we're going to a movie. As friends. If I had your eyelashes, I'd be famous, she tells me. The Giants start losing real bad. I still love you, she says and I'm embarrassed for the two of us, the way I'm embarrassed at those afternoon talk shows where broken couples and unhappy families let their hearts hang out.

We're friends, I say and Yes, she says, yes we are.

There's not much space so I have to put my heels on the edge of the bathtub. The cross I've given her dangles down on its silver chain so I put the cross in my mouth to keep it from poking me in the eye. By the time we finish my legs are bloodless, broomsticks inside my rolled-down baggies and while her breathing gets smaller and smaller against my neck, she says, I do, I still do.

Each payday I take out the old calculator and figure how long it would take me to buy a pool table honestly. A top of the line, three-piece slate affair doesn't come cheap. You have to buy sticks and balls and chalk and a score keeper and triangles and French tips if you're a fancy

shooter. Two and a half years if I give up buying underwear and eat
only pasta but even this figure's bogus. Money has never stuck to me; it
trails away like piles of dry leaves.

Most people don't realize how amazing pool tables are. Yes, tables
have bolts and staples on the rails but these suckers hold together
mostly by gravity and the precision of their construction. If you treat a
good table right it will outlast you. Believe me. Cathedrals are built like
that. There are Incan roads in the Andes that even today you couldn't
work a knife between two of the cobblestones. The sewers that the Romans built in Bath, England, were so good that they weren't replaced
until the 1950s. That's the sort of thing I can admire.

These days I can build a table with my eyes closed and depending
on how rushed we are I might build the table alone, let Wayne watch
until I need help putting on the slate. It's better when the customers
stay out of our faces, how they react when we're done, they run fingers
on the lacquered rails and suck in their breath, the felt so tight over the
slate you couldn't pluck it if you tried. Beautiful, is what they say and
we always nod, talc on our fingers, nod again, a bit wistfully.

The boss nearly kicked our asses over the Gold Crown. The customer,
an asshole named Pruitt, called up crazy, said we were delinquent.
That's how the boss put it. Delinquent. So we knew that's what the customer called us because the boss doesn't use words like that. Look boss,
I said, we knocked like crazy. I mean, we knocked like federal marshals.
Like Paul Bunyan. The boss wasn't having it. You fuckos, he said. You
butthogs. He tore into us for a good two minutes and then *dismissed* us.
For most of that night I didn't think I had a job so I hit the bars, fanta-
sizing that I would bump into this cabrón out with that black woman
while me and my boys were cranked but the next morning Wayne came
by with that Gold Crown again. Both of us had hangovers. One more
time, he said. An extra delivery, no overtime. We hammered on the
door for ten minutes but no one answered. I jimmied with the windows
and the back door and I could have sworn I heard her behind the patio
door. I knocked hard and heard footsteps.

We called the boss and told him what was what and the boss called the house but no one answered. Okay, the boss said. Get those card tables done. That night as we lined up the next day's paperwork we got a call from Pruitt and he didn't use the word delinquent. He wanted us to come late at night but we were booked. Two-month waiting list, the boss reminded him. I looked over at Wayne and wondered how much money this guy was pouring into the boss's ear. Pruitt said he was *contrite* and *determined* and asked us to come again. His maid was sure to let us in.

What the hell kind of name is Pruitt anyway? Wayne asks me when we swing onto the Parkway.

Pato name, I say. Anglic or some other bog people.

Probably a fucking banker. What's the first name?

Just an initial, C. Clarence Pruitt sounds about right.

Yeah, Clarence, Wayne yuks.

Pruitt. Most of our customers have names like this, court case names: Wooley, Maynard, Gass, Binder, but the people from my town, our names, you see on convicts or coupled together on boxing cards.

This time we take our time. We go to the Rio Diner. We blow an hour and all the dough we have in our pockets. Wayne is talking about Charlene and I'm leaning my head against a thick pane of glass.

Pruitt's neighborhood has recently gone up and only his court is complete. Gravel roams off this way and that, shaky. You can see inside the other houses, their newly formed guts, nailheads bright and sharp on the fresh timber. Wrinkled blue tarps protect wiring and fresh plaster. The driveways are mud and on each lawn stand huge stacks of sod. We park in front of Pruitt's house and bang on the door. I give Wayne a hard look when I see no car in the garage.

Yes? I hear a voice inside say.

We're the delivery guys, I yell.

A bolt slides, a lock turns, the door opens. She stands in our way, wearing black shorts and a gloss of red on her lips and I'm sweating.

Come in, yes? She stands back from the door, holding it open.

Sounds like Spanish, Wayne says.

No shit, I say, switching over. Do you remember me?

No, she says.

I look over at Wayne. Can you believe this?

I can believe anything, kid.

You heard us, didn't you? The other day, that was you.

She shrugs and opens the door wider.

You better tell her to prop that with a chair. Wayne heads back to unlock the truck.

You hold that door, I say.

We've had our share of delivery trouble. Trucks break down. Customers move and leave us with an empty house. Handguns get pointed. Slate gets dropped, a rail goes missing. The felt is the wrong color, the Dufferins get left in the warehouse. Back in the day the girlfriend and I made a game of this. A prediction game. In the mornings I rolled onto my pillow and said, What's today going to be like?

Let me check. She put her fingers up to her widow's peak and that motion would shift her breasts, her hair. We never slept under any covers, not in spring, fall or summer and our bodies were dark and thin the whole year.

I see an asshole customer, she murmured. Unbearable traffic. Wayne's going to work slow. And then you'll come home to me.

Will I get rich?

You'll come home to me. That's the best I can do. And then we'd kiss hungrily because this was how we loved each other.

The game was part of our mornings, the way our showers and our sex and breakfasts were. We stopped playing only when it started to go wrong for us, when I'd wake up and listen to the traffic outside without waking her, when everything was a fight.

She stays in the kitchen while we work. I can hear her humming. Wayne's shaking his right hand frantically like he's scalded his fingertips. Yes, she's a hottie. She has her back to me, her hands stirring around in a full sink, when I walk in.

I try to sound conciliatory. You're from the city?
A nod.
Where about?
Washington Heights.
Dominicana. Quisqueyana. She nods. What street?
I don't know the address. I have it written down. My mother and my brothers live there.
I'm Dominican, I say.
You don't look it.
I get a glass of water. We're both staring out at the muddy lawn.
I didn't answer the door because I wanted to piss him off.
Piss who off?
I want to get out of here, she says.
Out of here?
I'll pay you for a ride.
I don't think so, I say.
Aren't you from Nueva York?
No.
Then why did you ask the address?
Why? I have family near there.
Would it be that big of a problem?
I say in English that she should have her boss bring her but she stares blank at me. I switch over.
He's a pendejo, she says, suddenly angry. I put down the glass, move next to wash it. She's exactly my height and smells of liquid detergent and has tiny beautiful moles on her neck, an archipelago leading down into her clothes.
Here, she says; putting out her hand but I finish and go back to the den.
Do you know what she wants us to do? I say to Wayne.

Her room is upstairs, a bed, a closet, a dresser, yellow wallpaper. Spanish *Cosmo* and *El Diario* thrown on the floor. Four hangers worth of clothes in the closet and only the top drawer of the dresser is full. I put my hand on the bed and the cotton sheets are cool.

Pruitt has pictures of himself in his room. He's tan and probably has been to more countries than I know capitals for. Photos of him on vacations, on beaches, standing beside a wide-mouth Pacific salmon he has hooked. The size of his dome would make a phrenologist proud. The bed is made and his wardrobe spills out onto chairs and a line of dress shoes follows the far wall. A bachelor. I find an open box of Trojans in his dresser beneath a stack of boxer shorts. I put one of the condoms in my pocket and stick the rest under his bed.

I find her in her room. He likes clothes, she says.

A habit of money, I say but I can't translate it right; I end up agreeing with her. Are you going to need to pack?

She holds up her purse. I have everything I need. He can keep the rest of it.

You should take some of your things.

I don't care about that vaina. I just want to go.

Don't be stupid, I say. I open her dresser and pull out the jeans on top. A handful of soft bright panties comes out as well, starts to roll down the front of my jeans. There are more in the drawer. I try to catch the ones that fall but as soon as I touch their fabric I let everything go.

Leave it. She stands. Go on, she says and begins to put them back in the dresser, her square back to me, the movement of her hands smooth and easy.

Look, I say.

Don't worry. She doesn't look up.

I go downstairs. Wayne is sinking the bolts into the slate with the Makita. You can't do it, he says.

Why not?

Kid. We have to finish this.

I'll be back before you know it. A quick trip, in, out.

Kid. He stands up slowly; he's nearly twice as old as me.

I go to the window and look out. New ginkgos stand in fresh rows beside the driveway. A thousand years ago when I was still in college I learned something about them. Living fossils. Unchanged since their inception millions of years ago. You've tagged Charlene, haven't you?

Sure, he answers easily. I take the truck keys out of the toolbox.

I'll be right back, I promise him.

. . .

My mother still has pictures of the girlfriend in her apartment. The girlfriend's the sort of person who never looks bad. There's a picture of us at the bar where I taught her to play pool. She's leaning on the Schmelke I stole for her, nearly a grand worth of cue and frowning at the shot I left her, a shot she'd go on to miss.

The picture of us at Boca Raton is the largest—shiny, framed, nearly a foot tall. We're in our bathing suits and the legs of some stranger frame the right. She has her butt in the sand, knees folded up in front of her because she knew I was sending the picture home to my mom; she didn't want my mother to see her bikini, didn't want my mother to think her a whore. I'm crouching next to her, smiling, one hand on her thin shoulder, one of her moles showing between my thumb and pointer.

My mother won't look at the pictures or talk about her when I'm around but my sister says she still cries over the break-up. Around me my mother's polite, sits quietly on the couch while I tell her about what I'm reading and how work has been. Do you have anyone? she asks me sometimes.

Yes, I say.

She talks to my sister on the side, says, In my dreams they're still together.

We reach the Washington Bridge without saying a word. She's emptied his cupboards and refrigerator; the bags are at her feet. She's eating corn chips but I'm too nervous to join in.

Is this the best way? she asks. The bridge doesn't seem to impress her.

It's the shortest way.

She folds the bag shut. That's what he said when I arrived last year. I wanted to see the countryside. There was too much rain to see anything anyway.

I want to ask her if she loves her boss, but I ask instead, How do you like the States?

She swings her head across at the billboards. I'm not surprised by any of it, she says.

Traffic on the bridge is bad and she has to give me an oily fiver for the toll. Are you from the capital? I ask.

No.

I was born there. In Villa Juana. Moved here when I was a little boy.

She nods, staring out at the traffic. As we cross over the bridge I drop my hand into her lap. I leave it there, palm up, fingers slightly curled. Sometimes you just have to try, even if you know it won't work. She turns her head away slowly, facing out beyond the bridge cables, out to Manhattan and the Hudson.

Everything in Washington Heights is Dominican. You can't go a block without passing a Quisqueya Bakery or a Quisqueya Supermercado or a Hotel Quisqueya. If I were to park the truck and get out nobody would take me for a deliveryman; I could be like the guy who's on the street corner selling Dominican flags. I could be on my way home to my girl. Everybody's on the streets and the merengue's falling out of windows like TVs. When we reach her block I ask a kid with the sag for the building and he points out the stoop with his pinkie. She steps out of the truck and straightens the front of her sweatshirt before following the line that the kid's finger has cut across the street. Cuidate, I say.

Wayne works on the boss and a week later I'm back, on probation, painting the warehouse. Wayne brings me meatball sandwiches from out on the road, skinny things with a seam of cheese gumming the bread.

Was it worth it? he asks me.

He's watching me close. I tell him it wasn't.

Did you at least get some?

Hell yeah, I say.

Are you sure?

Why would I lie about something like that? Homegirl was an animal. I still have the teeth marks.

Damn, he says.

I punch him in the arm. And how's it going with you and Charlene?

I don't know, man. He shakes his head and in that motion I see him out on his lawn with all his things. I just don't know about this one.

We're back on the road a week later. Buckinghams, Imperials, Gold Crowns and dozens of card tables. I keep a copy of Pruitt's paperwork and when the curiosity finally gets to me I call. The first time I get the machine; we're delivering at a house in Long Island with a view of the Sound that would break you. Wayne and I smoke a joint on the beach and I pick a dead horseshoe crab up by the tail and heave it in the customer's garage. The next two times I'm in the Bedminster area and Pruitt picks up and says, Yes? But on the fourth time she answers and the sink is running on her side of the phone and she shuts it off when I don't say anything.

Was she there? Wayne asks in the truck.

Of course she was.

He runs a thumb over the front of his teeth. Pretty predictable. She's probably in love with the guy. You know how it is.

I sure do.

Don't get angry.

I'm tired, that's all.

Tired's the best way to be, he says. It really is.

He hands me the map and my fingers trace our deliveries, stitching city to city. Looks like we've gotten everything, I say.

Finally. He yawns. What's first tomorrow?

We won't really know until the morning, when I've gotten the paperwork in order but I take guesses anyway. One of our games. It passes the time, gives us something to look forward to. I close my eyes and put my hand on the map. So many towns, so many cities to choose from. Some places are sure bets but more than once I've gone with the long shot and been right.

You can't imagine how many times I've been right.

Usually the name will come to me fast, the way the numbered balls pop out during the lottery drawings, but this time nothing comes: no magic, no nothing. It could be anywhere. I open my eyes and see that Wayne is still waiting. Edison, I say, pressing my thumb down. Edison, New Jersey.

Issue 138, 1996

Edward P. Jones

✠

Marie

Every now and again, as if on a whim, the Federal government people would write to Marie Delaveaux Wilson in one of those white,
stampless envelopes and tell her to come in to their place so they could
take another look at her. They, the Social Security people, wrote to her
in a foreign language that she had learned to translate over the years,
and for all of the years she had been receiving the letters the same man
had been signing them. Once, because she had something important to
tell him, Marie called the number the man always put at the top of the
letters, but a woman answered Mr. Smith's telephone and told Marie
he was in an all-day meeting. Another time she called and a man said
Mr. Smith was on vacation. And finally one day a woman answered and
told Marie that Mr. Smith was deceased. The woman told her to wait
and she would get someone new to talk to her about her case, but Marie
thought it bad luck to have telephoned a dead man and she hung up.

Now, years after the woman had told her Mr. Smith was no more,
the letters were still being signed by John Smith. Come into our office
at Twenty-first and M Streets, Northwest, the letters said in that foreign
language. Come in so we can see if you are still blind in one eye. Come
in so we can see if you are still old and getting older. Come in so we can
see if you still deserve to get Supplemental Security Income payments.

She always obeyed the letters, even if the order now came from a
dead man, for she knew people who had been temporarily cut off from
SSI for not showing up or even for being late. And once cut off, you
had to move heaven and earth to get back on.

So on a not unpleasant day in March, she rose in the dark in the morning, even before the day had any sort of character, to give herself plenty of time to bathe, eat, lay out money for the bus, dress, listen to the spirituals on the radio. She was eighty-six years old and had learned that life was all chaos and painful uncertainty and that the only way to get through it was to expect chaos even in the most innocent of moments. Offer a crust of bread to a sick bird and you often draw back a bloody finger.

John Smith's letter had told her to come in at eleven o'clock, his favorite time, and by nine that morning she had had her bath and had eaten. Dressed by 9:30. The walk from Claridge Towers at Twelfth and M down to the bus stop at Fourteenth and K took her about ten minutes, more or less. There was a bus at about 10:30, her schedule told her, but she preferred the one that came a half hour earlier, lest there be trouble with the 10:30 bus. After she dressed, she sat at her dining room table and went over yet again what papers and all else she needed to take. Given the nature of life—particularly the questions asked by the Social Security people—she always took more than they might ask for: her birth certificate, her husband's death certificate, doctor's letters.

One of the last things she put in her pocketbook was a knife that she had, about seven inches long, which she had serrated on both edges with the use of a small saw borrowed from a neighbor. The knife, she was convinced now, had saved her life about two weeks before. Before then she had often been careless about when she took the knife out with her, and she had never taken it out in daylight, but now she never left her apartment without it, even when going down the hall to the trash drop.

She had gone out to buy a simple box of oatmeal, no more, no less. It was about seven in the evening, the streets with enough commuters driving up Thirteenth Street to make her feel safe. Several yards before she reached the store, the young man came from behind her and tried to rip off her coat pocket where he thought she kept her money, for she carried no purse or pocketbook after five o'clock. The money was in the other pocket with the knife, and his hand was caught in the empty pocket long enough for her to reach around with the knife and cut his hand as it came out of her pocket.

He screamed and called her an old bitch. He took a few steps up Thirteenth Street and stood in front of Emerson's Market, examining the hand and shaking off blood. Except for the cars passing up and down Thirteenth Street, they were alone, and she began to pray.

"You cut me," he said, as if he had only been minding his own business when she cut him. "Just look what you done to my hand," he said and looked around as if for some witness to her crime. There was not a great amount of blood, but there was enough for her to see it dripping to the pavement. He seemed to be about twenty, no more than twenty-five, dressed the way they were all dressed nowadays, as if a blind man had matched up all their colors. It occurred to her to say that she had seven grandchildren about his age, that telling him this would make him leave her alone. But the more filth he spoke, the more she wanted him only to come toward her again.

"You done crippled me, you old bitch."

"I sure did," she said, without malice, without triumph, but simply the way she would have told him the time of day had he asked and had she known. She gripped the knife tighter, and as she did, she turned her body ever so slightly so that her good eye lined up with him. Her heart was making an awful racket, wanting to be away from him, wanting to be safe at home. I will not be moved, some organ in the neighborhood of the heart told the heart. "And I got plenty more where that come from."

The last words seemed to bring him down some and, still shaking the blood from his hand, he took a step or two back, which disappointed her. I will not be moved, that other organ kept telling the heart. "You just crazy, thas all," he said. "Just a crazy old hag." Then he turned and lumbered up toward Logan Circle, and several times he looked back over his shoulder as if afraid she might be following. A man came out of Emerson's, then a woman with two little boys. She wanted to grab each of them by the arm and tell them she had come close to losing her life. "I saved myself with this here thing," she would have said. She forgot about the oatmeal and took her raging heart back to the apartment. She told herself that she should, but she never washed the fellow's blood off the knife, and over the next few days it dried and then it began to flake off.

Toward ten o'clock that morning Wilamena Mason knocked and let herself in with a key Marie had given her.

"I see you all ready," Wilamena said.

"With the help of the Lord," Marie said. "Want a spot a coffee?"

"No thanks," Wilamena said, and dropped into a chair at the table. "Been drinkin' so much coffee lately, I'm gonna turn into coffee. Was up all night with Calhoun."

"How he doin'?"

Wilamena told her Calhoun was better that morning, his first good morning in over a week. Calhoun Lambeth was Wilamena's boyfriend, a seventy-five-year-old man she had taken up with six or so months before, not long after he moved in. He was the best-dressed old man Marie had ever known, but he had always appeared to be sickly, even while strutting about with his gold-tipped cane. And seeing that she could count his days on the fingers of her hands, Marie had avoided getting to know him. She could not understand why Wilamena, who could have had any man in Claridge Towers or any other senior citizen building for that matter, would take such a man into her bed. "True love," Wilamena had explained. "Avoid heartache," Marie had said, trying to be kind.

They left the apartment. Marie sought help from no one, lest she come to depend on a person too much. But since the encounter with the young man, Wilamena had insisted on escorting her. Marie, to avoid arguments, allowed Wilamena to walk with her from time to time to the bus stop, but no farther.

Nothing fit Marie's theory about life like the weather in Washington. Two days before, the temperature had been in the forties, and yesterday it had dropped to the low twenties, then warmed up a bit with the afternoon, bringing on snow flurries. Today the weather people on the radio had said it would warm enough to wear just a sweater, but Marie was wearing her coat. And tomorrow, the weather people said, it would be in the thirties, with maybe an inch or so of snow.

Appointments near twelve o'clock were always risky, because the Social Security people often took off for lunch long before noon and returned sometime after one. And except for a few employees who seemed to work through their lunch hours, the place shut down. Marie had never been interviewed by someone willing to work through the lunch hour. Today, though the appointment was for eleven, she waited until 1:30 before the woman at the front of the waiting room told her she would have to come back another day, because the woman who handled her case was not in.

"You put my name down when I came in like everything was all right," Marie said after she had been called up to the woman's desk.

"I know," the woman said, "but I thought that Mrs. Brown was in. They told me she was in. I'm sorry." The woman began writing in a logbook that rested between her telephone and a triptych of photographs. She handed Marie a slip and told her again she was sorry.

"Why you have me wait so long if she whatn't here?" She did not want to say too much, appear too upset, for the Social Security people could be unforgiving. And though she was used to waiting three and four hours, she found it especially unfair to wait when there was no one for her at all behind those panels the Social Security people used for offices. "I been here since before eleven."

"I know," the woman behind the desk said. "I know. I saw you there, ma'am, but I really didn't know Mrs. Brown wasn't here." There was a nameplate at the front of the woman's desk and it said Vernelle Wise. The name was surrounded by little hearts, the kind a child might have drawn.

Marie said nothing more and left.

The next appointment was two weeks later, 8:30, a good hour, and the day before a letter signed by John Smith arrived to remind her. She expected to be out at least by twelve. Three times before eleven o'clock Marie asked Vernelle Wise if the man, Mr. Green, who was handling her case, was in that day, and each time the woman assured her that he was. At twelve, Marie ate one of the two oranges and three of the five slices of cheese she had brought. At one, she asked again if Mr. Green was indeed in that day and politely reminded Vernelle Wise that she had been waiting since about eight that morning. Vernelle was just as polite and told her the wait would soon be over.

At 1:15, Marie began to watch the clock hands creep around the dial. She had not paid much attention to the people about her, but more and more it seemed that others were being waited on who had arrived long after she had gotten there. After asking about Mr. Green at one, she had taken a seat near the front and, as more time went by, she found herself forced to listen to the conversation that Vernelle was having with the other receptionist next to her.

"I told him . . . I told him . . . I said just get your things and leave," said the other receptionist, who didn't have a nameplate.

"Did he leave?" Vernelle wanted to know.

"Oh, no," the other woman said. "Not at first. But I picked up some of his stuff, that Christian Dior jacket he worships. I picked up my cigarette lighter and that jacket, just like I was gonna do something bad to it, and he started movin' then."

Vernelle began laughing. "I wish I was there to see that." She was filing her fingernails. Now and again she would look at her fingernails to inspect her work, and if it was satisfactory, she would blow on the nails and on the file. "He back?" Vernelle asked.

The other receptionist eyed her. "What you think?" and they both laughed.

Along about two o'clock Marie became hungry again, but she did not want to eat the rest of her food because she did not know how much longer she would be there. There was a soda machine in the corner, but all sodas gave her gas.

"You-know-who gonna call you again?" the other receptionist was asking Vernelle.

"I hope so," Vernelle said. "He pretty fly. Seemed decent too. It kinda put me off when he said he was a car mechanic. I kinda like kept tryin' to take a peek at his fingernails and everything the whole evenin'. See if they was dirty or what."

"Well, that mechanic stuff might be good when you get your car back. My cousin's boyfriend used to do that kinda work and he made good money, girl. I mean real good money."

"Hmmmm," Vernelle said. "Anyway, the kids like him, and you know how peculiar they can be."

"Tell me 'bout it. They do the job your mother and father used to do, huh? Only on another level."

"You can say that again," Vernelle said.

Marie went to her and told her how long she had been waiting.

"Listen," Vernelle said, pointing her fingernail file at Marie. "I told you you'll be waited on as soon as possible. This is a busy day. So I think you should just go back to your seat until we call your name." The other receptionist began to giggle.

Marie reached across the desk and slapped Vernelle Wise with all her might. Vernelle dropped the file, which made a cheap, tinny sound when it hit the plastic board her chair was on. But no one heard the file because she had begun to cry right away. She looked at Marie as if, in the moment of her greatest need, Marie had denied her. "Oh, oh," Vernelle Wise said through the tears. "Oh, my dear God. . . ."

The other receptionist, in her chair on casters, rolled over to Vernelle and put her arm around her. "Security!" the other receptionist hollered. "We need security here!"

The guard at the front door came quickly around the corner, one hand on his holstered gun and the other pointing accusingly at the people seated in the waiting area. Marie had sat down and was looking at the two women almost sympathetically, as if a stranger had come in, hit Vernelle Wise, and fled.

"She slapped Vernelle!" said the other receptionist.

"Who did it?" the guard said, reaching for the man sitting beside Marie. But when the other receptionist said it was the old lady in the blue coat, the guard held back for the longest time, as if to grab her would be like arresting his own grandmother. He stood blinking and he would have gone on blinking had Marie not stood up.

She was too flustered to wait for the bus and so took a cab home. With both chains, she locked herself in the apartment, refusing to answer the door or the telephone the rest of the day and most of the next. But she knew that if her family or friends received no answer at the door or on the telephone, they would think something had happened to her. So the next afternoon, she began answering the phone and spoke with the chain on, telling Wilamena and others that she had a toothache.

For days and days after the incident she ate very little and asked God to forgive her. She was haunted by the way Vernelle's cheek had felt, by what it was like to invade and actually touch the flesh of another person. And when she thought too hard, she imagined that she was slicing through the woman's cheek, the way she had sliced through the young man's hand. But as time went on she began to remember the man's curses and the purplish color of Vernelle's fingernails, and all remorse would momentarily take flight. Finally, one morning nearly two weeks after she slapped the woman, she woke with a phrase she had not used or heard since her children were small: You whatn't raised that way.

It was the next morning that the thin young man in the suit knocked and asked through the door chains if he could speak with her. She thought that he was a Social Security man come to tear up her card and papers and tell her that they would send her no more checks. Even when he pulled out an identification card showing that he was a Howard University student, she did not believe.

In the end, she told him she didn't want to buy anything, not magazines, not candy, not anything.

"No, no," he said. "I just want to talk to you for a bit. About your life and everything. It's for a project for my folklore course. I'm talking to everyone in the building who'll let me. Please . . . I won't be a bother. Just a little bit of your time."

"I don't have anything worth talkin' about," she said. "And I don't keep well these days."

"Oh, ma'am, I'm sorry. But we all got something to say. I promise I won't be a bother."

After fifteen minutes of his pleas, she opened the door to him because of his suit and his tie and his tie clip with a bird in flight, and because his long, dark brown fingers reminded her of delicate twigs. But had he turned out to be death with a gun or a knife or fingers to crush her neck, she would not have been surprised. "My name's George. George Carter. Like the president." He had the kind of voice that old people in her young days would have called womanish. "But I was born right here in D.C. Born, bred and buttered, my mother used to say."

He stayed the rest of the day and she fixed him dinner. It scared her to be able to talk so freely with him, and at first she thought that at long last, as she had always feared, senility had taken hold of her. A few hours after he left, she looked his name up in the telephone book, and when a man who sounded like him answered, she hung up immediately. And the next day she did the same thing. He came back at least twice a week for many weeks and would set his cassette recorder on her coffee table. "He's takin' down my whole life," she told Wilamena, almost the way a woman might speak in awe of a new boyfriend.

One day he played back for the first time some of what she told the recorder:

> . . . My father would be sittin' there readin' the paper. He'd say whenever they put in a new president, "Look like he got the chair for four years." And it got so that's what I saw—this poor man sittin' in that chair for four long years while the rest of the world went on about its business. I don't know if I thought he ever did anything, the president. I just knew that he had to sit in that chair for four years. Maybe I thought that by his sittin' in that chair and doin' nothin' else for four years he made the country what it was and that without him sittin' there the country wouldn't be what it was. Maybe thas what I got from listenin' to father readin' and to my mother askin' him questions 'bout what he was readin'. They was like that, you see. . . .

George stopped the tape and was about to put the other side in when she touched his hand.

"No more, George," she said. "I can't listen to no more. Please . . . please, no more." She had never in her whole life heard her own voice. Nothing had been so stunning in a long, long while, and for a few moments before she found herself, her world turned upside down. There, rising from a machine no bigger than her Bible, was a voice frighteningly familiar and yet unfamiliar, talking about a man whom she knew as well as her husbands and her sons, a man dead and buried sixty years. She reached across to George and he handed her the tape. She turned it over and over, as if the mystery of everything could be discerned if she turned it enough times. She began to cry, and with her other hand she lightly touched the buttons of the machine.

Between the time Marie slapped the woman in the Social Security office and the day she heard her voice for the first time, Calhoun Lambeth, Wilamena's boyfriend, had been in and out of the hospital three times. Most evenings when Calhoun's son stayed the night with him, Wilamena would come up to Marie's and spend most of the evening sitting on the couch that was catty-corner to the easy chair facing the big window. She said very little, which was unlike her, a woman with more friends than hairs on her head and who, at sixty-eight, loved a good party. The most attractive woman Marie knew would only curl her legs up under herself and sip whatever Marie put in her hand. She looked out at the city until she took herself to her apartment or went back down to Calhoun's place. In the beginning, after he returned from the hospital the first time, there was the desire in Marie to remind her friend that she wasn't married to Calhoun, that she should just get up and walk away, something Marie had seen her do with other men she had grown tired of.

Late one night, Wilamena called and asked her to come down to the man's apartment, for the man's son had had to work that night and she was there alone with him and she did not want to be alone with him. "Sit with me a spell," Wilamena said. Marie did not protest, even though she had not said more than ten words to the man in all the time she knew him. She threw on her bathrobe, picked up her keys and serrated knife and went down to the second floor.

He was propped up on the bed, surprisingly alert, and spoke to Marie with an unforced friendliness. She had seen this in other dying people—a kindness and gentleness came over them that was often embarrassing for those around them. Wilamena sat on the side of the bed. Calhoun asked Marie to sit in a chair beside the bed and then he took her hand and held it for the rest of the night. He talked on throughout the night, not always understandable. Wilamena, exhausted, eventually lay across the foot of the bed. Almost everything the man had to say was about a time when he was young and was married for a year or so to a woman in Nicodemus, Kansas, a town where there were only black people. Whether the woman had died or whether he had left her, Marie could not make out. She only knew that the woman and Nicodemus seemed to have marked him for life.

"You should go to Nicodemus," he said at one point, as if the town was only around the corner. "I stumbled into the place by accident. But you should go on purpose. There ain't much to see, but you should go there and spend some time there."

Toward four o'clock that morning, he stopped talking and moments later he went home to his God. Marie continued holding the dead man's hand and she said the Lord's Prayer over and over until it no longer made sense to her. She did not wake Wilamena. Eventually the sun came through the man's venetian blinds, and she heard the croaking of the pigeons congregating on the window ledge. When she finally placed his hand on his chest, the dead man expelled a burst of air that sounded to Marie like a sigh. It occurred to her that she, a complete stranger, was the last thing he had known in the world and that now he was no longer in the world. All she knew of him was that Nicodemus place and a lovesick woman asleep at the foot of his bed. She thought that she was hungry and thirsty, but the more she looked at the dead man and the sleeping woman, the more she realized that what she felt was a sense of loss.

Two days later, the Social Security people sent her a letter, again signed by John Smith, telling her to come to them one week hence. There was nothing in the letter about the slap, no threat to cut off her SSI payments because of what she had done. Indeed, it was the same sort of letter John Smith usually sent. She called the number at the top of the letter, and the woman who handled her case told her that Mr. White would be expecting her on the day and time stated in the letter. Still, she suspected the Social Security people were planning something for her, something at the very least that would be humiliating. And, right up until the day before the appointment, she continued calling to confirm that it was okay to come in. Often, the person she spoke to after the switchboard woman and before the woman handling her case was Vernelle. "Social Security Administration. This is Vernelle Wise. May I help you?" And each time Marie heard the receptionist identify herself she wanted to apologize. "I whatn't raised that way," she wanted to tell the woman.

George Carter came the day she got the letter to present her with a cassette machine and copies of the tapes they had made about her life. It took quite some time for him to teach her how to use the machine, and after he was gone, she was certain it took so long because she really did not want to know how to use it. That evening, after her dinner, she steeled herself and put a tape marked "Parents/ Early Childhood" in the machine.

. . . My mother had this idea that everything could be done in Washington, that a human bein' could take all they troubles to Washington and things would be set right. I think that was all wrapped up with her notion of the gov'ment, the Supreme Court and the president and the like. "Up there," she would say, "things can be made right." "Up there" was her only words for Washington. All them other cities had names, but Washington didn't need a name. It was just called "up there." I was real small and didn't know any better, so somehow I got to thinkin' since things were on the perfect side in Washington, that maybe God lived there. God and his people. . . . When I went back home to visit that first time and told my mother all about my livin' in Washington, she fell into such a cry, like maybe I had managed to make it to heaven without dyin'. Thas how people was back in those days. . . .

The next morning she looked for Vernelle Wise's name in the telephone book. And for several evenings she would call the number and hang up before the phone had rung three times. Finally, on a Sunday, two days before the appointment, she let it ring and what may have been a little boy answered. She could tell he was very young because he said hello in a too-loud voice, as if he was not used to talking on the telephone.

"Hello," he said. "Hello, who this? Granddaddy, that you? Hello. Hello. I can see you."

Marie heard Vernelle tell him to put down the telephone, then another child, perhaps a girl somewhat older than the boy, came on the line. "Hello. Hello. Who is this?" she said with authority. The boy began to cry, apparently because he did not want the girl to talk if he couldn't. "Don't touch it," the girl said. "Leave it alone." The boy cried louder and only stopped when Vernelle came to the telephone.

"Yes?" Vernelle said. "Yes." Then she went off the line to calm the boy, who had begun to cry again. "Loretta," she said, "go get his bottle. . . . Well, look for it. What you got eyes for?"

There seemed to be a second boy, because Vernelle told him to help Loretta look for the bottle. "He always losin' things," Marie heard the second boy say. "You should tie everything to his arms." "Don't tell me what to do," Vernelle said. "Just look for that damn bottle."

"I don't lose noffin'. I don't," the first boy said. "You got snot in your nose."

"Don't say that," Vernelle said before she came back on the line. "I'm sorry," she said to Marie. "Who is this? . . . Don't you dare touch it if you know what's good for you!" she said. "I wanna talk to Granddaddy," the first boy said. "Loretta, get me that bottle!"

Marie hung up. She washed her dinner dishes. She called Wilamena because she had not seen her all day, and Wilamena told her that she would be up later. The cassette tapes were on the coffee table beside the machine, and she began picking them up, one by one. She read the labels: Husband No. 1, Working, Husband No. 2, Children, Race Relations, Early D.C. Experiences, Husband No. 3. She had not played another tape since the one about her mother's idea of what Washington was like, but she could still hear the voice, her voice. Without reading its label, she put a tape in the machine.

. . . I never planned to live in Washington, had no idea I would ever even step one foot in this city. This white family my mother worked for, they had a son married and gone to live in Baltimore. He wanted a maid, somebody to take care of his children. So he wrote to his mother and she asked my mother and my mother asked me about goin' to live in Baltimore. Well, I was young. I guess I wanted to see the world, and Baltimore was as good a place to start as anywhere.

This man sent me a train ticket and I went off to Baltimore. Hadn't ever been kissed, hadn't ever been anything, but here I was goin' farther from home than my mother and father put together. . . . Well, sir, the train stopped in Washington, and I thought I heard the conductor say we would be stoppin' a bit there, so I got off. I knew I probably wouldn't see no more than that Union Station, but I wanted to be able to say I'd done that, that I step foot in the capital of the United States. I walked down to the end of the platform and looked around, then I peeked into the station. Then I went in. And when I got back, the train and my suitcase was gone. Everything I had in the world on the way to Baltimore. . . .

. . . I couldn't calm myself down enough to listen to when the redcap said another train would be leavin' for Baltimore, I was just that upset. I had a buncha addresses of people we knew all the way from home up to Boston, and I used one precious nickel to call a woman I hadn't seen in years, 'cause I didn't have the white people in Baltimore number. This woman come and got me, took me to her place. I 'member like it was yesterday that we got on this streetcar marked 13TH AND D NE. The more I rode, the more brighter things got. You ain't lived till you been on a streetcar. The further we went on that streetcar— dead down in the middle of the street—the more I knowed I could never go live in Baltimore. I knowed I could never live in a place that didn't have that streetcar and them clackety-clack tracks. . . .

She wrapped the tapes in two plastic bags and put them in the dresser drawer that contained all that was valuable to her: birth and death certificates, silver dollars, life insurance policies, pictures of her husbands and the children they had given each other and the grandchildren those children had given her and the great-grands whose names she had trouble remembering. She set the tapes in a back corner of the drawer, away from the things she needed to get her hands on regularly. She knew that however long she lived, she would not ever again listen to them, for in the end, despite all that was on the tapes, she could not stand the sound of her own voice.

Issue 122, 1992

Alice Munro

✺

Circle of Prayer

Trudy threw a jug across the room. It didn't reach the opposite wall, it didn't hurt anybody, it didn't even break.

This was the jug without a handle, cement-colored, with brown streaks in it, rough as sandpaper to the touch, that Dan made the winter he took pottery classes. He made six little handleless cups, to go with it. The jug and the cups were supposed to be for saki, but the local liquor store doesn't carry saki. Once they brought some home from a trip, but they didn't really like it. So the jug Dan made sits on the highest open shelf in the kitchen, and a few odd items of value are kept in it. Trudy's wedding ring and her engagement ring, the medal Robin won for all-round excellence, in Grade Eight, a long, two-strand necklace of jet beads that belonged to Dan's mother and was willed to Robin. Trudy won't let her wear it yet.

Trudy came home from work a little after midnight, she entered the house in the dark. Just the little stove light was on—she and Robin always left that on for each other. Trudy didn't need any other light. She climbed up on a chair without even letting go of her bag, and got down the jug, fished around inside it.

It was gone. Of course. She had known it would be gone.

She went through the dark house to Robin's room, still with her bag over her arm, the jug in her hand. She turned on the overhead light. Robin groaned, and turned over, pulled the pillow over her head. Shamming.

"Your grandmother's necklace," Trudy said. "Why did you do that? Are you insane?"

Robin shammed a sleepy groan. All the clothes she owned, it seemed, old and new and clean and dirty, were scattered on the floor, on the chair, the desk, the dresser, even on the bed itself. On the wall was a huge poster showing a hippopotamus, with the words underneath "Why Was I Born So Beautiful?" and another poster showing Terry Fox running along a rainy highway, with a whole cavalcade of cars behind him. Dirty glasses, empty yogurt containers, school notes, a Tampax still in its wrapper, the stuffed snake and tiger Robin had had since before she went to school, a collage of pictures of her cat, Sausage, who had been run over two years ago. Red and blue ribbons that she had won for jumping, or running, or throwing basketballs.

"You answer me!" said Trudy. "You tell me why you did it!"

She threw the jug. But it was heavier than she'd thought, or else at the very moment of throwing it she lost conviction, because it didn't hit the wall, it fell on the rug beside the dresser, it rolled on the floor, undamaged.

You threw a jug at me that time. You could have killed me.

Not at you. I didn't throw it at you.

You could have killed me.

Proof that Robin was shamming:

She started up in a fright, but it wasn't the blank fright of somebody who'd been asleep. She looked scared, but underneath that childish scared look was another look—stubborn, calculating, disdainful.

"It was so beautiful. And it was valuable. It belonged to your grandmother."

"I thought it belonged to me," said Robin.

"That girl wasn't even your friend. Christ, you didn't have a good word to say for her, this morning."

"You don't know who is my friend!" Robin's face flushed a bright pink and her eyes filled with tears, but her scornful, stubborn expression didn't change. "I knew her. I talked to her. So get out!"

Trudy works at the Home for Mentally Handicapped Adults. Few people call it that. Older people in town still say, the Misses Weirs' house, and a number of others, including Robin, and presumably most of those her age, called it the Halfwit House.

The house has a ramp now, for wheelchairs, because some of the mentally handicapped may be physically handicapped as well, and it has a swimming pool in the backyard, which caused a certain amount of discussion, when it was installed at taxpayers' expense. Otherwise the house looks pretty much the way it always did—the white wooden walls, the dark-green curlicues on the gables, the steep roof and dark, screened side porch, and the deep lawn in front shaded by soft maple trees.

This month Trudy works the four-to-midnight shift. Yesterday afternoon she parked her car in front and walked up the drive thinking how nice the house looked, peaceful, as in the days of the Misses Weir, who must have served iced tea and read library books, or played croquet, whatever people did then.

Always some piece of news, some wrangle or excitement, once you get inside.

The men came to fix the pool but they didn't fix it, they went away again. It isn't fixed yet.

"We don't get no use of it, soon summer be over," Josephine said.

"It's not even the middle of June, you're saying summer'll be over," Kelvin said. "You think before you talk. Did you hear about the young girl that was killed, out in the country?" he said to Trudy.

Trudy had started to mix two batches of frozen lemonade, one pink and one plain. When he said that she smashed the spoon down on the frozen chunk so hard that some of the liquid spilled over.

"How, Kelvin?"

She was afraid she would hear that a girl was dragged off a country road, raped in the woods, strangled, beaten, left there. Robin goes running along the country roads, in her white shorts and T-shirt, a head-band on her flying hair. Robin's hair is golden, her legs and arms are golden. Her cheeks and limbs are downy, not shiny—you wouldn't be surprised to see a cloud of pollen delicately floating and settling behind her, when she runs. Cars hoot at her and she isn't bothered. Foul threats are yelled at her, and she yells foul threats back.

"Driving a truck," Kelvin said.

Trudy's heart eased. Robin didn't know how to drive yet.

"Fourteen years old, she didn't know how to drive," Kelvin said. "She got in the truck and the first thing you know, she ran it into a tree. Where was her parents, that's what I'd like to know? They weren't watching out for her. She got in the truck when she didn't know how to drive and ran it into a tree. Fourteen. That's too young."

Kelvin goes uptown by himself, he hears all the news. He is fifty-two years old, still slim and boyish-looking, well-shaved, with soft, short, clean, dark hair. He goes to the barbershop every day, because he can't quite manage to shave himself. Epilepsy, then surgery, an infected bone-flap, many more operations, a permanent mild difficulty with feet and fingers, a gentle head-fog. The fog doesn't obscure facts, just motives. Perhaps he shouldn't be in the Home at all, but where else? Anyway, he likes it. He says he likes it. He tells the others they shouldn't complain, they should be more grateful, they should behave themselves. He picks up the soft drink cans, or beer bottles, that people have thrown into the front yard—though of course it isn't his job to do that.

When Janet came in just before midnight, to relieve Trudy, she had the same story to tell.

"I guess you heard about that fifteen-year-old girl?"

When Janet starts telling you something like this, she always starts off with "I guess you heard." *I guess you heard Wilma and Ted are breaking up*, she says. *I guess you heard Alvin Stead had a heart attack.*

"Kelvin told me," Trudy said. "Only he said she was fourteen."

"Fifteen," Janet said. "She must've been in Robin's class at school. She didn't know how to drive. She didn't even get out of the lane."

"Was she drunk?" said Trudy. Robin won't go near alcohol, or dope, or cigarettes, or even coffee, she's so fanatical about what she puts into her body.

"I don't think so. Stoned, maybe. It was early in the evening. She was home with her sister, their parents were out. Her sister's boyfriend came over, it was his truck, and he either gave her the keys to the truck or she took them. You hear different versions. You hear that they sent her out for something, they wanted to get rid of her, and you hear she just took the keys and went. Anyway she ran it right into a tree, in the lane."

"Jesus," said Trudy.

"I know. It's so idiotic. It's getting so you hate to think about your kids growing up. Did they all take their medication okay? What's Kelvin watching?"

Kelvin was still up, sitting in the living room watching TV.

"It's somebody being interviewed. He wrote a book about schizo-phrenics."

Anything he comes across about mental problems, Kelvin has to watch, or try to read.

"I think it depresses him, the more he watches that kind of thing. Do you know I found out today I have to make five hundred roses out of pink Kleenex, for my niece Laurel's wedding? For the car. She said, you promised you'd make the roses for the car. Well I didn't. I don't remem-ber promising a thing. Are you going to come over and help me?"

"Sure," said Trudy.

"I guess the real reason I want him to get off the schizophrenics is, I want to watch the old *Dallas*," Janet said. She and Trudy disagree about this. Trudy can't stand to watch those old reruns of *Dallas*, to see the characters with their younger, plumper faces going through tribulations and bound up in romantic complications they and the au-dience have now forgotten all about. That's what's so hilarious, Janet says, it's so unbelievable it's wonderful. All that happens and they just forget about it and go on. But to Trudy it doesn't seem so unbelievable, that the characters would go from one thing to the next thing—forget-ful, hopeful, photogenic, forever changing their clothes. That it's not so unbelievable, is what she really can't stand.

Robin, the next morning, said, "Oh, probably. All those people she hung around with drink. They party all the time. They're self-destructive. It's her own fault. Even if her sister told her to go she didn't have to go. She didn't have to be so stupid."

"What was her name?" Trudy said.

"Tracy Lee," said Robin with distaste. She stepped on the pedal of the garbage-tin, lifted rather than lowered the container of yogurt she had just emptied, and dropped it in. She was wearing bikini underpants and a T-shirt that said, "If I Want to Listen to an Asshole, I'll Fart."

"That shirt still bothers me," Trudy said. "Some things are disgusting but funny, and some things are more disgusting than funny."

"What's the problem?" said Robin. "I sleep alone."

Trudy sat outside, in her wrapper, drinking coffee, while the day got hot. There is a little brick-paved space by the side door that she and Dan always called the patio. She sat there. This is a solar-heated house, with big panels of glass in the south-sloping roof, the oddest-looking house in town. It's odd inside, too, with the open shelves in the kitchen, instead of cupboards, and the living room up some stairs, looking out over the fields at the back. She and Dan, for a joke, gave parts of it the most conventional, suburban-sounding names—the patio, the powder room, the master bedroom. Dan always had to joke about the way he was living. He built the house himself—Trudy did a lot of the painting, and staining—and it was a success. Rain didn't leak in around the panels, and part of the house's heat really did come from the sun. Most people who have the ideas, or ideals, that Dan has, aren't very practical. They can't fix things, or make things, they don't understand wiring, or carpentry, or whatever it is they need to understand. Dan is good at everything—at gardening, cutting wood, building a house. He is especially good at repairing motors. He used to travel around, getting jobs as an auto mechanic, a small-engines repairman. That's how he ended up here. He came here to visit Marlene, got a job as a mechanic, became a working partner in an auto-repair business, and before he knew it—married to Trudy, not Marlene—he was a small-town businessman, a member of the Kinsmen. All without shaving off his sixties beard or trimming his hair any more than he wanted to. The town was too small, Dan was too smart, for that to be necessary.

Now Dan lives in a town house in Richmond Hill, with a girl named Genevieve. She is studying law. She was married when she was very young, and had three little children. Dan met her three years ago, when her camper broke down a few miles outside of town. He told Trudy about her, that night. The rented camper, the three little children, hardly more than babies, the lively little divorced mother with her hair in pigtails. Her bravery, her poverty, her plans to enter law school. If the camper hadn't been easily fixed, he was going to invite her and her children to spend the night. She was on her way to her parents' summer place at Pointe du Baril.

"Then she can't be all that poor," Trudy said.

"You can be poor and have rich parents," Dan said.

"No you can't."

Last summer, Robin went to Richmond Hill for a month's visit. She came home early. She said it was a madhouse. The oldest child has to go to a special reading clinic, the middle one wets the bed. Genevieve spends all her time in the Law Library, studying. No wonder. Dan shops for bargains, cooks, looks after the children, grows vegetables, drives a taxi on Saturdays and Sundays. He wants to set up a motorcycle-repair business in the garage, but he can't get a permit, the neighbors are against it.

He told Robin he was happy, Never happier, he said. Robin came home firmly grown-up—severe, sarcastic, determined. She had some slight, steady grudge she hadn't had before. Trudy couldn't worm it out of her, couldn't tease it out of her—the time when she could do that was over.

Robin came home at noon and changed her clothes. She put on a light, flowered cotton blouse and ironed a pale blue cotton skirt.

She said that some of the girls from the class might be going around to the funeral home, after school.

"I forgot you had that skirt," said Trudy.

If she thought that was going to start a conversation, she was mistaken.

. . .

The first time Trudy met Dan, she was drunk. She was nineteen years old, tall and skinny—as she still is—with a wild head of curly black hair (it is cropped short now and showing the grey as black hair does). She was very tanned, wearing jeans and a tie-dyed T-shirt. No brassiere and no need. This was in Muskoka, in August, in a hotel bar where they had a band. She was camping, with girlfriends. He was there with his fiancée, Marlene. He had taken Marlene home to meet his mother, who lived in Muskoka, on an island, in an empty hotel. When Trudy was nineteen, he was twenty-eight. She danced around by herself, giddy and drunk, in front of the table where he sat with Marlene, a meek-looking blonde with a big pink shelf of bosom all embroidered in little fake pearls. Trudy just danced in front of him until he got up and joined her. At the end of the dance he asked her name, and took her back and introduced her to Marlene.

"This is Judy," he said. Trudy collapsed, laughing, into the chair beside Marlene's. Dan took Marlene up to dance. Trudy finished off Marlene's beer and went looking for her friends.

"How do you do?" she said to them. "I'm Judy!"

He caught up with her at the door of the bar. He had ditched Marlene when he saw Trudy leaving. A man who could change course quickly, see the possibilities, flare up with new enthusiasm. He told people later that he was in love with Trudy before he even knew her real name. But he told Trudy that he cried when he and Marlene were parting.

"I have feelings," he said. "I'm not ashamed to show them."

Trudy had no feelings for Marlene at all. Marlene was over thirty, what could she expect? Marlene still lives in town, works at the Hydro office, is not married. When Trudy and Dan were having one of their conversations about Genevieve, Trudy said, "Marlene must be thinking I got what's coming to me."

Dan said he had heard that Marlene had joined the Fellowship of Bible Christians. The women weren't allowed makeup and had to wear a kind of bonnet to church on Sundays.

"She won't be able to have a thought in her head, but forgiving."
Trudy said, "I bet."

This is what happened at the funeral home, as Trudy got the story
from both Kelvin and Janet:

The girls from Tracy Lee's class all showed up together, after
school. This was during what was called the visitation, when the family
waited beside Tracy Lee's open casket, to receive friends. Her parents
were there, her married brother and his wife, her sister, and even her
sister's boyfriend, who owned the truck. They stood in a row and people lined up to say a few words to them. A lot of people came. They always do, in a case like this. Tracy Lee's grandmother was at the end of
the row, in a brocade-covered chair. She wasn't able to stand up for
very long.

All the chairs at the funeral home are upholstered in this white-and-
gold brocade. The curtains are the same, the wallpaper almost
matches. There are little wall-bracket lights behind heavy pink glass.
Trudy has been there, several times, she knows what it's like. But
Robin, and most of these girls, had never been inside the place before.
They didn't know what to expect. Some of them began to cry as soon
as they got inside the door.

The curtains were closed. Soft music was playing, not exactly
church music but it sounded like it. Tracy Lee's coffin was white, with
a gold trim, matching all the brocade and the wallpaper. It had a lining
of pleated pink satin. A pink satin pillow. Tracy Lee had not a mark on
her face. She was not made up quite as usual, because the undertaker
had done it. But she was wearing her favorite earrings, turquoise-
colored triangles and yellow crescents, two to each ear. (Some people
thought that was in bad taste.) On the part of the coffin that covered
her from the waist down there was a big heart-shaped pillow of pink
roses.

The girls lined up to speak to the family. They shook hands, they said
sorry-for-your-loss, just the way everybody else did. When they got
through that, when all of them had let the grandmother squash their cool
hands between her warm, swollen, freckled ones, they lined up again, in

a straggling sort of way, and began to go past the coffin. Many were crying now, shivering. What could you expect? Young girls.

But they began to sing as they went past. With difficulty at first, shyly, but with growing confidence in their sad, sweet voices, they sang.

"Now, while the blossom still clings to the vine,
I'll taste your strawberries, I'll drink your sweet wine—"

They had planned the whole thing, of course, beforehand, they had got that song off a record. They believed that it was an old hymn.

So they filed past, singing, looking down at Tracy Lee, and it was noticed that they were dropping things into the coffin. They were slipping the rings off their fingers and the bracelets from their arms, and taking the earrings out of their ears. They were undoing necklaces, and bowing to pull chains and long strands of beads over their heads. Everybody gave something. All this jewelry went flashing and sparkling down on the dead girl, to lie beside her, in her coffin. One girl pulled the bright combs out of her hair, let those go.

And nobody made a move to stop this. How could anyone interrupt? It was like a religious ceremony. The girls behaved as if they'd been told what to do, as if this was what was always done on such occasions. They sang, they wept, they dropped their jewelry. The sense of ritual made every one of them graceful.

The family wouldn't stop it. They thought it was beautiful.

"It was like church," Tracy Lee's mother said, and her grandmother said, "All those lovely young girls loved Tracy Lee. If they wanted to give their jewelry to show how they loved her, that's their business. It's not anybody else's business. I thought it was beautiful."

Tracy Lee's sister broke down and cried. It was the first time she had done so.

Dan said, "This is a test of love."

Of Trudy's love, he meant. Trudy started singing.

"Please release me, let me go—"

She clapped a hand to her chest, danced in swoops around the room, singing. Dan was near laughing, near crying. He couldn't help it, he came and hugged her and they danced together, staggering. They were fairly drunk. All that June (it was two years ago) they were drinking gin, in between and during their scenes. They were drinking, weeping, arguing, explaining, and Trudy had to keep running to the liquor store. Yet she can't remember ever feeling really drunk or having a hangover. Except that she felt so tired all the time, as if she had logs chained to her ankles.

She kept joking. She called Genevieve, "Jenny the Feeb."

"This is just like wanting to give up the business and become a potter," she said. "Maybe you should have done that. I wasn't really against it. You gave up on it. And when you wanted to go to Peru. We could still do that."

"All those things were just straws in the wind," Dan said.

"I should have known when you started watching 'The Ombudsman' on TV," Trudy said. "It was the legal angle, wasn't it? You were never so interested in that kind of thing before."

"This will open life up for you too," Dan said. "You can be more than just my wife."

"Sure. I think I'll be a brain surgeon."

"You're very smart. You're a wonderful woman. You're brave."

"Sure you're not talking about Jenny the Feeb?"

"No, you. You, Trudy. I still love you. You can't understand that I still love you."

Not for years had he had so much to say about how he loved her. He loved her skinny bones, her curly hair, her roughening skin, her way of coming into a room with a stride that shook the windows, her jokes, her clowning, her tough talk. He loved her mind and her soul. He always would. But the part of his life that had been bound up with hers was over.

"That is just talk, that is talking like an idiot!" Trudy said. "Robin, go back to bed!" For Robin in her skimpy nightgown was standing at the top of the steps.

"I can hear you yelling and screaming," Robin said.

"We weren't yelling and screaming," Trudy said. "We're trying to talk about something private."

"What?"

"I told you, it's something private."

When Robin sulked off to bed, Dan said, "I think we should tell her. It's better for kids to know. Genevieve doesn't have any secrets from her kids. Josie's only five, and she came into the bedroom one afternoon—"

Then Trudy did start yelling and screaming. She clawed through a cushion cover. "You stop telling me about your sweet fucking Genevieve and her sweet fucking bedroom and her asshole kids, you shut up, don't tell me any more! You're just a big dribbling mouth without any brains, I don't care what you do, just shut up!"

Dan left. He packed a suitcase, he went off to Richmond Hill. He was back in five days. Just outside of town he had stopped the car, to pick Trudy a bouquet of wild flowers.

He told her he was back for good, it was over.

"You don't say?" said Trudy.

But she put the flowers in water. Dusty pink milkweed flowers that smelled like face powder, black-eyed Susans, wild sweet peas, and orange lilies that must have got loose from old disappeared gardens.

"So, you couldn't stand the pace?" she said.

"I knew you wouldn't fall all over me," Dan said. "You wouldn't be you if you did. And what I came back to is you."

She went to the liquor store, and this time bought champagne. For a month—it was still summer—they were back together being happy. She never really found out what had happened at Genevieve's house. Dan said he'd been having a middle-aged fit, that was all, he'd come to his senses. His life was here, with her and Robin.

"You're talking like a marriage-advice column," Trudy said.

"Okay. Forget the whole thing."

"We better," she said. She could imagine the kids, the confusion, the friends, old boyfriends maybe, that he hadn't been prepared for. Jokes and opinions that he couldn't understand. That was possible. The music he liked, the way he talked, even his hair and his beard might be out of style.

They went on family drives, picnics. They lay out in the grass behind the house, at night, looking at the stars. The stars were a new interest of Dan's, he got a map. They hugged and kissed each other frequently and tried out some new things—or things they hadn't done for a long time—when they made love.

At this time the road in front of the house was being paved. They'd built their house on a hillside at the edge of town, past the other houses, but trucks were using this street quite a bit now, avoiding the main streets, so the town was paving it. Trudy got so used to the noise and constant vibration she said she could feel herself jiggling all night, even when everything was quiet. Work started at seven in the morning. They woke up at the bottom of a river of noise. Dan dragged himself out of bed then, losing the hour of sleep that he loved best. There was a smell of diesel fuel in the air.

She woke up one night to find him not in bed. She listened to hear noises in the kitchen or the bathroom, but she couldn't. She got up and walked through the house. There were no lights on. She found him sitting outside, just outside the door, not having a drink or a glass of milk or a coffee, sitting with his back to the street.

Trudy looked out at the torn-up earth and the huge stalled machinery.

"Isn't the quiet lovely?" she said.

He didn't say anything.

Oh. Oh.

She realized what she'd been thinking, when she found his side of the bed empty, and couldn't hear him anywhere in the house. Not that he'd left her, but that he'd done worse. Done away with himself. With all their happiness and hugging and kissing and stars and picnics, she could think that.

"You can't forget her," she said. "You love her."

"I don't know what to do."

She was glad just to hear him speak. She said, "You'll have to go and try again."

"There's no guarantee I can stay," he said. "I can't ask you to stand by."

"No," said Trudy. "If you go, that's it."

"If I go that's it."

He seemed paralyzed. She felt that he might just sit there, repeating what she said, never be able to move or speak for himself again.

"If you feel like this, that's all there is to it," she said. "You don't have to choose. You're already gone."

That worked. He stood up stiffly, he came over and put his arms around her. He stroked her back.

"Come back to bed," he said. "We can rest for a little while yet."

"No. You've got to be gone when Robin wakes up. If we go back to bed it'll just start all over again."

She made him a thermos of coffee. He packed the bag he had taken with him before. All Trudy's movements seemed skillful and perfect, as they never were, usually. She felt serene. She felt as if they were an old couple, moving in harmony, in wordless love, past injury, past forgiving. Their good-bye was hardly a ripple. She went outside with him. It was between four-thirty and five o'clock, the sky was beginning to lighten and the birds to wake, everything was drenched in dew. There stood the big harmless machinery, stranded in the ruts of the road.

"Good thing it isn't last night, you couldn't have got out," she said. She meant that the road hadn't been navigable. It was just yesterday that they had graded a narrow track, for local traffic.

"Good thing," he said.

Good-bye.

"All I want is to know why you did it. Did you just do it for show? Like your father, for show. It's not the necklace so much. But it was a beautiful thing, I love jet beads, it was the only thing we had of your grandmother's. It was your right but you have no right to take me by surprise like that, I deserve an explanation, I always loved jet beads. Why?"

"I blame the family," Janet says. "It was up to them to stop it. Some of the stuff was just plastic, those junk earrings and bracelets, but what Robin threw in, that was a crime. And she wasn't the only one. There were birthstone rings and gold chains. Somebody said a diamond cluster ring, but I don't know if I believe that. They said the girl inherited it, like Robin. You didn't ever have it evaluated, did you?"

"I don't know if jet is worth anything," Trudy says.

They are sitting in Janet's front room, making roses out of pink Kleenex.

"It's just stupid," Trudy says.

"Well. There is one thing you could do," says Janet. "I don't hardly know how to mention it."

"What?"

"Pray."

Trudy had the feeling, from Janet's tone, that Janet was going to tell her something serious and unpleasant, something about herself— Trudy—which was affecting her life, and which everybody knew except her. Now she wants to laugh, after bracing herself. She doesn't know what to say.

"You don't pray, do you?" Janet says.

"I haven't got anything against it," Trudy says. "I wasn't brought up to be religious."

"It's not strictly speaking religious," Janet says. "I mean, it's not connected with any church. This is just some of us that pray. I can't tell you the names of anybody in it but most of them you know. It's supposed to be secret. It's called the Circle of Prayer."

"Like at high school," Trudy says. "At high school there were secret societies, you weren't supposed to tell who was in them. Only I wasn't."

"I was in everything going." Janet sighs. "This is actually more on the serious side. Though some people in it don't take it seriously enough, I don't think. Some people, they'll pray that they'll find a parking spot, or they'll pray they get good weather for their holidays. That isn't what it's for. But that's just individual praying, what the Circle is really about is, you phone up somebody that is in it, and tell them what it is you're worried about, or upset about, and ask them to pray for you. And they do. And they phone one other person, that's in the Circle, and they phone another and it goes all around, and we pray for one person, all together."

Trudy throws a rose away. "That's botched. Is it all women?"

"There isn't any rule it has to be. But it is, yes. Men would be too embarrassed. I was embarrassed at first. Only the first person you phone knows your name, who it is that's being prayed for, but in a town like this nearly everybody can guess. But if we started gossiping and ratting on each other it wouldn't work, and everybody knows that. So we don't. And it does work."

"Like, how?" Trudy says.

"Well, one girl banged up her car, she did eight hundred dollars' damage, and it was kind of a tricky situation, where she wasn't sure her insurance would cover it, and neither was her husband, he was raging mad, but we all prayed, and the insurance came through without a hitch. That's only one example."

"There wouldn't be much point in praying to get the necklace back, when it's in the coffin and the funeral's this morning," says Trudy mildly.

"It's not up to you to say that. You don't say what's possible or impossible. You just ask for what you want. Because it says in the Bible, ask and it shall be given. How can you be helped if you won't ask? You can't, that's for sure. What about when Dan left, what if you'd prayed then? I wasn't in the Circle then, or I could have said something to you. Even if I knew you'd resist it, I would have said something. A lot of people resist. Now even, it doesn't sound too great with that girl, how do you know, maybe even now it might work. It might not be too late."

"All right," says Trudy in a calm, slow voice. "All right." She pushes all the floppy flowers off her lap. "I'll just get down on my knees right now and pray that I get Dan back. I'll pray that I get the necklace back and I get Dan back and why do I have to stop there? I can pray that Tracy Lee never died. I can pray that she comes back to life. Why didn't her mother ever think of that?"

Good news. The swimming pool is fixed. They'll be able to fill it tomorrow. But Kelvin is depressed. Early this afternoon—partly to keep them from bothering the men who were working on the pool—he took Marie and Josephine uptown. He let them get ice cream cones. He told them to pay attention and eat the ice cream up quickly, because the sun was hot, and it would melt. They ignored him. They licked at their cones now and then, as if they had all day. Ice cream was soon dribbling down their chins and down their arms. Kelvin had grabbed a handful of paper napkins but he couldn't wipe it up fast enough. They were a mess. A spectacle. They didn't care. Kelvin told them they weren't so pretty that they could afford to look like that.

"Some people don't like the look of us anyway," he said. "Some people don't even think we should be allowed uptown. People just get used to seeing us and not staring at us like freaks and you make a mess and spoil it."

They laughed at him. He could have cowed Marie if he had her alone, but not when she was with Josephine. Josephine was one who needed some old-fashioned discipline, in Kelvin's opinion. Kelvin had been in places where people didn't get away with anything like they got away with here. He didn't agree with hitting. He had seen plenty of it done, but he didn't agree with it, even on the hand. But a person like Josephine could be shut up in her room, she could be made to sit in a corner, she could be put on bread and water, and it would do a lot of good. All Marie needed was a talking-to, she had a weak personality. But Josephine was a devil.

"I'll talk to both of them," Trudy says. "I'll tell them to say they're sorry."

"I want for them to *be* sorry," Kelvin says. "I don't care if they say they are. I'm not taking them ever again."

Later, when all the others are in bed, Trudy gets him to sit down to play cards with her, on the screened verandah. They play Crazy Eights. Kelvin says that's all he can manage tonight, his head is sore.

Uptown, a man said to him, "Hey, which one of them two is your girlfriend?"

"Stupid," Trudy says. "He was a stupid jerk."

The man talking to the first man said, "Which one you going to marry?"

"They don't know you, Kelvin. They're just stupid."

But they did know him. One was Reg Hooper, one was Bud DeLisle. Bud DeLisle that sold real estate. They knew him, they had talked to him in the barbershop, they called him Kelvin. Hey, Kelvin, which one you going to marry?

"Nerds," says Trudy. "That's what Robin would say."

"You think they're your friend but they're not," says Kelvin, "how many times I see that happen."

Trudy goes to the kitchen to put on coffee. She wants to have fresh coffee to offer Janet, when Janet comes in. She apologized, this morning, and Janet said all right, I know you're upset. It really is all right. Sometimes, you think they're your friend, and they are.

She looks at all the mugs hanging on their hooks. She and Janet shopped all over to find them. A mug with each one's name. Marie, Josephine, Arthur, Kelvin, Shirley, George, Dorinda. You'd think Dorinda would be the hardest name to find, but actually, the hardest was Shirley. Even the people who can't read have learned to recognize their own mugs, by color and pattern.

One day two new mugs appeared, bought by Kelvin. They said Trudy, and Janet.

"I'm not going to be too overjoyed seeing my name in that line-up," Janet said. "But I wouldn't hurt his feelings for a million dollars."

For a honeymoon, Dan took her to an island on the lake, where the hotel was. The hotel was closed down, but his mother still lived there. Dan's father was dead. His mother lived there alone. She took the boat with the outboard motor across the water, to get her groceries. She sometimes made a mistake, and called Trudy, Marlene.

The hotel wasn't much. It was a white wooden box in a clearing by the shore. Some little boxes of cabins stuck behind it. Dan and Trudy stayed in one of the cabins. Every cabin had a wood stove. Dan built a fire at night to take off the chill. But the blankets were damp and heavy, when he and Trudy woke up in the morning.

Dan caught fish, and cooked them. He and Trudy climbed the big rock behind the cabins, and picked blueberries. He asked her if she knew how to make a piecrust, and she didn't. So he showed her, rolling out the dough with a whisky bottle.

In the morning there was a mist over the lake, just as you see in the movies, or in a painting.

One afternoon Dan stayed out longer than usual, fishing. Trudy kept busy for a while in the kitchen, rubbing the dust off things, washing some jars. It was the oldest, darkest kitchen she had ever seen, with wooden racks for the dinner plates to dry in. She went outside, and climbed the rock by herself, thinking she would pick some blueberries. But it was already dark under the trees, the evergreens made it dark, and she didn't like the idea of wild animals. She sat on the rock looking down on the roof of the hotel, the old dead leaves and broken shingles. She heard a piano being played. She scrambled down the rock and followed the music, around to the front of the building. She walked along the front verandah and stopped at a window, looking into the room that used to be the lounge. The room with the blackened stone fireplace, the lumpy leather chairs, the horrible mounted fish.

Dan's mother was there, playing the piano. A tall, straight-backed old woman, with her grey-black hair twisted into such a tiny knot. She sat and played the piano, without any lights on, in the half-dark, half-bare room.

Dan had said that his mother came from a rich family. She had taken piano lessons, dancing lessons, she had gone around the world, when she was a young girl. There was a picture of her, on a camel. But she wasn't playing a classical piece, the sort of thing you'd expect her to have learned. She was playing, "It's Three O'Clock in the Morning." When she got to the end she started in again. Maybe it was a special favorite of hers, something she had danced to, in the old days. Or maybe she wasn't satisfied yet, that she had got it right.

Why does Trudy now remember this moment? She sees her young self looking in the window at the old woman playing the piano. The dim room, with its oversize beams and fireplaces and the lonely leather chairs. The clattering, faltering, persistent, piano music. Trudy remembers that so clearly and it seems she stood outside her own body, which ached, then, from the punishing pleasures of love. She stood outside her own happiness, in a tide of sadness. And the opposite thing happened, the morning Dan left. Then she stood outside her own unhappiness in a tide of what seemed unreasonably like love. But it was the same thing, really, when you got outside. What are those times that stand out, clear patches in your life—what do they have to do with it? They aren't exactly promises. Breathing spaces. Is that all?

She goes into the front hall and listens for any noise from upstairs.
All quiet there, all medicated.

The phone rings, right beside her head.
"Are you still there?" Robin says.
"I'm still here."
"Can I run over and ride home with you? I didn't go for my run earlier because it was too hot."

You threw the jug. You could have killed me.
Yes.

Kelvin, waiting at the card table, under the light, looks bleached and old. There's a pool of light whitening his brown hair. His face sags, waiting. He looks old, sunk into himself, wrapped in a thick bewilderment, nearly lost to her. Nearly lost.
"Kelvin, do you pray?" says Trudy. Her voice sounds harsh, even panicky, though she didn't mean it to. Also, she didn't know she was going to ask him that. "I mean, it's none of my business. But like, for anything specific?"
He's got an answer for her, which is rather surprising. He pulls his face up, as if he might have felt the tug he needed, to bring him to the surface.
"If I was smart enough to know what to pray for," he says, "then I wouldn't have to."
He smiles at her, with some oblique notion of conspiracy, offering his halfway joke. It's not meant as comfort, particularly. Yet it radiates—what he said, the way he said it, just the fact that he's there

again, radiates, expands the way some silliness can, when you're very tired. In this way, when she was young, and high, a person or a moment could become a lily floating on the cloudy riverwater, perfect and familiar.

Karl Iagnemma

⌗

On the Nature of Human
Romantic Interaction

When students here can't stand another minute they get drunk and hurl themselves off the top floor of the Gehring Building, the shortest building on campus. The windows were tamper-proofed in August, so the last student forced open the roof-access door and screamed, *Pussy!* and dove spread-eagled into the night sky. From the TechInfo office I watched his body rip a silent trace through the immense snow dunes that ring the Gehring Building. A moment later he poked his head from the dune, dazed and grinning, and his four nervous frat brothers whooped and dusted him off and carried him on their shoulders to O'Dooley's, where they bought him shots of Jaegermeister until he was so drunk he slid off his stool and cracked his teeth against the stained oak bar.

In May a freshwoman named Deborah Dailey heaved a chair through a plate-glass window on the fifth floor of the Gray Building, then followed the chair down to the snowless parking lot, shattering both ankles and fracturing her skull. Later we learned—unsurprisingly—that her act had something to do with love: false love, failed love, mistimed or misunderstood or miscarried love. For no one here, I'm convinced, is truly happy in love. This is the Institute: a windswept quadrangle edged by charm-proofed concrete buildings. The sun disappears in October and temperatures drop low enough to flash-freeze saliva; spit crackles against the pavement like hail. In January whiteouts shut down the highways, and the outside world takes on a quality very much like oxygen: we know it exists all around us, but we can't see it.

It's a disturbing thing to be part of. My ex-Ph.D. advisor, who's been here longer than any of us, claims that the dormitory walls are abuzz with frustration, and if you press your ear against the heating ducts at night you can hear the jangling bedsprings and desperate whimpers of masturbators. Some nights my ex-advisor wanders the sub-basement hallways of the Gray Building and screams obscenities until he feels refreshed and relatively tranquil.

I used to be a Ph.D. student, but now my job is to sit all night at a government-issue desk in the TechInfo office, staring at a red TechHotline telephone. The TechHotline rings at 3:00 and 4:00 A.M., and I listen to distraught graduate students stammer about corrupted-file allocation tables and SCSI controller failures. I tell them to close their eyes and take a deep breath; I tell them everything will be all right. The TechInfo office looks onto the quadrangle, and just before dawn, when the sky has mellowed to the color of a deep bruise, the Institute looks almost peaceful. At those rare moments I love my job and I love this town and I love this institute. This is an indisputable fact: there are many, many people around here who love things that will never love them back.

A Venn diagram of my love for Alexandra looks like this:

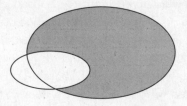

My inventory of love is almost completely consumed by Alexandra, while hers is shared by myself and others (or, more precisely: $|A|>|M|$; $\exists x$ s.t. $x \in (A \cap M)$; $\exists y$ s.t. $y \in A$, $y \xi M$; $\exists z$ s.t. $z \in A$, $z \xi M$). We live in a cabin next to the Owahee River and the Institute's research-grade nuclear power plant. Steam curls off the hyperboloidal cooling tower and settles in an icy mist on our roof, and some nights I swear I can see the reactor building glowing. Alexandra has hair the color of maple syrup, and she is sixteen years younger than me; she is twenty-five. She sips tea every morning in the front room of our cabin, and when I turn into the driveway and see her hair through the window I feel a deep, troubling urge.

Alexandra is the daughter of my ex-advisor, who has never claimed to be happy in love. On Wednesdays, at noon he meets a sophomore named Larissa in the Applied Optics Laboratory and scoots her onto the vibration isolation table and bangs her until the air pistons sigh. Every morning my ex-advisor straps on showshoes and clomps past our cabin on his way to the Institute, gliding atop the frozen crust like a Nordic vision of Jesus. I have given Alexandra an ultimatum: she has until commencement day to decide if she wants to marry me. If she does not want to marry me, I will pack my textbooks and electronic diagnostic equipment and move to Huntsville, Alabama.

When students jump off the Gehring Building, they curse and scream as though their hands are on fire. I can't say I blame them. This is the set of words I use when I talk about the Institute: hunger, numbness, fatigue, yearning, anger. Old photographs of this town show a cathedral of pines standing in place of the bare quadrangle, and a sawmill on the Owahee in place of the nuclear plant. People in the pictures stare at the camera with an unmistakable air of melancholy, and looking at them I wonder if there was ever a happy season on this peninsula.

Alexandra tells me I'm ungenerous toward the Institute; she tells me the cold has freeze-dried my kindness. Here is a fact I cannot refute: on nights when the TechHotline is quiet and snow is settling in swells around the Gehring Building, the silence is pure enough to make you want to weep. Windows in the Walsh Residence Hall blink off, one by one, until the quadrangle is lit only by moonlight. Icicles the size of children work loose and disappear into snowdrifts. Bark-colored hares hop lazily toward the Owahee. In the early-morning dark, before the sun climbs over the Gray Building and the Institute begins to stretch, you can wade into a drift and lie back like an angel and let snow sift down onto you, and the only sound you hear is the slow churn of your own unwilling heart.

Slaney is the name of this town: a few thousand houses and shops crushed up against the Institute like groupies. Slaney has a short but tragic history: founded in 1906 by a Swede as a company town for the Michigan Land and Lumber Company; within a year there were four hundred inhabitants, six boardinghouses, two general stores, a meat market, an icehouse, a whorehouse, seven saloons. The Swede, his heart full to bursting with pride, felled the tallest white pine in the county and propped it in the middle of Slaney's main drag as a monument to the town's greatness. By 1925 there was nothing left around Slaney except birch and tamarack and scrub poplar, and if tumbleweeds existed up here they'd have blown through the abandoned streets with a lonely rustle. The monumental white pine was dragged off to the sawmill in the middle of the night by timber thieves. The Swede drank himself into a stupor in Dan Dunn's empty saloon, then passed out during the twelve-block walk to his house and nearly froze to death.

That spring the hills hiccuped with dynamite blasts from prospectors looking for iron ore, and the Michigan state legislature chose Slaney as the location for a new institute of mining engineering. Every year in Slaney someone loses grip and commits an unspeakably self-destructive act. Here is something my ex-advisor does not think I know: seven years ago, when his ex-wife still lived in Slaney, he followed her to her house on Huron Street for eleven straight days, and one night as he crouched outside her kitchen window was knocked unconscious by a blow from a policeman's night stick. When he woke he was shackled to a stainless-steel toilet. Ontonagon County, I've heard, has the toughest anti-stalking laws in the state.

On Friday nights the TechHotline is quiet. Dormitory windows are dark as graves, and the quadrangle echoes with shouts of horny undergraduates. I lock the TechInfo office, and Alexandra meets me on Mill Street outside the Caribou Lounge, where a six-piece band called Chicken Little plays Benny Goodman and Cab Calloway and Nat King Cole. Twenty-one-year-olds wearing circle skirts and two-tone shoes jam the dance floor and Charleston like they're scaring off demons. Rusty, the bandleader, wears a white silk suit and by eleven is drenched with sweat. I lindy until my knees ache, but Alexandra's just getting started: she climbs onto the stage and whispers into Rusty's ear. He says, *We're gonna do one for the spitfire in the pretty pink blouse.* I sit at the bar and watch Alexandra press up against strange men, and think about how miserable it is to be alone.

On Saturday nights students throng to the Newett Ice Arena to watch the hockey team lose to future NHLers from Houghton and Escanaba. Bartenders on Middle Street stockpile pint glasses and rub their hands together, waiting for the post-game crush. My ex-advisor locks his office door and drinks a half-bottle of sherry, then calls his ex-wife in Sturgeon Falls. He waits until she says, *Hello? Who is this? John, please*—then hangs up. Afterwards he dials the TechHotline, stammering, and I tell him to close his eyes and take a deep breath; I tell him everything will be all right. He says, *I'm sorry, Joseph, good Christ*, and begins to sniffle. Snow ambles down outside the TechInfo window. One Saturday, drunk, my ex-advisor called and managed to say, *Listen, I'm not going to repeat this: my daughter can be somewhat difficult, and I frankly don't know if you're up to the challenge.*

The Swede kept a leather-bound journal detailing the events of his life from the day he arrived in Slaney until the day he died. *Town has grown faster than even my most incautious estimates*, he wrote in 1911. *Andrew Street now one-quarter mile long. Irish, Finns, Cousin Jacks have come, and for some reason a band of Sicilians. No chicken for eight months*. When Slaney was booming in the 1910s, lumberjacks from as far as Bruce Crossing would descend on the town on weekends and get knee-walking drunk on Yellow Dog whiskey, then smash pub stools to splinters with their peaveys. Their steel-calked boots punched holes in Slaney's plank sidewalks. A tenderloin sprang up along the eastern edge of town, and the Swede met a young prostitute named Lotta Scott at Hugh Logan's place on Thomas Street; she charged him two dollars. *Disarmingly frank*, he wrote. *Eyes dark as bituminous coal. Slim ankles. Short patience.*

Before I leave for the TechInfo office in the evening, Alexandra walks from room to room shedding her prim librarian's turtleneck and knee-length skirt and woolen tights, then lies back on the kitchen table, naked, ravenous. Her eyes follow my hands, nervous as squirrels, as I unbuckle myself. She tugs at the seam of my jeans. Outside, snow movers pound down the ice-packed street, their carbon-steel blades gouging the curb. Alexandra smells archival—glue and musty paper and indelible ink—and she loves sex as much as a snowman loves cold. This is what I do: I say a small prayer just before I begin, even though I am not religious. By her own count, Alexandra has had sex with more than thirty-five men.

Alexandra called the TechHotline one night and said, *Sometimes I wish you'd cool it a little bit. I mean, I love you, I love all the nerdy things you do, I just don't understand why you feel the need to control me. We can love each other and still lead normal, semi-independent lives.* I could hear the soft rush of her breathing, a sound that made me dizzy. Alexandra is stingy with love; she is afraid of ending up like her parents, who squandered their love like drunks at a craps table. *I don't want to control you,* I explained, *I'm just a little uncomfortable with the idea of you having sex with strange men.*

The Swede in his journal described the deep silence of the woods, which seemed to him a cruel and beautiful sound. *Streets filled with sweet smell of pitch. Pine as far as I can see. Have fallen in love with that dissolute woman, Lotta Scott. Consumed by thoughts of her.* His spindly, frugal hand filled the journal pages. On May third he recorded the purchase of a new frock coat, for four dollars, tailored by *a clever Polander from Detroit,* and a set of linens *of surpassing quality.* Then on the tenth of May, 1919, the Swede in deliriously shaky script wrote that he and Lotta Scott were married in Burke's Saloon by the justice of the peace with forty-four witnesses present. *I feel as the French explorers must have felt,* he wrote, *when they gazed for the first time upon the vast forests of this wondrous penisula. Glorious, glorious chicken.*

I have tried to convince myself that Alexandra is not a tramp, that she simply suffers from too much love—that she loves too much for her own good. My ex-advisor knocks on the TechInfo office door when he's too lonely to go home. One Saturday night, his shirt unbuttoned and a styrofoam cup of sherry balanced on his knee, he told me I am too particular when it comes to love, that I should accept love no matter how it appears and be grateful. He sipped a sherry in a languid, pensive manner. *There's a certain kind of imperfection that acts as a reference point, that gives a sense of perspective. Understand? The pockmark on the perfect cheek. The small, tragic flaw, like a beauty mark, but deeper.* He squinted out at the forlorn quadrangle. *I don't trust perfection.*

Alexandra's mother was so wonderfully, perfectly imperfect. I once snuck into an auditorium in the Gray Building and watched my ex-advisor deliver a Physics 125 lecture on kinetic and potential energy. As he lectured he smiled at a pair of sleepy-eyed sophomore girls, showing his artificially whitened teeth.

The harder I pull Alexandra toward me the harder she pushes away. It's heartbreaking. Every third Saturday in February the people of Slaney hold Winter Carnival, where they flood the Kmart parking lot and ice skate under a mosaic of stars. Teenaged boys in Red Wings jerseys skate backward and play crack-the-whip to show off. My ex-advisor dons a black beret and circles the rink in long, fluid strides. Last February Alexandra and I skated couples, and in the chilly night her skin was as smooth and luminous as a glass of milk. *What a world!* I found myself thinking, *where a failed engineer with a crooked nose can skate couples with a syrup-haired woman who smells archival.* On Andrew Street, we ate elephant ears and watched a muscular young townie lift people in his arms to guess their weight. Alexandra gave him a dollar, and he hoisted her up with one meaty arm and hugged her to his chest. Alexandra shouted *Whoa, hey! Wow!* and kicked her legs girlishly. When the townie put her down, she kissed him on the cheek, and when she came back and saw my face she said, *Oh, for God's sake, Joseph. Grow up.*

That night at 3:00 A.M. I turned on the bedroom light and knelt over Alexandra and asked her to be my wife. I felt tearful, exultant; I felt as vast and weightless as a raft of clouds; I felt all of Lake Superior welled inside my bursting chest. Sweat seeped from my trembling hands and dampened Alexandra's nightdress. *Joseph,* she said, *Joseph, Joseph, Joseph. Oh, God.* She kissed my cheek the same way she'd kissed the townie. *I just don't know, honey. I just don't know.*

This town: Everywhere I look I see equations. Ice floes tumbling in the Owahee, snowflakes skidding past the TechInfo window: Everywhere I look I see fractals and tensors and nonlinear differential equations. Some mornings when my TechInfo shift is over I stand in front of the Bradford Student Center and hand out pamphlets entitled "Proof of

God's Existence by Series Expansion," and "The Combinatorics of Ancient Roman Orgies." Undergraduates walk broad circles around me. They're bundled in scarves and wool hats; only their eyes show. Alexandra tells me I make people uneasy, that not everything can be described by mathematics, and I tell her she's probably wrong.

I have considered admitting to Alexandra that I hate dancing but worry that she'll find another partner. One night at the Caribou Lounge I ducked out for fresh air, and on a whim wandered into the meager woods; there were no lights in sight but the moonlit snow glowed bright enough to count change by. I laid down and stared up at the muddy streak of our galaxy. I thought—how to explain?—about the nature of imperfection. My ex-advisor every September stands before his Physics 125 class with his arms spread wide, like a preacher, and says, *Listen sharp, this is important: Nature. Hates. Perfection.* Alexandra says I sometimes remind her of her father, and this bothers her more than she can say.

In 1919 Slaney sent three million board feet of pine down the Owahee, and the sawmill howled from morning to dusk. Lumberjacks, tired of two-dollar whores on Thomas Street, sent agonized letters to *Heart and Hand* matrimonial newspaper and convinced scared young women to pack their lives into trunks and board the train north. The Swede on May 17—one week after his wedding—walked deep into the thinning woods and realized the pine would not last forever, that in four or five years it would be *cut out*, and Slaney would be *all caught up. Jacks will move westward, toward Ontonagon and Silver City*, he wrote. *Saloons will empty, sawmill will fall idle. Lotta departed for Hurley this morning at dawn to visit her mother. Declined my offer to accompany her.* Lotta Scott, before she left, borrowed two hundred dollars and a gold-plated pocket watch from the Swede.

I like my ex-advisor but worry that he cares too much about the wrong things. Larissa, the sophomore he bangs on Wednesdays in the Applied Optics Laboratory, has told him he'd better stop worrying about ancient history and start focusing on the here and now. *For Christ's sake*, my ex-advisor said, *she's nineteen years old—a child—telling me this. I love Larissa, but it's not the kind of love she thinks it is.*

Alexandra does not remember the names of some of the men she has slept with. *It was just sex,* she explains, *it wasn't this huge colossal thing.* The first time we made love, she stroked my hair afterwards and explained that I was not supposed to cry, that it was not supposed to be that way.

The tombstones in Slaney's cemetery have Finnish and Polish and Swedish names; they say COOPER and SAWYER and LUMBERJACK. Women who came to town, it seems, took a dismayed look around, then headed back south. The lumberjacks died alone. The Swede, two weeks after Lotta left for Hurley, wrote, *Met a man Masters from Sault St. Marie, who claims the entire eastern half of the peninsula is cut out, not a stick of white pine standing. Martinville, Maynard, Bartlow he claims are empty, the houses deserted and mill torn down for scrap. Queer fellow. Says land looks "naked and embarrassed" without the pine. No word from Lotta.*

The tenderloin was razed in a fit of prohibition righteousness in 1931 and lay vacant and weed-choked for twenty years. A Methodist church now stands where Dan Dunn's saloon used to be. Hugh Logan's whorehouse has been replaced by an electronics store called Circuit Shack. The Swede wrote nothing in his journal for two weeks, then, *Took train to Hurley to find no trace of Lotta. Walked all up and down the dusty streets. Back in Slaney, heard from John Davidson that Lotta was seen on the Sault St. Marie train as far along as Allouez. Davidson was drunk and perhaps not being truthful. Nevertheless I fear she is gone completely.* This is a fact: I live with a woman with syrup-colored hair who loves me in a hard, unknowable way. My ex-advisor one Sunday in the TechInfo office, his feet propped on my desk and a cup of sherry balanced on his knee, smiled cryptically and said, *I believe I can solve your problem with my daughter. I have an idea. A theory.*

Alexandra left to visit her mother in Sturgeon Falls two weeks after Winter Carnival. At the station I blinked back a swell of longing as her train dragged slowly north. Alexandra leaned out the window and blew me a kiss, then tossed a small white bundle into the snow. She was supposed to stay one week in Sturgeon Falls; she was supposed to tell me *yes* or *no* when she returned. I searched for almost two hours but never did find the bundle she threw out the window.

My ex-advisor that night, sprawled in front of the TechInfo radiator like a housecat, told me I cannot expect to understand Alexandra with mathematics alone, and that my view of love is analytical whereas his is romantic. My ex-advisor as he thawed smelled stale, like cooked cabbage. I set my mug of Seagrams down and on a wrinkled envelope wrote:

$$dJ\!/dt = aJ - \beta JA$$
$$dA\!/dt = \chi JA - \delta A$$

Where J is my love, A is Alexandra's. The predatory-prey equations— simple, but very elegant. My words were cold clouds of Canadian whiskey. I rattled the ice cubes in my glass like dice. *You should trust mathematics,* I told him. *Nothing is too complex to describe with mathematics.* Alexandra called early the next morning to tell me she'd decided to stay an extra week in Sturgeon Falls. I closed my eyes and listened to her syrup-colored voice. *I'm going to sit in my mother's sauna and think about everything. Have you ever been in a sauna, honey? It's incredible. First you feel like you're going to die, then you pass a certain point and feel like you're going to live forever.* She sighed. *And I'm helping my mother plan her wedding—she's getting remarried. Don't tell my father.*

I can build you a sauna. I can build it in the backyard, next to the big poplar.

His name is Harold. He breeds minks. There's hundreds of minks running around up here, honey. Her voice dropped to a whisper. *It makes me horny, in a weird way.*

I didn't say anything.

Joseph, I have never cheated on you, she said suddenly. Her voice held a thin edge of desperation. *I want you to understand that.* Alexandra, before she hung up, said that the bundle she threw out the train window contained a peach pit, nothing more.

My dissertation, which I never finished, was entitled "Nonlinear

Control of Biomimetic Systems." The first chapter, which I finished, was entitled "On the Nature of Human Romantic Interaction." It begins: *Consider a third-order system with three states corresponding to three distinct people, A, B, and C. A is attracted to B and C. B and C are both attracted to A but not to each other. We would like to describe the behavior of this system over time.*

One night while Alexandra was in Sturgeon Falls I sat staring into the darkened quadrangle for a long time. Finally I called her and said, *I can't wait forever, I can give you until commencement day, but then I'm moving to Huntsville, Alabama.* Alexandra was stunned, silent. *I don't know what else to do.* My ex-advisor convinced me to give Alexandra the Huntsville ultimatum. I had four handwritten pages of equations contradicting his advice, but he took the pencil from my hand and said, *Joseph, my friend, it's extremely simple: the only reason my daughter will not marry you is if she does not, in fact, love you.* Huntsville, Alabama. I chose Huntsville randomly off the map; I don't know what I'd do in a January without snow.

In my dissertation I proved analytically that it's possible to design a control system such that A's attraction to B grew exponentially, while A's attraction to C diminished exponentially. In the concluding paragraph, however, there is a caveat: *In practice the coupling factors are highly nonlinear and difficult to predict, and depend on phenomena such as shyness, boredom, desire, desperation, and self-knowledge, as well as numerous local conditions: the feeling of self-confidence gained from wearing a favorite pair of socks, the unexpected sorrow of seeing the season's first flock of geese flying south, etc.*

Alexandra returned from Sturgeon Falls five weeks before commencement day wearing a white muff, a gift from her mother's mink-breeder fiancé. She walked from the front door to the bedroom and dropped her suitcase on the bed, then walked back into the kitchen and gripped my shoulders and said, *Listen to me, Joseph: I love you. I love the shit out of you. But I'll never belong to you.*

That night I waited until Alexandra was asleep, then pulled on boots and a parka and walked the half-mile to the Institute. The Gehring Building was quiet except for a dull chorus of electronic devices. The TechInfo office was silent as a prayer. Suddenly I had an idea: I ran across the quadrangle to the Olssen Building, the tallest building on campus, and sprinted from classroom to empty classroom, turning on lights. I formed a three-story lit-up A, then an L, then an E, then part of an X—then I ran out of classrooms. The Olssen Building wasn't wide enough. Back in the TechInfo office, I threw open the window, breathless, and looked out across the quadrangle. ALE. The lights spelled Ale. A group of fraternity brothers had gathered and when I appeared as a silhouette in the TechInfo window they shouted, *Yo, hot-line man! Ale! Fuckin' A!*

I closed the office door and turned off the lights, picked up the telephone and dialed. The phone rang three times, four times, five—and then Alexandra answered. Her voice was husky and irritable, the voice of a confident young woman disturbed from sleep. She said, *Hello? Who the hell is this—Joseph?*

I hung up.

They found ore in the hills around Slaney in 1926—not the glittery hematite they were seeing in Ishpeming, but a muddy blue sludge that assayed at 60 percent iron. Overnight, Slaney was reborn: the front glass of Dan Dunn's saloon was replaced and the floor replanked; Hugh Logan's place on Thomas Street was scrubbed down and reopened. The Swede awoke from a monthlong bender, his handwriting looser and less optimistic. *Strange to see trains unloading again. Excitement even at the meat market; ore, they say, is everywhere. No chicken for nine months.* My ex-advisor, one chilly April Sunday in the TechInfo office, explained that his ex-wife had taken out a restraining order, and if he called her one more time he would be arrested. It took me two months to realize that *chicken* was the Swede's code word for intercourse.

Alexandra's mother, my ex-advisor said, *has the sort of posture you see in Victorian portraiture. Ivory skin, fingers that are almost impossibly delicate, yet strong. Beautifully strong, and that noble Victorian posture.* He stroked his stubbled chin and nodded, agreeing with himself. *And I treated her like shit on a heel.* My ex-advisor, one month before commencement day, somehow learned about his ex-wife's impending wedding, and he wandered into the quadrangle and slumped down in the dingy snow and refused to budge.

Alexandra was asked by her mother to be maid of honor. She sipped tea in the front room of our cabin, tearing pages from *Bride* magazine and acting like everything was okay. Alexandra does not understand the urgency that grips you at thirty; she does not understand the desperation that settles in at forty. I began staying late at work, wandering the Gehring Building's damp sub-basement tunnels. Down in the tunnels, I walked for hours without seeing a hint of the morning sky, and I felt how I imagined the old ore miners must have felt. One morning I told Alexandra that if she marries me she does not necessarily have to stop seeing other men, and she looked at me with confusion and deep pity and slapped my face.

The Institute graduated its first class of engineers in 1930, but the residents of Slaney had no use for book-taught miners. The Swede, caught up in the excitement, paid thirty dollars for a claim on fifteen acres he'd never seen, and his first week out found a nugget of what he thought was solid gold. He squatted in the snow outside his lean-to and threw his head back and shouted at the moon. He was sixty-two years old. *As much as I can haul out*, he wrote. *Nuggets size of fists. Rapture.*

The Slaney Mountain was a wet hole of a mine with a safety record that made the sawmill look like a nursery. A 1931 cave-in sent pressurized air pounding through the shaft, and thirteen miners were punched into the air, then flung down, uninjured. A moment later the creaking support timbers fell silent, and a blanket of rock crushed the breath from their lungs. All thirteen died. In 1932 an Italian accidentally stubbed his cigar into a tub of freshly thawed dynamite, and the blast rattled windows as far away as Andrew Street. The Swede on March 13, 1933, convinced he'd hit a mother lode, sold his house and hocked his gold family ring for three hundred acres and a pair of mules. He sat all night atop his tiny hill, staring at the forest draped in darkness and dreaming of Pierce-Arrow automobiles and English leather gloves, and when the sun broke over the frozen valley he began to dig.

Two weeks before commencement day I woke to find Alexandra sitting at the foot of the bed, teary-eyed. *Bride's* magazine lay tattered on her lap. She climbed beneath the comforter, sniffling, and said, *I wish you'd quit doing what you're doing. I wish you'd let things keep going the way they're going on.* It's crushing to remember the years before Alexandra: partial differential equations, cold beef pasties, the smell of melting solder and the heartless glow of a fluorescent lamp. I pulled Alexandra close and told her to close her eyes and take a deep breath, I told her everything would be all right, and she looked at me with confusion and deep pity and said, *Cut it out.*

The Swede stockpiled gold for five months, then one morning hitched his mules to a rented sledge and paraded his mound of nuggets down Slaney's main drag. Old broken prospectors with hematite in their hair and an alcoholic's tremble stared out through Dan Dunn's front window and muttered softly at the sight. *Celebrated with sirloin steak and Yellow Dog whiskey, then strolled over to Thomas Street. Feasted on chicken.*

One week before commencement day the snow in the quadrangle began to shrink; then as if by sleight of hand the sun appeared where there had been only clouds. Physical plant workers tucked geraniums into planter boxes and for the first time in months students unwrapped their scarves and looked around. One night I stayed sixteen hours at the TechInfo office. When I got home I packed my books into milk crates and stacked them next to the door; Alexandra waited until I was asleep then unpacked them and placed them neatly back on the bookshelf. The nuggets the Swede had spent everything to pull from the ground were not pure gold, he discovered, but copper spiked with fatty veins of pyrite. The rock he'd spent five months hauling from his plot was worth nine dollars and sixty-three cents.

The day before commencement day I purchased a nonrefundable ticket to Huntsville. I had not showered, and the TechInfo office reflected what must be my own human smell: lemon and sour milk and powdered cumin. That night, his feet resting on the TechInfo desk, my ex-advisor said, *You should not let yourself go like this, Joseph. It's undignified.* After he left, two Slaney policemen knocked on the door. Their furry snow hats were pulled low on their foreheads. They were looking for my ex-advisor. When I asked them what they wanted the smaller policeman pursed his lips and said, *We can't divulge that infor-*

mation. When I asked them if my ex-advisor was in trouble he said, *We can't divulge that information.*

The police, I learned eventually, were searching for a man who'd climbed into the heating ducts of the Benson Dormitory and watched an unnamed freshwoman apply lotion to her calves. The police had swept the Gray Building and sat for hours watching the Student Center, but no one had seen my ex-advisor. I told them I had no idea where he was. I told them it's not easy to hide in a town this small.

The ore around Slaney, it turned out, was not a single wide vein but pockety and impossible to follow. The D & C, Silver Lake and Petersen mines stopped drilling in 1937. The Slaney Mountain mine—the first mine—stayed stubbornly open, and in 1939 engineers thought they'd hit a million-ton ore body. But two months later the ore was gone. The mountain shut down. The last miners boarded the train west, for Houghton or Ishpeming. Dan Dunn nailed planks across the front window of his saloon and left Slaney for good. The Swede, penniless and without a home, took a bottle of Yellow Dog whiskey into the cut-out woods and sat down in the snow and put a .45 pistol to his mouth and pulled the trigger.

The pine around Slaney is gone. The ore is gone. The shaft house stands crumbling and windowless a half-mile from the Institute, and on Friday nights high-schoolers sneak inside and drink Boone's Farm Strawberry Hill and grope one another. My ex-advisor says that men never dig for iron or copper or coal; secretly, in their heart's heart, they're digging for gold. The Swede, before he shot himself in 1940, wrote: *Heard from a man Jonsson that Lotta is in Grand Rapids and married to a furniture magnate. Said he saw them two months ago in church, Lotta dressed in silk and singing a beautiful soprano. Not certain Jonsson was being truthful; told of Lotta only after securing a loan of thirty dollars. So be it. Wherever Lotta is I wish her happiness. I write these words without regret.*

On the morning of commencement day the air smelled salty, like trouble, and from nowhere a milk-gray sheet fell over the sky and the temperature dropped twenty degrees in twenty minutes. By 8:00 A.M. snow was swirling in the late-May breeze, and by nine there were four inches on the highway and the radio was saying it looked like we were going to get socked but good. Alexandra and I stayed in bed. I rolled her into a position we called the log drive, and she told me—she shouted—that she loves me, goddamnit, *yes*, and she wants to be with me forever. I stopped. Outside, the wind sobbed. Alexandra, her face flushed the color of ripe rhubarb, stumbled from the bedroom and closed the door. Forty minutes later, when it was clear she wasn't coming back, I bundled myself in a parka and thermal snow pants and set off for the Institute.

From outside the TechInfo office I heard a floorboard creak, then a moist sniffle. I opened the door: Alexandra was sitting in the TechHotline chair in front of the window, staring into the quadrangle. She looked at me; she looked back out the window; she shrugged awkwardly and said, *So, this is it. The famous office.*

In the quadrangle a stage had been erected near the Gray Building, and on the lawn an assembly of crimson-gowned seniors squirmed and hooted in the driving snow. Behind them, underdressed parents shivered in their seats, wondering what kind of people could live in a place like this. At the edge of the quadrangle the Caribou Brass Band sent up a frozen-lipped Sousa march. I drew the window shade, momentarily nostalgic at the sight of so much unbridled optimism, and as I did the crowd quieted and the provost took the podium and cleared her throat. *Students, parents, distinguished guests, fellow alumni and alumnae: Welcome. Today is a joyous day.*

Alexandra scooted onto the desk, her snow-booted feet not touching the floor, and pulled me down to her. *Just lie here*, she said, *Don't get funny*. Her breathing was loud in my ear: a seashore, a multitude. I kissed her smooth neck, and let myself believe that we were two strangers pressed together, shivering with possibility. Alexandra stroked my back, but when I began to stir she gripped my shoulders with heartbreaking finality. *Just don't*, she said. *Okay? Please. Just stay.*

From the quadrangle, the voice of the Institute's first female graduate drifted into the office. *I remember that my bedroom was in the infirmary, and boys would stand outside arguing over who would walk me to chemistry class. I remember walking to class and wondering how in the world a girl like myself ended up at a place with so many wonderful, wonderful boys.* Alexandra shifted beneath me. Suddenly there was a ripple of applause, and the microphone reverberated as if it had been dropped, then the tinny, shouted voice of my ex-advisor announced that he was having an immoral relationship with an undergraduate.

Alexandra struggled to her feet. The crowd hushed. Alexandra shoved aside the window shade and said, *Jesus Christ, fuck Dad*—then grabbed her parka and threw open the TechInfo door and clattered down the Gehring Building stairs.

Outside, the crowd had fractured into a jumble of bewildered voices. The provost stood at the podium, saying, *Okay, let's just be calm, people*—then a woman screamed and two people stood and pointed: I followed their gaze to the roof of the Gray Building, where my ex-advisor stood in full academic regalia, looking like an Arthurian pimp. His arms were hugged against his chest in a way that struck me as tremendously fragile. He shifted his weight from foot to foot, his crimson robes billowing in the snowy breeze; then I spotted Alexandra, a red-jacketed streak across the quadrangle. She sprinted past the brass band, past the podium, and burst through the Gray Building's tall front doors.

I threw open the window, half-expecting the TechHotline to ring, as a distant wail went up from the Slaney Firehouse. Atop the Gray Building, my ex-advisor tugged off his eight-cornered hat and tossed it limply over the edge. It fluttered down, down, down, then landed on the sidewalk, flopped once and lay flat. An anxious moan rose from the crowd. He climbed the safety railing and leaned over the roof edge, his wispy hair whipping in the breeze, and the provost over the loud-speaker said, *Please, please: Please.*

Then Alexandra appeared behind her father. She approached him slowly. He turned to her and spread his arms wide, his face a mask of nervous relief, then seemed to slip on the icy roof: he took a quick step backward and froze, arms thrown up to heaven, and then he was airborne. Down he went, his crimson robes rippling, as he bicycled in the frozen air then disappeared without a sound into a steep snowbank.

A chorus of screams rose up, and the provost whispered, *Sweet Jesus* into the microphone and covered her face. Alexandra rushed to the roof edge. A quartet of Slaney firemen jogged into the courtyard with a folded-up safety net and looked around, confused. I made a quick calculation: a 180-pound man, falling thirty feet at 32.2 feet per second squared—I drew the shade and turned away from the window and closed my eyes.

Wind howled past the TechInfo window. A baby broke into a restless wail. After what seemed like a long time I heard a hopeful shout, and I peeked around the shade: my ex-advisor was struggling out of the snowbank, clutching his left shoulder, surrounded by shocked firemen. I closed my eyes. I looked again: Alexandra, red parka gone and hair whipped into a cloud, rushed hip-deep into the snowbank and threw her arms around her father's neck. She touched his cheek, as if to make sure he was real and not some snowblown mirage. My ex-advisor, eyes squeezed shut with pain, slumped down in the drifting snow and hugged his daughter with his good arm and began to weep.

The Detroit train left at 11:13 P.M., and from there it was two connections and twenty-two hours to Huntsville. I sat in the TechInfo office until it was time to leave for the station, and when the TechHotline rang I didn't pick up. The CALL light threw jagged shadows against the dark office walls. I knew there were equations describing the contour of the shadows, the luminescent intensity of the CALL light, the heat distribution in my hands as I clasped them together, the stress distribution in my eyelids as I pressed my eyes shut. In the quadrangle, snow drifted down with perfect indifferent randomness. In thousands of dormitory bedrooms, young men and women were asleep and dreaming of numbers.

I would begin a new line of research in Alabama, I decided. I would throw away my textbooks and Institute notepads and start fresh. What effect does geography have on love? What effect does weather have on love? There are events in nature, I've noticed, that cannot be explained or reproduced, that simply *are*. It's enough to give a person hope.

Yiyun Li

❖

Immortality

His story, as the story of every one of us, started long before we were born. For dynasties, our town provided the imperial families their most reliable servants. Eunuchs they are called, though out of reverence we call them Great Papas. None of us is a direct descendant of a Great Papa, but traveling upstream in the river of our blood, we find uncles, brothers, and cousins who gave up their maleness so that our names would not vanish in history. Generations of boys, at the age of seven or eight, were chosen and castrated—*cleaned* as it was called—and sent into the palace as apprentices, learning to perform domestic tasks for the emperor and his family. At the age of thirteen or fourteen, they started to earn their allowances, silver coins that they saved and sent home to their parents. The coins were kept in a trunk, along with a small silk sack in which the severed male root was preserved with herbs. When the brothers of Great Papas reached the marriage age, their parents unlocked the trunk and brought out the silver coins. The money allowed the brothers to marry their wives; the wives gave birth to their sons; the sons grew up to carry on the family name, either by giving birth to more sons, or by going into the palace as cleaned boys. Years went by. When Great Papas could no longer serve the imperial masters on their wobbled knees, they were released from the palace and taken in by their nephews, who respected them as their own fathers. Nothing left for them to worry about, they sat all day in the sun and stroked the cats they had brought home from the palace, fat and slow as they themselves were, and watched the male dogs chasing the females in the alleys. In time death came for them. Their funerals were the most spectacular events in our town: sixty-four Buddhist monks in golden and red robes chanted prayers for forty-nine days to lead their souls into heaven; sixty-four Tao masters in blue and gray robes danced for forty-nine days to drive away any evils that dared to attach to their bodies. The divine moment came at the end of the forty-nine days, when the silk sacks containing their withered male roots were placed in the coffins. Now that the missing part had rejoined the body, the soul could leave without regret, to a place better than our town.

This was the story of every one of our Great Papas. For dynasties they were the most trustworthy members of the imperial family. They tended to the princesses' and the emperor's concubines' most personal tasks without tainting the noble blood with the low and dirty desires of men; they served the emperor and the princes with delicacy, yet, unlike those young handmaids who dreamed of seducing the emperor and his sons with their cheap beauties, Great Papas posed no threat to the imperial wives. There were wild rumors, though, about them serving as playthings for the princes before they reached the legal age to take concubines; and unfortunate tales of Great Papas being drowned, burned, bludgeoned, beheaded for the smallest mistakes—but such stories, as we all know, were made up to attack the good name of our town. What we believe is what we have seen—the exquisitely carved tombstones in our cemetery, the elegantly embroidered portraits in our family books. Great Papas filled our hearts with pride and gratitude. If not for them, who were we, the small people born into this no-name town?

The glory of our town has faded in the past century. But may I tell you one boy's story, before I reach the falling of Great Papas in history? As a tradition, the boys sent to the palace were not to be the only sons, who held the even more sacred duty of siring more boys. But the greatest among our Great Papas was an only son of his family. His father, also an only son, died young before he had the chance to plant more seeds in his wife's belly. With no uncle or brother to send them money from the palace, the boy and his widowed mother lived in poverty. At ten years old, after a fight with the neighbors' boys who had bragged about their brothers accepting gold bricks from the emperor's hands, the boy went into the cowshed and *cleaned* himself, with a rope and a sickle. According to the legend, the boy walked across the town, his male root dripping blood in his hand, and shouted to the people watching on with pity in their eyes, "Wait until I become the best servant of His Majesty!" Unable to endure the shame and the despair of living under a son-less and grandson-less roof, his mother threw herself into a well. Twenty years later the son became the master eunuch in the palace, taking under his charge 2,800 eunuchs and 3,200 handmaids. With no brothers to send his money to, he saved every coin and retired as the richest man in the region. He hired men to dig out his poor mother's coffin and gave her a second funeral, the most extravagant one ever to take place in our town. It was in the ninth month of 1904, and to this day our old people haven't stopped talking about every detail of the funeral: the huge coffin carved out of a sandalwood tree, stacks of gold bricks, trunks of silk clothes, and cases of jade bowls for her to use in the next life. Even more impressive were the four young girls the son had purchased from the poor peasants in the mountain, all of them twelve years old. They were put into satin dresses they would have never dreamed of wearing, and were each fed a cup of mercury. The mercury killed them instantly, so their peachy complexions were preserved when they were paraded in sedan chairs before the coffin. With burning incense planted in their curled fingers, the four girls accompanied the mother to the other world as her loyal handmaids.

This Great Papa's story was the brightest page in our history, like that one most splendid firework streaking the sky before darkness floods in. Soon the last dynasty was overthrown. The emperor was driven out of the Forbidden City; so were his most loyal servants, the last generation of our Great Papas. By the 1930s most of them lived in poverty in the temples around the Forbidden City. Only the smartest ones earned a fair living by showing their bodies to Western reporters and tourists, charging extra for answering questions, even more for having their pictures taken.

We have a short decade of republic; the warlords; two world wars, in both of which we fight on the winning side yet win nothing; the civil war; and finally we see the dawn of communism.

The day the dictator claims the communist victory in our country, a young carpenter in our town comes home to his newly wedded wife.

"It says we are going to have a new life from now on," the young wife tells the husband, pointing to a loudspeaker on their roof.

"New or old, life is the same," the husband replies. He gets his wife into bed and makes love to her, his eyes half-closed in ecstasy while the loudspeaker is broadcasting a new song, with men and women repeating the same lyrics over and over.

This is how the son is conceived, in a chorus of *Communism is so great, so great, and so great.* The same song is broadcast day after day, and the young mother hums along, touching her growing belly and cutting carefully the dictator's pictures from newspapers. Of course we never call him the dictator. We call him Our Father, Our Savior, the North Star of Our Lives, the Never Falling Sun of Our Era. Like most women of her generation, the mother is illiterate. Yet unlike others, she likes to look at newspapers, and she saves the pictures of the dictator in a thick notebook. Isn't she the woman with the greatest wisdom in our town? No other woman would ever think of looking at the dictator's face while pregnant with a son. Of course there has always been the saying that the more a pregnant woman studies a face, the greater the possibility of the baby owning that face. Years ago, young mothers in the cities liked to look at one kind of imported doll, all of them having the foreign name of Shirley Temple. Decades later, movie stars will be the most studied faces among the pregnant mothers. But at this time, the dictator is the only superstar in the media, so the mother has been gazing at the dictator's face for ten months before the baby's birth.

The son is born with the dictator's face, a miracle unnoticed by us at first. For the next ten years, we will avoid looking at him, for fear we will see his dead father in his face. The father was a hardworking man, nice to his neighbors, good to his wife. We would have never imagined that he would be an enemy of our newborn communist nation. Yet there are witnesses, not one, but a whole pub of evening drinkers.

What gets him killed is his comment about heroes and sows. At this time, we respect the communist power above us as our big brother. In our big-brother country, it is said, women are encouraged to produce babies for the communist cause, and those who have given birth to a certain number of babies are granted the title *mother hero*. Now that we are on the same highway to the same heaven, the dictator decides to adopt the same policy.

The young carpenter is a little drunk when he jokes aloud to his fellow drinkers, "Mother heroes? My sow has given birth to ten babies in a litter. Shouldn't she be granted a title, too?"

That's it, a malicious attack on the dictator's population policy. The carpenter is executed after a public trial. All but his wife attend the meeting, every one of us sticking our fists high and hailing the people's victory, our unanimous voice drowning out his wife's moans from her bed. We shout slogans when the bullet hits the young man's head. We chant revolutionary songs when his body is paraded in the street. When we finally lose our voices from exhaustion, we hear the boy's first cry, loud and painful, and for a moment, it is difficult for us to look into each other's eyes. What have we done to a mother and a baby? Wasn't the dead young man one of our brothers?

What we do not know, at the time, is that a scholar in the capital has been thrown in jail and tortured to death for predicting a population explosion and calling on the dictator to change the policy. Nor do we know that in a meeting with the leader of the big-brother country in Moscow, the dictator has said that we do not fear another world war or nuclear weapons: *Let the Americans drop the atomic bombs on our heads. We have five hundred million people in our nation. Even if half of us are killed, we still have two hundred and fifty million, and these two hundred and fifty million would produce another two hundred and fifty million in no time.*

Later, when we read his words in the newspaper, our blood boils. For the years to come, we will live with our eyes turned to the sky, waiting for the American bombs to rain down on us, waiting to prove to the dictator our courage, and our loyalty.

The boy grows up fast like a bamboo shoot. The mother grows old even faster. After the carpenter's death, upon her request, the Revolution Committee in our town gives her a job as our street sweeper. Every dawn, we lie in our beds and listen to the rustling of her bamboo broom. She has become a widow at the age of eighteen, as beautiful as a young widow could be, and naturally some of our bachelors cannot help but fantasize about her in their single beds. Yet none of our young men offers her another marriage. Who wants to marry a counterrevolutionary's widow, and spend the rest of his life worrying about being a sympathizer of the wrong person? What's more, even though the dictator has said that men and women are equal in our nation, we still believe a widow who wants another husband is a whore inside. Our belief is confirmed when we read in newspapers the dictator's comment about one of his close followers who has become an enemy of the nation: *A man cannot conceal his reactionary nature forever, just as a widow cannot hide her desire to be fucked.*

So the young mother withers in our eyes. Her face becomes paler each day, and her eyes drier. By the time the boy is ten, the mother looks like a woman of sixty. None of our bachelors bothers to lay his eyes on her face anymore.

The boy turns ten the year the famine starts. Before the famine, for three years, we have been doing nothing except singing of our communist heaven and vowing to liberate the suffering working class around the world. Farmers and workers have stopped toiling, their days spent in the pains and joys of composing yet another poem, competing to be the most productive proletarian poet. We go to the town center every day to discuss the strategy of how to conquer the world under the leadership of the dictator. When the famine catches us unprepared, we listen to the dictator's encouraging words in the loudspeakers. He calls for us to make our belts one notch tighter for our communist future, and we happily punch more holes in them. The second year of the famine, the dictator says in the loudspeakers: *Get rid of the sparrows and the rats; they are the thieves who stole our food, and brought hunger to us.*

Killing sparrows is the most festive event in the three long years of famine. After months of drinking thin porridges and eating weed roots, on the morning of the sparrow-killing day we each get two steamed buns from the municipal dining room. After breakfast, we climb to the roof of every house, and start to strike gongs and drums at the Revolution Committee's signal. From roof to roof, our arrhythmic playing drives the sparrows into the sky. All morning and all afternoon we play, in different shifts, and whenever a sparrow tries to rest in a treetop, we shoo him away with colorful flags bound to long bamboo poles. In the evening the sparrows start to rain down on us like little bombs, dying in horror and exhaustion. Kids decorated as little scarecrows run around, collecting the dead sparrows from the ground for our dinner.

The boy is trying to sneak a sparrow into his sleeve when a bigger boy snatches his hand. "He is stealing the property of the People," the big boy shouts to the town.

"My mom is sick. She needs to eat something," the boy says.

"Hey, boy, what your mom needs is not this kind of bird," a man says, and we roar with laughter. The buns in our stomachs and the sparrows in the baskets have put us in a good mood.

The boy stares at the man for a moment and smacks into him with his head.

"Son of a bitch," the man says, bending over and covering his crotch with his hands.

"Beat the little counterrevolutionary," someone says, and we swarm toward the boy with fists and feet. The famine has made us angrier each day, and we are relieved to have found someone to vent our nameless rage upon.

The mother rushes into the crowd and tries to push us away. Her presence makes us hit the boy even harder. Some of us pick up bricks and boulders, ready to knock him out. Some of us bare our teeth, ready to eat him alive.

"You all look at his face. Whoever dares to touch him one more time, I'll sue him for his disrespect for our greatest leader," the mother yells, charging at us like a crazy woman.

Our bodies freeze. We look at the boy's face. Even with his swollen face and black eyes, we have no problem telling that he has the face of the dictator, young and rebellious, just as in the illustrations in the books about the dictator's heroic childhood. The boy stands up and limps to his mother. We look at his face in awe, not daring to move when he spits bloody phlegm at our feet.

"Remember this face," the boy says. "You will have to pay for this one day." He picks up a couple sparrows and walks away with his mother. We watch them supporting each other like husband and wife.

For years we do not know if it is a blessing or a disaster that a boy with the dictator's face lives among us. We treat the boy and his mother as the most precious and fragile treasure we have, never breathing one word about them to an outsider.

"It may not be a good thing," our old people warn us, and tell us the story of one of our Great Papas, who happened to have the same nickname as the emperor and was thrown into a well to drown. "There are things that are not allowed to exist in duplicates," the old people say.

Yet none of us dares to say one disrespectful word about the boy's face. As he grows older, he looks more and more like the dictator. Sometimes, walking past him in the street, there is a surge of warmth in our chests, as if the dictator himself were with us. This is the time when the dictator becomes larger than the universe in our nation. Illiterate housewives, who have used old newspapers as wallpaper and who have, accidentally, reversed the titles with the dictator's name in them, are executed. Parents of little first-graders who have misspelled the dictator's name are sent to labor camps. With the boy living among us, we are constantly walking on a thin layer of ice above deep water. We worry about not paying enough respect to the face, an indication of our hidden hatred of the dictator. We worry about respecting that face too much, which could be interpreted as our inability to tell the false from the true, worshipping the wrong idol. In our school, the teachers never speak one harsh word to him. Whatever games the students play, the side without him is willing to lose. When he graduates from the high school, the Revolution Committee has meetings for weeks, to discuss what is an appropriate job for a young man with a face like his. None of the jobs we have in town is safe enough to be given to him. Finally we think we have come up with the best solution to the problem—we elect him as the director of the advisory board to the Revolution Committee.

The young man prospers. Having nothing to do, and not liking to kill his time over cups of tea with the old board members, he walks around town every day, talking to people who are flattered by his greetings, and watching the female sales assistants in the department store blush at his sight. His mother is in much better shape now, with more color in her face. The only inconvenience is that no girl will date the young man. We have warned our daughters that marrying him would either be the greatest fortune, or the greatest misfortune. Born into a town where gambling is genuinely disapproved of, none of us wants to marry a daughter off to a man like him.

The day the dictator dies, we gather at the town center and cry like orphans. On the only television set our town owns, we watch the whole nation howling with us. For three months, we wear black mourning armbands to work and to sleep. All entertainments are banned for six months. Even a year or two after his death, we still look sideways at those women who are growing bellies, knowing that they have been insincere in their mourning. Fathers of those children never receive respect from us again.

It is a difficult time for the young man. Upon seeing his face, some of us break into uncontrollable wails, and he himself has to spend hours crying with us. It must have tired him. For a year he stays in his own room, and the next time we see him, walking toward the town center with a small suitcase, he looks much older than his age of twenty-eight.

"Is there anything wrong?" we greet him with concern. "Don't let too much grief drag you down."

"Thank you, but I am in a fine state," the young man replies.

"Are you leaving for somewhere?"

"Yes, I am leaving."

"Where to?" We feel a pang of panic. Losing him at this time seems as unbearable as losing the dictator one year ago.

"It's a political assignment," the young man says with a mysterious smile. "Classified."

Only after he is driven away in a well-curtained luxury car (the only car most of us have ever seen in our life), do we catch the news that he is going to the capital for an audition as the dictator's impersonator. It takes us days of discussion among ourselves to figure out what words like *audition* and *impersonator* mean. In the end the only agreement we come to is that he is going to become a great man.

Now that he has disappeared from our sights, his mother becomes the only source for his stories. She is a proud mother, and every time we inquire of his whereabouts she repeats the story of how she gazed at the late dictator's face day and night when her son was growing inside her. "You know, it's like he is the son of our great leader," she says.

"Yes, all of us are sons of our great leader," we nod and say. "But surely he is the best son."

The mother sighs with great satisfaction. She remembers how in the first few years after her son was born, women of her age produced baby after baby, putting framed certificates of mother heroes on their walls and walking past her with their eyes turned to the sky. Let time prove who is the real hero, she would think, and smile to herself.

Then she tells us about her son, every bit of information opening a new door to the world. He rode in the first-class car in a train to the capital, where he and other candidates have settled down in a luxury hotel, and are taken to the dictator's memorial museum every day, studying for the competition.

"Are there other candidates?" we gasp, shocked that she may not be the only woman to have studied the dictator's face during pregnancy.

"I am sure he is the one they want," the mother says. "He says he has total confidence, when he looks at the leader's face, that he is going to be the chosen one."

In the years to come, some among us will have the chance to go to the capital, and wait in a long line for hours to take a look at the dictator's face. After his death, a memorial museum was built in the center of our nation's capital, and the dictator's body is kept there in a crystal coffin. *Let our great leader live for ten thousand years in the hearts of a hundred generations* is what the designer has carved into the entrance of the museum. Inside the entrance, we will pay a substantial fee for a white paper flower to be placed at the foot of the crystal coffin, among a sea of white flowers. For a brief moment, some of us will wonder whether the flowers are collected from the base and resold the next day, but instantly we will feel ashamed of ourselves for thinking such impure thoughts in the most sacred place in the world. With the flowers in hand, we will walk into the heart of the memorial, in a single hushed file, and we will see the dictator, lying in the transparent coffin, covered by a huge red flag decorated with golden stars, his eyes closed as if in sleep, his mouth in a smile. We will be so impressed with this great man's body that we will ignore the unnatural red color in his cheeks, and his swollen neck as thick as his head.

Our young man must have walked the same route and looked at his face with the same reverence. What else has passed through his heart that does not occur to us? We will wonder.

He must have felt closer to the great man than any one of us. He has the right to feel so, chosen among tens of candidates as the dictator's impersonator. How he beat his rivals his mother never tells us in detail, just saying that he was born for the role. Only much later do we hear the story: our young man and the other candidates spend days in training, and those who are too short or too weakly built for the dictator's stature (even they, too, have the dictator's face) are eliminated in the first round, followed by those who cannot master the dictator's accent. Then there are the candidates who have everything except a clean personal history, like those born to the landlord class. Thanks to the Revolution Committee in our town, which has concealed the history of our young man being the son of an executed counterrevolutionary, he makes it into the final round with three other men. On the final day, when asked to do an improvised performance, the other three candidates all choose to quote the dictator announcing the birth of our communist nation (which is, as you remember, also the beginning of our young man's own journey), while he, for some unknown reason, says, *"A man cannot conceal his reactionary nature forever, just as a widow cannot hide her desire to be fucked."*

For a moment, he is horrified by his blunder, and feels the same shame and anger he once felt as a dead sparrow turned cold between his fingers. To his surprise, he is chosen, the reason being that he has caught the essence of the dictator, while the other three only got the rough shape. The three of them are sent with the rest of the candidates for plastic surgery, for, as our old men have said, there are things that are not allowed to exist in duplicate.

Our young man becomes the sole face that represents the dictator in the nation, and thus starts the most glorious years of his life. Movies about the dictator, starring our young man, are filmed by the government-run movie factories. Back in town, we cram into our only theater and watch the movies, secretly blaming our mothers or wives for not having given birth to a great face.

The marriage of the young man becomes our biggest concern. He is over thirty now, an age generally considered indecent for our young daughters. But who will care about the age of a great man? The old-style ones among us hire matchmakers for our daughters, and send with them expensive gifts to his mother. Others, more modern and aggressive, knock on his mother's door with blushing daughters trailing behind. Dazed by the choices, his mother goes to the town center and makes long-distance calls to him every other day, reporting yet another suitable candidate. But he is no longer a man of our town. He has been flying all over the nation for celebrations and movies; he has seen more attractive women than our town can provide. Through his apologetic mother, he rejects all of our offers. Accepting that our town is too shallow a basin to contain a real dragon, most of us give up and marry our daughters off to local young men. Yet some among us cling to the nonexistent hope, waiting for the days when he will realize the incomparable beauties and virtues of our daughters. For a number of years, scores of girls in our town are kept untouched by their parents. Too much looking forward makes their necks grow longer each year. It is not an unfamiliar sight to see a girl with a cranelike neck walk past us in the street, guarded by her parents who have grown to resemble giraffes.

The young man is too occupied with his new role to know such stories. He appears in the national celebrations for all the holidays. His most loyal audience, we sit all night long in front of the television and wait for his appearance. On the screen, men and women sing and dance with hearty smiles on their faces like well-trained kindergarteners. Children four or five years old flirt with one another, singing love songs like many joyful parrots. At such moments, those of us who think a little more than others start to feel uneasy, haunted by a strange fear that our people are growing down, instead of growing up. But the worry vanishes when our young man, the dictator's impersonator, shows up. People on the screen stand up in ovation and hold out their hands to be shaken. Young women with the prettiest faces rush to him with bouquets of flowers. Kids swarm around him and call him by the name of the dictator. Nostalgic tears fill everyone's eyes. For a moment, we believe time has stopped. The dictator is still alive among us, and we are happily living as his sons.

But time has sneaked by while we were mesmerized by our young man's face. Now we have Sony and Panasonic; we have Procter & Gamble, Johnson & Johnson. We have imported movies in which men and women hold hands freely in the street, and they even kiss each other without a trace of fear in their eyes. Our life, we realize, is not as happy as we have been taught to think. People in those capitalist countries are not waiting for us to be their liberators. They never knew of our love for them.

This must be a difficult period for our young man as well. Biographies and memoirs about the dictator appear overnight like spring grass. Unlike the books written collectively by the government-assigned writing groups, these books spell trouble the moment they appear. Soon they are decided to be illegal publications, and are confiscated and burned in great piles. Yet some of the words have spread out, bad words about the dictator. Mouth to mouth the rumors travel, how under his reign fifty million people have died from famine and political persecution. But if you looked at the number closely, you would realize it is far less than what the dictator was once willing to sacrifice to American nuclear bombs. So what is all the fuss about?

Still, we start to think about what we have been led to believe all these years. Once doubt starts, it runs rampant in our hearts like wildfire. Our young man's face appears on the television regularly, but the face has lost its aura. Those of us who have been waiting for his proposal are eager to sell our daughters to the first offer available. The young man's mother, now a garrulous old woman, walks in the street and grabs whomever she can to tell his stories, none of which impresses us anymore. From his mother, we have learned that he is touring across the nation with our present leader, a tour designed to inspire our national belief in communism. So what? we ask, and walk away before the mother has the chance to elaborate.

The tour ends early when a protest breaks out in the capital. Thousands of people rally for democracy in the center of the capital, where the dictator's memorial museum is less and less visited. Threatened and infuriated, our present leader orders the army to fire machine guns at the protesters. Astonishing as the event is, it slips out of our memory as soon as the dead are burned to ashes in the state-supervised crematoriums. The leader has said, as we later read in newspapers, that he is willing to kill two hundred thousand lives in exchange for twenty years of communist stability. Numbed by such numbers, we will echo his words and applaud his wisdom when we are required to publicly condemn those killed in the incident.

In no time the big-brother country above us no longer exists. Then one by one, our comrades-in-arms take turns exiting the historical stage. Confused as we are, we do not know what to think of them, whether we should envy, despise or pity them.

Life is presenting a big problem to our young man at this time. Although out of habit we still call him our young man, he is no longer young but in his forties. Even worse, he is a man in his forties who has never tasted a woman in his life. Can you believe it? We will ask one another. Incredible, we will shake our heads. But it is true: our young man spent most of his twenties wanting a woman, but we were unwilling to hand our daughters to him; when we were ready, he had become a man too great for our daughters. Time passes ruthlessly. Now that none of our daughters is available anymore, he starts to fantasize about the women he should have had long ago.

Once the desire is awakened, he is no longer able to live in peace. He watches women walking in the streets, their bare arms and legs in summer dresses deliciously attractive, and wonders how it would feel to have a woman of his own. Yet which woman is worthy of his greatness? Sometimes his blood is so unruly that he feels the urge to grab anyone passing by and make her his woman. But once his desire is subdued, after successful masturbation, he is no longer driven by blind craving. At such moments, he sees his life more clearly than ever, and he knows that no woman is great enough to match him.

"But you need a wife to give birth to a son," his mother, eager for a grandson, reminds him when he calls long distance to speak to her.

"Remember, the first and the foremost duty of a man is to make a son, and pass on his family name."

He mumbles indistinct words and hangs up. He knows that no woman's womb will nurture a son with a face as great as his own.

Now that the dictator's life has been explored and filmed thoroughly, our young man has more time on his hands. When there is no celebration to attend, he wanders in the street with a heavy coat, his face covered by a high collar and a pair of huge dark glasses. Sometimes he feels the temptation to walk with his face completely bare to the world, but the memory of being surrounded by hundreds of people asking for autographs stops him from taking the risk.

One day he walks across the capital, in search of something he is eager to have but unable to name. When he enters an alley, someone calls to him from behind a cart of newspapers and magazines.

"Want some books, friend?"

He stops and looks at the vendor from behind his dark glasses. "What kind of books?"

"What kind do you want?"

"What kind do you have?"

The vendor moves some magazines and uncovers the plastic sheet beneath the magazines. "Yellows, reds, whatever you want. Fifty yuan a book."

He bends over and looks from above his dark glasses. Underneath the plastic sheet are books with colorful covers. He picks one up and looks at a man and a woman, both naked, copulating in a strange position on the cover. His heart starts to beat in his chest, loud and urgent.

"That's a good yellow one," the vendor says, "as yellow as you want."

He clasps the book with his fingers. "What else do you have?"

"How about this red one?" the vendor hands him another book, the dictator's face on the cover. "Everybody loves this book."

He has heard of the book, a memoir written by the dictator's physician of thirty years, banned when it was published abroad, and smuggled into the country from Hong Kong and America.

He pays for the two books and walks back to his room. He studies the dictator's portrait, and compares it with his own face in the mirror, still perfect from every angle. He sighs and plunges into the yellow book, devouring it like a starved man. When his erection becomes too painful, he forces himself to drop the book and pick up the red one.

He feels an emptiness that he has never felt before, switching between the books when one becomes too unbearable. In the yellow book he sees a world he has missed all his life, in which a man has an endless supply of women, all of them eager to please him. Yet for all he knows, the only man who could have as many women as he wants is the dictator. He leafs through the red book one more time, looking at the pictures of the dictator in the company of young attractive nurses, and realizes that he has misunderstood his role all these years. To be a great man means to have whatever he wants from the world. Blaming himself for this belated understanding, he stands up and goes out into the night.

He has no difficulty locating a prostitute in the dimly lit karaoke-and-dance bar. As a precaution, he keeps his dark glasses and heavy coat on the whole time they are bargaining. Then he goes away with the young woman to a nearby hotel, sneaking through a side door into a room the woman has reserved while she deals with the receptionist.

What comes next is perplexing to us. All we can figure out from the rumors is that, when he is asked to undress, he refuses to take off either his dark glasses or his heavy coat. To be a great man means to have a woman in whatever way he wants, our young man must be thinking. But how is a man like him able to resist the skillful fingers of a professional like the woman he has hired? In a confusing moment, he is as naked as the woman, his face bare and easy to recognize. Before he realizes it, the woman's pimp, dressed up in police uniform, rushes in with a pair of handcuffs and a camera. Lights flash and snapshots are taken, his hands cuffed and clothes confiscated. Only then does the couple recognize his face, and we can imagine how overjoyed they must be by such a discovery. Instead of the usual amount, they ask for ten times what others pay, on account that our young man is a celebrity, and should pay a celebrity price for the pictures.

To this day we still disagree on how our young man should have reacted. Some of us think he should have paid and let himself go free, money being no problem for him. Others think he did nothing wrong by refusing to cooperate, but he should have gone to the police and reported the couple, instead of thinking such things would pass unnoticed. After that night, rumors start to spread across the capital, vivid stories about our young man's regular visits to the illegal brothels. The pictures he has failed to secure are circulated in different circles, until everyone in the capital claims that he has seen them. None of us in town has seen the pictures. Still, our hearts are broken when we imagine his body, naked and helpless, and we try our best to keep our mind's eyes away from the familiar face in those pictures.

He is considered unsuitable to continue as the impersonator of the dictator, for, as it is put in the letter addressed to him by the Central Committee of Cultural Regulation, he has soiled the name he is representing. Never before had it occurred to him that a man like him could be fired. There is no other face as his in the world, and who would replace him, the most irreplaceable man in the nation? He goes from office to office, begging for another chance, vowing never to touch a woman again. What he does not understand is that his role is no longer needed. A new leader has come into power and claimed himself the greatest guide of our communist cause in the new millennium. Talent scouts are combing through the nation for a new perfect face different from his own.

So our no longer young man comes home on a gloomy winter day. Stricken by shame, his mother has turned ill overnight and left us before he makes his way back. The day he arrives, some of us—those who remember him as the boy with a sparrow in his hand, who have secretly wished him to be our son-in-law, who have followed his path for years as the loyal audience of his mother, and who have, despite the pains of seeing him fall, lived for the joy of seeing his face—yes, those of us who have been salvaged from our mundane lives by loving him, we gather at the bus stop and hold out our hands for him to shake. He gets off the bus and ignores our earnest smiles, his dark glasses and high collar covering his face. Watching him walk to his mother's grave, with a long shadow limping behind him, we decide we will forgive him for his rudeness. Who would have the heart to blame a son like him? No matter what has happened to him, he is still the greatest man in our history, our boy and our hero.

. . .

Trust us, it breaks our hearts when he *cleans* himself by his mother's tomb. How such a thought occurred to him we will never understand, especially since, if we are not mistaken, he is still a virgin who has so much to look forward to in life. The night it happens, we hear a long howl in our sleep. We rush outside into the cold night, and find him in our cemetery. Even though we have grown up listening to the legends of our Great Papas, the scene makes us sick to our bones. We wonder what the meaning of such an act is. No one in our town—not we the small people, not our Great Papas—has reached the height that he has. Even our greatest Great Papa was only the best servant of the emperor, while he, with the face of the dictator, was once the emperor himself. Watching him roll on the ground, his face smeared with tears and blood, we remember the story of the ten-year-old boy, his male root in his hand, his face calm and proud. This is a sad moment for us, knowing that we, the children of our Great Papas, will never live up to their legends.

But lamenting aside, we still have a newly cleaned man to deal with. Some of us insist on sending him to the hospital for emergency treatment; others consider such a move unnecessary, for the act is done and there is no more harm left. Confused as we are, none of us remembers to collect the most important thing at the scene. Later, when we realize our mistake, we spend days searching every inch of our cemetery. Yet the missing part from his body has already disappeared, to whose mouth we do not want to imagine.

He survives, not to our surprise. Hadn't all our Great Papas survived and lived out their heroic stories? He is among us now, with a long barren life ahead. He sits in the sun and watches the dogs chasing each other, his face hidden behind the dark glasses and high collar of his coat. He walks to the cemetery in the dusk and talks to his mother until the night falls.

As for us, we have seen him born in pain and we will, in time, see him die in pain. The only thing we worry about is his next life. With his male root forever missing, what will we put into the silk sack to bury with him? How will we be able to send a soul to the next world in such incompleteness?

For the peace of our own minds, every day we pray for his health. We pray for him to live forever as we prayed for the dictator. He is the man whose story we do not want to end, and, as far as we can see, there will be no end to his story.

Helen Schulman

✠

The Revisionist

It had been a hundred years since Hershleder had taken in a late afternoon movie, a hundred years since he had gone to the movies by
himself. It was 5:45. There was a 6:15 train Hershleder could still
make. But why give in, why not not do something as inevitable as being
home on time for dinner? At heart he was a rebel. Hershleder walked
up the avenue to Kips Bay. There, there was a movie house. He could
enter the theater in daylight. When was the last time he had done that—
gone from a dazzling summer afternoon, when the air was visible and
everything looked like it was in a comic book, only magnified, broken
down into a sea of shimmering dots—into the dark, cool mouth of a
movie theater? It was a dry July day. It was hot out. Who cared what
was playing? Porno. Action. Comedy. All Hershleder wanted was to
give himself over to something.

He was drawn to the box office as if the gum-chewing bored girl behind the counter was dispensing pharmaceutical cocaine and he was
still a young and reckless intern—the kind he had always planned on
being, the kind Hershleder was only in his dreams. She had big hair.
Brown hair, sprayed and teased into wings. She had a dark mole beneath her pink lips on the left-hand side of her face. It looked like the
period that marks a dotted quarter in musical notation. She was a beautiful girl in an interesting way. Which means if the light were right
(which it wasn't quite then), if she held her chin at a particular angle
(which she didn't, her chin was in a constant seesaw on account of the

gum) when she laughed or when she forgot about pulling her lips over her teeth (which were long and fine and, at the most reductive—canine) she was a lovely, cubist vision.

Hershleder bought two tickets from this young girl. He bought two tickets out of force of habit. He entered the building, passed the two tickets toward the ticket taker and realized that he was alone.

Back at the box office, the girl wouldn't grant Hershleder a refund. She said: "It's a done deal, doll." But she smiled at him.

Hershleder gave the extra ticket to a bag lady who sat under the marquee where the sidewalk was slightly more shaded than the street, where the open and close of the glass doors to the air-conditioned theater provided the nearest thing to an ocean breeze that she would feel on this, her final face.

Hershleder the blind, Hershleder the dumb—oblivious to the thrill of a beautiful big-haired girl's lyrical smile, a smile a musician could sight-read and play. Blind and stuck with an extra ticket, Hershleder gave it away to the old lady. He wasn't a bad guy, really. Hadn't the old woman once been somebody's baby? Wasn't it possible, also, that she was still somebody's mother? Were there ever two more exalted roles in this human theater? This woman had risen to the pinnacle of her being; and she'd fallen. She suffered from La Tourette. Hershleder held the glass door open for her; he'd been well raised by his own mother, a woman with a deep residing respect for the elderly.

"Bastard," said the old lady, smiling shyly. "Cocksucker."

Hershleder smiled back at her. Here was someone who spoke his language. Hadn't he seen a thousand and one patients like her before?

"Fucking Nazi prick," the woman said, her voice trailing low as she struggled to gain control of herself. Her face screwed up in concentration; she wrestled with her inner, truer self. "Faggot," she said through clenched teeth; she bowed her head now, trying to direct her voice back into her chest. The next word came out like an exhalation of smoke, in a puff, a whisper: "Motherfucker."

The old lady looked up at Hershleder from beneath hooded lids— in her eyes was a lifetime of expressions unfortunately not held back, of words unleashed, epithets unfettered—there was a locker room of vile language in her head, but her face seemed apologetic. When Hershleder met her gaze, she fluttered her lashes, morse-coding like the quadriplegic on Ward A, then turned and shuffled away from him.

It was delicious inside the theater. Cold enough for Hershleder to take off his jacket and lay it flat like a blanket across his chest. His hand wandered across his crotch, stroked his belly. In the flirtation of film light, Hershleder felt himself up under the curtain of his jacket. There were a couple of teenagers in the back of the house who talked throughout the movie, but what did Hershleder care? It was dark, there was music. Stray popcorn crunched beneath his feet. A side door opened, and he got high off the smell of marijuana wafting on a cross breeze. An old man dozed in an end seat across the aisle. A beautiful girl on screen displayed a beautiful private birthmark. A bare-chested man rolled on top of her, drowning Hershleder's view. Above war planes flew, bombs dropped, the girl moaned, fire fire fire. Something was burning. On screen? Off screen? The exit sign was the reddest thing he'd ever seen. It glowed on the outskirts of his peripheral vision. Time passed in a solid leap, as in sleep, as in coma. When the lights came up, Hershleder was drowsily aware that much had happened to him—but what? Couldn't the real world have jumped forward at the rate of onscreen time in quantum leaps of event and tragedy and years? The movies. Like rockets hurtling a guy through space.

It was a way to make the hours pass, that's for sure, thought Hershleder. For a moment he had no clue as to what day it was.

Grand Central Station.

Hershleder waited for information. On the south wall was a huge photo essay, Kodak's, presenting the glories of India. A half-naked child, his brown outstretched hand, an empty bowl, his smile radiant. A bony cow. A swirl of sari, a lovely face, a red dot like a jewel amidst the light filigree of a happy forehead. A blown-up piece of poori: a bread cloud. The Taj Mahal . . . *In All Its Splendor*.

The lobby of Bellevue looked something like this. The women in their saris, the homeless beggars, the drug addicts that punctuated the station like restless exclamation marks. Inge, his chief lab technician, had told him that at the hospital, in the ground-floor women's bathrooms, mothers bathed their babies in the sinks. Hershleder could believe this. There, like here, was a place to come in out of the cold, the rain, the heat.

The signboard fluttered its black lids, each train announcement inched its way up another slot. Hershleder's would depart from Track 11. There was time for half a dozen oysters at the Oyster Bar. He headed out past Zaro's Bakery, the bagels and the brioche, the pies of mile-high lemon frosting. Cholesterol—how it could slather the arteries with silken ecstacy! (Hershleder had to watch himself. Oysters would do the trick—in more ways than one. What was that old joke . . . the rules of turning forty: Never waste an erection, never trust a fart.) He hung a left, down the curved, close passageway—the tunnel that felt like an inner tube, an underground track without the track, an alimentary canal, a cool stone vagina. Vagrants sagged against the walls, sprawled beneath the archways. There was a souvenir stand. A bookstore. A florist! Daisies, bright white for Itty, beckoned from earthenware vases. This was a must-stop on his future trek to Track 11. The passageway smelled like a petstore. The horrible inevitable decay of everything biological, the waste, the waste! Hershleder did a little shocked pas de bourrée over a pretzel of human shit, three toe-steps, as lacy as a dancer's.

They slid down easy, those Wellfleets, Blue Points. Hershleder leaned against the polished wood and ordered another half dozen. Not liquid, not solid—a fixed transitional state. A second beer. So what if he missed his train? There would always be another. Death and taxes. Conrail and the Erie Lackawanna. The fact that oysters made him horny.

They slid down cold and wet. Peppery. Hershleder wasn't one to skimp on hot sauce. The shell against his upper lip was blue and smooth, his lower lip touched lichen or was it coral? Pinstripes made up his panorama. The other slurpers were all like him. Commuters. Men who traveled to and from their wives, their children, "the Office." Men with secret lives in a foreign land: the city. Men who got off on eating oysters, who delayed going home by having yet another round of drinks. They all stood in a row at the bar the way they would stand at a row of urinals. Each in his private world. "Aaach," said Hershleder, and tipped another briny shell to his lips. His mouth was flooded by ocean.

Delays, delays. A lifetime full of delays. Hershleder the procrastinator, the putter-offer. Hershleder of the term papers started the night before, the grant proposals typed once into the computer, the postmarks fudged by the hospital's friendly postmaster. He was the kind of man to leave things to the last minute, to torture himself every moment that he did not attend to what needed attending to, his tasks, but also the type always to get them done. While in his heart he lusted after irresponsibility, he was never bad enough. Chicken-shit. A loser.

Hershleder's neighbor at the bar was reading *The New York Times*.

"Hey, mister," said Hershleder, sounding like he was seven. "Would you mind letting me look at the C section?" Now he spoke like a gynecologist.

The neighbor slid the paper over without even glancing up.

Hershleder turned to the book review.

David Josephson. His old pal from college. A picture of the sucker. A picture; why a picture? Hershleder thought. It wasn't even Josephson's book. He was just a translator, that schlep was.

Josephson had not fared well over time, although to be fair, the reproduction was kind of grainy. A hook nose. A high forehead. He still looked brainy. That forehead hung over his eyes like an awning at a fancy club. Hershleder read the article for himself.

A 1,032-page study of the Nazi gas chambers has been published. . . . The study is by Jacques LeClerc, a chemist who began his work doubting that the Holocaust even took place. . . . The book, written in French [translated by that bald rat Josephson!] . . . presents as proof, based entirely on technical analysis of the camps, that the Holocaust was every bit as monstrous and sweeping as survivors have said. . . . It is also a personal story of a scientific discovery during which, as Mr. LeClerc writes in a postscript, he was converted from "revisionist" to "exterminationist."

Exterminationist. What a hell of an appellative. Hershleder shook his head, in public, at the Oyster Bar, at no one in particular. Exterminationist. Is that what he himself was? His beloved mother, Adela Hershleder, just a child, along with her sister and her mother, her father recently dead of typhus, smuggled out of Germany on Kristallnacht. His mother's mother lost six brothers and sisters in Hitler's crematoria. And the friends, the extended family, even the neighbors they didn't like—all gone, gone. Hershleder's grandfather Chaim and his grandfather's brother, Abe, came to this country from Austria as refugees after World War I, the sole survivors of the sweeping tragedies of Europe that did away with their entire extended family.

And *heerre* . . . was Hershleder, the beneficiary of all that compounded survival; Hershleder the educated, the privileged, the beloved, the doctor! Hershleder the first generation New York Jew, Hershleder the bar mitzvahed, the assimilated, Hershleder with the shiksa wife, the children raised on Christmas, bacon in their breakfast, mayonnaise spread across their Wonder Bread, the daughter who once asked him if calling a person a Jew was really just another way to insult him.

He was lucky; his ancestors were not. What could you do? Isn't this the crux of it all (the history of civilization): those of us who are lucky juxtaposed against those of us who are not?

Mindy and Lori, his sisters, married with children, each active in her own temple, one out on Long Island, one on the Upper West Side. Irv, his father, retired now, remarried now, donating his time to the Jewish Home for the Blind. Were they any more Jewish than he was? Wasn't it true, what his own mother had told him, that what mattered in life was not religion per se, but that one strived to be a good person? Wasn't he, Hershleder—the researcher and, on Tuesdays and Thursdays, the healer (albeit a reluctant one), the father, the husband, the lawn mower, the moviegoer (he did show that bag lady a good time), the friend to Josephson (at least in theory)—a good person?

My God, thought Hershleder, just imagine being this chemist, this LeClerc, having the courage to disprove the very tenets upon which you've built your life. But Hershleder knew this kind, he had seen them before: LeClerc's accomplishments were probably less about bravery than they were about obsessive compulsion: LeClerc was probably a man who practiced a strict adherence to facts, to science. After all, Hershleder had spent much of his adult life doing research. You let the data make the decisions for you. You record what you observe. You synthesize, yes, you interpret; but you don't theorize, create out of your own imagination needs and desires. He knew him, LeClerc, LeClerc the compulsive, the truth-teller. They were alike these two men, rational, exact, methodical. Science was their true religion. Not the ephemeral mumbo jumbo of politicians, philosophers, poets.

Hershleder and LeClerc: they told the truth, when they were able, when it stared them in the face.

Hershleder folded up the paper and left it on the counter, its owner, his neighbor, having vanished in the direction of the New Haven Line some time ago. Paid up and exited the comforts of the Oyster Bar and headed out into the festering subterranean world. He stopped at the florist to pick up those daisies, two dozen, a field of them, a free-floating urban meadow. He held the bouquet like a cheerleader's pom-pom in his hands.

"Daisies are wildflowers," said the florist when he wrapped them up, those hothouse posies, in a crinkly paper cone. What did he think, that Hershleder was a poster child? He'd been to summer camp, away to college. Didn't he live in the suburbs and have a wife who cultivated daisies of her own? Daisies smell awful, but their faces are so sunny and bright, so fresh, so clean, petals as white as laundry detergent.

As he made his way to Track 11, Hershleder had a musical association: "Daisy, Daisy, give me your answer true." He had a poetic association: "She loves me, she loves me not." He had a visual association: the daisy stickers on the leaded glass windows that faced his yard, the plastic daisy treads that his mother had stuck to the bottom of his bathtub so that he, Hershleder, her precious boy-child, the third born and most prized, wouldn't slip, hit his head and drown. The big bright patent-leather daisies that dressed the thongs of his own daughter's dress-up sandals. The golden yolk, the pinky white of Itty's eyes when she'd been crying.

Hershleder walked through the vaulted, starred, amphitheater of Grand Central Station with a sensual garden, his human history, flowering bitterly in his hands.

"Smoke," hissed a young man in a black concert T-shirt. "Thai stick, dust, coke." The young man stood outside Track 11. Hershleder saw this dealer there, this corrupter of the young and not so young, this drugpusher, almost every day for months and months. Hershleder nodded at him, started down the ramp to the train tracks, then stopped. He had been a good boy. At Bronx Science he had smoked pot, at Cornell he'd done magic mushrooms once in awhile at a Dead show—then usually spent the rest of the night in the bathroom throwing up. For the most part, he'd played it safe; a little blow on a prom night or some graduation, but no acid, no ups, no downs (well, that wasn't true, there were bennies in med school, Valiums after), no needles in the arm, no track marks. No long velvety nights of swirling hazy rock songs. Drugwise, he was practically a virgin. Hadn't this gone on long enough?

Hershleder backtracked up the ramp.

"How much?" asked Hershleder.

"For what?" said Mr. Black Concert T-shirt.

For what? For what?

"Heroin?" asked Hershleder, with hope.

Mr. Black Concert T-shirt looked away in disgust.

"Pot?" asked Hershleder, humbly, in his place.

"Smoke," hissed the young man, "Thai stick, dust, coke."

"Thai stick," said Hershleder. Decisively. "Thai fucking stick," said Hershleder the reckless, the bon vivant.

And then, even though he was in danger of missing his train (again) Hershleder went back into the lobby of the station and officially bought cigarettes. He bought Merit Ultra Lights, thought better of it, backtracked to the kiosk and traded in the Merits for a pack of Salems.

.   .   .

The john was small enough that if you were to sit your knees would be in your armpits and your elbows in your ears. Hershleder and his daisies floated in a cloud of smoke, mentholated, Asiatic (the Thai stick). The chemical smell of toilets on trains and airplanes permeated all that steam. The resultant odor was strong enough to etherize an elephant, but Hershleder the rebel was nose-blind to it. He was wasted.

The MetroNorth rumbled through the tunnel. Outside the scenery was so familiar Hershleder had it memorized. First the rude surprise of 125th Street, all those broken windows, empty eyeholes, the flash of grafitti, of murals, loud paint. The decals of curtains and cozy cats curled up on cheery sills pasted to crumbling bricked-up tenements, the urban renewal. Then onward, the Bronx, Riverdale, Spuyten Duyvil. The scramble of weedy green, the lumberyards, factories, houses that line the train tracks in the suburbs. At night, all of this would be in shadow; what he'd see would be the advertisements for *Cats*, for Big Mac attacks, for Newport cigarettes: usually of a man gleefully dumping a bucket of something over an equally gleeful woman's head. The lonely maid still in uniform waiting for the train to carry her home two towns away. A couple of emasculated teenagers without driver's licenses. A spaced-out commuter who had stumbled off at the wrong station. Hershleder knew this route by heart.

In the train car itself, there was always the risk of running into one of his neighbors, or worse yet the aging parents of a chum from college. Better to hang out in that safe smoky toilet pondering the meaning of life, his humble existence. He was stoned for the first time in years. Drunken synapse fired awkwardly to drunken synapse. His edges were rounded, his reflexes dulled. The ghosts that lived inside him spiraled around in concentric circles. Hershleder's interior buzzed. His head hung heavy off his neck, rested in the field of daisies. A petal went up his nose, pollen dusted his mouth. He couldn't really think at all—he was full to the brim with nothing.

It was perfect.

"Laaarchmont," cried the lockjawed conductor. "Laaarchmont," ruining everything.

. . .

Hershleder lit up a cigarette and coughed up a chunk of lung. Larchmont. The Station. A mile and a half from Casa Hershleder, a mile and a half from Itty and the kids, a mile and a half from his home and future heart failures. His eyes roved the Park and Ride. Had he driven his car this morning or had Itty dropped him off at the train? Had he called for a cab, hitched a ride with a neighbor? Where was that beat-up Mazda? His most recent history dissolved like a photograph in water, a dream upon awakening, a computer screen when the power suddenly shuts down. It receded from his inner vision. Must have been the weed. . . . It really knocked him out.

Good shit, thought Hershleder.

He decided to walk. What was a mile and a half? He was in the prime of his life. Besides, Hershleder couldn't arrive home like this, stoned, in front of his innocent children, his loving wife. A long stroll would surely be enough to sober him; it would be a head-clearing, emotional cup of coffee.

Larchmont. Westchester, New York. One curvy road segueing into another. A dearth of streetlights. The Tudor houses loomed like haunted mansions. They sat so large on their tiny lots, they swelled over their property lines the way a stout man's waist swells above his belt. A yuppie dog, a dalmatian, nosed its way across a lawn and accompanied Hershleder's shuffling gait. Hershleder would have reached down to pat its spotty head if he could have, but his arms were too full of daisies. He made a mental note to give in to Itty; she'd been begging him to agree to get a pup for the kids. There had been dogs when Hershleder was a child. Three of them. At different times. He had had a mother who couldn't say no to anything. He had had a mother who was completely overwhelmed. The longest a dog had lasted in their home had been about a year; Mrs. Hershleder kept giving those dogs away. Three dogs, three children. Was there some wish fulfillment involved in her casting them aside? His favorite one had been called Snoopy. A beagle. His sister Mindy, that original thinker, had been the one to name her.

Hershleder remembered coming home from camp one summer to find that Snoopy was missing. His mother had sworn up and down that she had given the dog to a farm, a farm in western Pennsylvania. Much better for the dog, said Mrs. Hershleder, than being cooped up in some tiny apartment. Better for the dog, thought Hershleder now, some twenty-eight years later, better for the dog! What about me, a dogless boy cooped up in some tiny apartment! But his mother was dead, she was dead; there was no use in raging at a dead mother. Hershleder the motherless, the dogless, walked the streets of Larchmont. His buzz was beginning to wear off.

Why neurology? Mrs. Hershleder had asked. How about a little pediatrics? Gynecology? Family practice? Dovidil, don't make the same mistakes I made, a life devoted to half-lives, a life frozen in motion. But Hershleder had been drawn to the chronic ward. Paralysis, coma. He could not stand to watch a patient suffer, the kick and sweat, the scream of life battling stupidly for continuation. If he had to deal with people—and wasn't that what a doctor does, a doctor deals with people—he preferred people in a vegetative state, he preferred them non-cognizant. What had attracted him in the first place had been the literature, the questions: What was death? What was life, after all? Did the answers to these lie, as Hershleder believed, not in the heart but in the brain? He liked to deal in inquiries; he didn't like to deal in statements. It was natural then that he'd be turned on by research. Books and libraries, the heady smell of ink on paper. He'd been the kind of boy who had always volunteered in school to run off things for the teacher. He'd stand close to the Rexograph machine, getting giddy, greedily inhaling those toxic vapors. He'd walk back slowly to his classroom, his nose buried deep in a pile of freshly printed pages.

Hershleder was not taken with the delivering of babies, the spreading of legs, the searching speculum, the bloody afterbirth like a display of raw ground meat. But the brain, the brain, that fluted, folded mushroom, that lovely intricate web of thought and tissue and talent and dysfunction, of arteries and order. The delicate weave of neurons, that thrilling spinal cord. All that communication, all those nerves sending and receiving orders. A regular switchboard. Music for his mind.

A jogger passed him on the right, his gait strong and steady. Hershleder's dalmatian abandoned him for the runner.

Hershleder turned down Fairweather Drive. He stepped over a discarded red tricycle. He noticed that the Fishmans had a blue Jag in their carport. The Fishman boy was his own boy's nemesis. Charlie Fishman could run faster, hit harder. No matter that Hershleder's own boy could speak in numbers—a = 1 b = 2, for example, when Hershleder arrived home at night the kid said: "8-9 4-1-4" (translation: Hi Dad!)—the kid was practically a savant, a genius! So what, the Fishman boy could kick harder, draw blood faster in a fight. Could Charlie Fishman bring tears to his own father's eyes by saying, "9 12-15-22-5 25-15-21" when Fishman's father tucked him in at night? (Even though it had taken Hershleder seven minutes and a pad and pencil to decode the obvious.) Charlie Fishman had just beaten out Hershleder's Jonathan for the lead in the second-grade play. The Fishman father was a famous nephrologist. He commuted to New Haven every morning on the highway, shooting like a star in that blue Jag out of the neighborhood, against the traffic, in the opposite direction. Hershleder admired the Jag from afar. It was a blue blue. It glowed royally against the darkness.

The jogger passed him again, on the right. The dalmatian loped after the runner, his spotted tongue hanging from his mouth. The jogger must have circled around the long circuitous block in record time. A powerful motherfucker. Bearded. And young. Younger than Hershleder. The jogger had a ponytail. It sailed in the current of his own making. His legs were strong and bare. Ropy, tendoned. From where he stood, Hershleder admired them. Then he moved himself up the block to his own stone Tudor.

Casa Hershleder. It was written in fake Spanish tile on the front walk, a gift from his sisters. Hershleder walked up the slate steps and hesitated on his own front porch. Sometimes it felt like only an act of courage could get him to turn the knob and go inside. So much tumult awaited. Various children: on their marks, getting set, ready to run, to hurl themselves into his arms. Itty, in this weather all soft and steamed and plumped—dressed in an undulation of circling Indian shmatas—hungry for connection, attention, the conversation of a living, breathing adult. Itty, with tiny clumps of clay still lodged like bird eggs in the curly red nest of her hair. Itty with the silt on her arms, the gray slip-like slippers on her bare feet. Itty, his wife, the potter.

By this point, the daisies were half-dead. They'd wilted in the heat. Hershleder lay them in a pile on his front shrub then lowered himself onto a slate step seat. If he angled his vision past the O'Keefes' mock turret, he would surely see some stars.

The steam of summer nights, the sticky breath of the trees and their exhalation of oxygen, the buzz of the mosquitoes and the cicadas, the sweaty breeze, the rubbing of his suit legs against his thighs. The moon above the O'Keefe's turret was high, high, high.

The jogger came around again. Angled right and headed up the Hershleder walk. His face was flushed with all that good clean high-octane blood that is the result of honest American exertion. He looked young—far younger than Hershleder, but hadn't Hershleder noted this before? Must be wanting to know the time, or in need of a glass of water, a bathroom, a phone, Hershleder thought. The jogger was jogging right towards him.

In a leap of blind and indiscriminate affection the dalmatian bounded past the runner and collided with Hershleder's head, his body, his lap. David was stunned for a second, then revived by the wet slap of the dog's tongue. He was showered with love and saliva. "Hey," said Hershleder. "Hey there, Buster. Watch it." Hershleder fended off the beast by petting him, by bowing under to all that animal emotion. The dalmatian wagged the bottom half of his spinal column like a dissected worm would, it had a life all its own. His tail beat the air like a wire whisk. His tongue was as soft and moist as an internal organ. "Hey, Buster, down." Hershleder's arms were full of dog.

The jogger jogged right past them. He wiped his feet on Hershleder's welcome mat. He opened Hershleder's door and entered Hershleder's house. He closed Hershleder's door behind him. There was the click of the lock Hershleder had installed himself. That old bolt sliding into that old socket.

What was going on? What was going on around here?

Buster was in love. He took to Hershleder like a bitch in heat, this same fancy mutt that had abandoned him earlier for the runner. A fickle fellow, thought Hershleder, a familiar fickle fellow.

"Hey," said Hershleder. "Hey," he called out. But it was too late. The runner had already disappeared inside his house.

The night was blue. The lawns deep blue-green, the asphalt blue-black, the trees almost purple. Jaundiced yellow light, like flames on an electric menorah, glowed from the Teretskys' leaded windows. At the Coens', from the second-floor family room, a TV flickered like a weak pulse. Most of the neighborhood was dark. Dark, hot, blue and yellow. Throbbing like a bruise.

A car backfired in the distance. Buster took off like a shot.

Hershleder sat on his front step feeling used. He was like a college girl left in the middle of a one-night stand. The dog's breath was still hot upon his face. His clothes were damp and wrinkled. The smell of faded passion clung to him. His hair—what was left of it—felt matted. He'd been discarded. Thrown-over. What could he do?

Stand up, storm into the house, demand: What's the meaning of this intrusion? Call the cops? Were Itty and the kids safe inside, locked up with that handsome, half-crazed stranger? Was it a local boy, home on vacation from college, an art student perhaps, hanging around to glean some of his wife's infinite and irresistible knowledge? The possibilities were endless. Hershleder contemplated the endless possibilities for a while.

Surely, he should right himself, climb his own steps, turn his key in his lock, at least ring his own bell, as it were. Surely, Hershleder should do something to claim what was his: "If I am not for me, who will be for me? If I am not for mine, who will be for mine?" Surely, he should stop quoting, stop questioning, and get on with the messy thrill of homeownership. After all, his wife, his children were inside.

The jogger was inside.

Hershleder and LeClerc, they told the truth when it stared them in the face. In the face! Which was almost enough but wasn't enough, right then at that exact and awful moment to stop him, the truth wasn't, not from taking his old key out of his pocket and jamming it again and again at a lock it could not possibly ever fit. Which wasn't enough, this unyielding frustration, to stop him from ringing the bell, again and again, waking his children, disturbing his neighbors. Which wasn't enough to stop him, the confusion, the shouting that ensued, that led Itty *his wife* to say: "Please, Sweetheart," to the jogger (Please, Sweetheart!) and usher him aside, that ponytailed bearded athlete who was far, far younger than Hershleder had ever been, younger than was biologically possible.

She sat on the slate steps, Itty, her knees spread, the Indian shmata pulled discreetly down between them. She ran her silt-stained hands through her dusty strawberry cloud of hair. There were dark, dirty half-moons beneath her broken fingernails. She was golden-eyed and frustrated and terribly pained. She was beautiful, Itty, at her best really when she was most perplexed, her expression forming and reforming like a kaleidescope of puzzled and passionate emotion, when she patiently and for the thousandth time explained to him, Dr. David Hershleder, M.D., that this was no longer his home, that the locks had been changed for this very reason. He had to stop coming around here, upsetting her, upsetting the children, that it was time, it was time, Dave, to take a good look at himself; when all Hershleder was capable of looking at was her, was Itty, dusty, plump and sweaty, sexy-sexy Itty, his wife, his wife, sitting with him on the stoop of his house in his neighborhood, while his children cowered inside.

Until finally, exhausted (Hershleder had exhausted her), Itty threatened to call the police if he did not move, and it was her tiredness, her sheer collapsibility that forced Hershleder to his feet—for wasn't being tired one thing Itty went on and on about that Hershleder could finally relate to—that pushed him to see the truth, to assess the available data and to head out alone and ashamed and apologetic to his suburban slip of a sidewalk, down the mile and a half back to the station to catch the commuter rail that would take him to the city and to the medical student housing he'd wrangled out of the hospital, away from everything he'd built, everything he knew and could count on, out into everything unknown, unreliable and yet to be invented.

Philip Roth

꙰

Epstein

Michael, the weekend guest, was to spend the night in one of the twin beds in Herbie's old room, where the baseball pictures still hung on the wall. Lou Epstein slept with his wife in the room with the bed pushed catter-corner. His daughter Sheila's bedroom was empty; she was at a meeting with her fiancé the folk singer. In the corner of her room a childhood teddy bear balanced on its bottom, a "*Vote Socialist*" button pinned to its left ear; on her bookshelves, where once volumes of Louisa May Alcott gathered dust, now were collected the works of Howard Fast. The house was quiet. The only light burning was downstairs in the dining room where the *shabus* candles flickered in their tall golden holders and Herbie's *jahrzeit* candle trembled in its glass.

Epstein looked at the dark ceiling of his bedroom and let his head that had been bang-banging all day go blank for a moment. His wife Goldie breathed thickly beside him, as though she suffered from eternal bronchitis. Ten minutes before she had undressed and he had watched as she dropped her white nightdress over her head, over the breasts which had funneled down to her middle, over the behind like a bellows, the thighs and calves veined blue like a road map. What once could be pinched, what once was small and tight, now could be poked and pulled. Everything hung. He had shut his eyes while she had dressed for sleep and had tried to remember the Goldie of 1927, the Lou Epstein of 1927. Now he rolled his stomach against her backside, remembering, and reached around to hold her breasts. The nipples were dragged down like a cow's. He rolled back to his own side.

A key turned in the front door—there was whispering, then the door gently shut. He tensed and waited for the noises—it didn't take those Socialists long. At night the noise from the zipping and the unzipping was enough to keep a man awake. "What are they doing down there?" he had screamed at his wife last Friday night, "Trying on clothes?" Now, once again, he waited. It wasn't that he was against their playing. He was no puritan, he believed in young people enjoying themselves. Hadn't he been a young man himself? But in 1927 he and his wife were handsome people. Lou Epstein had never resembled that chinless, lazy, smart-alec whose living was earned singing folk songs in a saloon, and who once had asked Epstein if it hadn't been "thrilling" to have lived through "a period of great social upheaval" like the thirties.

And his daughter, why couldn't she have grown up to be like—like the girl across the street whom Michael had the date with, the one whose father had recently died. Now there was a pretty girl. But not his Sheila. What happened, he wondered, what happened to that little pink-skinned baby? What year, what month did those skinny ankles grow thick as logs, the peaches-and-cream turn to pimples? That lovely child was now a twenty-three-year-old woman with "a social conscience!" Some conscience, he thought. She hunts all day for a picket line to march in so that at night she can come home and eat like a horse. . . . For her and that guitar-plucker to touch each other's unmentionables seemed worse than sinful—it was disgusting. When Epstein tossed in bed and heard their panting and the zipping it sounded in his ears like thunder.

Zip!

They were at it. He would ignore them, think of his other problems. The business . . . here he was a year away from the retirement he had planned but with no heir to Epstein Paper Bag Company. He had built the business from the ground, suffered and bled during the Depression and Roosevelt, only, finally, with the War and Eisenhower to see it succeed. The thought of a stranger taking it over made him sick. But what could be done? Herbie, who would have been twenty-eight, had died of polio, age eleven. And Sheila, his last hope, had chosen as her intended a lazy man. What could he do? Does a man of fifty-nine all of a sudden start producing heirs?

Zip! Pant-pant-pant! Ahh!

He shut his ears and mind, tighter. He tried to recollect things and drown himself in them. For instance, dinner . . .

He had been startled when he arrived home from the shop to find the soldier sitting at his dinner table. Surprised because the boy, whom he had not seen for ten or twelve years, had grown up with the Epstein face, as his own son would have, the small bump in the nose, the strong chin, dark skin, and shock of shiny black hair that, one day, would turn gray as clouds.

"Look who's here," his wife shouted at him the moment he entered the door, the day's dirt still under his fingernails. "Sol's boy."

The soldier popped up from his chair and extended his hand. "How do you do, Uncle Louis?"

"A Gregory Peck," Epstein's wife said, "a Monty Clift your brother has. He's been here only three hours already he has a date. And a regular gentleman . . ."

Epstein did not answer.

The soldier stood at attention, square, as though he'd learned courtesy long before the Army. "I hope you don't mind my barging in, Uncle Louis. I was shipped to Monmouth last week and Dad said I should stop off to see you people. I've got the weekend off and Aunt Goldie said I should stay . . ." he waited.

"Look at him," Goldie was saying, "a Prince!"

"Of course," Epstein said at last. "Stay. How is your father?" Epstein had not spoken to his brother Sol since 1945 when he had bought Sol's share of the business and his brother had moved to Detroit, with words.

"Dad's fine," Michael said. "He sends his regards."

"Sure, I send mine too. You'll tell him."

Michael sat down, and Epstein knew that the boy must think just as his father did: that Lou Epstein was a coarse man whose heart beat faster only when he was thinking of Epstein Paper Bag.

When Sheila came home they all sat down to eat, four, as in the old days. Goldie Epstein jumped up and down, up and down, slipping each course under their noses the instant they had finished the one before. "Michael," she said historically, "Michael, as a child you were a very poor eater. Your sister, Ruthie, God bless her, was a nice eater. Not a good eater, but a nice eater."

For the first time Epstein remembered his little niece Ruthie, a little dark-haired beauty, a Bible Ruth. He looked at his own daughter and heard his wife go on. "No, Ruthie wasn't such a good eater. But she wasn't a picky eater. Our Herbie, he should rest in peace, was a picky eater. . . ." Goldie looked toward her husband as though he would remember precisely what category of eater his beloved son had been; he stared into his pot roast.

"But," Goldie Epstein resumed, "you should live and be well, Michael, you turned out to be a good eater. . . ."

Ahhh! Ahhh!

The noises snapped Epstein's recollection in two.

Aaahhhh!

Enough was enough. He got out of bed, made certain that he was tucked into his pajamas, and started down to the living room. He would give them a piece of his mind. He would tell them that—that 1927 was not 1957! No, that was what they would tell him.

But in the living room it was not Sheila and the folk singer. Epstein felt the cold from the floor rush up the loose legs of his pajamas and chill his crotch, raising goose flesh on his thighs. They did not see him. He retreated a step, back behind the archway to the dining room. His eyes, however, remained fixed on the living room floor, on Sol's boy and the girl from across the street.

The girl had been wearing shorts and a sweater. Now they were thrown over the arm of the sofa. The light from the candles was enough for Epstein to see that she was naked. Michael lay beside her, squirming and potent, wearing only his army shoes and khaki socks. The girl's breasts were like two small white cups. Michael kissed them, and more. Epstein tingled; he did not dare move, he did not want to move, until the two, like cars in a railroad yard, slammed fiercely together, coupled, shook. In their noise Epstein tiptoed, trembling, up the stairs and back to his wife's bed.

He could not force himself to sleep for what seemed like hours, not until the door had opened downstairs and the two young people had left. When, a minute or so later, he heard another key turn in the lock he did not know whether it was Michael returning to go to sleep, or—

Zip!

Now it was Sheila and the folk singer! The whole world, he thought, the whole young world, the ugly ones and the pretty ones, the fat and the skinny ones, zipping and unzipping! He grabbed his great shock of gray hair and pulled it till his scalp hurt. His wife shuffled, mumbled a noise. *"Brrr . . . brrrr . . ."* She captured the blankets and pulled them over her. *"Brrr . . ."*

Butter! She's dreaming about butter. Recipes she dreams while the world zips. He closed his eyes and pounded himself down down into an old man's sleep.

How far back must you go to discover the beginning of trouble? Later, when Epstein had more time he would ask himself this question. When did it begin? That night he'd seen those two on the floor? Or the summer night seventeen years before when he had pushed the doctor away from the bed and put his lips to his Herbie's? Or, Epstein wondered, was it that night fifteen years ago when instead of smelling a woman between his sheets he smelled Bab-O? Or the time when his daughter had first called him "capitalist" as though it were a dirty name, as though it were a crime to be successful? Or was it none of these times? Maybe to look for a beginning was only to look for an excuse. Hadn't the trouble, the big trouble, begun simply when it appeared to begin, the morning he saw Ida Kaufman waiting for the bus?

And about Ida Kaufman, why in God's name was it a stranger, nobody he loved or ever could love, who had finally changed his life?— she, who had lived across the street for less than a year, and who (it was revealed by Mrs. Katz, the neighborhood Winchell) would probably sell her house now that Mr. Kaufman was dead and move all-year-round into the summer cottage she owned at Barnegat? Up until that morning Epstein had no more than noticed the woman: dark, good-looking, a big chest. She hardly spoke to the other housewives, but spent every moment, until a month ago, caring for her cancer-eaten husband. Once or twice Epstein had tipped his hat to her, but even then he had been more absorbed in the fate of Epstein Paper Bag than in the civility he was practicing. Actually then, on that Monday morning, it would not have been unlikely for him to have driven right past the bus stop. It was a warm April day, certainly not a bad day to be waiting for a bus. Birds fussed and sang in the elm trees, and the sun glinted in the sky like a young athlete's trophy. But the woman at the bus stop wore a thin dress and no coat. Epstein saw her waiting, and beneath the dress, the stockings, the imagined underthings he saw again the body of the girl on his living room rug—for Ida Kaufman was the mother of Linda Kaufman, the girl Michael had befriended. So Epstein pulled slowly to the curb and, stopping for the daughter, picked up the mother.

"Thank you, Mr. Epstein," she said. "This is kind of you."

"It's nothing," Epstein said. "I'm going to Market Street."

"Market Street will be fine."

He pressed down too hard on the accelerator and the big Chrysler leaped away, noisy as a hot-rodder's Ford. Ida Kaufman rolled down her window and let the breeze waft in; she lit a cigarette. After a while she asked, "That was your nephew, wasn't it, that took Linda out Saturday night?"

"Michael? Yes." Epstein flushed, for reasons Ida Kaufman did not know. He felt the red on his neck and coughed to make it appear that some respiratory failure had caused the blood to rush up from his heart.

"He's a very nice boy, extremely polite," she said.

"My brother Sol's," Epstein said. "In Detroit." And he shifted his thoughts to Sol so that the flush might fade: If there had been no words with Sol it would be Michael who would be heir to Epstein Paper Bag. Would he have wanted that? Was it any better than a stranger . . . ?

While Epstein thought, Ida Kaufman smoked, and they drove on without speaking, under the elm trees, the choir of birds, and the new spring sky unfurled like a blue banner.

"He looks like you," she said.

"What? Who?"

"Michael."

"No," Epstein said, "him, he's the image of Sol."

"No, no, don't deny it—" and she exploded with laughter, smoke dragoning out of her mouth; she jerked her head back mightily, "No, no, no, he's got your face!"

Epstein looked at her, wondering: the lips, big and red, over her teeth, grinning. Why? Of course—your little boy looks like the ice man, she'd made that joke. He grinned, mainly at the thought of going to bed with his sister-in-law, whose everything had dropped even lower than his wife's.

Epstein's grin provoked Ida Kaufman into more extravagant mirth. What the hell, he decided, he would try a joke himself.

"Your Linda, who does *she* look like?"

Ida Kaufman's mouth straightened; her lids narrowed, killing the light in her eyes. Had he said the wrong thing? Stepped too far? Defiled the name of a dead man, a man who'd had cancer yet? But no, for suddenly she raised her arms in front of her, and shrugged her shoulders as though to say, "Who knows, Epstein, who knows?"

Epstein roared. It was so long since he had been with a woman who had a sense of humor; his wife took everything he said seriously. Not Ida Kaufman, though—she laughed so hard her breasts swelled over the top of her tan dress. They were not cups but pitchers. The next thing Epstein knew he was telling her another joke, and another, in the middle of which a cop screamed up alongside him and gave him a ticket for a red light which, in his joy, he had not seen. It was the first of three tickets he received that day; he earned a second racing down to Barnegat later that morning, and a third speeding up the Parkway at dusk, trying not to be too late for dinner. The tickets cost him $32 in all, but as he told Ida, when you're laughing so hard you have tears in your eyes, how can you tell the green lights from the red ones, fast from slow?

At seven o'clock that evening he returned Ida to the bus stop on the corner and squeezed a bill into her hands.

"Here," he said, "here—buy something"; which brought the day's total to fifty-two.

Then he turned up the street, already prepared with a story for his wife: A man interested in buying Epstein Paper Bag had kept him away all day, a good prospect. As he pulled into his driveway he saw his wife's square shape in back of the venetian blinds; she ran one hand across a slat, checking for dust while she awaited her husband's homecoming.

Prickly heat?

He clutched his pajama trousers around his knees and looked at himself in the bedroom mirror. Downstairs a key turned in the lock but he was too engaged to hear it. Prickly heat is what Herbie always had—a child's complaint. Was it possible for a grown man to have it? He shuffled closer to the mirror, tripping on his half-hoisted pajamas. Maybe it was a sand rash. Sure, he thought, for during those three warm, sunny weeks, he and Ida Kaufman, when they were through, would rest on the beach in front of the cottage. Sand must have gotten into his trousers and irritated him on the drive up the Parkway. He stepped back now and was squinting at himself in the mirror when Goldie walked into the bedroom. She had just emerged from a hot tub—her bones ached, she had said—and her flesh was boiled red. Her entrance startled Epstein, who had been contemplating his blemish with the intensity of a philosopher; when he turned swiftly from his reflection, his feet caught in the pant legs, he tripped, and the pajamas slipped to the floor. So there they were, naked as Adam and Eve, except that Goldie was red all over, and Epstein had prickly heat, or a sand rash, or—and it came to him as a first principle comes to a metaphysician. Of course! His hands shot down to cover his crotch.

Goldie looked at him, mystified, while Epstein searched for words appropriate to his posture.

At last: "You had a nice bath?"

"Nice, shmise, it was a bath," his wife mumbled.

"You'll catch a cold," Epstein said. "Put something on."

"I'll catch a cold? *You'll* catch a cold!" She looked at the hands laced across his crotch. "Something hurts?"

"It's a little chilly," he said.

"Where?" She motioned towards his protection. "There?"

"All over."

"Then cover all over."

He leaned over to pick up his pajama trousers; the instant he dropped the fig leaf of his hands Goldie let out a short airless gasp. "What is *that*?"

"What?"

"That!"

He could not look into the eyes of her face, so concentrated instead on the purple eyes of her droopy breasts. "A sand rash, I think."

"*Vus far* sand!"

"A rash then," he said.

She stepped up closer and reached out her hand, not to touch but to point. She drew a little circle of the area with her index finger. "A rash, there?"

"Why not there?" Epstein said. "It's like a rash on the hand or the chest. A rash is a rash."

"But how come all of a sudden?" his wife said.

"Look, I'm not a doctor," Epstein said. "It's there today, maybe tomorrow it'll be gone. How do I know! I probably got it from the toilet seat at the shop. The *shvartzes* are pigs—"

Goldie made a clicking sound with her tongue.

"You're calling me a liar?"

She looked up. "Who said liar?" And she gave her own form a swift looking-over, checked limbs, stomach, breasts, to see if she had caught the rash from him. She looked back at her husband, then at her own body again, and suddenly her eyes widened. "You!" she screamed.

"Shah," Epstein said, "you'll wake Michael."

"You pig! Who was it!"

"I told you who, the *shvartzes*—"

"Liar! Pig!" Wheeling her way back to the bed, she flopped on to it so hard the springs squeaked as they rarely had in their last decade of lovemaking. "Liar!" And then she was off the bed pulling the sheets from it. "I'll burn them, I'll burn every one!"

Epstein stepped out of the pajamas that roped his ankles and raced to the bed. "What are you doing—it's not catching. Only on the toilet seat. You'll buy a little ammonia . . ."

"Ammonia!" she yelled, "you should *drink* ammonia!"

"No," Epstein shouted, "no," and he grabbed the sheets from her and threw them back over the bed, tucking them in madly. "Leave it be—" He ran to the back of the bed but as he tucked there Goldie raced around and ripped up what he had tucked in the front; so he raced back to the front while Goldie raced around to the back. "Don't touch me," she screamed, "don't come near me, you filthy pig! Go touch some filthy whore!" Then she yanked the sheets off again in one swoop, held them in a ball before her and spat. Epstein grabbed them back and the tug-of-war began, back and forth, back and forth, until they had torn them to shreds. Then, for the first time Goldie cried. With white strips looped over her arms she began to sob. "My sheets, my nice clean sheets—" and she threw herself on the bed.

Two faces appeared in the doorway of the bedroom. Sheila Epstein groaned, "Holy Christ!"; the folk singer peeked in, once, twice, and then bobbed out, his feet scuttling down the stairs. Epstein whipped some white strands about him to cover his privates. He did not say a word as his daughter entered.

"Mama, what's the matter?"

"Your father," the voice groaned from the bed, "he has—a rash!" And so violently did she begin to sob that the flesh on her white buttocks rippled and jumped.

"That's right," Epstein said, "a rash. That's a crime? Get out of here! Let your mother and father get some sleep."

"Why is she crying?" Sheila demanded. "I want an answer!"

"How do I know! I'm a mind reader? This whole family is crazy, who knows what they think!"

"Don't call my mother crazy!"

"Don't you raise your voice to me! Respect your father!" He pulled the white strips tighter around him. "Now get out of here!"

"No!"

"Then I'll throw you out." He started for the door; his daughter did not move, and he could not bring himself to reach out and push her. Instead he threw back his head and addressed the ceiling. "She's picketing my bedroom! Get out, you lummox!" He took a step toward her and growled, as though to scare away a stray cat or dog. With all her

160 pounds she pushed her father back; in his surprise and hurt he dropped the sheet. And the daughter looked on the father; under her lipstick she turned white.

Epstein looked up at her; he pleaded, "I got it from the toilet seat. The *shvartzes*—"

Before he could finish, a new head had popped into the doorway, hair messed and lips swollen and red; it was Michael, home from Linda Kaufman, his regular weekend date. "I heard the noise, is any—" and he saw his aunt naked on the bed; when he turned his eyes away, there was Uncle Lou.

"All of you," Epstein shouted. "Get out!"

But no one obeyed. Sheila blocked the door, politically committed: Michael's legs were rooted, one with shame, the other curiosity.

"Get out!"

Feet now came pounding up the stairs. "Sheila, should I call somebody—" And then the guitar-plucker appeared in the doorway, eager, big-nosed. He surveyed the scene and his gaze, at last, landed on Epstein's crotch; the beak opened.

"What's he got? The syph?"

The words hung for a moment, bringing peace. Goldie Epstein stopped crying and raised herself off the bed. The young men in the doorway lowered their eyes. Goldie arched her back, flopped out her breasts, and began to move her lips. "I want . . ." she said. "I want . . ."

"What Mama?" Sheila demanded. "What is it?"

"I want . . . a divorce!" She looked amazed when she said it, though not as amazed as her husband; he smacked his palm to his head.

"Divorce! Are you crazy?" Epstein looked around; to Michael he said, "She's crazy!"

"I want one," she said, and then her eyes rolled up into her head and she passed out across the sheetless mattress.

After the smelling salts, Epstein was ordered to bed in Herbie's room. He tossed and turned in the narrow bed which he was unused to; in the twin bed beside him he heard Michael breathing. Monday, he thought, Monday he would seek help. A lawyer. No, first a doctor. Surely in a

minute a doctor could take a look and tell him what he already knew—
that Ida Kaufman was a clean woman. Epstein would swear by it—he
had smelled her flesh! The doctor would reassure him: His blemish re-
sulted simply from their rubbing together. It was a temporary thing,
produced by two, not transmitted by one. He was innocent! Unless
what made him guilty had nothing to do with some dirty bug. But either way the doctor would prescribe for him. And then the lawyer
would prescribe. And by then everyone would know, including, he
suddenly realized, his brother Sol who would take special pleasure in
thinking the worst. Epstein rolled over and looked to Michael's bed.
Pinpoints of light gleamed in the boy's head; he was awake, and wearing the Epstein nose, chin, and brow.

"Michael?"

"Yes."

"You're awake?"

"Yes."

"Me too," Epstein said, and then apologetically, "all the excitement . . ."

He looked back to the ceiling. "Michael?"

"Yes?"

"Nothing . . ." But he was curious as well as concerned. "Michael,
you haven't got a rash, have you?"

Michael sat up in bed; firmly he said, "No."

"I just thought," Epstein said quickly. "You know, I have this
rash . . ." He dwindled off and looked away from the boy, who, it occurred to him again, might have been heir to the business if that stupid Sol hadn't . . . But what difference did the business make now.
The business had never been for him, but for them. And there was no
more them.

He put his hands over his eyes. "The change, the change," he began. "I don't even know when it began. Me, Lou Epstein, with a rash. I
don't even feel anymore like Lou Epstein. All of a sudden, *pffft!* and
things are changed." He looked at Michael again, speaking slowly now,
stressing every word, as though the boy were more than a nephew,
more, in fact, than a single person. "All my life I tried. I swear it, I

should drop dead on the spot, if all my life I didn't try to do right, to give my family what I didn't have. . . ."

He stopped; it was not exactly what he wanted to say. He flipped on the bedside light and started again, a new way. "I was seven years old, Michael. I came here I was a boy seven years old, and that day, I can remember it like it was yesterday. Your grandparents and me—your father wasn't born yet, this stuff believe me he doesn't know. With your grandparents I stood on the dock, waiting for Charlie Goldstein to pick us up. He was your grandfather's partner in the old country, the thief. Anyway, we waited, and finally he came to pick us up, to take us where we would live. And when he came he had a big can in his hand. And you know what was in it? Kerosene. That's right, kerosene. We stood there and Charlie Goldstein poured it on all our heads. He rubbed it in, to delouse us. It tasted awful. For a little boy it was awful. . . ."

Michael shrugged his shoulders.

"Eh! How can you understand?" Epstein grumbled. "What do you know? Twenty years old . . ."

Michael shrugged again. "Twenty-two," he said softly.

There were more stories Epstein could tell, but he wondered if any of them would bring him closer to what it was he had on his mind but could not find the words for. He got out of bed and walked to the bedroom door. He opened it and stood there listening; on the downstairs sofa he could hear the folk singer snoring. Some night for guests! He shut the door and came back into the room, scratching his thigh. "Believe me, *she's* not losing any sleep. . . . She doesn't deserve me. What, she cooks? That's a big deal? She cleans? That deserves a medal? One day I should come home and the house should be a *mess*. I should be able to write my initials in the dust, somewhere, in the basement at least. Michael, after all these years that would be a pleasure!" He grabbed at his gray hair. "How did this happen? My Goldie, that such a woman should become a cleaning machine. Impossible." He walked to the far wall and stared into Herbie's baseball pictures, the long jaw-muscled faces, faded technicolor now, with signatures at the bottom: Charlie Keller, Lou Gehrig, Red Ruffing . . . a long time. How Herbie had loved his Yankees.

"One night," Epstein started again, "it was before the Depression even . . . you know what we did, Goldie and me?" He was staring at Red Ruffing now, through him. "You didn't know my Goldie, what a beautiful beautiful woman she was. And that night we took pictures, photos. I set up the camera—it was in the old house—and we took pictures, in the bedroom." He stopped, remembered. "I wanted a picture of my wife naked, to carry with me. I admit it. The next morning I woke up and there was Goldie tearing up the negatives. She said God forbid I should get in an accident one day and the police would take out my wallet for identification, and then oy-oy-oy!" He smiled. "You know, a woman, she worries. . . . But at least we took the pictures, even if we didn't develop them. How many people even do that?" He wondered, and then turned away from Red Ruffing to Michael, who was, faintly, at the corners of his mouth, smiling.

"What, the photos?"

Michael started to giggle.

"Huh?" Epstein smiled. "What, you never had that kind of idea? I admit it. Maybe to someone else it would seem wrong, a sin or something, but who's to say—"

Michael stiffened, at last his father's son. "Somebody's got to say. Some things just aren't right."

Epstein was willing to admit a youthful lapse. "Maybe," he said, "maybe she was even right to tear—"

Michael shook his head vehemently. "No! Some things aren't right. They're just not!"

And Epstein saw that the finger was pointed not at Uncle Lou, the Photographer, but at Uncle Lou, the Adulterer. Suddenly he was shouting. "Right, wrong! From you and your father that's all I ever hear. Who are you, what are you, King Solomon! He gripped the bedposts. Should I tell you what else happened the night we took pictures? That my Herbie was started that night, I'm sure of it. Over a year we tried and tried till I was *oysgamitched*, and that was the night. After the pictures, because of the pictures. Who knows!"

"But—"

"But what! But *this*?" He was pointing at his crotch. "You're a boy, you don't understand. When they start taking things away from you,

you reach out, you *grab*—maybe like a pig even, but you grab. And right, wrong, who knows! With tears in your eyes, who can even see the difference!" His voice dropped now, but in a minor key the scolding grew more fierce. "Don't call *me* names. I didn't see you with Ida's girl, there's not a name for that? For *you* it's right?"

Michael was kneeling in his bed now. *"You—saw?"*

"I saw!"

"But it's different—"

"Different?" Epstein shouted.

"To be married is different!"

"What's different you don't know about. To have a wife, to be a father, twice a father—and then they start taking things away—" and he fell weak-kneed across Michael's bed. Michael leaned back and looked at his uncle, but he did not know what to do or how to chastise, for he had never seen anybody over fifteen years old cry before.

Usually Sunday morning went like this: at nine-thirty Goldie started the coffee and Epstein walked to the corner for the lox and the Sunday *News.* When the lox was on the table, the bagels in the oven, the rotagravure section of the *News* two inches from Goldie's nose, then Sheila would descend the stairs, yawning, in her toe-length housecoat. They would sit down to eat, Sheila cursing her father for buying the *News* and "putting money in a Fascist's pocket." Outside, the Gentiles would be walking to church. It had always been the same, except, of course, that over the years the *News* had come closer to Goldie's nose and further from Sheila's heart; she had the *Post* delivered.

This Sunday when he awoke Epstein smelled coffee bubbling in the kitchen, and when he sneaked down the stairs, past the kitchen— he had been ordered to use the basement bathroom until he'd seen a doctor—he could smell lox. And, at last, when he entered the kitchen, shaved and dressed, he heard newspapers rattling. It was as if another Epstein, his ghost, had risen an hour earlier and performed his Sunday duties. Beneath the clock, around the table, sat Sheila, the folksinger, and Goldie. Bagels toasted in the oven, while the folk singer, sitting backwards in a chair, strummed his guitar and sang—

I've been down so long
It look like up to me . . .

Epstein clapped his hands and rubbed them together, preparatory to eating. "Sheila, you went out for this?" He gestured towards the paper and the lox. "Thank you."

The folk singer looked up, and in the same tune, improvised—

I went out for the lox

and grinned, a regular clown.

"Shut up!" Sheila told him.

He echoed her words, *plunk! plunk!*

"Thank *you*, then, young man," Epstein said.

"His name is Marvin," Sheila said, "for your information."

"Thank you, Martin."

"Mar*vin*," the young man said.

"I don't hear so good."

Goldie Epstein looked up from the paper. "Syphilis softens the brain."

"What!"

"Syphilis softens the brain. . . ."

Epstein stood up, raging. "Did you tell her that?" he shouted at his daughter. "Who told her that!"

The folk singer stopped plucking his guitar. Nobody answered; a conspiracy. He grabbed his daughter by the shoulders. "You respect your father, you understand!"

She jerked her shoulder away. "You're not *my* father!"

And the words hurled him back, to the joke Ida Kaufman had made in the car, to her tan dress, the spring sky . . . He leaned across the table to his wife. "Goldie, Goldie, look at me! Look at *me*, Lou!"

She stared back into the newspaper, though she held it far enough from her nose for Epstein to know she could not see the print; with everything else, the optometrist said the muscles in her eyes had loosened. "Goldie," he said, "Goldie, I did the worst thing in the world?

Look me in the eyes, Goldie. Tell me, since when do Jewish people get a divorce? Since when?"

She looked up at him, and then to Sheila. "Syphilis makes soft brains. I can't live with a pig!"

"We'll work it out. We'll go to the rabbi—"

"He wouldn't recognize you—"

"But the children, what about the children?"

"What children?"

Herbie was dead and Sheila a stranger; she was right.

"A grown-up child can take care of herself," Goldie said. "If she wants, she can come to Florida with me. I'm thinking I'll move to Miami Beach."

"Goldie!"

"Stop shouting," Sheila said, anxious to enter the brawl whatever way she could. "You'll wake Michael."

Painfully polite, Goldie addressed her daughter. "Michael left early this morning. He took his Linda to the beach for the day, to their place in Belmar."

"Barnegat," Epstein grumbled, retreating from the table.

"What did you say?" Sheila demanded.

"Barnegat." And he decided to leave the house before any further questions were asked.

At the corner luncheonette he bought his own paper and sat alone, drinking coffee and looking out the window beyond which the people walked to church. A pretty young *shiksa* walked by, holding her white round hat in her hand; she bent over to remove her shoe and shake a pebble from it. Epstein watched her bend, and he spilled some coffee on his shirt front. The girl's small behind was round as an apple beneath the close-fitting dress. He looked, and then as though he were praying, he struck himself on the chest with his fist, again and again. "What have I done! Oh, God!"

When he finished his coffee, he took his paper and started up the street. To home? What home? Across the street in her backyard he saw Ida Kaufman, who was wearing shorts and a halter and was hanging her daughter's underwear on the clothesline. Epstein looked around and saw only the Gentiles walking to church. Ida saw him and smiled. Growing angry, he stepped off the curb and, passionately, began to jay-walk.

At noon in the Epstein house those present heard a siren go off. Sheila looked up from the *Post* and listened; she looked at her watch. "Noon? I'm fifteen minutes slow. This lousy watch, my father's present."

Goldie Epstein was leafing through the ads in the travel section of the *New York Times*, which Marvin had gone out to buy for her. She looked at her watch. "I'm fourteen minutes slow. Also," she said to her daughter, "a watch from him. . . ."

The wail grew louder. "God Almighty," Sheila said, "it sounds like the end of the world."

And Marvin, who had been polishing his guitar with his red hand-kerchief, immediately broke into song, a high-pitched, shut-eyed, Ne-gro tune about the end of the world.

"Quiet!" Sheila said. She cocked her ear. "But it's Sunday. The sirens are Saturday—"

Goldie shot off the couch. "It's a real air raid? Oy, that's all we need!"

"It's the police," Sheila said, and fiery-eyed she raced to the front door, for she was politically opposed to police. "It's coming up the street—an ambulance!"

She raced out the door, followed by Marvin, whose guitar still hung around his neck. Goldie trailed behind, her feet slapping against her slippers. On the street she suddenly turned back to the house to make sure the door was shut against daytime burglars, bugs, and dust. When she turned again she had not far to run. The ambulance had pulled up across the street in Kaufman's driveway.

Already a crowd had gathered, neighbors in bathrobes, housecoats, carrying the comic sections with them; and, too, churchgoers, *shiksas* in white hats. Goldie could not make her way to the front where her daughter and Marvin stood, but even from the rear of the crowd she could see a young doctor leap from the ambulance and race up to the porch, his stethoscope wiggling in his back pocket as he took two steps at a time.

Mrs. Katz arrived. A squat red-faced woman whose stomach seemed to start at her knees, she tugged at Goldie's arm. "Goldie, more trouble here?"

"I don't know, Pearl. All that racket. I thought it was an atomic bomb."

"When it's that, you'll know," Pearl Katz said. She surveyed the crowd, then looked at the house. "Poor woman," she said, remembering that only three months before, on a windy March morning, an ambulance had arrived to take Mrs. Kaufman's husband to the nursing home, from which he never returned.

"Troubles, troubles . . ." Mrs. Katz was shaking her head, a pot of sympathy. "Everybody has their little bundle, believe me. I'll bet she had a nervous breakdown. That's not a good thing. Gallstones, you have them out and they're out. But a nervous breakdown, it's very bad. . . . You think maybe it's the daughter who's sick?"

"The daughter isn't home," Goldie said. "She's away with my nephew, Michael."

Mrs. Katz saw that no one had emerged from the house yet; she had time to gather a little information. "He's who, Goldie? The son of the brother-in-law that Lou doesn't talk to? That's his father?"

"Yes, Sol in Detroit—"

But she broke off, for the front door had opened, though still no one could be seen. A voice at the front of the crowd was commanding, "A little room here. Please! A little room, damn it!" It was Sheila. "A little room! Marvin, help me!"

"I can't put down my guitar—I can't find a place—"

"Get them back!" Sheila said.

"But my instrument—"

The doctor and his helper were now wiggling and tilting the stretcher through the front door. Behind them stood Mrs. Kaufman, a man's white shirt tucked into her shorts. Her eyes peered out of two red holes; she wore no make-up, Mrs. Katz noted.

"It must be the girl," said Pearl Katz, up on her toes. "Goldie, can you see, who is it—it's the girl?"

"The girl's *away*—"

"Stay back!" Sheila commanded. "Marvin, for crying out loud, help!"

"My instrument—"

The young doctor and his attendant held the stretcher steady as they walked sideways down the front steps.

Mrs. Katz jumped up and down. "Who *is* it?"

"I can't see," Goldie said. "I can't—" she pushed up on her toes, out of her slippers. "I—oh God! My God!" And she was racing forward, screaming, "Lou! Lou!"

"Mama, stay back." Sheila found herself fighting off her mother. The stretcher was sliding into the ambulance now.

"Sheila, let me go, it's your father!" She pointed to the ambulance, whose red eye spun slowly on top. For a moment Goldie looked back to the steps. Ida Kaufman stood there yet, her fingers fidgeting at the buttons of the shirt. Then Goldie broke for the ambulance, her daughter beside her, propelling her by her elbows.

"Who are you?" the doctor said. He took a step towards them to stop their forward motion, for it seemed as if they intended to dive right into the ambulance on top of his patient.

"The wife—" Sheila shouted.

The doctor pointed to the porch. "Look, lady—"

"I'm the *wife*," Goldie cried. "Me!"

The doctor looked at her. "Get in."

Goldie wheezed as Sheila and the doctor helped her into the ambulance, and she let out a gigantic gasp when she saw the white face sticking up from the gray blanket; his eyes were closed, his skin grayer than his hair. The doctor pushed Sheila aside, climbed in, and then the ambulance was moving, the siren screaming. Sheila ran after the ambulance a moment, hammering on the door.

Goldie turned to the doctor. "He's dead?"

"No, he had a heart attack."

She smacked her face.

"He'll be all right," the doctor said.

"But a heart attack. Never in his life."

"A man sixty, sixty-five, it happens." The doctor snapped the answers back while he held Epstein's wrist.

"He's only fifty-nine."

"Some only," the doctor said.

The ambulance zoomed through a red light and made a sharp right turn that threw Goldie to the floor. She sat there and spoke. "But how does a healthy man—"

"Lady, don't ask questions. A grown man can't act like a boy."

She put her hands over her eyes, as Epstein opened his.

"He's awake now," the doctor said. "Maybe he wants to hold your hand or something."

Goldie crawled to his side and looked at him. "Lou, you're all right? Does anything hurt?"

He did not answer. "He knows it's me?"

The doctor shrugged his shoulders. "Tell him."

"It's me, Lou."

"It's your wife, Lou," the doctor said. Epstein blinked his eyes. "He knows," the doctor said. "He'll be all right. All he's got to do is live a normal life, normal for sixty."

"You hear the doctor, Lou. All you got to do is live a normal life."

Epstein opened his mouth. His tongue hung over his teeth like a dead snake.

"Don't you talk," his wife said. "Don't you worry about anything. Not even the business. That'll work out. Our Sheila will marry Marvin and that'll be that. You won't have to sell, Lou, it'll be in the family. You can retire, rest, and Marvin can take over. He's a smart boy, Marvin, a *mensch*."

Lou rolled his eyes in his head.

"Don't try to talk. I'll take care. You'll be better soon and we can go someplace. We can go to Saratoga, to the mineral baths, if you want. We'll just go, you and me—" Suddenly she gripped his hand. "Lou, you'll live normal, won't you? *Won't you?*" She was crying. " 'Cause what'll happen, Lou, is you'll kill yourself! You'll keep this up and that'll be the end—"

"All right," the young doctor said, "you take it easy now. We don't want two patients on our hands."

The ambulance was pulling down and around into the side entrance of the hospital and the doctor knelt at the back door.

"I don't know why I'm crying," Goldie wiped her eyes. "He'll be all right? You say so, I believe you, you're a doctor." And as the young man swung open the door with the big red cross painted on the back, she asked, softly, "Doctor, you have something that will cure what else he's got—this rash?" She pointed.

The doctor looked at her. Then he lifted for a moment the blanket that covered Epstein's nakedness.

"Doctor, it's bad?"

Goldie's eyes and nose were running.

"An irritation," the doctor said.

She grabbed his wrist. "You can clean it up?"

"So it'll never come back," the doctor said, and hopped out of the ambulance.

Issue 19, 1958

TRAINS

Raymond Carver

⚬

Why Don't You Dance?

In the kitchen, he poured another drink and looked at the bedroom suite in his front yard. The mattress was stripped and the candy-striped sheets lay beside two pillows on the chiffonier. Except for that, things looked much the way they had in the bedroom—nightstand and reading lamp on his side of the bed, nightstand and reading lamp on her side.

His side, her side.

He considered this as he sipped the whiskey.

The chiffonier stood a few feet from the foot of the bed. He had emptied the drawers into cartons that morning, and the cartons were in the living room. A portable heater was next to the chiffonier. A rat-tan chair with a decorator pillow stood at the foot of the bed. The buffed aluminum kitchen-set took up a part of the driveway. A yellow muslin cloth, much too large, a gift, covered the table and hung down over the sides. A potted fern was on the table, along with a box of sil-verware and a record player, also gifts. A big console-model television set rested on a coffee table, and a few feet away from this, stood a sofa and a chair and a floor lamp. The desk was pushed against the garage door. A few utensils were on the desk, along with a wall clock and two framed prints. There was also in the driveway a carton with cups, glasses, and plates, each object wrapped in newspaper. That morning he had cleared out the closets and, except for the three cartons in the living room, all the stuff was out of the house. He had run an extension cord on out there and everything was connected. Things worked, no different from how it was when they were inside.

Now and then a car slowed and people stared. But no one stopped. It occurred to him that he wouldn't either.

"It must be a yard sale," the girl said to the boy.

This girl and boy were furnishing a little apartment.

"Let's see what they want for the bed," the girl said.

"And the TV," the boy said.

The boy pulled into the driveway and stopped in front of the kitchen table.

They got out of the car and began to examine things, the girl touching the muslin cloth, the boy plugging in the blender and turning the dial to MINCE, the girl picking up a chafing dish, the boy turning on the television set and making adjustments. He sat down on the sofa to watch. He lit a cigarette, looked around, and flipped the match into the grass. The girl sat on the bed. She pushed off her shoes and lay back. She thought she could see the evening star.

"Come here, Jack. Try this bed. Bring one of those pillows," she said.

"How is it?" he said.

"Try it," she said.

He looked around. The house was dark.

"I feel funny," he said. "Better see if anybody's home."

She bounced on the bed.

"Try it first," she said.

He lay down on the bed and put the pillow under his head.

"How does it feel?" the girl said.

"Feels firm," he said.

She turned on her side and put her hand to his face.

"Kiss me," she said.

"Let's get up," he said.

"Kiss me," she said.

She closed her eyes. She held him.

He said, "I'll see if anybody's home."

But he just sat up and stayed where he was, making believe he was watching the television.

Lights came on in houses up and down the street.

"Wouldn't it be funny if," the girl said and grinned and didn't finish.

The boy laughed, but for no good reason. For no good reason, he switched on the reading lamp.

The girl brushed away a mosquito, whereupon the boy stood up and tucked in his shirt.

"I'll see if anybody's home," he said. "I don't think anybody's home. But if anybody is, I'll see what things are going for."

"Whatever they ask, offer ten dollars less. It's always a good idea," she said. "And, besides, they must be desperate or something."

"It's a pretty good TV," the boy said.

"Ask them how much," the girl said.

The man came down the sidewalk with a sack from the market. He had sandwiches, beer, and whiskey. He saw the car in the driveway and the girl on the bed. He saw the television set going and the boy on the porch.

"Hello," the man said to the girl. "You found the bed. That's good."

"Hello," the girl said, and got up. "I was just trying it out." She patted the bed. "It's a pretty good bed."

"It's a good bed," the man said, and put down the sack and took out the beer and the whiskey.

"We thought nobody was here," the boy said. "We're interested in the bed and maybe the TV. Maybe the desk. How much do you want for the bed?"

"I was thinking fifty dollars for the bed," the man said.

"Would you take forty?" the girl asked.

"Okay, I'll take forty," the man said.

He took a glass out of the carton. He took the newspaper off it. He broke the seal on the whiskey.

"How about the TV?" the boy said.

"Twenty-five."

"Would you take fifteen?" the girl said.

"Fifteen's okay. I could take fifteen," the man said.

The girl looked at the boy.

"You kids, you'll want a drink," the man said. "Glasses in the box. I'm going to sit down. I'm going to sit down on the sofa."

The man sat on the sofa, leaned back, and stared at the boy and the girl.

The boy found two glasses and poured whiskey.

"That's enough," the girl said. "I think I want water in mine."

She pulled out a chair and sat at the kitchen table.

"There's water in the spigot over there," the man said. "Turn on that spigot."

The boy came back with the watered whiskey. He cleared his throat and sat down at the kitchen table. He grinned. But he didn't drink anything.

Birds darted overhead for insects, small birds that moved very fast.

The man gazed at the television. He finished his drink and started another, and when he reached to turn on the floor lamp, his cigarette dropped from his fingers and fell between the cushions.

The girl got up to help him find it.

"So what do you want?" the boy said to the girl.

The boy took out the checkbook and held it to his lips as if thinking.

"I want the desk," the girl said. "How much money is the desk?"

The man waved his hand at this preposterous question.

"Name a figure," he said.

He looked at them as they sat at the table. In the lamplight, there was something about their faces. It was nice or it was nasty. There was no telling which.

"I'm going to turn off this TV and put on a record," the man said. "This record player is going, too. Cheap. Make me an offer."

He poured more whiskey and opened a beer.

"Everything goes."

The girl held out her glass and the man poured.

"Thank you," she said. "You're very nice."

"It goes to your head," the boy said. "I'm getting it in the head." He held up his glass and jiggled it.

The man finished his drink and poured another, and then he found the box with the records.

"Pick something," the man said to the girl, and he held the records out to her.

The boy was writing the check.

"Here," the girl said, picking something, picking—anything—for she did not know the names on these records. She got up from the table and sat down again. She did not want to sit still.

"I'm making it out to cash," the boy said.

"Sure," the man said.

They drank. They listened to the record. And then the man put on another.

Why don't you kids dance? he decided to say, and then he said it. "Why don't you dance?"

"I don't think so," the boy said.

"Go ahead," the man said. "It's my yard. You can dance if you want to."

Arms about each other, their bodies pressed together, the boy and girl moved up and down the driveway. They were dancing. And when the record was over, they did it again, and when that one ended, the boy said, "I'm drunk."

The girl said, "You're not drunk."

"Well, I'm drunk," the boy said.

The man turned the record over and the boy said, "I am."

"Dance with me," the girl said to the boy and then to the man, and when the man stood up, she came to him with her arms open.

"Those people over there, they're watching," she said.

"It's okay," the man said. "It's my place," he said. "We can dance."

"Let them watch," the girl said.

"That's right," the man said. "They thought they'd seen everything over here. But they haven't seen this, have they?" he said.

He felt her breath on his neck. "I hope you like your bed," he said.

The girl closed and then opened her eyes. She pushed her face into the man's shoulder. She pulled the man closer.

"You must be desperate or something," she said.

Weeks later she said: "The guy was about middle-aged. All his things right there in his yard. No lie. We got real pissed and danced. In the driveway. Oh, my God. Don't laugh. He played us these records. Look at this record player. The old guy gave it to us. These crappy records, too. Will you look at this shit?"

She kept talking. She told everyone. There was more to it, but she couldn't get it all talked out. After a time, she quit trying.

Issue 79, 1981

T. Coraghessan Boyle

❊

Greasy Lake

It's about a mile down on the dark side of Route 88.
                                                        —Bruce Springsteen

There was a time when courtesy and winning ways went out of style, when it was good to be bad, when you cultivated decadence like a taste. We were all dangerous characters then. We wore torn-up leather jackets, slouched around with toothpicks in our mouths, sniffed glue and ether and what somebody claimed was cocaine. When we wheeled our parents' whining station wagons out into the street, we left a patch of rubber half a block long. We drank gin and grape juice, Tango, Thunderbird and Bali Hai. We were nineteen. We were bad. We read André Gide and struck elaborate poses to show that we didn't give a shit about anything. At night, we went up to Greasy Lake.

Through the center of town, up the strip, past the housing developments and shopping malls, streetlights giving way to the thin streaming illumination of the headlights, trees crowding the asphalt in a black unbroken wall: that was the way out to Greasy Lake. The Indians had called it Wakan, a reference to the clarity of its waters. Now it was fetid and murky, the mud banks glittering with broken glass and strewn beer cans and the charred remains of bonfires. There was a single ravaged island a hundred yards from shore, so stripped of vegetation it looked as if the Air Force had strafed it. We went up to the lake because everyone went there, because we wanted to snuff the rich scent of possibility on the breeze, watch a girl take off her clothes and plunge into the festering murk, drink beer, smoke pot, howl at the stars, savor the incongruous full-throated roar of rock and roll against the primeval susurrus of frogs and crickets. This was nature.

I was there one night, late, in the company of two dangerous characters. Digby wore a gold star in his right ear and allowed his father to pay his tuition at Cornell; Jeff was thinking of quitting school to become a painter/musician/head-shop proprietor. They were both expert in the social graces, quick with a sneer, able to manage a Ford with lousy shocks over a rutted and gutted blacktop road at eighty-five while rolling a joint as compact as a Tootsie Pop stick. They could lounge against a bank of booming speakers and trade "man's" with the best of them or roll out across the dance floor as if their joints worked on bearings. They were slick and quick and they wore their mirror shades at breakfast and dinner, in the shower, in closets and caves. In short, they were bad.

I drove. Digby pounded the dashboard and shouted along with Toots & the Maytals while Jeff hung his head out the window and streaked the side of my mother's Bel Air with vomit. It was early June, the air soft as a hand on your cheek, the third night of summer vacation. The first two nights we'd been out till dawn, looking for something we never found. On this, the third night, we'd cruised the strip sixty-seven times, been in and out of every bar and club we could think of in a twenty-mile radius, stopped twice for bucket chicken and forty-cent hamburgers, debated going to a party at the house of a girl Jeff's sister knew, and chucked two dozen raw eggs at mailboxes and hitchhikers. It was 2:00 A.M., the bars were closing. There was nothing to do but take a bottle of lemon-flavored gin up to Greasy Lake.

The taillights of a single car winked at us as we swung into the dirt lot with its tufts of weed and washboard corrugations: '57 Chevy, mint, metallic blue. On the far side of the lot, like the exoskeleton of some gaunt chrome insect, a chopper leaned against its kickstand. And that was it for excitement: some junkie half-wit biker and a car freak pumping his girlfriend. Whatever it was we were looking for, we weren't about to find it at Greasy Lake. Not that night.

But then all of a sudden Digby was fighting for the wheel. "Hey, that's Tony Lovett's car! Hey!" he shouted, while I stabbed at the brake pedal and the Bel Air nosed up to the gleaming bumper of the parked Chevy. Digby leaned on the horn, laughing, and instructed me to put my brights on. I flicked on the brights. This was hilarious. A joke. Tony would experience premature withdrawal and expect to be confronted by grim-looking state troopers with flashlights. We hit the horn, strobed the lights and then jumped out of the car to press our witty faces to Tony's windows: for all we knew we might even catch a glimpse of some little fox's tit, and then we could slap backs with red-faced Tony, rough-house a little, and go on to new heights of adventure and daring.

The first mistake, the one that opened the whole floodgate, was losing my grip on the keys. In the excitement, leaping from the car with the gin in one hand and a roach clip in the other, I spilled them in the grass—in the dark, dank, mysterious nighttime grass of Greasy Lake. This was a tactical error, as damaging and irreversible in its way as Westmoreland's decision to dig in at Khe Sanh. I felt it like a jab of intuition, and I stopped there by the open door, peering vaguely into the night that puddled up round my feet.

The second mistake—and this was inextricably bound up with the first—was in identifying the car as Tony Lovett's. Even before the very bad character in greasy jeans and engineer boots ripped out of the driver's door, I began to realize that this chrome blue was much lighter than the robin's egg of Tony's car and that Tony's car didn't have rear-mounted speakers. Judging from their expressions, Digby and Jeff were privately groping toward the same inevitable and unsettling conclusion that I was.

In any case, there was no reasoning with this bad greasy character—clearly he was a man of action. The first lusty Rockettes' kick of his steel-toed boot caught me under the chin, chipped my favorite tooth and left me sprawled in the dirt. Like a fool, I'd gone down on one knee to comb the stiff hacked grass for the keys, my mind making connections in the most dragged-out, testudinal way, knowing that things had gone wrong, that I was in a lot of trouble, and that the lost ignition key was my Grail and my salvation. The three or four succeeding blows were mainly absorbed by my right buttock and the tough piece of bone at the base of my spine.

Meanwhile, Digby vaulted the kissing bumpers and delivered a savage kung fu blow to the greasy character's collarbone. Digby had just finished a course in martial arts for phys. ed. credit and had spent the better part of the past two nights telling us apocryphal tales of Bruce Lee types and of the raw power invested in lightning blows shot from coiled wrists, ankles and elbows. The greasy character was unimpressed. He merely backed off a step, his face like a Toltec mask, and laid Digby out with a single whistling roundhouse blow . . . but by now Jeff had got into the act, and I was beginning to extricate myself from the dirt, a tinny compound of shock, rage and impotence wadded in my throat.

Jeff was on the guy's back, biting at his ear. Digby was on the ground, cursing. I went for the tire iron I kept under the driver's seat. I kept it there because bad characters always keep tire irons under the driver's seat, for just such an occasion as this. Never mind that I hadn't been involved in a fight since sixth grade when a kid with a sleepy eye and two streams of mucus depending from his nostrils hit me in the knee with a Louisville slugger, never mind that I'd touched the tire iron exactly twice before, to change tires: it was there. And I went for it.

I was terrified. Blood was beating in my ears, my hands were shaking, my heart turning over like a dirt bike in the wrong gear. My antagonist was shirtless, and a single cord of muscle flashed across his chest as he bent forward to peel Jeff from his back like a wet overcoat. "Motherfucker," he spat, over and over, and I was aware in that instant that all four of us—Digby, Jeff and myself included—were chanting "motherfucker, motherfucker," as if it were a battle cry. (What happened next? the detective asks the murderer from beneath the turned-down brim of his porkpie hat. I don't know, the murderer says, something came over me. Exactly.)

Digby poked the flat of his hand in the bad character's face and I came at him like a kamikaze, mindless, raging, stung with humiliation— the whole thing, from the initial boot in the chin to this murderous primal instant involving no more than sixty hyperventilating, gland-flooding seconds—I came at him and brought the tire iron down across his ear. The effect was instantaneous, astonishing. He was a stunt man and this was Hollywood; he was a big grimacing toothy balloon and I was a man with a straight pin. He collapsed. Wet his pants. Went loose in his boots.

A single second, big as a zeppelin, floated by. We were standing over him in a circle, gritting our teeth, jerking our necks, our limbs and hands and feet twitching with glandular discharges. No one said anything. We just stared down at the guy, the car freak, the lover, the bad greasy character laid low. Digby looked at me, then Jeff. I was still holding the tire iron, a tuft of hair clinging to the crook like dandelion fluff, like down. Rattled, I dropped it in the dirt, already envisioning the headlines, the pitted faces of the police inquisitors, the gleam of handcuffs, clank of bars, the big black shadows rising from the back of the cell . . . when suddenly a raw torn shriek cut through me like all the juice in all the electric chairs in the country.

It was the fox. She was short, barefoot, dressed in panties and a man's shirt. "Animals!" she screamed, running at us with her fists clenched and wisps of blow-dried hair in her face. There was a silver chain round her ankle, and her toenails flashed in the glare of the headlights. I think it was the toenails that did it. Sure, the gin and the cannabis and even the Kentucky Fried may have had a hand in it, but it was the sight of those flaming toes that set us off—the toad emerging from the loaf in *Virgin Spring*, lipstick smeared on a child: she was already tainted. We were on her like Bergman's deranged brothers—see no evil, hear none, speak none—panting, wheezing, tearing at her clothes, grabbing for flesh. We were bad characters, and we were scared and hot and three steps over the line—anything could have happened.

It didn't.

Before we could pin her to the hood of the car, our eyes masked with lust and greed and purest primal badness, a pair of headlights swung into the lot. There we were, dirty, bloody, guilty, dissociated from humanity and civilization, the first of the Ur-crimes behind us, the second in progress, shreds of nylon panty and spandex brassiere dangling from our fingers, our flies open, lips licked—there we were, caught in the spotlight. Nailed.

We bolted. First for the car, and then, realizing we had no way of starting it, for the woods. I thought nothing. I thought escape. The headlights came at me like accusing fingers. I was gone.

Ram-bam-bam, across the parking lot, past the chopper and into the feculent undergrowth at the lake's edge, insects flying up in my face, weeds whipping, frogs and snakes and red-eyed turtles splashing off into the night: I was already ankle-deep in muck and tepid water and still going strong. Behind me, the girl's screams rose in intensity, disconsolate, incriminating, the screams of the Sabine women, the Christian martyrs, Anne Frank dragged from the garret. I kept going, pursued by those cries, imagining cops and bloodhounds. The water was up to my knees when I realized what I was doing: I was going to swim for it. Swim the breadth of Greasy Lake and hide myself in the thick clot of woods on the far side. They'd never find me there.

I was breathing in sobs, in gasps. The water lapped at my waist as I looked out over the moon-burnished ripples, the mats of algae that clung to the surface like scabs. Digby and Jeff had vanished. I paused. Listened. The girl was quieter now, screams tapering to sobs, but there were male voices, angry, excited, and the high-pitched ticking of the second car's engine. I waded deeper, stealthy, hunted, the ooze sucking at my sneakers. As I was about to take the plunge—at the very instant I dropped my shoulder for the first slashing stroke—I blundered into something. Something unspeakable, obscene, something soft, wet, moss-grown. A patch of weed? A log? When I reached out to touch it, it gave like a rubber duck, it gave like flesh.

In one of those nasty little epiphanies for which we are prepared by films and TV and childhood visits to the funeral home to ponder the shrunken painted forms of dead grandparents, I understood what it was that bobbed there so inadmissibly in the dark. Understood, and stumbled back in horror and revulsion, my mind yanked in six different directions (I was nineteen, a mere child, an infant, and here in the space of five minutes I'd struck down one greasy character and blundered into the waterlogged carcass of a second), thinking the keys, the keys, why did I have to go and lose the keys? I stumbled back, but the muck took hold of my feet—a sneaker snagged, balance lost—and suddenly I was pitching face forward into the buoyant black mass, throwing out my hands in desperation while simultaneously conjuring the image of rotting frogs and muskrats revolving in slicks of their own deliquescing juices. AAAAArrrgh! I shot from the water like a torpedo, the dead man rotating to expose a mossy beard and eyes cold as the moon. I must have shouted out, thrashing around in the weeds, because the voices behind me suddenly became animated.

"What was that?"

"It's them, it's them: they tried to, tried to . . . *rape* me!" Sobs.

A man's voice, flat midwestern accent. "You sons a bitches, we'll kill you!"

Frogs, crickets.

Then another voice, harsh, r-less, lower East Side: "Motherfucker!" I recognized the verbal virtuosity of the bad greasy character in the engineer boots. Tooth chipped, sneakers gone, coated in mud and slime and worse, crouching breathless in the weeds waiting to have my ass thoroughly and definitively kicked and fresh from the hideous stinking embrace of a three-days-dead corpse. I suddenly felt a rush of joy and vindication: the son of a bitch was alive! Just as quickly, my bowels turned to ice. "Come on out of there you pansy motherfuckers!" the bad greasy character was screaming. He shouted curses till he was out of breath.

The crickets started up again, then the frogs. I held my breath. All at once there was a sound in the reeds, a swishing, a splash: *thunk-a-thunk*. They were throwing rocks. The frogs fell silent. I cradled my head. *Swish, swish, thunk-a-thunk*. A wedge of feldspar the size of a cue ball glanced off my knee. I bit my finger.

It was then that they turned to the car. I heard a door slam, a curse, and then the sound of the headlights shattering—almost a good-natured sound, celebratory, like corks popping from the necks of bottles. This was succeeded by the dull booming of the fenders, metal on metal, and then the icy crash of the windshield. I inched forward, elbows and knees, my belly pressed to the muck, thinking of guerrillas and commandos and *The Naked and the Dead*. I parted the weeds and squinted the length of the parking lot.

The second car—it was a Trans-Am—was still running, its high beams washing the scene in a lurid stagey light. Tire iron flailing, the greasy bad character was laying into the side of my mother's Bel Air like an avenging demon, his shadow riding up the trunks of the trees. *Whomp. Whomp. Whomp-whomp.* The other two guys—blond types, in fraternity jackets—were helping out with tree branches and skull-sized boulders. One of them was gathering up bottles, rocks, muck, candy wrappers, used condoms, pop-tops and other refuse and pitching it through the window on the driver's side. I could see the fox, a white bulb behind the windshield of the '57 Chevy. "Bobbie," she whined over the thumping, "come *on.*" The greasy character paused a moment, took one good swipe at the left taillight and then heaved the tire iron halfway across the lake. Then he fired up the '57 and was gone.

Blond head nodded at blond head. One said something to the other, too low for me to catch. They were no doubt thinking that in helping to annihilate my mother's car they'd committed a fairly rash act, and thinking, too, that there were three bad characters connected with that very car watching them from the woods. Perhaps other possibilities occurred to them as well—police, jail cells, justices of the peace, reparations, lawyers, irate parents, fraternal censure. Whatever they were thinking, they suddenly dropped branches, bottles and rocks and sprang for their car in unison, as if they'd choreographed it. Five seconds. That's all it took. The engine shrieked, the tires squealed, a cloud of dust rose from the rutted lot and then settled back on darkness.

I don't know how long I lay there, the bad breath of decay all around me, my jacket heavy as a bear, the primordial ooze subtly reconstituting itself to accommodate my upper thighs and testicles. My jaw ached, my knee throbbed, my coccyx was on fire. I contemplated suicide, wondered if I'd need bridgework, scraped the recesses of my brain for some sort of excuse to give my parents—a tree had fallen on the car, I was blindsided by a bread truck, hit and run, vandals had got to it while we were playing chess at Digby's. Then I thought of the dead man. He was probably the only person on the planet worse off than I was. I thought about him, fog on the lake, insects chirring eerily, and felt the tug of fear, felt the darkness opening up inside me like a set of jaws. Who was he, I wondered, this victim of time and circumstance bobbing sorrowfully in the lake at my back. The owner of the chopper, no doubt, a bad older character come to this. Shot during a murky drug deal, drowned while drunkenly frolicking in the lake. Another headline. My car was wrecked, he was dead.

When the eastern half of the sky went from black to cobalt and the trees began to separate themselves from the shadows, I pushed myself up from the mud and stepped out into the open. By now the birds had begun to take over for the crickets, and dew lay slick on the leaves. There was a smell in the air, raw and sweet at the same time, the smell of the sun firing buds and opening blossoms. I contemplated the car. It lay there like a wreck along the highway, like a steel sculpture left over from a vanished civilization. Everything was still. This was nature.

I was circling the car, as dazed and bedraggled as the sole survivor of an air blitz, when Digby and Jeff emerged from the trees behind me. Digby's face was crosshatched with smears of dirt, Jeff's jacket was gone and his shirt was torn across the shoulder. They slouched across the lot, looking sheepish, and silently came up beside me to gape at the ravaged automobile. No one said a word. After awhile Jeff swung open the driver's door and began to scoop the broken glass and garbage off the seat. I looked at Digby. He shrugged. "At least they didn't slash the tires," he said.

It was true; the tires were intact. There was no windshield, the headlights were staved in and the body looked as if it had been sledgehammered for a quarter a shot at the county fair, but the tires were inflated to regulation pressure. The car was driveable. In silence, all three of us bent to scrape the mud and shattered glass from the interior. I said nothing about the biker. When we were finished, I reached in my pocket for the keys, experienced a nasty stab of recollection, cursed myself, and turned to search the grass. I spotted them almost immediately, no more than five feet from the open door, glinting like jewels in the first tapering shaft of sunlight. There was no reason to get philosophical about it: I eased into the seat and turned the engine over.

It was at that precise moment that the silver Mustang with the flame decals rumbled into the lot. All three of us froze, then Digby and Jeff slid into the car and slammed the door. We watched as the Mustang rocked and bobbed across the ruts and finally jerked to a halt beside the forlorn chopper at the far end of the lot. "Let's go," Digby said. I hesitated, the Bel Air wheezing beneath me.

Two girls emerged from the Mustang. Tight jeans, stiletto heels, hair like frozen fur. They bent over the motorcycle, paced back and forth aimlessly, glanced once or twice at us and then ambled over to where the reeds sprang up in a green fence round the perimeter of the lake. One of them cupped her hands to her mouth. "Al," she called. "Hey, Al!"

"Come on," Digby hissed. "Let's get out of here."

But it was too late. The second girl was picking her way across the lot, unsteady on her heels, looking up at us and then away. She was older—twenty-five or six—and as she came closer we could see there was something wrong with her—she was stoned or drunk, lurching now and waving her arms for balance. I gripped the steering wheel as if it were the ejection lever of a flaming jet, and Digby spat out my name, twice, terse and impatient.

"Hi," the girl said.

We looked at her like zombies, like war veterans, like deaf and dumb pencil peddlers.

She smiled, her lips cracked and dry. "Listen," she said, bending from the waist to look in the window, "you guys seen Al?" Her pupils were pinpoints, her eyes glass. She jerked her neck. "That's his bike over there—Al's. You seen him?"

Al. I didn't know what to say. I wanted to get out of the car and retch, I wanted to go home to my parents' house and crawl into bed. Digby poked me in the ribs. "We haven't seen anybody," I said.

The girl seemed to consider this, reaching out a slim veiny arm to brace herself against the car. "No matter," she said, slurring the t's, "he'll turn up." And then, as if she'd just taken stock of the whole scene—the ravaged car and our battered faces, the desolation of the place—she said: "Hey, you guys look like some pretty bad characters—been fightin', huh?" We stared straight ahead, rigid as catatonics. She was fumbling in her pocket and muttering something. Finally she held out a handful of tablets in glassine wrappers: "Hey, you want to party, you want to do some of these with me and Sarah?"

I just looked at her. I thought I was going to cry. Digby broke the silence. "No thanks," he said, leaning over me. "Some other time."

I put the car in gear and it inched forward with a groan, shaking off pellets of glass like an old dog shedding water after a bath, heaving over the ruts on its worn springs, creeping toward the highway. There was a sheen of sun on the lake. I looked back. The girl was still standing there, watching us, her shoulders slumped, hand outstretched.

William Maxwell

The Lily-White Boys

The Follansbees' Christmas party was at teatime on Christmas Day, and it was for all ages. Ignoring the fire laws, the big Christmas tree standing between the two front windows in the living room of the Park Avenue apartment had candles on it. When the last one was lit, somebody flipped a light switch, and in the hush that fell over the room the soft yellow candlelight fell on the upturned faces of the children sitting on the floor in a ring around the base of the tree, bringing tears to the eyes of the susceptible. The tree was strung with loops of gold and silver tinsel and popcorn and colored paper, and some of the glass ornaments—the hardy tin soldier, the drum, the nutmeg, and the Man in the Moon—went all the way back to Beth Follansbee's childhood. While the presents were being distributed, Mark Follansbee stood by with a bucket of water and a broom. The room smelled of warm wax and balsam.

The big red candles on the mantlepiece burned down slowly in their nest of holly. In the dining room, presiding over the cut-glass punch bowl, Beth Follansbee said, "You let the peaches sit all day in a quart of vodka, and then you add two bottles of white wine and a bottle of champagne. Be a little careful. It isn't as innocuous as you might think," and with her eyebrows signaled to the maid that the plate of watercress sandwiches needed refilling. Those that liked to sing had gathered around the piano in the living room and, having done justice to all the familiar carols, were singing with gusto, "Seven for the seven stars in the sky and six for the six proud walkers. Five for the symbols at your door and four for the Gospel makers, Three, three, the rivals, Two, two, two the lily-white boys, clothed all in green-ho. One is one and all alone and evermore shall *be* so." And an overexcited little boy with a plastic spaceship was running up and down the hall and shouting "Blast off!"

The farewells at the elevator door were followed by a second round down below on the sidewalk while the doorman was blowing his whistle for cabs.

"Can we drop you?" Ellen Hunter called.

"No. You're going downtown, and it would be out of your way," Celia Coleman said.

The Colemans walked two blocks north on Park and then east. The sidewalks of Manhattan were bare, the snow the weatherman promised having failed to come. There were no stars, and the night sky had a brownish cast. From a speaker placed over the doorway of a darkened storefront human voices sang "O Little Town of Bethlehem." The drugstore on the corner was brightly lighted but locked, with the iron grating pulled down and no customers inquiring about cosmetics at the cash register or standing in front of the revolving Timex display unable to make up their minds.

The Venetian red door of the Colemans' house was level with the sidewalk and had a Christmas wreath on it. In an eerie fashion it swung open when Dan Coleman tried to fit his key in the lock.

"Did we forget to close it?" Celia said and he shook his head. The lock had been jimmied.

"I guess it's our turn," he said grimly as they walked in. At the foot of the stairs they stood still and listened. Nothing on the first floor was disturbed. There was even a silver spoon and a small silver tray on the dining room sideboard. Looking at each other they half managed to believe that everything was all right: The burglars had been frightened by somebody coming down the street, or a squad car perhaps, and had cleared out without taking anything. But the house felt queer, not right somehow, not the way it usually felt, and they saw why when they got to the top of the first flight of stairs.

"Sweet Jesus!" he exclaimed softly, and she thought of her jewelry.

The shades were drawn to the sills, so that people on the sidewalk or in the apartments across the way could not see in the windows. One small detail caught his eye in the midst of the general destruction. A

Limoges jar that held potpourri lay in fragments on the hearth and a faint odor of rose petals hung on the air.

With her heart beating faster than usual and her mouth as dry as cotton she said, "I can understand why they might want to look behind the pictures, but why walk on them?"

"Saves time," he said.

"And why break the lamps?"

"I don't know," he said. "I have never gone in for house-breaking."

A cigarette had been placed at the edge of a tabletop, right next to an ashtray, and allowed to burn all the way down. The liquor cupboard was untouched. In the study, on that same floor at the back of the house, where the hi-fi, the tape deck, and the TV should have been there was a blank space. Rather than bother to unscrew the cable, the burglars had snipped it with wire cutters. All the books had been pulled from the shelves and lay in mounds on the floor.

"Evidently they are not readers," he said, and picked up volume seven of *Hakluyt's Voyages* and stood it on an empty shelf.

She tried to think of a reason for not going up the next flight to the bedrooms, to make the uncertainty last a little longer. Rather than leave her jewelry in the bank and never have the pleasure of wearing it, she had hidden it in a place that seemed to her very clever.

It was not clever enough. The star ruby ring, the cabuchon emeralds, the gold bracelets, the moonstones, the garnet necklace that had been her father's wedding present to her mother, the peridot and tourmaline pin that she found in an antiquity shop on a back street in Toulon, the diamond earrings—gone. All gone. Except for the things Dan had given her they were all inherited and irreplaceable, and so what would be the point of insuring them.

"In a way it's a relief," she said, in what sounded to her, though not to him, like her normal voice.

"Meaning?"

"Meaning that you can't worry about possessions you no longer have."

She opened the top right-hand drawer of her dressing table and saw that the junk jewelry was still there. As she pushed the drawer shut he said, "The standard procedure," and took her in his arms.

The rest was also pretty much the standard procedure. Mattresses were pulled half off the beds and ripped open with a razor blade, drawers turned upside down, and his clothes closet completely empty, which meant that his wardrobe now consisted of the dark blue suit he had put on earlier this evening to go to the Follansbees' Christmas party. Her dresses lay in a colored confusion that spilled out into the room from the floor of her walk-in closet. Boxes from the upper shelves had been pulled down and ransacked—boxes containing hats, evening purses, evening dresses she no longer had occasion to wear, since they seldom went out at night except to go to the theater or dine with friends.

When the police came she let him do the talking. Christmas Eve, Christmas Day, were the prime moments for break-ins, they said. The house had probably been watched. They made a list of the more important things and suggested that Dan send them an inventory. They were pleasant and held out no hope. There were places they could watch, they said, to see if anything belonging to the Colemans turned up, but chances were that . . . When they left he put the back of a chair against the doorknob of the street door and started up the stairs.

From the stairs he could see into their bedroom. To his astonishment Celia had on an evening dress he hadn't seen for twenty years. Turning this way and that, she studied her reflection in the full-length mirror on the back of a closet door. Off the dress came, over her head, and she worked her way into a scarlet chiffon sheath that had a sooty footprint on it. Her hair had turned from dark brown to grey and when she woke up in the morning her back was as stiff as a board, but the dress fit her perfectly. While he stood there, watching, and unseen, she tried them on, one after another—the black taffeta with the bouffant skirt, the pale sea-green silk with bands of matching silk fringe, all her favorite dresses that she had been too fond of to take to a thrift shop, and that had been languishing on the top shelf of her closet. As she stepped back to consider critically the effect of a white silk evening suit, her high heels ground splinters of glass into the bedroom rug.

Its load lightened by a brief stop in the Bronx at a two-story warehouse that was filled from floor to ceiling with hi-fi sets and color TVs, the

Chrysler sedan proceeded along the Bruckner Elevated Expressway to Route 95. When the car slowed down for the tollgate at the Connecticut state line, the sandy-haired recidivist, slouched down in the right-hand front seat, opened his eyes. The false license plates aroused no interest whatever as the car came to a stop and then drove on.

In the middle of the night, the material witnesses to the breaking and entering communicated with one another, a remark at a time. A small spotlight up near the ceiling that was trained on an area over the living room sofa said, *When I saw the pictures being ripped from the walls I was afraid. I thought I was going to go the same way.*

So fortunate, they were, the red stair-carpet said, and the stair-rail said, *Fortunate? How?*

The intruders were gone when they came home.

I had a good look at them, said the mirror over the lowboy in the downstairs hall. *They were not at all like the Colemans' friends or the delivery boys from Gristede's and the fish market.*

The Colemans' friends don't break in the front door, the Sheraton sideboard said. *They ring and then wait for somebody to come and open it.*

She will have my top refinished, said the table with the cigarette scar. *The number is in the telephone turnaround. She knows about that sort of thing and he doesn't. But it will take a while. And the room will look odd without me.*

It took a long time to make that star ruby, said a small seashell on the mantelpiece.

Precious stones you can buy, said the classified directory. *Van Cleef and Arpels. Harry Winston. And auctions at Christie's and Sotheby Parke-Bernet. It is the Victorian and Edwardian settings that were unusual. I don't suppose the thieves will know enough to value them.*

They will be melted down, said the brass fire irons, *into unidentifiability. It happens every day.*

Antique jewelry too can be picked up at auction places. Still, it is disagreeable to lose things that have come down in the family. It isn't something one would choose to have happen.

There are lots of things one would not choose to have happen that do happen, said the fire irons.

With any unpleasantness, said the orange plastic Design Research kitchen wall clock, *it is better to take the long view.*

Very sensible of them to fall asleep the minute their heads hit the pillow, said the full-length mirror in the master bedroom. *Instead of turning and tossing and going over in their minds the things they have lost, that are gone forever.*

They have each other, a small bottle of Elizabeth Arden perfume spray said. *They will forget about what happened this evening. Or, if they remember, it will be something they have ceased to have much feeling about, a story they tell sometimes at dinner parties, when the subject of robberies comes up. He will tell how they walked home from the Follansbees' on Christmas night and found the front door ajar, and she will tell about the spoon and the silver tray the thieves didn't take, and he will tell how he stood on the stairs watching while she tried on all her favorite evening dresses.*

Issue 100, 1986

Joy Williams

✠

Marabou

The funeral of Anne's son Harry had not gone smoothly. Other burials were taking place at the same hour, including that of a popular singer several hundred yards away whose mourner fans carried on loudly under a lurid, striped tent. Still more fans pressed against the cemetery's wrought-iron gates screaming and eating potato chips. Anne had been distracted. She gazed at the other service with disbelief, thinking of the singer's songs that she had heard now and then on the radio.

Her own group, Harry's friends, was subdued. They were pale, young, and all wore sunglasses. Most of them were classmates from the prep school he had graduated from two years before, and all were addicts, or former addicts, of some sort. Anne couldn't tell the difference between those who were recovering and those who were still hard at it. She was sure there was a difference, of course, and it only appeared there wasn't. They all had a manner. There were about twenty of them, boys and girls, strikingly alike in black. Later she took them all out to a restaurant. "Death . . . by none art thou understood . . ." one boy kept saying. "Henry Vaughan."

They were all bright enough, Anne supposed. After awhile he stopped saying it. They had calamari, duck, champagne, everything. They were on the second floor of the restaurant and had the place to themselves. They stayed for hours. By the time they left, one girl was saying earnestly, "You know, a word I like is *interplanetary*."

Then she brought them back to the house, although she locked Harry's rooms. Young people were sentimentalists, consumers. She didn't want them carrying off Harry's things, his ties and tapes, his jackets, anything at all. They sat in the kitchen. They were beginning to act a little peculiar, Anne thought. They didn't talk about Harry much, though one of them remembered a time when Harry was driving, and he stopped at all the green lights and proceeded on the red. They all acted as though they'd been there. This seemed a fine thing to remember about Harry. Then someone, a floppy-haired boy who looked frightened, remembered something else, but it turned out that this was associated with a boy named Pete who was not even present.

About one o'clock in the morning, Anne said that when she and Harry were in Africa, during the very first evening at the hotel in Victoria Falls, Harry claimed that he had seen a pangolin, a peculiar anteater-like animal. He described it, and that's what it was clearly, but a very rare thing, an impossible thing for him to have seen really, no one in the group they would be traveling with believed him. He had been wandering around the hotel grounds by himself, there were no witnesses to it. The group went on to discuss the Falls. Everyone could verify the impression the Falls made. So many hundreds of millions of gallons went over each minute or something, there was a drop of four hundred feet. Even so, everyone was quite aware it wasn't like that, no one was satisfied with that. The sound of the Falls was like silence, total amplified silence, the sight of it exclusionary. And all that could be done was to look at it, this astonishing thing, the Falls, then eventually stop looking, and go on to something else.

The next day Harry had distinguished himself further by exclaiming over a marabou stork, and someone in the group told him that marabous were gruesome things, scavengers, "morbidity distilled" in the words of this fussy little person, and certainly nothing to get excited about when there were hundreds of beautiful and strange creatures in Africa that one could enjoy and identify and point out to the others. Imagine, Anne said, going to an immense new continent for the first time and being corrected as to one's feelings, one's perceptions in such a strange place. . . . And it was not as though everything was known. Take the wild dogs for example. Attitudes had changed utterly about the worth of wild dogs. . . .

Abruptly, she stopped. She had been silent much of the evening, and she felt that this outburst had not gone over particularly well.

Harry's friends were making margaritas. One of them had gone out and just returned with more tequila. They were watching her uncomfortably, as though they felt she should fluff up her stories on Harry a bit.

Finally one of them said, "I didn't know Harry had been to Africa."

This surprised her. The trip to Africa hadn't worked out particularly well, but it hadn't been a disaster either, it could very well have been worse. They had been gone a month, and this had been very recently. But it didn't matter. She would probably never see these children again.

They sat around the large kitchen. They were becoming more and more strange to her. She wondered what they were all waiting for. One of them was trying to find salt. There was no salt? He opened a cupboard and peered inside, bringing out a novelty set, a plastic couple, Amish or something, she supposed the man was pepper, the woman salt. They were all watching him as he turned the things over and shook them against his cupped hand. Anne never cooked, never used anything in this kitchen, she and Harry ate out, these things were barely familiar to her. Then, it was really quite a normal gesture, the boy unscrewed the head off the little woman and poured the salt inside onto a saucer.

Someone shrieked in terror. It was the floppy-haired boy, he was yelling, horrified. Anne was confused for an instant. Was Harry dying again? Was Harry all right? The boy was howling, his eyes were rolling in his head. The others looked at him dully. One of the girls giggled. "Uh-oh," she said.

Two of the boys were trying to quiet him. They all looked like Harry, even the boy who was screaming.

"You'd better take him to the emergency room," Anne said.

"Maybe if he just gets a little air, walks around, gets some air," a boy said.

"You'd all better go now," Anne said.

It was not even dawn yet, of course, it was still very dark. Anne sat there, alone in the bright kitchen in her black dress. There was a run in her stocking. The dinner in the restaurant had cost almost a thousand dollars, and Harry probably wouldn't even have liked it. She hadn't liked it. She wanted to behave differently now for Harry's sake. He hadn't been perfect, Harry, he had been a very troubled boy, a very misunderstood boy, but she had never let him go, never, until now. She knew that he couldn't be aware of that, that she had let him go now. She knew that between them, from now on, she alone would be the one who realized things. She wasn't going to deceive herself in that regard. Even so, she knew she wasn't thinking clearly about this.

After some time, she got up and packed a bag for Africa, exactly the way she had done before. It was a gray duffle. The contents could weigh no more than twenty-two pounds. When she was finished, she put it in the hallway by the door. Outside it was still dark, as dark as it had been hours ago, it scarcely seemed possible.

Perhaps she would go back to Africa.

There was a knock on the door. Anne looked at it, startled, a thick door with locks. Then she opened it. A girl was standing there, not the *interplanetary* one but another one, one who had particularly relished the dinner. She had been standing there smoking for awhile before she knocked. There were several cigarette butts ground into the high-gloss cerulean of the porch.

"May I come in?" the girl asked.

"Why no," Anne said, "no you may not."

"Please," the girl said.

Anne shut the door.

She went into the kitchen and threw the two parts of the salt shaker into the trash. She tossed the small lady's companion in as well. Harry had once said to her, "Look this is amazing, I don't know how this could have happened actually, but I have these spikes in my head. They must have been there for awhile, but I swear, I swear to you, I just noticed them. But I got them out! On the left side. But on the right side it's more difficult because they're in a sort of helmet, and the helmet is fused to my head see. Can you help me?"

She had helped him then. She had stroked his hair with her fingers for a long, long time. She had been very careful, very thorough. But that had been a unique situation. Usually, she couldn't help him.

There was a sound at the door again, a determined knocking. Anne walked to it quickly and opened it. There were several of Harry's friends there, not just the girl, but not all of them either. "You don't have to be so rude," one of them said.

They were angry. They had lost Harry, she thought, and they missed him.

"We loved Harry, too, you know," one of them said. His tie was loose, and his breath was sweet and dry, like sand.

"I want to rest now," Anne told them. "I must get some rest."

"Rest," one of them said in a soft, scornful voice. He glanced at the others. They ignored him.

"Tell us another story about Harry," one of them said. "We didn't get the first one."

"Are you frightening me?" Anne said. She smiled. "I mean, are you trying to frighten me?"

"I think Harry saw that thing, but I don't think he was ever there. Is that what you meant?" one of them said with effort. He turned and as though he were dancing, it looked as though he were dancing, moved down the steps and knelt on the ground where he lowered his head and began spitting up quietly, like a baby. The black grass winked and glittered with it.

"Harry will always be us," one of them said. "You better get used to it. You better get your stories straight."

"Good night," Anne said. She did not feel frightened. There was an ugly sound in her head was all. It seemed to be falling through her, filling her.

"Good night, *please*," they said, and Anne shut the door.

She turned off all the lights and sat in the darkness of the house. Before long, as she knew it would, the phone began to ring. It rang and rang, but she didn't have to answer it. She wouldn't do it. It would never be that once, again, when she'd learned that Harry died, no matter how much she knew in her heart that the present was but a past in that future to which it belonged, that the past, after all, couldn't be everything.

Issue 126, 1993

Vijay Seshadri

Lifeline

As soon as he realized he was lost, that
in kicking around his new job in his head,
the new people he'd met, and how
he could manage a week in Seaside,
he'd stumbled past the muddy fork of road
that slithered down in switchbacks
to Highway 20, and now couldn't tell,
through rainclouds coarse as pig iron,
and about as cold, which languished
over each of the scarred mountaintops,
where west was, or east, or north,
or feel the sun's direction,
he stopped, as he knew he should,
and doubled back. An hour at the worst
would bring him to the International
inert in a ditch with its radiator
punctured, its axle broken, and blood
from his temple on the steering wheel.
He wished he'd never set eyes on that truck . . .
here he was, trudging like an idiot
through a thousand-square-mile dead spot
of Douglas fir, soaked to the bone
and hungry, with his head throbbing.

He wasn't up to this, he said to himself,
staring disconsolately outward
to the numberless ridges and valleys, singed
with the bitter green of the firs.
But why hadn't he reached the truck yet,
or at least somewhere familiar,
where he could get his bearings again?
He didn't recognize the ridge he was on.
He'd never seen this particular patch—
glinting with wild crocus prongs—
of clear-cut ground, torched and scarified.
Should he keep going, or return again?
There and then he made his third mistake.
Hearing, or thinking he heard,
deep in the valley below him plunged
in mist, a chain saw start and sputter,
he made off down toward the sound.
It would be a gypo logger, scrounging
deadfall cedar for shake-bolt cords,
or a civilian with a twenty-dollar permit
to cut firewood for sale at a roadside stand.
Either way, he could get directions
and hitch home by dark. Hours later,
night found him in a hollow, shouting
until he was hoarse for someone, anyone.
The weekend was almost here, and no one
at work would miss him before Monday . . .
he lived alone, idiot, he lived alone
and couldn't count on a single person
to send out an alarm. Those first hours
he spent shivering under a lip of rock,
wide awake, startling at each furtive,
night-hunting animal sound, each flap
of the raptors in the branches overhead.
On the second day he lost his glasses.

It happened like this: As he struggled
over the cryptic terrain all morning—
terrain that would seem, if looked at
from high above, from a helicopter
or a plane flying low enough to pierce
the dense, lazy foliage of clouds,
created, finessed, meticulously contrived
to amaze, like a marvelous relief map
of papier-mâché, revealing its artifice only
in the improbable dramas of its contours,
its extravagant, unlikely colors—
he had what amounted to a real insight.
All this was the brainchild of water.
Stretching back beyond the Pleistocene—
how many millions of years?—
imperial rain had traced without pity,
over and over again, its counter-image
on the newborn, jagged mountains
until the length of the coast had been
disciplined to a system on purpose designed
to irrigate and to nourish the soil.
He decided he'd follow the water down.
He'd use each widening tributary
like the rung of a ladder, to climb down
from his awful predicament, and soon
work his way to the ocean—though, of course,
long before that he'd run across people.
With this in mind, he came to a stream
heavy and brown with the spring runoff,
its embankment on his side steep
to the point of perpendicularity, thick
with brush, though on the other side
a crown of ferns tumbled gently down
to the next watershed. It seemed like
a good idea to cross, and farther on

he found a logged fir with a choker cable
still attached (it must have snapped
when they tried to yard the falled tree
to the road high above) straddling
the stream. A little more than halfway over
he slipped on the treacherous wood
and would have gone in but for the cable
which he lunged at just in time.
That was his lifeline, though flailing
to save himself, he knocked the glasses
from his head. Now they'd reach the sea
long before him, if he ever would.
He knelt down in the ferns, exhausted,
by fits growing determined never
to leave that spot. They'd find his bones
fifty years from now, clothes and ID
rotted away, a trillium poking through
his rib cage, a cucumber vine trellised
by the seven sockets in his skull.
The play of the thin, unending drizzle
on the overlapping leaves he sank below,
on the bark of the impassive trees
looming around him, grew indistinguishable
from the pulse turning loud in his head.
The ugly bruise on his forehead throbbed.
There were rents and gashes everywhere
down the length of his rain gear, which
let the mist and the dampness in.
Beyond a scant dozen inches, the world
looked blurry, smeared bright, unattainable.
Nothing in his life, up until then
(and if this had been pointed out to him
he would have acknowledged pride in it),
suggested that anything resembling
a speculative turn of mind cannibalized

the adequate, rhythmic, progressive
movements of his thoughts and feelings.
But, still, as almost everyone does,
he'd occasionally had inklings, stirrings,
promptings, and strange intuitions
about something just beyond the radius
of his life—not divine, necessarily,
but what people meant when they referred
to such things—which gave to the least
of his actions its dream of complicity.
Now he recognized, with a shock
almost physical, that those inklings
were just the returning, reanimated echo
(on a different scale but similar
to the echo we sometimes hear in our skulls
which leads us to the uncanny feeling
that an experience we're having is one
we've had before, at some other time—
but does anything ever repeat itself?)
of the vibrations his life made
bouncing off the things around him
sunk deep in their own being;
and that life, his life, blossoming now
in this daisy chain of accident and error,
was nothing more or less than what there was.
There was nothing hidden underneath this,
but it was small, so small, as the life
of his family was, his people, his species
among the other species—firs, owls,
plants whose names he didn't know—
all of them minute, and the earth itself,
its four billion plus years of life
just the faint, phosphorescent track
of a minute sea creature on an ocean
for the annihilating dimensions of which

words such as "infinite" and "eternal"
were ridiculous in their inadequacy.
He lay on his back inside the ferns
and listened to the rain's clepsydral ticking.
He tried to grasp—what was it?—
but it clattered away, that slight change
in the pressure binding thing to thing,
as when an upright sleeper shifts
just a little, imparting to his dreams
an entirely different train of meaning.
Beyond those clouds, the blue was there
which shaded to blackness, and beyond
that blackness the uncounted, terrifying
celestial entities hung suspended only
by the influence they had on one another.
And all of this was just a seed
inside a seed inside a seed. . . .
So that when, finally, late the next morning
he half-crawled out of the woods, and came
in time to a wire fence in a clearing,
less than two feet high and decorated
with gleaming ceramic insulators,
which indicated that a mild current,
five volts at the most, ran through it
to keep the foraging animals off
the newly sown vegetable garden
enclosed inside its perimeter, and saw
beyond it the sprawl of the lawn,
the 4-by-4 parked in the driveway,
the Stars and Stripes on the flagpole,
and the house, he stopped, paralyzed.
The wind was blowing northwest, the clouds
were breaking up under its steady persuasion,
but, try as he did, he couldn't will
himself to step lightly over that wire,

and cross the garden's sweet geometry,
and go up to the door and ask to be
fed and made warm and taken home.
By that small fence, he sat down and wept.

Issue 137, 1995

Lydia Davis

✠

Break It Down

He's sitting there staring at a piece of paper in front of him. He's trying to break it down. He says.

I'm breaking it all down. The ticket was $600 and then after that there was more for the hotel and food and so on, for just ten days. Say $80 a day, no, more like $100 a day. And we made love, say, once a day on the average. That's $100 a shot. And each time it lasted maybe two or three hours so that would be anywhere from $33 to $50 an hour, which is expensive.

Though of course that wasn't all that went on, because we were together almost all day long. She would keep looking at me and every time she looked at me it was worth something, and she smiled at me and didn't stop talking and singing, something I said, she would sail into it, a snatch, for me, she would be gone from me a little ways but smiling too, and tell me jokes, and I loved it but didn't exactly know what to do about it and just smiled back at her and felt slow next to her, just not quick enough. So she talked and touched me on the shoulder and the arm, she kept touching and stayed close to me. You're with each other all day long and it keeps happening, the touches and smiles, and it adds up, it builds up, and you know where you'll be that night, you're talking and every now and then you think about it, no, you don't think, you just feel it as a kind of destination, what's coming up after you leave wherever you are all evening and you're happy about it and you're planning it all, not in your head, really, somewhere inside your body, or all through your body, it's all mounting up and coming together so that when you get in bed you can't help it, it's a real performance, it all pours out, but slowly, you go easy until you can't anymore, or you hold back the whole time, you hold back and touch the edges of everything, you edge around until you have to plunge in and finish it off, and when you're finished, you're too weak to stand but after a while you have to go the bathroom and you stand, your legs are trembling, you hold the doorways, there's a little light coming in through the window, you can see your way in and out, but you can't really see the bed.

So it's not really $100 a shot because it goes on all day, from the start when you wake up and feel her body next to you, and you don't miss a thing, not a thing of what's next to you, her arm, her leg, her shoulder, her face, that good skin, I have felt other good skin, but this skin is just the edge of something else, and you're going to start going, and no matter how much you crawl all over each other it won't be enough, and when your hunger dies down a little then you think how much you love her and that starts you off again, and her face, you look over at her face and can't believe how you got there and how lucky and it's still all a surprise and it never stops, even after it's over, it never stops being a surprise.

It's more like you have a good sixteen or eighteen hours a day of this going on, even when you're not with her it's going on, it's good to be away because it's going to be so good to go back to her, so it's still there, and you can't go off and look at some old street or some old painting without still feeling it in your body and a few things that happened the day before that don't mean much by themselves or wouldn't mean much if you weren't having this thing together, but you can't forget and it's all inside you all the time, so that's more like, say, sixteen into a hundred would be $6 an hour, which isn't too much.

And then it really keeps going on while you're asleep, though you're probably dreaming about something else, a building, maybe, I kept dreaming, every night, almost, about this building, because I would spend a lot of every morning in this old stone building and when I closed my eyes I would see these cool spaces and have this peace inside me, I would see the bricks of the floor and the stone arches and the space, the emptiness between, like a kind of dark frame around what I could see beyond, a garden, and this space was like stone, too, because of the coolness of it and the gray shadow, that kind of luminous shade, that was glowing with the light of the sun falling beyond the arches, and there was also the great height of the ceiling, all this was in my mind all the time though I didn't know it until I closed my eyes, I'm asleep and I'm not dreaming about her but she's lying next to me and I wake up enough times in the night to remember she's there, and notice, say, once she was lying on her back but now she's curled around me, I look at her closed eyes, I want to kiss her eyelids, I want to feel that soft skin under my lips, but I don't want to disturb her, I don't want to see her frown as though in her sleep she has forgotten who I am and feels just that something is bothering her and so I just look at her and hold onto it all, these times when I'm watching over her sleep and she's next to me and isn't away from me the way she will be later, I want to stay awake all night just to go on feeling that, but I can't, I fall asleep again, though I'm sleeping lightly, still trying to hold onto it.

But it isn't over when it ends, it goes on after it's all over, she's still inside you like a sweet liquor, you are filled with her, everything about her has kind of bled into you, her smell, her voice, the way her body moves, it's all inside you, at least for a while after, then you begin to lose it, and I'm beginning to lose it, you're afraid of how weak you are, that you can't get her all back into you again and now the whole thing is going out of your body and it's more in your mind than your body, the pictures come to you one by one and you look at them, some of them last longer than others, you were together in a very white clean place, a coffeehouse, having breakfast together and the place is so white that against it you can see her clearly, her blue eyes, her smile, the colors of her clothes, even the print of the newspaper she's reading when she's not looking up at you, the light brown and red and gold of her hair when she's got her head down reading, the brown coffee, the brown rolls, all against that white table and those white plates and silver urns and silver knives and spoons, and against that quiet of the sleepy people in that room sitting alone at their tables with just some chinking and clattering of spoons and cups in saucers and some hushed voices her voice now and then rising and falling. The pictures come to you and you have to hope they won't lose their life too fast and dry up though you know they will and that you'll also forget some of what happened because already you're turning up little things that you nearly forgot.

We were in bed and she asked me, Do I seem fat to you? and I was surprised because she didn't seem to worry about herself at all in that way and I guess I was reading into it that she did worry about herself so I answered what I was thinking and said stupidly that she had a very beautiful body, that her body was perfect, and I really meant it as an answer, but she said kind of sharply, That's not what I asked, and so I had to try to answer her again, exactly what she had asked.

And once she lay over against me late in the night and she started talking, her breath in my ear, and she just went on and on, and talked faster and faster, she couldn't stop, and I loved it, I just felt that all that life in her was running into me too, I had so little life in me, her life, her fire, was coming into me, in that hot breath in my ear, and I just wanted her to go on talking forever right there next to me, and I would go on living, like that, I would be able to go on living, but without her I don't know.

Then you forget some of it all, maybe most of it all, almost all of it, in the end, and you work hard at remembering everything now so you won't ever forget, but you can kill it too even by thinking about it too much, though you can't help thinking about it nearly all the time.

And then when the pictures start to go you start asking some questions, just little questions, that sit in your mind without any answers, like why did she have the light on when you came in to bed one night, but it was off the next, but she had it on the night after that and she had it off the last night, why, and other questions, little questions that nag at you like that.

And finally the pictures go and these dry little questions just sit there without any answers and you're left with this large heavy pain in you that you try to numb by reading or you try to ease it by getting out into public places where there will be people around you, but no matter how good you are at pushing that pain away, just when you think you're going to be all right for a while, that you're kind of holding it off with all your strength and you're staying in some little bare numb spot of ground, then suddenly it will all come back, you'll hear a noise, maybe it's a cat crying or a baby, or something else like her cry, you hear it and make that connection in a part of you you have no control over and the pain comes back so hard that you're afraid, afraid of how you're falling back into it again and you wonder, no, you're terrified to ask how you're ever going to climb out of it.

And so it's not only every hour of the day while it's happening, but it's really for hours and hours every day after that, for weeks, though less and less, so that you could work out the ratio if you wanted, maybe after six weeks you're only thinking about it an hour or so in the day altogether, a few minutes here and there spread over, or a few minutes here and there and half an hour before you go to sleep, or sometimes it all comes back and you stay awake with it half the night.

So when you add up all that you've only spent maybe $3 an hour on it.

If you have to figure in the bad times too, I don't know. There weren't any bad times with her, though maybe there was one bad time, when I told her I loved her. I couldn't help it, because this was the first time this had happened with her, now I was half falling in love with her or maybe completely if she had let me but she couldn't or I couldn't completely because it was all going to be so short and other things too, and so I told her, and didn't know of any way to tell her first that she didn't have to feel this was a burden, the fact that I loved her, or that she didn't have to feel the same about me, or say the same back, that it was just that I had to tell her, that's all, because it was bursting inside me, and saying it wouldn't even begin to take care of what I was feeling, really I couldn't say anything of what I was feeling because there was so much, words couldn't handle it, and making love only made it worse because then I wanted words badly but they were no good, no good at all, but I told her anyway, I was lying on top of her and her hands were up by her head and my hands were on hers and our fingers were locked and there was a little light on her face from the window but I couldn't really see her and I was afraid to say it but I thought I better say it because I want her to know, it was the last night, I had to tell her then or I'd never have another chance, I just said, before you go to sleep, I just said, I have to tell you before you go to sleep that I love you, and immediately, right away after, she said, I love you too, and it sounded to me as if she didn't mean it, a little flat, but then it usually sounds a little flat when someone says, I love you too, because they're just saying it back even if they do mean it, and the problem is, that I'll never know if she meant it, or maybe some day she'll tell me whether she meant it or not, but there's no way to know now, and I'm sorry I did that, it was a trap I didn't mean to put her in, because it was a trap, if she hadn't said anything at all I know that would have hurt too, as though she were taking something from me and just accepting it and not giving anything back, so she really had to, even just to be kind to me, she had to say it, and I don't really know now if she meant it.

Another bad time, but it wasn't exactly bad, but it wasn't easy either, was when I had to leave, the time was coming, and I was beginning to tremble and feel empty, nothing in the middle of me, nothing inside, and nothing to hold me up on my legs and then it came, everything was ready, and I had to go, and so it was just a kiss, a quick one, as though we were afraid of what might happen after a kiss, and she was almost wild then, she reached up to a hook by the door and took an old shirt, a green and blue shirt from the hook and put it in my arms, for me to take away, the soft cloth was full of her smell, and then we stood there close together looking at a piece of paper she had in her hand and I didn't lose any of it, I was holding it tight, that last minute or two, because this was it, we'd come to the end of it, things always change, so this was really it, over.

Maybe it works out all right, maybe you haven't lost for doing it, I don't know, no, really, sometimes when you think of it you feel like a prince really, you feel just like a king, and then other times you're afraid, you're afraid, not all the time but now and then, of what it's going to do to you, and it's hard to know what to do with it now.

Walking away I looked back once and the door was still open, I could see her standing far back in the dark of the room, I could only really see her white face still looking out at me, and her white arms.

I guess you get to a point where you look at that pain as if it were there in front of you three feet away lying in a box, an open box, in a window somewhere. It's hard and cold, like a bar of metal. You just look at it there and say all right, I'll take it, I'll buy it. That's what it is. Because you know all about it before you even go into this thing. You know the pain is part of the whole thing. And it isn't that you can say afterwards the pleasure was greater than the pain and that's why you would do it again. That has nothing to do with it. You can't measure it, because the pain comes after and it lasts longer. So the question really is, why doesn't that pain make you say, I won't do it again? When the pain is so bad that you have to say that, but you don't.

So I'm just thinking about it, how you can go in with $600, more like $1,000, and how you can come out with an old shirt.

V. P'yetsukh

❦

Killer Miller

Androusha Miller—the great-great-grandson, by the way, of the very same General Evgeny Karlovich Miller, head of the Russian All-General Military union, whom Chekists rubbed out in Paris in 1937—received, tenth hand, the assignment to gun down a certain dealer. He was given an envelope, which contained the victim's address and a snapshot, a pistol—a TT—and a three-thousand-dollar advance, in the new denominations. First Androusha counted the money; then he looked at the snapshot, and was stunned—having recognized his PE teacher, who in seventh grade had given him an F for his exercises on the horse. For some reason, that F burned into his memory; and gazing at the snapshot, he thought with distaste, Oh well, serves you right, fool; you shouldn't stick your nose in commerce if your profession is teaching. And he clearly imagined how he would meet his former teacher in the elevator, slowly withdraw the pistol, plant half a clip in the old dumbbell, then take a check shot to the head, blow in the barrel—for style—and say in a sepulchral voice, "Now you'll think twice before giving Fs to killers."

In general, Androusha was an okay guy, but stupid. He was destined to become a husband, a father and the manager of a haberdashery shop, but, as is well known, the movement of heavenly bodies was disrupted by our frantic times. And so Androusha set his sights on the romantic profession of hit man, not realizing this choice was, to say the least, not divinely ordained and that he would pay for it one day.

*   *   *

And Sasha Measurman, a resident of a small workers' village in the Vladimirsky district, has a dream: The god Savaoth presents herself, for some reason, in the form of a proper old woman—wearing a white, glossy floor-length dress, a white kerchief with fringed edges on her head—sits down opposite his bed and says, "Soon, a new Deluge will burst, in which all humanity will perish for innumerable sins. So you, Measurman, build an ark, pick out seven clean pairs, seven unclean pairs of animals and wait for the rain." Sasha Measurman asks, "What did I do to deserve this?" "What you did," she answers, "is that you never harmed a fly in your life, even your daughter-in-law bosses you around and looks haughty. . . ."

Measurman was a suspicious man—twice a year, he would go into Vladimir for a check-up at a tuberculosis dispensary—and therefore believed the dream. A week hadn't passed before he quit at the dairy plant, where he worked as a boiler operator, and undertook the construction of an ark from material at hand. He had about three cubic meters of timber—having taken apart the summer-kitchen roof, borrowed several carts from a neighbor and torn down a fence. The whole village made fun of him, but he hacked away with his ax, not giving a damn, and kept murmuring, "He who laughs last laughs best," while nails, sticking out of his mouth, wiggled as if alive. By the summer, in his backyard, directly on the garden plot meant for potatoes, lying heavily sideways, there was a vessel of gigantic proportions for Vladimirsky district—which is entirely landlocked, where even a tiny boat like a *kazanka* is a rarity and considered almost a ship. Having built it, Measurman began waiting for the torrential rain. Fall was just around the corner, and here and there mushrooms took over his ark, but not a sign of the flood at all.

Meanwhile, Nikolai Ivanovich Spiridonov, chief engineer of the Bakunin Moscow Button Factory, felt somewhat sick that day. For no apparent reason, something started to tickle in his nostrils, his ears stuffed up, tiny worms floated before his eyes and a strange hollow formed in his stomach. Nikolai Ivanovich immediately broke off a conference on the results of the second quarter, summoned his car and left for home.

At home, he paced for a long time back and forth between a glass door and his desk, listening to the beating of his heart and pondering what kind of sickness had befallen him. Then he decided to take his temperature and lie down. Ten minutes later, when he took the thermometer out from under his tongue, he was so horrified that he almost fainted: The mercury had climbed to 106.4. "This is the end," Nikolai Ivanovich's inner voice said to him, and he felt his legs grow cold. Anguish seized his heart, tears came to his eyes and suddenly he was so sorry for the life he was leaving—for the trees beyond the window, for the happy sparrows chirping at the top of their lungs, for his wife, Nina, who would be left in the cold and, even worse, might jump hastily into a marriage with some vulgar guy from the Bakunin Button Factory—that he felt like howling. He would have howled from the bottom of his heart, stricken with grief, had it not been for his next-door neighbors, who, at the merest trifle, would immediately dial 02 for the police. He realized that he should write his will and, overcoming the nausea rising in his throat from time to time, Nikolai Ivanovich got up from the sofa and sat at the table. He reached for a sheet of paper, took out a Parker fountain pen from a jade holder, unpleasantly quacked and wrote down the obligatory beginning words: "Being in sound mind and control of my faculties, I bequeath . . ."

What a surprise: laying out his last wishes, he used the most uncomplicated style, which still here and there bore traces of red tape; but little by little the style became lofty and luxurious; he went for hyperbole and allegory; all of a sudden, rhyme hatched out by itself and—Nikolai Ivanovich didn't even notice—verses began to flow from under his pen. They were about old age, about the inevitability of departure, about unbearable anguish; and what had begun as "Being in sound mind . . ." concluded in a fantastical manner with the following stanza:

> And here another old lady
> like a sack on the counter lies,
> in her eyes the summer has faded;
> a light snow falls in her eyes.

"I'm a poet, á real poet!" exclaimed Nikolai Ivanovich in his inner voice when he reread the verses. And he felt so sorry that his poetic gift had been awakened on the eve of his death, and that he would leave behind only a poem of two hundred lines that he dropped his head on the paper and sobbed.

Meanwhile, at about nine in the morning, the killer, Androusha Miller—while Nikolai Ivanovich Spiridonov was sobbing, his head on the paper—waited for his former PE teacher on the staircase landing, worrying the TT pistol in the pocket of his short coat. The door slammed on the floor above, and Androusha pulled the safety off the gun, bolted up one level in a flash and touched his teacher on the shoulder. The former PE teacher recognized him immediately.

"Aha! Miller, you poor hooky-playing, F-student, good-for-nothing!" he said, smiling gaily and a little nastily. "So, what are you up to, how's life treating you?"

Androusha's hand faltered; his teacher's question could not be left unanswered, and the pistol remained in his pocket.

"I'm doing okay," Androusha answered, "on five million a month. I'm a killer by profession. I'm an on-call liquidator, like the Twilight Company when they hire people to wash windows."

"Look what an idiotic word they've come up with: *killer*," the PE teacher said, knitted his brow and added, "Some killer you are, Androusha; you're a thug, a con; you're predatory riffraff."

"Hey you, Sergei Sergeevich, stop putting me down," Androusha said seriously. "Fuck it; first they flunk you, then they use insulting words."

"Look, I'm not putting you down; I'm telling you the truth: thug, con, predatory riffraff."

Androusha's face suddenly became very drawn; his shoulders sagged; the fire in his eyes went out; and, as happens to people when they're dumbfounded by a doctor's diagnosis, he turned around and slowly began to descend the stairs, tracing a zigzag on the banister with his nails, wondering: if he wasn't really a killer but a con, then probably he should change his line of work.

By the way, words still have weight in our society. If, let's say, you're a call girl, then your life is joyous and carefree; but you feel entirely different if you're a whore.

Meanwhile, Nikolai Ivanovich's wife returned from work, saw her teary spouse and grabbed her cheeks.

"Farewell, Nina!" Nikolai Ivanovich said to her. "I'm going to kick off any minute now. My temperature is 106.4."

"What a fool you are! A fool!" Nina said. "This old thermometer should have been tossed out long ago. It's been showing 106.4 for two years already!"

It's truly hard to comprehend a man's psychology: Nikolai Ivanovich was saddened by this information; he became gloomy. Somehow he pulled himself together and, after walking back and forth between the glass door and the desk for a while, took up the pages he'd written, winced, then crumpled and threw them in the wastebasket.

Meanwhile, Sasha Measurman's ark became a real attraction; it was even entered into a *Golden Ring* guidebook, and tourists who arrived in Vladimir would make a special detour to satisfy their curiosity about the wonder and also its creator. Soon they began to chip off pieces from the ark for souvenirs; Sasha Measurman didn't mind. The only thing that depressed him was the Flood hadn't come yet. Over the radio they announced that Holland had been submerged and Germany flooded, but in Vladimirsky district there was a drought. . . .

—translated from the Russian by
Dinara Georgeoliani and Mark Halperin

Issue 161, 2002

J. G. Ballard

The Index

EDITOR'S NOTE. From abundant internal evidence it seems clear that the text printed below is the index to the unpublished and perhaps suppressed autobiography of a man who may well have been one of the most remarkable figures of the twentieth century. Yet of his existence nothing is publicly known, although his life and work appear to have exerted a profound influence on the events of the past fifty years. Physician and philosopher, man of action and patron of the arts, sometime claimant to the English throne and founder of a new religion, Henry Rhodes Hamilton was evidently the intimate of the greatest men and women of our age. After World War II he founded a new movement of spiritual regeneration, but private scandal and public concern at his growing megalomania, culminating in his proclamation of himself as a new divinity, seem to have led to his downfall. Incarcerated within an unspecified government institution, he presumably spent his last years writing his autobiography of which this index is the only surviving fragment.

A substantial mystery still remains. Is it conceivable that all traces of his activities could be erased from our records of the period? Is the suppressed autobiography itself a disguised *roman à clef*, in which the fictional hero exposes the secret identities of his historical contemporaries? And what is the true role of the indexer himself, clearly a close friend of the writer, who first suggested that he embark on his autobiography? This ambiguous and shadowy figure has taken the unusual step of indexing himself into his own index. Perhaps the entire compilation is nothing more than a figment of the overwrought imagination of some deranged lexicographer. Alternatively, the index may be wholly genuine, and the only glimpse we have into a world hidden from us by a gigantic conspiracy, of which Henry Rhodes Hamilton is the greatest victim.

Ira Sadoff

✣

Seven *Romances*

The Romance of the Rose

I could not help myself, I fell in love with the florist. Each day he handed me arrangements of flowers: lilies-of-the-valley, chrysanthemums and roses, exotic willows and violets. As a lover he was strange and melancholy: He had an intense hatred for the out-of-doors and almost never left the house; the mention of sports made him dizzy and a car moving too fast would bring him close to tears. He was deathly afraid of heights and he was not homosexual. When he found me talking to another man he brought me a wreath and said he would leave me, though he did not. In the winter, though, it was I who could not leave my bed: My robe seemed to grow roots on the sheets and I made him bring me my meals on a tray. When he threatened to leave I became the carnation in his lapel, I was his brooch. When the weather became warm and clear, somehow it was he who wrapped me in a blanket, dragged me outside to a park; and when we made love I was the one who wilted, I felt my color brush off on his chin. And when he took me home for the last time, I could not help but stare at the limp stems of flowers, the discolored water, the fragrance of my own immobility, the fear that all this could happen again, and when it did, nothing would blossom, nothing would spoil.

THE ROMANCE OF THE RACER

The race-car driver was different. He made love with all his clothes on. Always the smell of grease, a trailing vapor of gasoline. He drove circles around me and when it was over I was tired and dizzy, his tongue in my mouth was a memory, a thin slice of dirt road. When he spoke he was like an engine idling, he could never talk fast enough; but whatever he said was unexpected. "I enjoy being sad," he once told me. "I wish there were more sadness in the world." In bed he was not much of a man, once was always enough.

He was an insomniac who read long books and never said a word about them. He took me to the opera and asked me not to raise my voice. He hummed arias he said had not been written yet. Once he took me to a party where all his former lovers were, and they never stopped talking about him. Two of them he still made love to on big occasions: the night before a race, the afternoon of Verdi's birthday. And when he took me home he was unusually cautious, driving way below the speed limit, stopping at intersections where he had the right of way. When he got into bed he curled up like a wheel; in the dark I could have sworn he was spinning. In the end, what he had to prove he could not, and we all loved him the more for it, at least for a short while. When I drove out of his driveway for the last time I did not look back; but on the road I had the feeling I was constantly being passed, no matter how fast I went, no matter how many cars were filled with whistling men.

THE ROMANCE OF THE REGIMENT

The general was always giving orders: clean up this mess, have your hair done this way, let me enter from the rear. He had an intense dislike for insects, clumps of dirt, anything small. His hatred of long hair extended only to men: He wanted his women to have hair that would run all the way down their backs, the way a river would divide a battlefield. He'd spend whole nights stroking my hair and whistling military tunes, even if the only thoughts that crossed his mind were the next day's maneuvers, which medals he should pin on his chest. He was reluctant to perform his marital duty, with his wife, with me, or with anyone else.

He went to sleep with his boots off, perfectly erect, his hands at his sides, his feet pointing upward toward heaven like a dead man. He did not love war, and he never struck me in the face, in moments of passion or otherwise. He would do anything for his men short of an act of mercy.

With the general I always ate the best of food, wore gorgeous clothes and rode in limousines. We took short trips to Venezuela to meet the oil magnates, and all his friends called me his paramour. He forbade me to use vulgar language and always made me wear a dress. In public he was attentive and mildly affectionate: always with a kiss on the back of the neck, his arm entwined with mine. Sadly, it was all a camouflage; to be perfectly frank, the general was stiff when he should have been soft and vice versa.

The Romance of the Evening

I remember the night I fell in love with the evening. I was driving on a mountain road, a few moments after dusk: The trees' shadows were merging with the background of the sky, the cool air was a whisper in my ear. I did not abandon myself uncontrollably, I did not lose sight of the road. Rather the evening surrounded me the way a footprint surrounds a foot, the way a star is surrounded by empty space. I lost the notion of preference: I did not care for darkness over light, I could not tell my left hand from my right. Later I drove through the forest knocking down small trees; rabbits were caught frozen in my headlights, the car's engine gave off the smell of fear: fear released, fear repulsed, fear returning. I got out of the car in a small clearing and turned off the lights. The evening made no demands; I did not have to remove my clothes, there were no promises made or broken. I did not have to give up my other lovers, nor did the idea of fidelity even occur to me: No matter how many times I left the evening it would always come back to me, by choice or otherwise.

THE ROMANCE OF THE RORSCHACH

The psychiatrist was the dullest, the man with the least imagination. For days we'd look at his strange inkblots, he became angry when I did not see what he saw, when I confused an elephant's head with a child lost in fog. We made love on Tuesdays, on the condition we did not speak. Always one hour exactly, never more and never less. I never saw his couch and he always liked to be on top.

When I told him about the other men I had known, at first he blushed, then he asked me why I felt this desperate need for men, what was so wrong with spending nights all by myself? When I asked if he were jealous he huffed out of the room and only later simpered back; he insisted he was the psychiatrist, it was he who knew what was best for me. But perhaps I'd have to find this out for myself. To punish me he said he saw no need to see me for awhile, now was the time to test what we'd discussed. For weeks after that he'd call me on the phone, ask me if I were all right, then he'd tell me all his problems, how he found it difficult to rise in the morning, how he no longer desired his wife.

Our affair did not end because I found him with another woman: He was the one man I was sure of, he held no power over me. Rather, when I was tired of all his questions, when I said my love of words was limited, he told me my time was up. I went down the elevator without regret, touching everything I could get my hands on: other men, the walls of tall buildings, the lips of a glass. And if I never gave him another thought, if I never had to share the air he breathed, it would still be too soon, I'd never share my nightmares again.

ROMANCE OF THE REAL WORLD

I decided to give up on the world of metaphor: I would become the rose itself. The world would not exceed its own dimensions, nothing would be more or less than it seemed. The streets were deserted and no one would speak to me; luncheonettes were left with their doors open, their half-empty saucers and plates. It was always cloudy out and the cold, gray air hung over the city like a cloud of smoke, a drawn-up net. If someone struck a match, the hiss would be heard for miles. If a dress were unzipped, it could set a child on edge.

At first I took everything at face value: I believed the promises of politicians, the husband who happened to come home late. I forgot the nuances between women, the open window of the penthouse looking over the river. I could see everything but I could not touch. If I were prepared to register a feeling, it was without approximation. When a drop of rain reached up from my roots it was like . . . when the sun went down the air was somewhat different: Scientists like to call it photosynthesis, but what is that like? And if I speculated on my own death, the moment of my wilting, I would be like the mute actor whose words had failed him once again.

Yes, my frustrations were too numerous to mention: In someone's lapel I smelled pastries rising from the bakery, how would I communicate that? Growing wild in the country, listening to the varieties of weather, there were endless trails of animals who stood above me, who blocked my view. Always my petals seemed like an enormous ear: I could not help but hear what was going on around me. There were teenagers on a small park bench, acting out a movie they must have seen: "Is it too soon to tell our parents?" "You'll never leave me, will you?" "My intentions are the best." Out of boredom I had to hum myself a tune: an aria of Handel's, a ballad about the agitation of water, the changing seasons, the soft powder of snow.

O the flat world could hold nothing of me, it was like water without the glass. I knew I had to return to the world of metaphor, my own domain: to the flower's fragrant desires, the dangerous thorns of the stem, the petal's opening lips. And I would lose my passion for daily life, its vague and helpless watering, its withering speech and slowly spreading weeds. I would save my kiss for the pollination of the dreamlife, the windless orchard, the landscape which would not end.

THE ROMANCE OF THE REMAINDER

At last I've fallen in love with endings. I've begun to dream of being the last woman on earth—by some miracle, disaster or divine plan, only men have survived the holocaust. To satisfy themselves, they had to seek me out. At first I found it thrilling, I slept with anyone, the youngest first and then the strongest. But suddenly I had more power than I was accustomed to, I had too much to choose from! To keep my composure I had to get away from myself. If I sat in a chair a man's hand would be underneath it. If I decided to take a shower a man would be peering from behind the curtain. I covered myself the best I could, I never accepted favors from anyone; I opened doors for myself, I lifted heavy objects from room to room.

The world was not a desert as you might expect; far from it. When the smoke cleared the foliage was lush, there were weeds growing out of the concrete. I found a million ways to enjoy myself. Empty buildings and staircases spoke to me alone; I communed with the empty cars, or the women slumped over the steering wheels. My temperament shortly became less extreme, I never wept or raised my voice: I was like the surveyor's plumb in the middle of a valley. I walked into movie houses and empty screens became my mirrors. When it snowed over the dead bodies and piles of rubble, it was as though the old world had been erased, smeared off-white or slightly gray. And if the end of the world was near, then the beginning of something else I did not yet understand would soon begin. In the distance I hear someone playing music on a comb. Two tin cans and a drum. Someone small is lying down with someone else. Like it or not, as though we had a choice, we'll love to survive, we'll refuse anything that refuses to move.

Joyce Carol Oates

⌖

Nairobi

Early Saturday afternoon the man who had introduced himself as
Oliver took Ginny to several shops on Madison Avenue above 70th
Street to buy her what he called an appropriate outfit. For an hour and
forty-five minutes she modeled clothes, watching with critical interest
her image in the three-way mirrors, unable to decide if this was one of
her really good days or only a mediocre day. Judging by Oliver's expression she looked all right but it was difficult to tell. The salesclerks
saw too many beautiful young women to be impressed, though one told
Ginny she envied her her hair—not just that shade of chestnut red but
the thickness too. In the changing room she told Ginny that her own
hair was "coming out in handfuls" but Ginny told her it didn't show. It
will begin to show one of these days, the salesgirl said.

Ginny modeled a green velvet jumpsuit with a brass zipper and
oversized buckles, and an Italian knit dress with bunchy sleeves in a
zigzag pattern of beige, brown, and cream, and a ruffled organdy "tea
dress" in pale orange, and a navy blue blazer made of Irish linen, with
a pleated white linen skirt and a pale blue silk blouse. Assuming she
could only have one costume, which seemed to be the case, she would
have preferred the jumpsuit not just because it was the most expensive
outfit (the price tag read $475) but because the green velvet reflected in
her eyes. Oliver decided on the Irish linen blazer and the skirt and
blouse, however, and told the salesclerk to remove the tags and to pack
up Ginny's own clothes, since she intended to wear the new outfit.

Strolling uptown he told her that with her hair down like that, and her bangs combed low on her forehead, she looked like a "convent schoolgirl." In theory, that was. Tangentially.

It was a balmy windy day in early April. Everyone was out. Ginny kept seeing people she almost knew, Oliver waved hello to several acquaintances. There were baby buggies, dogs being walked, sports cars with their tops down. In shop windows—particularly in the broad windows of galleries—Ginny's reflection in the navy blue blazer struck her as unfamiliar and quirky but not bad: The blazer with its built-up shoulders and wide lapels was more stylish than she'd thought at first. Oliver too was pleased. He had slipped on steel-frame tinted glasses. He said they had plenty of time. A pair of good shoes—really good shoes—might be an idea.

But first they went into a jewelry boutique at 76th Street where Oliver bought her four narrow silver bracelets, engraved in bird and animal heads, and a pair of conch-shaped silver earrings from Mexico. Ginny slipped her gold studs out and put on the new earrings as Oliver watched. Doesn't it hurt to force those wires through your flesh? He was standing rather close.

No, Ginny said. My earlobes are numb, I don't feel a thing. It's easy.

When did you get your ears pierced? Oliver asked.

Ginny felt her cheeks color slightly—as if he were asking a favor of her and her instinct wasn't clear enough, whether to acquiesce or draw away just perceptibly. She drew away, still adjusting the earrings, but said: I don't have any idea, maybe I was thirteen, maybe twelve, it was a long time ago. We all went out and had our ears pierced.

In a salon called Michel's she exchanged her chunky-heeled red shoes for a pair of kidskin sandals that might have been the most beautiful shoes she'd ever seen. Oliver laughed quizzically over them: They were hardly anything but a few straps and a price tag, he told the salesman, but they looked like the real thing, they were what he wanted. The salesman told Oliver that his taste was "unerring."

Do you want to keep your old shoes? Oliver asked Ginny.

Of course, Ginny said, slightly hurt, but as the salesman was packing them she changed her mind. No, the hell with them, she said.

They're too much trouble to take along.—Which she might regret afterward: But it was the right thing to say at that particular moment.

In the cab headed west and then north along the park Oliver gave her instructions in a low casual voice. The main thing was that she should say very little. She shouldn't smile unless it was absolutely necessary. While he and his friends spoke—if they spoke at any length, he couldn't predict Marguerite's attitude—Ginny might even drift away, pick up a magazine and leaf through it if something appropriate was available, not nervously, just idly, for something to do, as if she were bored: better yet she might look out the window or even step out on the terrace since the afternoon was so warm. Don't even look at me, Oliver said. Don't give the impression that anything I say—anything the three of us say—matters very much to you.

Yes, said Ginny.

The important thing, Oliver said, squeezing her hand and releasing it, is that you're basically not concerned. I mean with the three of us. With Marguerite. With anyone. Do you understand?

Yes, said Ginny. She was studying her new shoes. Kidskin in a shade called "vanilla," eight straps on each shoe, certainly the most beautiful shoes she'd ever owned. The price had taken her breath away too. She hadn't any questions to ask Oliver.

When Ginny had been much younger—which is to say, a few years ago, when she was new to the city—she might have had some questions to ask. In fact she had had a number of questions to ask, then. But the answers had invariably disappointed. The answers had contained so much less substance than her own questions, she had learned, by degrees, not to ask.

So she told Oliver a second time, to assure *him*: Of course I understand.

The apartment building they entered at Fifth and 88th was older than Ginny might have guessed from the outside—the mosaic murals in the lobby were in a quaint ethereal style unknown to her. Perhaps they were meant to be amusing but she didn't think so. It was impressive that the uniformed doorman knew Oliver, whom he called "Mr.

Leahy," and that he was so gracious about keeping their package for them while they visited upstairs; it was impressive that the black elevator operator nodded and murmured hello in a certain tone. Smiles were measured and respectful all around but Ginny didn't trouble to smile, she knew it wasn't expected of her.

In the elevator—which was almost uncomfortably small—Oliver looked at Ginny critically, standing back to examine her from her toes upward and finding nothing wrong except a strand of hair or two out of place. The Irish linen blazer was an excellent choice, he said. The earrings too. The bracelets. The shoes. He spoke with assurance though Ginny had the idea he was nervous, or excited. He turned to study his own reflection in the bronze-frosted mirror on the elevator wall, facing it with a queer childlike squint. This was his "mirror face," Ginny supposed, the way he had of confronting himself in the mirror so that it wasn't *really* himself but a certain habitual expression that protected him. Ginny hadn't any mirror face herself. She had gone beyond that, she knew better, those childish frowns and half-smiles and narrowed eyes and heads turned coyly or hopefully to one side—ways of protecting her from seeing "Ginny" when the truth of "Ginny" was that she required being seen head-on. But it would have been difficult to explain to another person.

Oliver adjusted his handsome blue-striped cotton tie and ran his fingers deftly through his hair. It was pale, fine, airily colorless hair, blond perhaps, shading into premature silver, rather thin, Ginny thought, for a man his age. (She estimated his age at thirty-four, which seemed "old" to her in certain respects, but she knew it was reasonably "young" in others.) Oliver's skin was slightly coarse; his nose wide at the bridge, and the nostrils disfigured by a few dark hairs that should have been snipped off; his lower jaw was somewhat heavy. But he was a handsome man. In his steel-rimmed blue-tinted glasses he was a handsome man and Ginny saw for the first time that they made an attractive couple.

Don't trouble to answer any questions they might ask, Oliver said. In any case the questions won't be serious—just conversation.

I understand, Ginny said.

A Hispanic maid answered the door. The elevator and the corridor had been so dimly lit, Ginny wasn't prepared for the flood of sunlight in the apartment. They were on the eighteenth floor overlooking the park and the day was still cloudless.

Oliver introduced Ginny to his friends Marguerite and Herbert—the last name sounded like Crews—and Ginny shook hands with them unhesitatingly, as if it were a customary gesture with her. The first exchanges were about the weather. Marguerite was vehement in her gratitude since the past winter, January in particular, had been uncommonly long and dark and depressing. Ginny assented without actually agreeing. For the first minute or two she felt thrown off balance, she couldn't have said why, by the fact that Marguerite Crews was so tall a woman—taller even than Ginny. And she was, or had been, a very beautiful woman as well, with a pale olive-dark complexion and severely black hair parted in the center of her head and fixed in a careless knot at the nape of her neck.

Oliver was explaining apologetically that they couldn't stay. Not even for a drink, really: They were in fact already late for another engagement in the Village. Both the Crews expressed disappointment. And Oliver's plans for the weekend had been altered as well, unavoidably. At this announcement the disappointment was keener, and Ginny looked away before Marguerite's eyes could lock with hers.

But Oliver was working too hard, Marguerite protested.

But he *must* come out to the Point as they'd planned, Herbert said, and bring his friend along.

Ginny eased discreetly away. She was aloof, indifferent, just slightly bored, but unfailingly courteous: a mark of good breeding. And the Irish linen blazer and skirt were just right.

After a brief while Herbert Crews came over to comment on the view and Ginny thought it wouldn't be an error to agree: The view of Central Park was, after all, something quite real. He told her they'd lived here for eleven years "off and on." They travelled a good deal, he was required to travel almost more than he liked, being associated with an organization Ginny might have heard of—the Zieboldt Foundation. He had just returned from Nairobi, he said. Two days ago. And still feeling the strain—the fatigue. Ginny thought that his affable talkative "social" manner showed not the least hint of fatigue but did not make this observation to Herbert Crews.

She felt a small pinprick of pity for the way Marguerite Crews's collarbones showed through her filmy muslin "Indian" blouse, and for the extreme thinness of her waist (cinched tight with a belt of silver coins or medallions), and for the faint scolding voice—so conspicuously a "voice"—with which she was speaking to Oliver. She saw that Oliver, though smiling nervously, and standing in a self-conscious pose with the thumb of his right hand hooked in his sports-coat pocket, was enjoying the episode very much—she noted for the first time something vehement and cruel though at the same time unmistakably boyish in his face. Herbert Crews was telling her about Nairobi but she couldn't concentrate on his words. She was wondering if it might be proper to ask where Nairobi was—she assumed it was a country somewhere in Africa—but Herbert Crews continued, speaking now with zest of the wild animals, including great herds of "the most exquisitely beautiful gazelles," in the Kenya preserves. Had she ever been there, he asked. No, Ginny said. Well, said Herbert, nodding vigorously, it really *is* worth it. Next time Marguerite promised to come along.

Ginny heard Oliver explain again that they were already late for an appointment in the Village, unfortunately they couldn't stay for a drink, yes it was a pity but he hoped they might do it another time: with which Marguerite warmly agreed. Though it was clearly all right for Oliver and Ginny to leave now, Herbert Crews was telling her about the various animals he'd seen—elands, giraffes, gnus, hippopotami, crocodiles, zebras, "feathered monkeys," impalas—he had actually eaten impala and found it fairly good. But the trip was fatiguing and his business in Nairobi disagreeable. He'd discovered—as in fact the Foundation had known from certain clumsily fudged reports—that the microbiological research being subsidized there had not only come to virtually nothing, but that vast sums of money had "disappeared" into nowhere. Ginny professed to feel some sympathy though at the same time, as she said, she wasn't surprised. Well, she said, easing away from Herbert Crews's side, that seems to be human nature, doesn't it. All around the world.

Americans and Swedes this time, Herbert Crews said,—equally taken in.

It couldn't be avoided that Herbert tell Oliver what he'd been saying—Oliver in fact seemed to be interested, he might have had some indirect connection with the Foundation himself—but unfortunately they were late for their engagement downtown, and within five minutes they were out of the apartment and back in the elevator going down.

Oliver withdrew a handkerchief from his breast pocket, unfolded it, and carefully wiped his forehead. Ginny was studying her reflection in the mirror and felt a pinprick of disappointment—her eyes looked shadowed and tired, and her hair wasn't really all that wonderful, falling straight to her shoulders. Though she'd shampooed it only that morning it was already getting dirty—the wind had been so strong on their walk up Madison.

On Fifth Avenue, in the gusty sunlight, they walked together for several blocks. Ginny slid her arm through Oliver's as if they were being watched but at an intersection they were forced to walk at different paces and her arm slipped free. It was time in any case to say good-bye: She sensed that he wasn't going to ask her, even out of courtesy, to have a drink with him: and she had made up her mind not to feel even tangentially insulted. After all, she hadn't been insulted.

He signalled a cab for her. He handed over the pink cardboard box with her denim jumper and sweater in it and shook her hand vigorously. You were lovely up there, Oliver said,—just perfect. Look, I'll call you, all right?

She felt the weight, the subtle dizzying blow, of the "were." But she thanked him just the same. And got into the cab. And wasn't so stricken by a sudden fleeting sense of loss—of loss tinged with a queer cold sickish knowledge—that, as the cab pulled away into the traffic stream, she couldn't give him a final languid wave of her hand, and even shape her mouth into a puckish kiss. All she had really lost, in a sense, was her own pair of shoes.

Issue 87, 1983

V. S. Naipaul

✠

My Aunt Gold Teeth

I never knew her real name and it is quite likely that she did have one, though I never heard her called anything but Gold Teeth. She did, indeed, have gold teeth. She had sixteen of them. She had married early and she had married well, and shortly after her marriage she exchanged her perfectly sound teeth for gold ones, to announce to the world that her husband was a man of substance.

Even without her gold teeth my aunt would have been noticeable. She was short, scarcely five foot, and she was fat, horribly, monstrously fat. If you saw her in silhouette you would have found it difficult to know whether she was facing you or whether she was looking sideways.

She ate little and prayed much. Her family being Hindu, and her husband being a pundit, she too was an orthodox Hindu. Of Hinduism she knew little apart from the ceremonies and the taboos, and this was enough for her. Gold Teeth saw God as a Power, and religious ritual as a means of harnessing that Power for great practical good, her good.

I fear I may have given the impression that Gold Teeth prayed because she wanted to be less fat. The fact was that Gold Teeth had no children, and she was almost forty. It was her childlessness, not her fat, that oppressed her, and she prayed for the curse to be removed. She was willing to try any means—any ritual, any prayer—in order to trap and channel the supernatural Power.

And so it was that she began to indulge in surreptitious Christian practices.

She was living at the time in a country village called Cunupia, in County Caroni. Here the Canadian Mission had long waged war against the Indian heathen, and saved many. But Gold Teeth stood firm. The Minister of Cunupia expended his Presbyterian piety on her; so did the headmaster of the Mission school. But all in vain. At no time was Gold Teeth persuaded even to think about being converted. The idea horrified her. Her father had been in his day one of the best-known Hindu pundits, and even now her husband's fame as a pundit, as a man who could read and write Sanskrit, had spread far beyond Cunupia. She was in no doubt whatsoever that Hindus were the best people in the world, and that Hinduism was a superior religion. She was willing to select, modify and incorporate alien eccentricities into her worship; but to abjure her own faith—never!

Presbyterianism was not the only danger the good Hindu had to face in Cunupia. Besides, of course, the ever-present threat of open Muslem aggression, the Catholics were to be reckoned with. Their pamphlets were everywhere and it was hard to avoid them. In them Gold Teeth read of novenas and rosaries, of squads of saints and angels. These were things she understood and could even sympathize with, and they encouraged her to seek further. She read of the mysteries and the miracles, of penances and indulgences. Her scepticism sagged, and yielded to a quickening, if reluctant, enthusiasm.

One morning she took the train for the county town of Chaguanas, three miles, two stations and twenty minutes away. The church of St. Philip and St. James in Chaguanas stands imposingly at the end of the Caroni Savannah Road, and although Gold Teeth knew Chaguanas well, all she knew of the church was that it had a clock, at which she had glanced on her way to the Railway Station nearby. She had hitherto been far more interested in the drab ochre-washed edifice opposite, which was the Police Station.

She carried herself into the churchyard, awed by her own temerity, feeling like an explorer in a land of cannibals. To her relief, the church was empty. It was not as terrifying as she had expected. In the gilt and the images and the resplendent cloths she found much that reminded her of her Hindu temple. Her eyes caught a discreet sign: CANDLES TWO CENTS EACH. She undid the knot in the end of her veil, where she kept her money, took out three cents, popped them into the box, picked up a candle and muttered a prayer in Hindustani. A brief moment of elation gave way to a sense of guilt, and she was suddenly anxious to get away from the church as fast as her weight would let her.

She took a bus home, and hid the candle in her chest of drawers. She had half feared that her husband's Brahminical flair for clairvoyance would have uncovered the reason for her trip to Chaguanas. When after four days, which she spent in an ecstasy of prayer, her husband had mentioned nothing, Gold Teeth thought it safe to burn the candle. She burned it secretly, at night, before her Hindu images and sent up, as she thought, prayers of double efficacy.

Every day her religious schizophrenia grew, and presently she began wearing a crucifix. Neither her husband nor her neighbors knew she did so. The chain was lost in the billows of fat around her neck, and the crucifix was itself buried in the valley of her gargantuan breasts. Later she acquired two holy pictures, one of the Virgin Mary, the other of the crucifixion, and took care to conceal them from her husband. The prayers she offered to these Christian things filled her with new hope and buoyancy. She became an addict of Christianity.

Then her husband, Ramprasad, fell ill.

Ramprasad's sudden, unaccountable illness alarmed Gold Teeth. It was, she knew, no ordinary illness, and she knew, too, that her religious transgression was the cause. The District Medical Officer at Chaguanas said it was diabetes but Gold Teeth knew better. To be on the safe side, though, she used the insulin he prescribed, and, to be even safer, she consulted Ganesh Pundit, the masseur with mystic leanings, celebrated as a faith-healer.

Ganesh came all the way from Feunte Grove to Cunupia. He came in great humility, anxious to serve Gold Teeth's husband, for Gold Teeth's husband was a Brahmin among Brahmins, a *Panday*, a man who knew all five Vedas; while he, Ganesh, was a mere *Chaubay* and knew only four.

With spotless white *koortah*, his dhoti cannily tied, and a tasselled green scarf as a concession to elegance, Ganesh exuded the confidence of the professional mystic. He looked at the sick man, observed his pallor, sniffed the air inquiringly. "This man," he said slowly, "is bewitched. Seven spirits are upon him."

He was telling Gold Teeth nothing she didn't know. She had known from the first that there were spirits in the affair, but she was glad that Ganesh had ascertained their number.

"But you mustn't worry," Ganesh added. "We will 'tie' the house—in spiritual bonds—and no spirit will be able to come in."

Then without being asked, Gold Teeth brought out a blanket, folded it, placed it on the floor and invited Ganesh to sit on it. Next she brought him a brass jar of fresh water, a mango leaf and a plate full of burning charcoal.

"Bring me some ghee," Ganesh said, and after Gold Teeth had done so, he set to work. Muttering continuously in Hindustani he sprinkled the water from the brass jar around him with the mango leaf. Then he melted the ghee in the fire and the charcoal hissed so sharply that Gold Teeth could not make out his words. Presently he rose and said, "You must put some of the ash of this fire on your husband's forehead, but if he doesn't want you to do that, mix it with his food. You must keep the water in this jar and place it every night before your front door."

Gold Teeth pulled her veil over her forehead.

Ganesh coughed. "That," he said, rearranging his scarf, "is all. There is nothing more I can do. God will do the rest."

He refused any payment for his services. It was enough honor, he said, for a man as humble as he was to serve Pundit Ramprasad, and she, Gold Teeth, had been singled out by fate to be the spouse of such a worthy man. Gold Teeth received the impression that Ganesh spoke from a firsthand knowledge of fate and its designs, and her heart, buried deep down under inches of mortal, flabby flesh, sank a little.

"Baba," she said hesitantly, "Revered father, I have something to say to you." But she couldn't say anything more and Ganesh, seeing this, filled his eyes with charity and love. "What is it, my child?"

"I have done a great wrong, Baba."

"What sort of wrong?" he asked, and his tone indicated that Gold Teeth could do no wrong.

"I have prayed to Christian things."

And to Gold Teeth's surprise, Ganesh chuckled benevolently. "And do you think God minds, daughter? There is only one God and different people pray to Him in different ways. It doesn't matter how you pray, but God is pleased if you pray at all."

"So it is not because of me that my husband has fallen ill?"

"No, to be sure, daughter."

In his professional capacity Ganesh was consulted by people of many faiths, and with the license of the mystic he had exploited the commodiousness of Hinduism, and made room for all beliefs. In this way he had many clients, as he called them, many satisfied clients.

Henceforward Gold Teeth not only pasted Ramprasad's pale forehead with the sacred ash Ganesh had prescribed, but mixed substantial amounts with his food. Ramprasad's appetite, enormous even in sickness, diminished; and he shortly entered into a visible and alarming decline that mystified his wife.

She fed him more ash than before, and when it was exhausted and Ramprasad perilously macerated, she fell back on the Hindu wife's last resort. She took her husband home to her mother. That venerable lady, my grandmother, lived with us in Port of Spain, in Woodbrook.

Ramprasad was tall and skeletal, and his face was grey. The virile voice that had expounded a thousand theological points and recited a hundred *puranas* was now a wavering whisper. We cooped him up in a room called, oddly, "the pantry." It had never been used as a pantry and one can only assume that the architect, in the idealistic manner of his tribe, had so designated it some forty years before. It was a tiny room. If you wished to enter the pantry you were compelled, as soon as you opened the door, to climb on to the bed: It fitted the room to a miracle. The lower half of the walls were concrete, the upper close latticework; there were no windows.

My grandmother had her doubts about the suitability of the room for a sick man. She was worried about the lattice-work. It let in air and light, and Ramprasad was not going to die from these things if she could help it. With cardboard, oilcloth and canvas she made the lattice-work air-proof and light-proof.

And, sure enough, within a week Ramprasad's appetite returned, insatiable and insistent as before. My grandmother claimed all the credit for this, though Gold Teeth knew that ash she had fed him had not been without effect. Then she realized with horror that she had ignored a very important thing. The house in Cunupia had been tied and no spirits could enter, but the house in Woodbrook had been given no such protection and any spirit could come and go as it chose. The problem was pressing.

Ganesh was out of the question. By giving his services free, he had made it impossible for Gold Teeth to call him in again. But thinking in this way of Ganesh, she remembered his words: "It doesn't matter how you pray, but God is pleased if you pray at all."

Why not, then, bring Christianity into play again?

She didn't want to take any chances this time. She decided to tell Ramprasad.

He was propped up in bed, and eating. When Gold Teeth opened the door, he stopped eating and blinked at the unwonted light. Gold Teeth, stepping into the doorway and filling it, shadowed the room once more and he went on eating. She placed the palms of her hands on the bed. It creaked.

"Man," she said.

Ramprasad continued to eat.

"Man," she said in English, "I thinking about going to the chu'ch to pray. You never know, and it better to be on the safe side. After all, the house here ain't tied—"

"I don't want you to pray in no chu'ch," he whispered, in English too.

Gold Teeth did the only thing she could do. She began to cry.

Three days in succession she asked his permission to go to church, and his opposition weakened in the face of her tears. He was now, besides, too weak to oppose anything. Although his appetite had returned he was still very ill and very weak, and every day his condition became worse.

On the fourth day he said to Gold Teeth, "Well, pray to Jesus and go to chu'ch if it will put your mind at rest."

And Gold Teeth straightaway set about putting her mind at rest. Every morning she took the trolley bus to the Holy Rosary Church, to offer worship in her private way. Then she was emboldened to bring a crucifix and pictures of the Virgin and the Messiah into the house. We were all somewhat worried by this, but Gold Teeth's religious nature was well known to us, her husband was a learned pundit and when all was said and done this was an emergency, a matter of life and death. So we could do nothing but look on. Incense and camphor and ghee burned now before the likenesses of Krishna and Shiva as well as Mary and Jesus. Gold Teeth revealed an appetite for prayer that equalled her husband's for food, and we marvelled at both, if only because neither prayer nor food seemed to be of any use to Ramprasad.

One evening, shortly after bell and gong and conch-shell had announced that Gold Teeth's official devotions were almost over, a sudden chorus of lamentation burst over the house, and I was summoned to the room reserved for prayer. "Come quickly, something dreadful has happened to your aunt."

The prayer-room, still heavy with the fumes of incense, presented an extraordinary sight. Before the Hindu shrine, flat on her face, Gold Teeth lay prostrate, rigid as a sack of flour, a large amorphous mass. I had only seen Gold Teeth standing or sitting, and the aspect of Gold Teeth prostrate, so novel and so grotesque, was disturbing.

My grandmother, an alarmist by nature, bent down and put her ear to the upper half of the body on the floor. "I don't seem to hear her heart," she said.

We were all somewhat terrified. We tried to lift Gold Teeth but she seemed as heavy as lead. Then, slowly, the body quivered. The flesh beneath the clothes rippled, then billowed, and the children in the room sharpened their shrieks. Instinctively we all stood back from the body and waited to see what was going to happen. Gold Teeth's hand began to pound the floor and at the same time she began to gurgle.

My grandmother had grasped the situation. "She's got the spirit," she said.

At the word "spirit," the children shrieked louder, and my grandmother slapped them into silence.

The gurgling resolved itself into words pronounced with a lingering ghastly quaver. "Hail Mary, Hara Ram," Gold Teeth said, "the snakes are after me. Everywhere snakes. Seven snakes. Rama! Rama! Full of grace. Seven spirits leaving Cunupia by the four o'clock train for Port of Spain."

My grandmother and my mother listened eagerly, their faces lit up with pride. I was rather ashamed at the exhibition, and annoyed with Gold Teeth for putting me into a fright. I moved towards the door.

"Who is that going away? Who is the young *daffar*, the unbeliever?" the voice asked abruptly.

"Come back quickly, boy," my grandmother whispered, "Come back and ask her pardon."

I did as I was told.

"It is all right, son," Gold Teeth replied, "You don't know. You are young."

Then the spirit appeared to leave her. She wrenched herself up to a sitting position and wondered why we were all there. For the rest of that evening she behaved as if nothing had happened and she pretended she didn't notice that everyone was looking at her and treating her with unusual respect.

"I have always said it, and I will say it again," my grandmother said, "that these Christians are very religious people. That is why I encouraged Gold Teeth to pray to Christian things."

Ramprasad died early next morning and we had the announcement on the radio after the local news at one o'clock. Ramprasad's death was the only one announced and so, although it came between commercials, it made some impression. We buried him that afternoon in Mucurapo Cemetery.

As soon as we got back my grandmother said, "I have always said it, and I will say it again: I don't like these Christian things. Ramprasad would have got better if only you, Gold Teeth, had listened to me and not gone running after these Christian things."

Gold Teeth sobbed her assent; and her body squabbered and shook as she confessed the whole story of her trafficking with Christianity. We listened in astonishment and shame. We didn't know that a good Hindu, and a member of our family, could sink so low. Gold Teeth beat her breast and pulled ineffectually at her long hair and begged to be forgiven. "It is all my fault," she cried. "My own fault, Ma. I fell in a moment of weakness. Then I just couldn't stop."

My grandmother's shame turned to pity. "It's all right, Gold Teeth. Perhaps it was this you needed to bring you back to your senses."

That evening Gold Teeth ritually destroyed every reminder of Christianity in the house.

"You have only yourself to blame," my grandmother said, "if you have no children now to look after you."

Issue 19, 1958

ELEVATORS

Richard Wilbur

✠

Piccola Commedia

He is no one I really know,
The sun-charred, gaunt young man
By the highway's edge in Kansas
Thirty-odd years ago.

On a tourist-cabin veranda
Two middle-aged women sat;
One, in a white dress, fat,
With a rattling glass in her hand,

Called "Son, don't you feel the heat?
Get up here into the shade."
Like a good boy, I obeyed,
And was given a crate for a seat

And an Orange Crush and gin.
"This state," she said, "is hell."
Her thin friend cackled, "Well, dear,
You've gotta fight sin with sin."

"No harm in a drink; my stars!"
Said the fat one, jerking her head.
"And I'll take no lip from Ed,
Him with his damn cigars."

Laughter. A combine whined
On past, and dry grass bent
In the backwash; liquor went
Like an ice pick into my mind.

Beneath her skirt I spied
Two sea cows on a floe.
"Go talk to Lucy Jo, son,
She's reading a book inside."

As I gangled in at the door
A pink girl, curled in a chair,
Looked up with an ingénue stare.
Screenland lay on the floor.

Amazed by her starlet's pout
And the way her eyebrows arched,
I felt both drowned and parched.
Desire leapt up like a trout.

"Hello," she said, and her gum
Gave a calculating crack.
At once, from the lightless back
Of the room there came the grumble

Of someone heaving from bed,
A Zippo's click and flare,
Then, more and more apparent,
The shuffling form of Ed,

Who neither looked nor spoke
But moved in profile by,
Blinking one gelid eye
In his elected smoke.

This is something I've never told,
And some of it I forget.
But the heat! I can feel it yet,
And that conniving cold.

Issue 61, 1975

Stuart Dybek

❦

Nighthawks

The moon, still cooling off from last night, back in the sky—a bulb insects can't circle. Instead, they teem around a corner street-light, while down the block air conditioners crank, synchronized with katydids.

There's a light on in a garage where a man's legs, looking lonely, stick out from under a Dodge. What is it that's almost tender about someone tinkering with a car after midnight? The askew glare of the extension lamp propped in the open engine reminds me of how once, driving through the dark in Iowa, I saw a man and women outlined in light, kissing in a wheat field. They stood pressed against each other before the blazing bank of headlamps from a giant combine. It must have been threshing in the dark, for dust and chaff hung smoldering in the beams, making it seem as if the couple stood in smoke or fog.

I was speeding down a gravel-pinging road and caught only a glimpse of them, but took it as an omen to continue following the drunken divor-cée I'd met earlier in a roadside bar and grill where I'd stopped for a cof-fee on my way back to Chicago. Divorcée was her word, the way she'd introduced herself. "I'm celebrating becoming an official, gay divorcée," she'd told me. I must have looked a little surprised because she quickly added, as if I'd gotten the wrong idea, "You know, not *gay* like with other women, but gay, like, you know, wild." We had several drinks, danced to the jukebox, and ended up in the parking lot, necking in her pickup. When I started to unbutton her blouse, she asked, "You intend to sit out here all night like teenagers or do you want to follow me home?"

I didn't know the countryside. I followed her down highways, one veering into another, so many turns that I thought she must be taking a shortcut. I had the windows rolled down, hoping the streaming night air would clear my head. Beyond the narrow beams of my headlights, I could feel the immensity of prairie buoying us up, stretching in the dark without the limit of a horizon, and I felt suddenly lost in its vastness in a way I'd only felt before on the ocean, rocking at night in a small boat. She kept driving faster, and I could imagine the toe of her high heel pressing down on the workboot-sized gas pedal of her truck. I wasn't paying attention to where she was leading me and couldn't have kept track if I'd tried. Unlit blacktop tunneled through low-hanging trees. By the time we hit the dirt roads she was driving like a maniac, bouncing over railroad crossings and the humps of drainage pipes, dust swirling behind her so that her taillights were only red pin-points, and I wondered what radio station she must be listening to, wondered if she was drunker than I'd realized and she thought we were racing, or if she'd had a sudden change of heart and was trying to lose me on those backroads, and I wondered if I ought to let her.

Tonight, a lot of people are still up watching the nighthawks hunt through the streetlights. The white bars on their wings flash as they dip through the lights, then glide off against the dark trees that line the street. The trees seem more like shadows except where the inverted cones of light catch their leaves and heighten their green. And despite all the people still up, unable to let go of the evening, leaning from windows, smoking on steps or rocking on front porches, it's quiet—no small talk, or gossip, no stories, or lullabies—only the whir of insects and the stabbing cries of birds, as if we all know we should be sleeping now, leaving the nighthawks to describe the night.

Robert Pinsky

✣

Immortal Longings

Inside the silver body
Slowing as it banks through veils of cloud
We float separately in our seats

Like the cells or atoms of one
Creature, needs
And states of a shuddering god.

Under him, a thirsty brilliance.
Pulsing or steady,
The fixed lights of the city

And the flood of carlights coursing
Through the grid: Delivery,
Arrival, Departure. Whim. Entering

And entered. Touching
And touched: down
The lit boulevards, over the bridges

And the river like an arm of night.
Book, cigarette. Bathroom.
Thirst. Some of us are asleep.

ROBERT PINSKY

We tilt roaring
Over the glittering
Zodiac of intentions.

Issue 112, 1989

Paul Hoover

In Berlin

At the center of the city I come upon a hill, at the top of which is a very large bird. I see it resembles an eagle. Though it's about 14 stories high, it's as docile as a rabbit. Its foot, I see, is tied to a stout nearby building. The rope used for this purpose is thick, the knot alone having the bulk of a cottage, or a pleasant bungalow. I see also, as night falls, that all over the miraculous bird there are windows from which the residents, framed in the warm yellow light of their domiciles, peer down into the street or out into the star-filled night. I suspect they are kept warm by the heat of its body, suspect also they lead precarious lives, as even the slightest movement, the lifting of a wing, would send their well-stacked dishes spinning into havoc. Yet as long as I watch, the bird gives but one indication that it lives. When the wind blows with great force against its feathers, it seems to shift its weight from one leg to the other, and once or twice its enormous eye blinks like an eclipse.

Issue 62, 1975

A. R. Ammons

from "Strip"

1.

wdn't it be silly to be serious, now:
I mean, the hardheads and the eggheads

are agreed that we are an absurd
irrelevance on this slice of curvature

and that a boulder from the blue
could confirm it: imagine, mathematics

wiped out by a wandering stone, or
Grecian urns not forever fair when

the sun expands: can you imagine
cracking the story off we've built

up so long—the simian ancestries,
the lapses and leaps, the discovery

of life in the burial of grains:
the scratch of pictorial and syllabic

script, millennia of evenings around
the fires: nothing: meaninglessness

our only meaning: our deepest concerns
such as death or love or child-pain

arousing a belly laugh or a witty
dismissal: a bunch of baloney: it's

already starting to feel funny: I
think I may laugh: few of the dead

lie recalled, and they have not
cautioned us: we are rippers and

tearers and proceeders: restraint`
stalls us still—we stand hands

empty, lip hung, dumb eyes struck
open: if we can't shove at the

trough, we don't understand: but is
it not careless to become too local

when there are four hundred billion
stars in our galaxy alone: at

least, that's what I heard: also,
that there are billions of such

systems spread about, some older,
some younger than ours: if the

elements are the elements throughout,
I daresay much remains to be learned:

however much we learn, tho, we may
grow daunted by our dismissibility

in so sizable a place: do our gods
penetrate those reaches, or do all

those other places have their godly
nativities: or if the greatest god

is the stillness all the motions add
up to, then we must ineluctably be

included: perhaps a dribble of
what-is is what what-is is: it is

nice to be included, especially from
so minor a pew: please turn, in yr

hymnals, to page "Archie carrying on
again:" he will have it his way

though he has no clue what his way
is: after such participations as

that with the shrill owl in the
spruce at four in the morning with

the snow ended and the moon come
out, how am I sagely to depart from

all being (universe and all—by
that I mean material and immaterial

stuff) without calling out—just a
minute, am I not to know at last

what lies over the hill: over the
ridge there, over the laps of the

ocean, and out beyond the plasmas
of the sun's winds, and way out

where the bang still bubbles in the
longest risings: no, no: I must

get peanut butter and soda crackers
and the right shoe soles (for ice)

and leave something for my son and
leave these lines, poor things, to

you, if you will have them, can they
do you any good, my trade for my

harm in the world: come, let's
celebrate: it will all be over

Issue 139, 1996

Patricia Storace

※

Still Life

Somehow, the two of us sit in a café
bordering the park. Its grass succumbs
again to chronic green, and I see,
obedient, what I don't want to see—
lacerating tulips, leaf-racked trees,
hear steps as gunshots on the street,
heel and pavement sniping at each other.
The corner of your mouth bleeds geography
in the form of Côtes du Rhône.
And the sunset is Cossack,
reddening the West with its pogrom.
I should be sipping the Riesling of an April evening,
the minutes sweet and disappearing on my palate,
mouth smoothing out, from time to time,
the folds of your neck's mortal velvet.
I should admire, not endure, the hyacinth, the campanelle
developing their color photographs of light.
But an hour not this one has stiffened
on the clock, and will not pass;
and eternity, twelve-armed goddess
revealed to me, appears in her aspect of hell.

Issue 90, 1983

Heather McHugh

This Is the Life

His watch is wicked, going on
without him. Pass your hand
across the blue man's lips and
Q.E.D. We know we breathe

(and quite without our help) but then
we know we know, and so forget.
It's strange to be alive but we
have not felt awe since we were someone's

kid, and that was once
upon a time. In time we taught ourselves
to find the world mundane, and all
the unknown unsurprising, like

next Sunday, for example.
God himself gets bored, God knows.

On holidays we like to make
some sugar on a rope, some fallout

in the form of rocks,
the Science City someone gave

to Junior, Christmas Day. And you can etch
your name in the petri dish with pure

bacteria, or in the virgin snow with piss.
We draw the line at skin, for different,
at heart for dead; the EEG goes on all by itself. We used
to sing, and when we did, we sensed

the air itself was lively; then we fell
back into dream, we froze. And all night long
in the drawing room, after the household's asleep,
the crystal grows.

Issue 97, 1985

Sharon Olds

12 years old

When my girl and her friend walk away from me
at the swimming pool, I see her friend's
sweet stick legs, thin as
legs drawn by a child, and then I
see my daughter's curved hocks and
haunches, her hips that behind my back have
swelled until they taper delicious as
chicken legs, the liquid meat of the
thigh. Her joints gently grind and
suck and rock as she walks in rich
innocence toward the diving board, her
chest flat as a plank, the front of her
torso meek and raw as a kid's, but her
ass delicately flashes its signals:
Soon, now, the gold glow of the
warning lights. She mounts the ladder, her
skin twinkling wet as the basted
broiler halfway done to a turn, she
sways her frail way down the board
waving its wand in the air, the water
far below her rich with college boys, she
grins toward me, her head slick, and

takes the plunge, her pale body
plummeting through the air in silence and then
entering the water with the charged thrust of her
knife into the chicken when she is really hungry.

Albert Goldbarth

⌘

Lithium Sonnet

Judith, I've seen the CPA. She showed me two
indomitable columns, numbers rising like the legs
of a statue god. And where they add up, where
they meet in a kind of pedestal at their bottom, they
declared such a sense of solidity and completion, you,
especially you, would have wept at the beauty.

And Judith, the carpenter visited. We joked about her
many minor trials, making a go of it in
a "man's world," then she got down to the monstrousness
of chainsaw, and the nearly-pubic delicacy of shavings.
At the end, she had an instrument: its bubble centers
whenever the work is centered enough to be done.

Let them be totems, let them be invoked.
For the balance. For the level.

Issue 112, 1989

James Lasdun

※

First Bodies

All evening the herds stream from the woods
Down the Interstate, the Palisades,
Dreamy-eyed, tiptoeing does and coral-crowned bucks
Crossing over the water to Manhattan,
Strapped onto roof-racks and the backs of pickup trucks,
Scooped muzzles open as if to nibble
Ribbons of bark, sprigs of bittersweet.

Still more themselves than anything else
(Scut-hearts flush as milkweed under tails),
They flare through the city in a soft, slow-motion
Fusillade; as estranging, as out of place
Among the iron and cobbles, the callipygian
Bubble-strut of graffiti, as the lead
Lodged in their tight flesh, or as the men,

The blue- or white-collared blood brothers
Who got up early in the boroughs
To take their thirsty souls into the wilderness
And drink to the dregs its elixir of bright
Silence and ungridded space, from the tipped back glass
Of cross-hair sights angled through flensed white birch,
Maple scrub and crimson-burred sumac

With a sudden sweet kick of betrayal,
Half-wished, half not what was meant at all,
Gun-smoke and dropped knees insufficient to express
The vanishing tumult of consummation
Or that in spite of appearances tenderness
Was probably the point: love as violence;
Its usual name in the fallen world.

Issue 120, 1991

William S. Burroughs

✠

The Cat Inside

Animal contact can alter what Castaneda calls "assemblage points." Like mother-love. It's been slobbered over by Hollywood. Andy Hardy goes down on his knees by his mother's bed. What's wrong with that? A decent American kid praying for his mother. What's wrong with that?

"I'll tell you what's wrong with it, B.J. It's shit. It's dead mawkish muck and it destroys the truth under it."

Here is a mother hooded seal on an ice floe with her cub. Thirty-mile-an-hour winds, thirty degrees below zero. Look into her eyes, slitted, yellow, fierce, crazed, sad and hopeless. End line of a doomed planet. She can't lie to herself, she can't pull any pathetic rags of verbal self-glorification about her. There she is, on this ice floe with her cub. She shifts her five-hundred-pound bulk to make a dug available. There's a cub with its shoulder ripped open by one of the adult males. Probably won't make it. They all have to swim to Denmark, fifteen hundred miles away. Why? The seals don't know why. They have to get to Denmark. They all have to get to Denmark.

Issue 124, 1992

Deborah Warren

❖

Airplane

Now, as you board the airplane, is there latent
in its thorax—nestled near the spine—
some wiring awry, a hose not tightened?
Embolisms inching up the fuel line?
One loose part that's starting to abrade
a second part—a third—without a sign
that some essential fabric's growing frayed?
Or else, in *you*, does some flaw undermine

(undiagnosed) the operation of
the force—and the fragility—that arcs
from fingertip to fingertip above
us on the Sistine ceiling? Let one spark
misfire, and the oxygen won't move
to fire the lungs and drive the heart that bears
you up . . . Now as we stand so hale in love,
some valve is rotting, some small linchpin wears

that holds some cotter pin, mechanics err,
a bolt corrodes; a radon plume delivers
traces to some deficient gene. A mere
omission, fissure, mist can stop whatever
keeps you above the ground: What engineer

invented a machine so frail its breath
depends on something casual as the air
you cruise on, asymptotic to your death?

X. J. Kennedy

In a Prominent Bar
in Secaucus One Day

*With thanks to Claire McAllister for pointing out that these
words may be sung to the tunes of "The Old Orange Flute"
and "Sweet Betsy from Pike."*

In a prominent bar in Secaucus one day
Rose a lady in skunk with a top-heavy sway,
Raised a knobby red finger—all turned from their beer—
While with eyes bright as snowcrust she sang high and clear:

"Now who of you'd think from an eyeful of me
That I once was a princess, and proud as could be?—
Oh I'd never sit down by a tumble-down drunk
If it wasn't, my dears, for the high cost of junk.

"All the gents used to swear that the white of my calf
Beat the down of the swan by a length and a half—
In the kerchief of linen I caught to my nose
Ah, there never fell snot, but a little gold rose.

"I had seven gold teeth and a toothpick of gold,
My Virginia cheroot was a leaf of it rolled,
And I'd light it each time with a hundred in cash—
Why the bums used to fight if I flicked them an ash.

"In a car like the Roxy I'd roll to the track,
A steel-guitar trio, a bar in the back,
And the wheels made no noise, they turned over so fast—
It would take you ten minutes to see me go past.

"When the horses bowed down to me that I might choose
I bet on them all, for I hated to lose—
Now I'm saddled each night for my butter and eggs
And the broken threads race down the backs of my legs.

"Let you hold in mind, girls, that your beauty must pass
Like a lovely white clover that rusts with its grass—
Keep your bottoms off barstools and marry you young
Or you'll end—an old barrel with many a bung.

"For when time takes you out for a spin in his car
You'll be hard-pressed to stop him from going too far
And be left by the roadside, for all your good deeds,
Two toadstools for tits and a face full of weeds."

All the house raised a cheer, but the man at the bar
Made a phone call and up pulled a red patrol car
And she blew us a kiss as they copped her away
From that prominent bar in Secaucus, N.J.

Issue 25, 1961

Jim Carroll

Heroin

Sat for three days in a white room
a tiny truck of white flowers
was driving through the empty window
to warn off your neighbors
and their miniature flashlights.

by afternoon
across the lake
a blind sportsman had lost his canoe.
He swam,
by evening
toward the paper cup
of my hand.

At dawn,
clever housewives tow my Dutch kitchen
across the lawn.
and in the mail a tiny circus
filled with ponies
had arrived.

You,
a woman with feathers
have come so often lately
under my rubber veranda,

that I'm tearing apart all those tactless warnings
embroidered across your forehead.

Marc,
I'm beginning to see those sounds
that I never even thought
I would hear.

Over there a door is knocking
for example
with someone you hate.
and here I beg another to possess somehow
the warmth of these wooden eyes

so beside me
a lightbulb is revolving
wall to wall,
a reminder of the great sun
which had otherwise completely collapsed
down to the sore toe of the white universe.

its chalky light
rings
like a garden of tiny vegetables
to gather the quiet of these wet feelings
together

once again

like the sound of a watch
on your cold white wrist
which is reaching for a particular moment
to reoccur . . .

which is here . . . now.

Issue 48, 1969

Philip Larkin

❖

Referred Back

That was a pretty one, I heard you call
From the unsatisfactory hall
To the unsatisfactory room where I
Played record after record, idly,
Wasting my time at home, that you
Looked so much forward to.

Oliver's *Riverside Blues*, it was. And now
I shall, I suppose, always remember how
The flock of notes those antique negroes blew
Out of Chicago air into
A huge remembering pre-electric horn
The year after I was born
Three decades later made this sudden bridge
From your unsatisfactory age
To my unsatisfactory prime.

Truly, though our element is time,
We are not suited to the long perspectives
Open at each instant of our lives.
They link us to our losses: worse,
They show us what we have as it once was,
Blindingly undiminished; just as though
By acting differently we could have kept it so.

Issue 19, 1958

Lucy Grealy

✠

Ward 10

Nothing melodramatic, it's just when the sunlight
came in through the wired windows and laid itself
down on the green floor, it was nice, we liked it
there, then, playing our games. And like kids
anywhere, we were bad, always sneaking off
to buy chocolate in the lobby, over to Maternity
to make faces at babies, and one morning,
after a previous evening of hushed, excited planning
based on an overheard conversation,
we took the elevator all the way down to the lower basement
to wind our way through the deserted tunnels linking buildings,
nervous, fearless explorers among the bare floodlights
and echoes, looking for signs pointing
toward the animal labs. The night before
we'd lain in our beds unable to sleep with the image
of what we must have thought would be
some sort of petting zoo. We got giggly lost three times
before the stink of sheep's pee found us,
and then we found them, bleating in their concrete
strawless pens, raw geometrics shaved
in their sides. In the next room were cages
and cages of cats, most of them silent, some
with electrodes sewn in their heads.
We could hear monkeys nearby, but instead chose

to finally read the signs we'd laughed at minutes before:
we *were* unauthorized personnel, we weren't
supposed to be there. We went back to the ward
to find the nurses laughing, scolding.
They thought we'd somehow found out
the hated technician who took blood
was coming that morning, and that we'd sneaked off
to buy Hershey's bars in the gift shop instead.
Always loving, they applauded our ingenuity:
"How did you know?" We hadn't, but
played along anyway.
"Guess," we told them.

Before I knew high school I knew words
like vincristine, cytotoxin, sarcoma, failing.
I understood the basic theory of radiation,
the vacuum principle of hypodermics,
that it would be a long time
before I would say out loud
the names of my friends again.

Listen, Michael, Tina: I'm the one who made it.
I don't know the reason for this.

Issue 121, 1991

Ben Sonnenberg

꙰

The Crease

He was in the bathtub when she came in and when he got out, he went into the bedroom and started putting on his shorts. She said, "I have lost all respect for you."

"Isn't it about time?"

"You must have known I'd find out."

"I don't like confrontations."

"Were there others?" she said.

"Look here—" he said.

"I want you to tell me."

He picked out a shirt.

"I want *you* to tell me," she said again.

And so he told her. While getting dressed, he listed a number of women, including an underground actress who lived in the same hotel. "Brought her baby with her," he added and grinned.

Her last words took him by surprise. She said, "Wasn't *that* cavalier."

After she left, he knotted his tie and made a cold face in the mirror. A short affair remarkable for her sweetness, his sharpness and its abrupt end. An affair much shorter to him than to her, he was certain of that. She would be obsessed with him for a time, calling him up at all hours, following him at night. . . . Still, the affair had been long enough to include summer weekends with her wealthy Connecticut family, much going out as a couple, a planned trip to the south of France, as well as an abortion.

Now that it was over, he felt a sour pride.

• • •

Soon after that he got married and soon after that he left his wife. And soon after that he moved into the young girl's apartment, on Hudson Street in the Village. She let him store his belongings there and use her car whenever he liked. They went out a lot as a couple again. People who saw them together were frightened for her and if they knew her, they told her so. This time they were planning a trip to Turkey and Greece.

One night, with another couple, they went to a restaurant for dinner. Downey's on Eighth Avenue. Downey's was crowded and noisy. The women were still at the table and the two men were walking out when she distinctly heard him say, "Do you happen to know an apartment where I could take Kate for the night?"

"I never said that," he said in the car.

"I heard you distinctly."

"I don't believe it." He was incredulous. Truly, he was. "Downey's was just too noisy."

"I'm telling you," she said. "And I'll tell you something else." They were parked in front of his parents' house on Gramercy Park. "My boyfriend before you—"

"Spare me," he said.

But she wouldn't and she didn't.

At her place the following morning he told her he was sorry. They were eating biscuits and drinking tea. "I didn't want you to hear in that way. But the fact is, I've decided that I'm going to Greece with Kate."

At lunch he told Kate what happened next. "She threw hot tea on my trousers. Took the crease right out of them. Look," he said. He stood up, he sat down. Then he said to Kate, "Serves me right, I suppose."

Suji Kwock Kim

✦

The Korean Community Garden
in Queens

In the vacant lot nobody else wanted to rebuild,
dirt scumbled for years with syringes and dead
weed-husks, tire-shreds and smashed beer bottles,
the first green shoots of spring spike through—

bullbrier, redroot, pokeweed, sowthistle,
an uprising of grasses whose only weapons are themselves.
Blades slit through scurf. Spear-tips spit dust
as if thrust from the other side. They spar and glint.

How far can they climb, grappling for light?
Inside I see coils of fern-bracken called *kosari*,
bellflower cuts named *toraji* in the old country.
Knuckles of ginger and mugwort dig upward,

working through soil and woodlice until they break
the surface. Planted by immigrants, they survive,
like their gardeners, though ripped from their
native plot. What is it that they want, driving

toward a foreign sky? How not to mind the end
they'll come to. Imaging the garden underground,
where gingko and ailanthus grub cement rubble.
They tunnel slag for foothold. Wring crumbs of rot

for water. Of shadows, seeds foresung as *Tree
of Heaven* and *Silver Apricot* in ancient Mandarin,
their roots tangle now with plum and weeping willow,
their branches mingling with tamarack and oak.

I love how nothing in these furrows grows unsnarled,
nothing stays unscathed. How last year's fallen stalks,
withered to pith, cleave to this year's crocus bulbs,
each infant knot burred with bits of garbage and tar.

Fist to fist with tulips, glads, selving and unselving
daffodils, they work their metamorphoses in loam
pocked with rust-flints, splinters of rodent-skull—
a ground so mixed, so various that everything's born

of what it is not. Who wouldn't want to flower
like this? Look how strangely they become
themselves, this gnarl of azaleas and roses-of-Sharon,
native to both countries, blooming here as if drunk

with blossoming. Green buds suck and bulge.
Stem-nubs thicken. Sepals swell and crack their cauls.
Lately, every time I walk down this street and peer
through the fence, I'm surprised by something new.

Yesterday hydrangea and chrysanthemums burst
their calyxes, corolla-skins blistering into welts.
Today jonquils slit blue shoots from their sheaths.
Tomorrow daylilies and wild-asters will flame petals,

each incandescent color unlike: indigo, blood, ice,
coral, fire-gold, violet the hue of shaman's robes—
every flower with its unique glint and slant, faithful
to each particular. Each one lit by what it neighbors

but is not, each tint flaring without a human soul,
without human rage at its passing. In the summer
there will be scallions, mung-beans, black sesame,
muskmelons, to be harvested into zinc buckets

and sold at market. How do they live without wanting
to live forever? Unlike their gardeners in the old world,
who die for warring dreams and warring heavens,
who stop at nothing, life the one paradise they wanted.

Issue 148, 1998

Carl Phillips

❈

Of That City, the Heart

You lived here once. City—remember?—
of formerly your own, of the forever beloved,
of the dead.

        for some part of you, this part,
is dead, you have said so, and it is fitting:
a city of monuments, monuments to what is

gone, leaving us with our human need always
to impose on memory a body language, some
shape that holds.

        I can picture you walking
this canal, this park, this predictably steep
gorge through which predictably runs a river,

in which river, earlier today, I saw stranded
a bent hubcap, spent condoms, a cup by
someone crushed, said *enough* to, tossed . . .

City in which—what happened? or did not
happen? what chance (of limbs, of spoils)
escaped you?

And yet . . . I have sometimes
imagined you nowhere happier than here, in
that time before me.

I can even, from what
little you have told me, imagine your first
coming here, trouble ahead but still far,

you innocent—of disappointment, still
clean. In those historical years preceding
the sufferings

of Christ, there were cities
whose precincts no one could enter unclean,
be their stains those of murder, defilement

of the wrong body, or at what was holy some
outrage. There were rituals for cleaning;
behind them, unshakeable laws, or—

they seemed so . . . But this city is not
ancient. And it is late inside a century
in which clean and unclean,

less and less,
figure. At this hour of sun, in clubs of
light, in broad beams failing, I do not

stop it: I love you. Let us finally, un-
daunted, slow, with the slowness that a
jaded ease engenders, together

step into
—this hour, this sun: city of trumpets,
noteless now; of tracks whose end is here.

Issue 148, 1998

Agha Shahid Ali

✵

The Purse-Seiner *Atlantis*

Black Pacific. "Shahid, come here, quick." A ship,
giant lantern held in its own light, the dark
left untouched, a phantom-ship with birds, no, moths,

giant moths that cannot die. Which world has sent
it? And which awaits its cargo's circling light,
staggered halo made of wings? The dark is still,

fixed around that moving lamp which keeps the light
so encased it pours its milk into itself,
sailing past with moths that cannot put themselves

out. What keeps this light from pouring out as light?
Beautiful in white, she says, "I'll just be back."
She goes inside. I fill my glass till I see

everything and nothing stare back at me, fill
me with longing, the longing to long, to be
flame, and mouth, and ash. What light now startles me?

Neighbor's window. *Turn it off, God, turn it off*.
When they do, a minute later, I am—what?
Ash completely, yet not ash, I see I am

what is left of light, what light leaves me, what light
always leaves of me. "Oh, Shahid" (from inside
her voice is light), "could you light the candles, please?"

"Come back out, the ship is close." Moths, one by one,
dive into the light, dive deep to catch the light,
then return to keep the halo. Ship, what ghost

keeps you moving north? Your light is pouring flames
down your sides—yet all the sea keeps dark. What waits
for you beyond—seas and continents erased

from every map? The halo thickens. Yet what
keeps the sky untouched, so dark? She comes outside.
"Do you like the wine? I bought it years ago."

"It is the best ever." When I next look out
("Nothing lasts, of course"), the ship has disappeared.
The dark completes itself. What light now strikes us?

"Look, the phosphorus." It streaks the shore, it shines
green, bottle green, necklace darkened round the shore
where we now are walking by Time's stray wreckage

(broken planks, black glass) while the waves, again,
repeat each rumor the sea, out there, denies—
chilled necklaces, lost continents, casks of wine.

Issue 158, 2001

Lawrence Raab

⚭

Why It Often Rains in the Movies

Because so much consequential thinking
happens in the rain. A steady mist
to recall departures, a bitter downpour
for betrayal. As if the first thing
a man wants to do when he learns his wife
is sleeping with his best friend, and has been
for years, the very first thing
is *not* to make a drink, and drink it,
and make another, but to walk outside
into bad weather. It's true
that the way we look doesn't always
reveal our feelings. Which is a problem
for the movies. And why somebody has to smash
a mirror, for example, to show he's angry
and full of self-hate, whereas actual people
rarely do this. And rarely sit on benches
in the pouring rain to weep. Is he wondering
why he didn't see it long ago? Is he wondering
if in fact he did, and lied to himself?
And perhaps she also saw the many ways
he'd allowed himself to be deceived. In this city
it will rain all night. So the three of them
return to their houses, and the wife
and her lover go upstairs to bed

while the husband takes a small black pistol
from a drawer, turns it over in his hands,
then puts it back. Thus demonstrating
his inability to respond to passion
with passion. But we don't want him
to shoot his wife, or his friend, or himself.
And we've begun to suspect
that none of this is going to work out,
that we'll leave the theater feeling
vaguely cheated, just as the movie,
turning away from the husband's sorrow,
leaves him to be a man who must continue,
day after day, to walk outside into the rain,
outside and back again, since now there can be
nowhere in this world for him to rest.

C. K. Williams

From My Window

Spring: the first morning when that one true block of sweet,
    laminar, complex scent arrives
from somewhere west and I keep coming to lean on the sill,
    glorying in the end of the wretched winter.
The scabby-barked sycamores ringing the empty lot across
    the way are budded—I hadn't even noticed—
and the thick spikes of the unlikely urban crocuses have
    already broken the gritty soil.
Up the street, some surveyors with tripods are waving each
    other left and right the way they do.
A girl in a gymsuit jogged by a while ago, some kids passed,
    playing hooky, I imagine, and now the paraplegic
    Vietnam vet who lives in a half-converted warehouse
    down the block
and the friend who stays with him and seems to help him
    out come weaving towards me, their battered
    wheelchair lurching uncertainly from one edge of the
    sidewalk to the other.
I know where they're going—to the "Legion"; once, when I
    was putting something out, they stopped,
both drunk that time, too, both reeking—it wasn't ten
    o'clock—and we chatted for a bit.
I don't know how they stay alive—on benefits most likely. I
    wonder if they're lovers.

They don't look it. Right now, in fact, they look a wreck,
        careening haphazardly along.
contriving as they reach beneath me to dip a wheel from the
        curb so that the chair skewers, teeters,
tips, and they both tumble, the one slowly, almost gracefully
        sliding in stages from his seat,
his expression hardly marking it, the other staggering over
        him, spinning heavily down, to lie on the asphalt, his
        mouth working, his feet shoving weakly and fruitlessly
        against the curb.
In the storefront office on the corner, Reed and Son, Real
        Estate, have come to see the show:
gazing through the golden letters of their name, they're not,
        at least, thank god, laughing.
Now the buddy, grabbing at a hydrant, gets himself erect
        and stands there for a moment, panting.
Now he has to lift the other one, who lies utterly still, a
        forearm shielding his eyes from the sun.
He hauls him partly upright, then hefts him almost all the
        way into the chair but a dangling foot
catches a support-plate, jerking everything around so that he
        has to put him down, set the chair to rights and hoist
        him again and as he does he jerks the grimy jeans right
        off him.
No drawers, shrunken, blotchy thighs; under the thick white
        coils of belly blubber the poor, blunt pud, tiny,
        terrified, retracted, is almost invisible in the sparse
        genital hair,
then his friend pulls his pants up, he slumps wholly back as
        though he were, at last, to be let be,
and the friend leans against the cyclone fence, suddenly
        staring up at me as though he'd known
all along that I was watching and I can't help wondering if
        he knows that in the winter, too,
I watched, the night he went out to the lot and walked,
        paced rather, almost ran, for how many hours

It was snowing, the city in that holy silence, the last we have,
    when the storm takes hold,
and he was making patterns that I thought at first were
    circles then realized made a figure eight,
what must have been to him a perfect symmetry but which,
    from where I was, shivered, bent,
ad lay on its side: a warped, unclear infinity, slowly, as the
    snow came faster, going out.
Over and over again, his head lowered to the task, he
    slogged the path he'd blazed but the race was lost, his
    prints were filling faster than he made them now and I
    looked away,
up across the skeletal trees to the tall center-city buildings,
    some, though it was midnight,
with all their offices still gleaming, their scarlet warning-
    beacons signaling erratically
against the thickening flakes, their smouldering auras
    softening portions of the dim, milky sky.
In the morning, nothing; every trace of him effaced, all the field
    pure white, its surface glittering, the dawn,
    glancing from its glaze, oblique, relentless, unadorned.

Jamaica Kincaid

⬥

What I Have Been Doing Lately

What I have been doing lately: I was lying in bed and the doorbell rang. I ran downstairs. Quick. I opened the door. There was no one there. I stepped outside. Either it was drizzling or there was a lot of dust in the air and the dust was damp. I stuck out my tongue and the drizzle or the damp dust tasted like government-school ink. I looked north. I looked south. I decided to start walking north. While walking north I decided that I didn't have any shoes on my feet and that is why I was walking so fast. While walking north I looked up and saw the planet Venus and said, "It must be almost morning." I saw a monkey in a tree. The tree had no leaves. I said, "Aa, monkey. Must look at that. A monkey." I walked for I don't know how long before I came up to a big body of water. The big body of water was blue and silver and rippled and looked as if it had been a painting painted by a woman. I wanted to get across it but I couldn't swim. I wanted to get across it but it would take me years to build a boat. I wanted to get across it but it would take me I didn't know how long to build a bridge. Years passed and then one day, feeling like it, I got into my boat and rowed across. When I got to the other side it was noon and my shadow was small and fell parallel to me. I set out on a path that stretched out straight ahead of me. I passed a house and a dog was sitting on the verandah but looked the other way when it saw me coming. I passed a goat eating green grass in a pasture but the goat looked the other way when it saw me coming. I walked and I walked but I couldn't tell if I walked a long time because my feet didn't feel as if they would drop off. I turned around to look behind me to see what I had left behind but nothing was familiar. Instead of the straight path, I saw hills. Instead of the green grass in a pasture, I saw tall flowering trees. I looked up and the sky was without clouds and seemed near as if it were the ceiling in my house and if I stood on a chair I could touch it with the tips of my fingers. I turned around and looked ahead of me again. A deep hole had opened up in front of me. I looked in but the hole was so deep and so dark that I couldn't see the bottom. I thought, What's down there?, so on purpose I fell in. I fell and I fell, over and over as if I were an old suitcase. On the sides of the deep hole I could see things written but perhaps it was in a foreign language because I couldn't read them. Still I fell, for I don't know how long. As I fell I began to see that I didn't like the way falling made me feel. Falling made me feel sick and I missed all the people I had loved. I said, I don't want to fall anymore and I reversed myself. I was standing again on the edge of the deep hole. I looked at the deep hole and I said, You can close up now and it did. I walked some more without knowing distance, I only knew that I passed through days and nights, I only know that I passed through rain and shine, light and darkness. I was never thirsty and I felt no pain. Looking at the horizon I made a joke for myself: I said, "The earth has thin lips" and I laughed. Looking at the horizon again, I saw a lone figure coming towards me but I wasn't frightened because I was sure it was my mother. As I got closer to the figure I could see that it wasn't my mother but still I wasn't frightened because I could see that it was a woman.

When I got closer to this woman I saw that I had never seen her face before so I looked hard at it because what if I saw it again. When this woman got closer to me she looked at me hard and then she threw up her hands and I realized that she had seen me before because she said, "It's you. Just look at that. It's you. And just what it is you have been doing lately?"

I could have said, "A school of fish, though each of them completely different, swam together aimlessly."

I could have said, "A number of men, some bald, some wearing wigs, attended a boxing match."

I could have said, "A pack of dogs, tired from chasing each other all over town, slept in the moonlight."

Instead I said, What I have been doing lately: I was lying in bed on my back, my hands drawn up, my fingers interlaced lightly at the nape of my neck. Someone rang the doorbell. I went downstairs and opened the door but there was no one there. I stepped outside. Either it was drizzling or there was a lot of dust in the air and the dust was damp. I stuck out my tongue and the drizzle or the damp dust tasted like government-school ink. I looked north and I looked south. I started walking north. While walking north I wanted to move fast, so I removed the shoes from my feet. While walking north I looked up and saw the planet Venus and I said, "If the sun went out it would be eight minutes before I would know it." I saw a monkey sitting in a tree that had no leaves and I said, "A monkey. Just look at that. A monkey." So I picked up a stone and I threw it at the monkey. The monkey seeing the stone quickly moved out of its way. Three times I threw a stone at the monkey and three times it moved away. Then the fourth time I threw the stone the monkey caught it and then threw it back at me. The stone struck me on my forehead and over my right eye, making a deep gash. The gash healed immediately but now the skin on my forehead felt false to me. I walked for I don't know how long before I came to a big body of water. The big body of water was blue and silver and rippled and looked as if it had been a painting painted by a woman. I wanted to get across so when the boat came I paid my fare. When I got to the other side I saw a lot of people sitting on the beach and they were having a picnic. They were the most beautiful people I had ever seen. Everything about them was black and shiny. Their skin was black and shiny. Their shoes were black and shiny. Their hair was black and shiny. The clothes they wore were black and shiny. I could hear them laughing and chatting and I said, I would like to be with these people, so I started to walk towards them, but when I got up close to them I saw that they weren't at a picnic and they weren't beautiful and they weren't chatting and laughing. All around me was black mud and the people all looked as if they had been made up out of the black mud. I looked up and saw that the sky seemed far away and nothing I could stand on would make me able to touch it with my fingertips. I thought, If only I could get out of this, so I started to walk. I must have walked for a long time because my feet hurt and felt as if they would drop off. I thought, If only just around the bend I would see my house and inside my house I would find my bed freshly made at that, and in the kitchen I would find my mother or anyone else that I loved making me a custard. I thought, If only it was a Sunday and I was sitting in a church and I had just heard someone sing a psalm. I sat down because I wanted to see myself but then I couldn't find a mirror and that made me sad. I felt so sad that I rested my head on my knees and smoothed my own head. I felt so sad I couldn't imagine feeling any other way again. So I said, I don't like this. I don't want to do this anymore. And I went back to lying in bed, just before the doorbell rang.

Issue 82, 1981

Billy Collins

※

On Turning Ten

The whole idea of it makes me feel
like I'm coming down with something,
something worse than any stomach ache
or the headaches I get from reading in bad light—
a kind of measles of the spirit,
a mumps of the psyche,
or a disfiguring chicken pox of the soul.

You tell me it is too early to be looking back,
but that is because you have forgotten
the perfect simplicity of being one
and the beautiful complexity introduced by two.
But I can lie on my bed and remember every digit.
At four I was an Arabian wizard.
I could make myself invisible
by drinking a glass of milk a certain way.
At seven I was a soldier, at nine a prince.

But now I am mostly at the window
watching the late afternoon light.
Back then it never fell so solemnly
against the side of my tree house,

and my bicycle never leaned against the garage
as it does today,
all the dark blue speed drained out of it.

WAITING ROOMS

Charles D'Ambrosio

⌗

Open House

The last time I'd seen my father he behaved like one of those wolf-boys, those kids suckled and reared in the wild by animals, and I was never sure, during the ten confusing minutes I stood on the lawn outside the house, whether or not he recognized me. The security chain on the back door remained slotted. Inside, through the crack, he asked me when I was going to relinquish my disease, which made me think either he was speaking rhetorically or confusing me with my brother Miles, who is schizophrenic and lives in a halfway. Then he seemed to have a moment of lucidity and called me a loser for dropping out of college. He had trouble breathing and rasped and swore like someone twitched by demons on a downtown corner. All the flowers, in the hanging baskets, in the clay pots, in the whiskey barrel, were dead and hissing dryly in the wind, so it was true, apparently, that he had watered the garden with gasoline. He gasped, he yelled, he mixed the latinate with potty talk, calling my sisters complicitous cunts and my mother a vituperative bitch. His shouting had always had the effect of diminishing me, the sheer volume of it taking away the ground I stood on, for it would sound as if he were screaming across the country or into the past, to someone, at any rate, who was not present, and the longer I remained there, listening, the more invisible I felt. He had a certain emotional vigor that turned his head purple, and all during that most recent visit his head was purple. When I was a kid he'd put that purple head in my face and grab my jaw and tell me, "If you were me you'd be dead because my father

273

ould have killed you." Driving away, I had that feeling, of echoes within echoes.

Certain he was finally and forever crazy, and in need of professional help, I called his shrink, Dr. Headberry, but that poor, harassed pill-dispenser had been fired, or dismissed, and then, about a week later, my father tried to take his suffering public. He came to church dressed in his version of sackcloth and ashes—tin pants, snake boots, a wool coat with suede ovals at the elbows and a plaid cap with foam earflaps. These things had long ago been banished to hooks in the garage, and smelled, I knew, of motor oil and grass clippings and dusty, forgotten fabrics that have gone damp and dried, then gone damp again and dried again, end-lessly over the years. He'd locked away his guns after my brother Jackie (as my father liked to say) sucked a barrel—shoved a twelve-gauge Moss-berg back in his tonsil area and opened his skull against the bedroom wall. While both my older brothers were evidently fucked up, I, as the baby of the family, was luckily buffered by my four sisters. If it wasn't for them, I knew I'd be way more of a mental clodhopper than I was, or dead or crazy like my brothers. Karen, Lucy, Meg and especially Roxy, they all had this special way, this oddball interest in good places to paddle ca-noes, and herb remedies, and parks where you could take safe walks in the dark, and sardonyx and black fire opals, and weird healing practices, and crow feathers and chips of eggshells, and numerology, and playing records backwards, and food that didn't come out of a can or box. My fa-ther thought they were witches. Roxy carried a bull thistle in a tea infuser chained around her neck. The Salish believed thistles would ward off back luck, and the Scots believed they would keep away the enemy. Roxy gave me a thistle of my own and once she gave me a pomegranate. I'd never seen one before, and I was shocked that someone could think of me, sitting downstairs in Jackie's room, on Jackie's old bed, and bring me a gift out of nowhere, and for no reason. A pomegranate. *Out of nowhere, and for no reason!* Isn't it perfect, she asked, and it was.

I watched my father from across the aisle. He knelt in a pew with his head bowed, and his hands hung limply over the backrest as though he'd been clamped into a pillory. Lawyers for both sides had called me, asking if I'd testify if the divorce went to trial, but I had no idea what

I'd say if I were being deposed. He looked drunk and sleepy and wired, and also penitent in this odd, remembered way, as if he were still trying to fool some buzzard-backed nun from his childhood. He wiped sweat from his brow with a wrinkled hanky, mopped the back of his neck, held the thing like a flag of truce as he folded his hands for prayer. During the offertory he began crying or weeping—weeping, I guess, because there was something stagey about it. He beat the butt of his palm against his head, lifted his eyes to the cross, and said, "Oh God, oh God, my God."

"I wish I could be crucified," my father had told me over the phone, the day after he was served papers. "That's really the only way to settle these things."

Despite the lunacy of pitting his agony against the agony of Jesus Christ, I now decided he wasn't crazy. This was calculated. He'd come to menace and harass my mother. For years church had been her only bastion and retreat and he'd come as a trespasser to violate it, to pollute its purity and calm, to take it away from her, and make it ugly like everything else in our life, and that's what I'd tell the lawyers. I was no disciple or defender of the church and no big fan of the snobs who weekly attended mass. With its pale green walls and polished pine benches and high windows of distorted glass it seemed a place for lame rummage sales, a place where fussy old men sold boxes of yesterday's bestsellers, soup ladles and wide neckties. The young seemed old, and the old seemed ancient—widowers in pleated pants who had retired into a sallow golden age, bereft men with nothing to do but sip their pensions like weak tea in a waiting room whose only door opened on death. And the women—some so frantically dedicated to a pre-Vatican II universe they still wore hats within the nave, and if they'd forgotten a scarf or hat, they'd unclasp their purses and find a Kleenex and bobby-pin that to their hair. Arranged in the pews these women with toilet paper on their heads looked like planted rows of petunias. Yet that Saturday, as my father crudely interrupted the service, I considered the possibility that the heart and soul of any faith is absurdity, and that these ridiculous, otherworldly women, with their silly gestures, might just be saints.

The mass stopped and everyone turned from the altar and stared at him. Everyone—the Greys, the Hams, the Wooleys, Mrs. Kayhew and the Grands and the Stones. Also the priest, the altar boys. It was a caesura that filled with whisperings of disbelief and doubt, and only my mother, who was the eucharistic minister and sat in the sanctuary, remained quiet and calm. She laced her hands together and set them like a dead bird in her lap. Sitting in her chair, icily withdrawn, she looked as she did when I was a child and dinner was not going well, evenings when my father occupied the head of the table like a cigar-store Indian and silence settled in our bones and we could hear little else but the tink-tink of fork tines and the sound of chewing and it was painful to swallow. Those nights I wouldn't eat the hard things, the raw carrots or breadsticks, for fear of making a noise, and my mother wouldn't eat at all. My mother liked to say that silence had made her a very slender woman, and it was true, she was slim and at sixty still looked girlish in blue jeans.

The priest drank wine from the chalice and, wiping the rim, held the cup to my mother's lips. He leaned toward her, whispered something in her ear, and she nodded her head deliberately. Together they stepped down to the communion rail. My father waited until the line dwindled down, then lifted himself awkwardly, stumbling up the aisle alone. I saw Mrs. Grand lay a hand on her husband, restraining him. My father stood, swaying a little, before my mother. Later, after my mother returned from her trip to Texas, she would tell me it was not her place to judge, and certainly not her role as the morning's eucharistic minister. Her faith gave her the ability not to judge anything, even movies. To me, as an outsider, and someone without any faith at all, the scene at the communion rail seemed a show of profound strength, but my father, later, would say he only went up there to prove what a chickenshit she was. The church was dead quiet. My mother lifted the eucharist as you would a bright, promised coin, holding it slightly above eye level, and my father looked up. "Body and Blood of Christ," she said, and he responded, "Amen," and then she very carefully set the host on his waiting tongue.

After the blessing my mother left the sanctuary and knelt in the front pew. The door in the vestibule had been jammed open with a rubber wedge and a cool wet wind circulated through church, stirring the lace edge of the altar cloth and the sprigs of white gladiolas in their fluted gold standards. Her friends filed out, and cars left the lot. She remained kneeling on the padded hassock and prayed with her eyes shut and with her eyes shut she heard, from the vestibule, the ruffle of the priest's soutane as the black skirt swept the floor, and then the hurried, heavy steps of my father. She remained still and continued to pray.

"She denied me and she denied me," my father said to the priest. "She denied me even the simplest things a husband requires."

The priest gestured helplessly toward the confessionals—the penalty boxes, my father called them, those two upright coffins in the corner of the church. Probably it crossed the priest's mind that the formality of this arrangement might help contain my father's apparent madness. A closed door, at the very least, might muffle his complaint. My father didn't often go out in public because he thought people didn't like him, and when he did socialize, out of nervousness and excessive drinking, he was a terrible gasbag, and most people did try to avoid him, and so the fact that he'd come to church, and made such an awful ruckus, now swayed me back in the direction of the idea that he must be crazy. I was about to step in, but the priest waved me away.

"Even bedtime pleasures."

The priest said, "I'm sure there's more to the story."

"Don't tell me about stories," my father responded. "Calumny is one of the seven deadly sins."

"No it isn't," the priest said, firmly.

My father ignored him, shouting at my mother.

"How dare you judge me! You call yourself Christians!"

The altar boy returned to snuff the candles and collect the cruets of wine and water. My mother could smell the curls of black smoke rising from the burnt wicks. With her eyes closed, she felt as though she could lift herself up, she could rise away and soar, as she said her prayers, on the whispered fluttering wingbeat of words, away, away, away . . . while my father stared after her from what then seemed a lifetime of hatred. She did not move. Her skin was pale to the point of appearing blue. Her fingers, interlaced, were delicate and weak. She was as still in her pew as the pale crucified Christ floating high above the sanctuary, but she was gone.

"Goddamn you to hell," my father screamed on his way out the door.

I hadn't dropped out of school. In early March the bursar asked me to withdraw until the outstanding balance on my tuition bill was paid. I stuffed a rucksack with clothes and left campus that night. I was relieved. My lisp made me quiet and shy, embarrassed at the sound of myself, and also something of a hostile shit. People gathered in their dorms, smoked bong hits under batik bedspreads that breathed and endlessly analyzed their families. I couldn't get into it. The soft sibilance of my voice didn't square with what I had to say, and I felt paralyzed by a pressure, a sense that if I started talking there was a good chance I'd never stop. To cure this, or get around it, I had signed up for a writing course, but dropped it when I couldn't figure out the economy of a story, the lifeboat ethics of it—who got pitched in with the sharks, who got rescued. By the end of January I had stopped attending classes, and only turned in the written assignments, and sometime in February I pulled the curtains and lay in bed for a week.

I left school without telling anyone, in part because as a rule, a policy, I never say good-bye. The night I walked off campus was quiet, I remember, that country quiet where every sound seems to have a distinct place in the world, and by the next morning I'd hitched to Altoona, Wisconsin. From there I hopped a freight train home to Seattle. Twice, as the train crossed trestles over the Yellowstone and then later over the Clark Fork, I considered jumping off to do some fishing, but the divorce was already in progress and I was convinced my father was going to destroy the contents of our house. (He did: he burned the christening dress we'd been baptized in, he tossed our photo albums.) Back in Seattle I rented a shoebox room and got a job busing tables at a restaurant owned by two lesbians I knew from day one would eventually fire me. (They did.) I spent most nights hunched over my vice, drinking beer and tying flies, filling one box with hare's ears and pheasant tails, and another with size 16 blue-winged olives and pale morning duns. My only plan in the world right then was to hop a train to Livingston, head into the park and fish the Firehole near the west end of Fountain Flats, a place that was a favorite of both Miles and Jackie. After that, after Memorial Day, I planned to take my tent and stove and live in the park all season. (Which I did, until in mid-October I woke one morning with my tent sagging like a collapsed parachute and was driven out by snow.)

The only things I wanted out of our house were Miles's old fly rod and the original fifteen and a half pages of Jackie's suicide note.

Realtor's signs had been staked into the front and side yards, and a sandwich board stood spraddled on the sidewalk. OPEN HOUSE, it said, SUNDAY, and the lead agent's name was Cynthia. My father's beat spy car was parked in the drive, the passenger door lashed shut with loops of clothesline, the landau top half-scalped, peeling back to raw metal. For weeks he'd been tailing my mother around town in this battered, rust-bitten Plymouth. Was this corny or dangerous? In the last days, as the end drew near, he'd thrown her down the stairs, grated her arm with a grapefruit knife—but the end had been drawing near regularly for twenty years; my entire life, and the tragic end of it all was the very rhythm of all our hearts, and if two of my sisters, Roxy and Karen, hadn't finally abducted my mother, hadn't dragged her out of the house, she would have stayed, I bet, and would still be getting chased around the house with knives and screamed at.

As the youngest of seven children, my family's history had always been my future, a past I was growing into and inheriting, a finished world, a place where the choices had been made, irrevocably. As a result I was never very interested in the riddle of heredity or the way dysteleology can become design. I arrived too late to believe any other world existed. I was fourteen when Miles started living either on Western Avenue behind the Skyway coat factory or at the V.A. or in a series of ratty halfway houses, and by now I just assumed the voices Miles heard would speak to me also. I was sixteen when Jackie killed himself. At twenty, I assumed madness would visit me, and so would suicide. I assumed they would approach quietly and hold out their hands and claim me and take me where they had taken my brothers. Miles had tried to kill himself too, driven by his voices to jump off the Aurora Bridge, but he'd survived. Frequently, obsessively, I fantasized sitting on the bridge railing and shooting myself in the head. That way in one moment I'd bring my brothers together in me. I was convinced I'd know them in that way. And my father? Would I know him? Could I even describe him? Often my father couldn't take a shit unless my mother held his hand. But I couldn't really imagine that.

I looked up, and there he was, framed in the open window of Miles's old bedroom.

"You can't come in," he shouted. "My lawyer guy said nobody can come in the house. Not you, not anybody. I'm sorry, I know it sounds stupid, but too many negative things redound in my direction."

"I came to get my stuff," I said.

"I have to insulate me totally."

He disappeared from the window and reappeared at the back door. He opened it a crack, steel chain still slotted.

"We did this last week," I said.

"You can't come in. I'm sorry, too many negative things. You're all complicitous with your mother. I didn't want this. It wasn't my idea. I wanted to work it out. There's family solutions to family problems, but this, this is appalling and obscene, it's immoral."

"I have a key," I said.

"Not anymore you don't. I changed the locks."

The back porch was lined with clay pots full of dead marigolds, woolly brown swabs on bent black stalks.

"What's wrong?" I asked.

"Wrong? Nothing's wrong except your mother's got me by the fucking balls. She's got her hooks in me, but I'm fine."

I picked up one of the clay pots and put my nose to the soil and it had the cold smell of gasoline.

"Did you pour gas on the flowers?"

"That's just more of your mother's calumny."

"I think we should call Dr. Headberry," I said.

"Headberry? I just talked with him. Headberry says I have no real problems. He's got your mother analyzed perfectly, though. It's ugly. She's got control of my life."

He was lying about Headberry, of course, and unless something happened we were going to continue having the kind of conversation that you have when there's only one seat left on the bus.

"Let me in."

"I don't understand the ugliness—the enormity of the entire process. So many hooks there—they've got control of my life."

I dropped the pot, letting it shatter on the porch, and started walking back out to my truck.

"This is against my better instinct," my father said. He closed the door and slipped the chain off. "It's against everything I know and against my lawyers's advice too."

"Thanks," I said. I nodded out toward the Realtor's sign. "There's an open house tomorrow."

"Yeah, yeah," he said. "Well, I guess you're here and you're coming in and we'll talk and maybe have a drink and then you'll leave. So let's start. Come on in."

Except for boxers drooping off his ass, he was naked. His hunting outfit was piled on a shelf in the kitchen.

He shook his head, and scratched the thick, knotted hair on his chest, then rubbed his arms, his stubbled face.

"Feel like my veins are turning into worms," he said.

"Why'd you come to church?"

"Hey, don't forget I let you in," he said. He fumbled inside his coat and pulled out a piece of paper. "I got the restraining order right here. I take it with me everywhere I go. I felt the need to talk to a priest." He scratched the pale inside of his arm, and examined the legal document. "I don't think the law applies to a church," he said. "Once you get inside you get asylum."

He returned the paper to his coat pocket and then picked up the kitchen garbage can, reached his hand in, and pushed aside newspapers, a tuna can, a melon rind.

"See?" he said.

He meant to show me a prescription bottle at the bottom of the can. I lifted it out, gave it a rattle, and held it to the light.

"There's one left," I said.

"I quit," he said. "Thirty-five years and now I've kicked 'em cold turkey."

My father never talked about his own father, and the oldest story he ever told me about himself was of the way snow whipped off Lake Erie in August of 1953, great blinding gusts and rolling drifts, the summer landscape sculpted into a sea of white. Fantastic! A miracle! Naturally, of course, it hadn't been August. He'd been hospitalized, locked up in a Cleveland sanatorium and then shocked out of his mind for six months, and it was January, the day of his release. Why, in telling me this, had he left the story in its state of confusion? Now I thought of the snow in August. At the time, electro-convulsive therapy was an experimental procedure and current thinking called for barbituates in long-term intractable cases. That, then, was science and the bold sci-fi future. My father, the day of his release, filled his prescription at a corner druggist and renewed it regularly, like his subscription to the *Wall Street Journal*, for the next thirty-five years.

"When d'you quit?"

"It's a booger, man," he said, clawing at his arms and again at the matted hair on his chest. "I tried watching TV. Then I tried taking a shower and banging my head against the wall."

"You just now tossed these," I said.

"Why the fuck do you think I'm traipsing around the house naked?" he shouted. "My clothes were driving me crazy, that's why."

"I'd like to call Headberry."

He scratched himself some more. "Worms, man. I feel like I could explode. You want a drink?"

The gin and limes and a tray of melting ice were already out on the sink counter. He fixed us two drinks and we sat at the dining table. Across the street the Grand and Wooley families walked out onto their adjoining lawns. A badminton net was strung across the property line on metal stakes. The kids, some of them my age, stood on one side, and the parents stood on the other. Everybody carried rackets and Mr.

Wooley, in chinos and a pink shirt, opened a cannister of birdies. Bill Grand said something and Bill Wooley leaned back and aimed a silent laugh at the sky.

"I hate those redundant bastards," my father commented.

"You don't even know them."

"Sure I do, you know one you know 'em all." He sipped his drink with fine relish. "Where's your mother going?"

It surprised me that he knew she was going anywhere, and I was caught off guard.

"I'm not saying," I said, and now there was a secret between us.

"She's having an affair."

"Mom? Mom's not having an affair."

"What makes you so sure?"

"Who with then?"

My father looked away, out the window. "Jesus Christ, probably." He sucked an ice cube out of his drink and bit it, spitting glassy splinters. "She's got me by the nuts."

"Hardly," I said. "You're free."

"Free? Free my ass. You know, I've never been to the rainforest—isn't that a phenomena? She's mortgaged my work effort."

For the longest time I thought this was an old bromide all fathers told their kids. Don't mortgage my work effort. No one in this house is going to mortgage my work effort. Roxy took me to the dictionary and explained. *Mort*, she said, means dead. And *gage*, she said, means security.

"That doesn't make any sense," I told him now.

"No? Okay, fine. What's up with you?"

I guessed we were going to ignore the scene at church. Somehow we had agreed to forget it.

"I had a dream about you last night."

"Other people's dreams are boring."

"I was over here, in the kitchen. You were trying to give me some medicine, like when I was a kid, with a squeeze dropper. Like liquid aspirin. But I wasn't a kid anymore. You were holding the back of my head and telling me to open my mouth. Open up, you said, and when I did, you put a gun in my mouth and kept saying, take your medicine. Take your medicine, you'll feel better."

"Goddamnit," he said.

"It's just a dream."

"Let's talk about something else. You hear the latest about Mr. Kayhew?"

"No, what?"

"You knew a blood vessel popped in his head? Up in an airplane, up there behind the curtain, first class, knowing the Kayhews. He wasn't dead, just in a coma. I heard they rented him his own apartment and he lived there in a coma."

"I didn't know."

"I'm practically there myself."

I must have made a face.

"What? I'm serious. When I die I'll be exploded to shit. People'll look in the box and say, 'Good God, what the hell killed him?'"

My dad sipped his drink again, keeping an eye on me over the lip of his glass.

"Just everything," he said, answering himself. "Anyway, Kayhew's out."

"Out?"

"He was in a coma."

"You told me that," I said. "So he's out of it now?"

"I guess. I guess you could say that. He's dead."

"That's not what people usually mean when they say someone comes out of a coma."

"Well, it's a little discussed medical fact, but dying is the other way out."

After a moment, he said, "We were friends, you know, me and Kayhew. Not great friends, but I liked him all right, and he liked me. I think he liked me. He never actually said he liked me, but—anyway, the point is, I read his obit—he was much beloved, survived by, et cetera—and only sixty-five years old. Sixty-five. That's five years older than me. You know how many days that is?"

"Do you?" I said.

"2,190," my father said. "Given my habits, I figure I've got 2,000 days left." He raised his eyebrows. "This is one of them." He shrugged. "How's your drink? You want another? I'm having another."

"I'll hold off," I said.

But he made me a drink anyway. When he returned to the table, a cigarette dangled from his lips.

"Smoking?"

"2,000 days, man. Who gives a crap?"

I left the split seeds and floating pulp of my old drink and started the new one. I held the glass to the light and the fresh gin at that moment seemed to be the clearest thing I'd ever seen in my life.

"Miles used to say certain streams were gin clear," I said, "That's how he'd describe them."

"I hate fishing."

"I was only remembering. It was just something to say."

"I've worked in insurance all my life," he said. "The actuarial tables are incredibly accurate. They'll nail you to the wall just about every time. You can read those things and then call a mortician and make an appointment. Like Jackie."

Jackie's last day, his last hour, was an obsessive concern of mine. I'd reconstructed it. I knew where he went, who he talked to, the last tape he played in his stereo ("Johnny Was," by Stiff Little Fingers). The night Jackie shot himself my mother had come into his bedroom. He was at his desk, writing. It was shortly after 8:30. He wore a green-and-gray flannel shirt, blue jeans with blown-out knees, black army boots. Jackie wouldn't turn around and face her. She went back upstairs to tell my father something was strange, that Jackie had a shotgun in his room. "I'm watching a TV show," he said, "don't interrupt me. And close the door when you leave." But that doesn't really explain. What he told my mother that night he told her every night. Without the punctuation of Jackie's death the night of November 26, and all the information I'd gathered about it, it would mean nothing. But at 4:30 in the morning, when the police lights pulsed in the graying air and a couple cops stood on the lawn discussing the case, I ran out there in my p.j.'s. "It wasn't suicide," I screamed at them. "It was murder!"

"You want a smoke?" My dad waved his pack of Pall Malls at me. He went to the kitchen and fished in the garbage can and set the tuna can between us. "No ashtrays. I quit these buggers to save money. I calculated it out that I was spending two hundred bucks a year on cigs. That was when I only made two hundred a month. A whole month's salary. So I quit."

"Where's the rug?" I asked.

I had just felt with my feet below the dining table that the oriental rug wasn't there.

"What? The rug, I don't know."

"That's weird," I said. "All my life it was under the table and now it's gone."

"Crazy, huh?"

I finished my drink, stood and said, "I'm gonna split. First I want to get some stuff."

"Stay here," my dad said. "I can't have you running around the house."

"It's my house too."

"On what piece of paper does it say this is your house?"

"There's only two things I want."

"Look, sit down. Okay? Sit down. Let's have another drink."

"I want Miles's fly rod. You don't fish and I want it."

"It's yours, you can have it. Okay? Jesus. I hate fishing. Fishing makes me feel fucking hopeless."

"And the christening dress, I want that too."

"I'm not sure where that is," my dad said.

"Crazy, huh?"

"It's fucking nuts," he said, "the way things get lost."

Out the window the Grands and Wooleys were still playing badminton in the lowering light. I could faintly hear their shouts and cries as they chased the birdie. The gray air seemed to be filling the house like rising water.

My dad said, "It's wild."

I waited for him to say what was wild, but he only looked out the window.

"What?"

"I can't make the data stand still."

My father sipped his drink meditatively and watched.

"So what's your mother doing in Texas?" he asked.

"How do you know she's going to Texas?"

"She went to the travel agent. She used our credit card to charge the ticket. That's how."

"You put on quite a show at church this afternoon."

"A show?"

I was starting to feel hazy, blurred. "Yeah, a show. You almost looked like somebody in need of pity."

I shook a Pall Mall from the pack, lit it. My dad watched the badminton game wind down. The Wooleys and the Grands seemed to be running around their lawn swatting flies. Cheers went up, moans, cries, but I could no longer see what they were chasing. It was too dark. A clock ticked in the living room and the refrigerator buzzed and a wind must have risen because behind me a branch scratched the window. A car passed.

"I'll get that stuff," I said.

"You know what the agent told me? Cynthia—that's her name, Cynthia—she told me the place had bad vibes."

"I don't get it."

"We'll have to sell below the appraised value," my dad said. "We won't get near the asking price. They all know Jackie killed himself in the basement, they know Miles is crazy, they know all that shit."

"They? Who's they?"

"People." He looked at me. He smiled, grimly. "Do what you have to do. I'm having another drink. This gin is something, huh?"

Our basement was a museum housing a collection of all the usual artifacts. In bins and racks, we had baseball bats, broken skis, tennis rackets with warped guts, wingless gliders, golf clubs, aquariums, hula hoops, a bowling ball and several orange life jackets my dad had purchased at a lawn sale, along with an old O'Brien water ski and a gas can, all with the idea, a very sudden, impulsive idea, that he'd buy a boat, too. For weeks after we saw boats gleaming in showrooms or parked on trailers in someone's driveway or heading out to sea or docked at a slip in the Union Bay Marina. I don't know what happened to that idea, but here were four faded life jackets, hooked on tenpenny nails. Along a rickety wooden shelf were cases of canned peas and corn and thirty-weight oil, a box of powdered milk, several bottles of novitiate wine—bulk items of a big family. In boxes were tools, tools to fix everything, from loose chair legs to leaky faucets. C-clamps, crimpers, a circular saw. With a tool in his hand, my dad was no better than a caveman. He couldn't fix anything. He usually ended up clubbing whatever wouldn't work, breaking it worse. But he loved tools, he strolled through hardware stores handling trouble lights and blue hacksaw blades with the enthusiasm other people might reserve for the Louvre.

I found what I was looking for: a polished cherry wood case, narrow and about two and a half feet long. I brought it upstairs and turned on a light. I popped the hasp, and opened the box. The inside was lined with crushed velvet, and hand-carved bridges at either end held the rod in place. I lifted the butt end out, cradled the sanded cork in my hand. The cane was pale blond, unmarred by knots or coarse grain, and the lacquer, gin clear, seemed only to draw out the bamboo's simplicity; the reel seat was rosewood, the fittings nickel-plated; the guides gleamed; the ferrules were wrapped in blue and green thread, winding in a spiral pattern. I heard the ice in my dad's glass clink, and then he was there, looking at the rod over my shoulder. I turned the rod in my hand. Miles had called us all down to his workbench in the basement the day he signed it. He used a Chinese brush from which he'd clipped all but a single horsehair. I remember watching him do it, the way he held one hand steady with the other while, miraculously, his name looped across the cane in a single stroke.

"That's art, man. That's a piece of work," I said.

"Not bad for a crazy fuck," my dad said.

"He wasn't crazy then." I angled the rod in the light. "It's just the opposite of how he is now. It's simple."

"Have another drink?"

"No thanks," I said.

From the kitchen, Dad said, "You planning a trip?"

"Wyoming," I said. "I'm gonna live in the park all season."

"That's stupid," Dad said. "Here's your gin."

"I said no. What's stupid about it? I go there every year."

"What about school?"

"What about it?"

"Don't look at me that way," my father said. "I'm broke."

"Anyway, it's where I tossed Jackie's ashes," I said. After he'd been cremated, we were each given an envelope of ashes, just a pinch—you'd throw more oregano in a pot of spaghetti sauce.

"Where?"

"Well, you've never been there, so it's hard to describe."

"Hey guy," my father said, "it's good to see you."

"You're drunk."

"Sure. Been drunk. I don't think I've talked to anyone for ten days, two weeks."

"You're talking pretty good tonight."

"I guess I am. Imagine if you were God and had to listen to all this."

And then I must have said yes. I should have gone back to the shoe-box, and there were four or five opportunities to say I'd had enough, I got what I wanted, see you. But the evening kept opening up, wider and wider, accepting every vague word and half-assed idea. Everything was finding a place; there was a room at every inn. The night became like a fairy tale in which every juncture is answered with a yes, and the children hold hands and merrily march down the dark trail into a furnace. The gin ran clear, the tuna can was full of stubbed Pall Malls, I was drunk and awake and my dad was drunk and awake, and the space was there, yawning, and something had to happen.

"Tell me where your mother is?" Dad was saying.

"No way," I insisted.

"Tell me."

"Okay," I said. I squinted a teasing look across the table. "I'll trade you."

"You already got the fly rod."

"I want the original of Jackie's letter."

"Can't do it. I don't know where it is."

"Oh well—"

"All right."

"Get it," I said.

"You don't trust me?"

"Oh, I don't think so."

When he brought the letter back I checked to make sure all fifteen and a half pages were there, licking my fingers and counting them like bills.

Then I said, "She's gone to see an angel."

"An angel, huh?"

"In the bark of a tree, a cottonwood. In the middle of a junkyard somewhere in Texas. There's been reports, so she's going to see for herself."

"It's been in the papers. I've read about that angel." He lit a cigarette, waved the smoke from his face. "Hey, we got coffee stains in the carpet look like angels. We got angels in this house."

A bus passed out front. An old habit, I looked through the window to see if any of my brothers or sisters were coming home.

"Your mother was never anything but a whore. She got me fired off my job. All slander."

"The reason you were fired is because no one likes you. You're an asshole—that's actually a quote."

"Who said that? Markula?"

"I'm not telling."

"I got something else to give you," my father said.

He disappeared again and when he returned to the table he set the shotgun and a box of shells in front of me.

I said, "That's the gun."

"Cops took this as evidence," my father said. "Suicide's a crime. Evidence? Heigh-ho—but I got it back."

In the garage we gathered up gunnysacks, some twine and a flashlight, and loaded everything into the Plymouth.

"Me and Miles used to do this," my dad said, as we drove away.

Again I thought he was confusing me with my brother. "I'm not too big on guns," I reminded him.

"Neither was Jackie. You took after him on that."

I thought there was a joke in there somehow, but I couldn't find it.

"A gun doesn't mean anything."

"Huh?"

"Take a caveman," my father said. "You put a short-arm of some sort, a .38 or what have you, you put it on the ground with some other stuff, like a rock and a sewing machine and a banana. Ordinary things. What's the caveman going to do? Huh? He's not going to look at the banana and think, Oh, this'd be good on cornflakes. He's not going to take the sewing machine and stitch up a tutu. And he's not going to look at the gun and think, Maybe I'll blow my head off. You see what I'm saying."

I thought I did, and then I was sure I didn't.

"I'm nearly broke," my dad said.

"No you're not."

"I thought I'd be living with more dignity by this time, but it's not turning out that way."

"You're lying," I said again. It wasn't an accusation, more like a statement. We were stopped at a four-way intersection. My father curled his hands tightly around the wheel to steady them.

"Maybe I should do the Jackie thing," he said.

"Fuck you," I said. The words just popped out of my mouth, like a champagne cork. Now my hands were trembling, and I put them in my coat pocket. "Don't ever say that again."

"Why are you so pissed all of a sudden?"

"Let's just go. Let's get those birds."

I've read and reread Jackie's letter to us, I've searched the final paragraph for a summation. Now I had the original. The letter is long. In it he lists the things he likes: wolves and trains, the Skagit River, coasting a bike down Market Street in Ballard. He talks about my mom, Dad, my four sisters and Miles, but at no time does he mention me. Toward the last few pages I sense a creepy mortmain, as if my father's hand is folded over his, guiding the pen across the page, line by line, word by word. Is he trying to say something about himself, or about my father? I look at the last word and think of the moment when he put down the pen and picked up the gun and pulled the trigger. How much time passed? Had he been thinking it over? To pull the trigger he would have used the same finger he used to press the pen against the paper. What went on in that space? Between the pen and the gun?

Under the freeway we found a cement ledge. A sleepy cooing came from the recess, the occasional flutter of beating wings. It sounded like a nursery at nap time.

"You stay down here," Dad said. "I'll hand the birds to you."

He chinned himself onto the ledge, grunting loudly. He wiped shit off his hands, and I passed him the flashlight. He aimed the beam at the birds, a row of them squatting along the ledge. The first bird was mottled gray and brown with beady eyes like drops of melted chocolate. Its eyes remained wide open, stunned and tranced, staring into the beam, unable to move or turn away from the white light. Dad stroked the bird's throat gently. "Come to papa," he said, and when he'd soothed it somewhat he grabbed it by the neck and passed it down to me. I could feel its heart beating in my hand. I slipped the bird into the gunnysack. The pigeon flopped around, trying to orient itself. Dad jacklit another and another. Some were white, others black as crows. After we'd bagged five birds I tied off the first sack with twine and started a new one. Dad handed me five more paralyzed pigeons and then jumped down.

"That ought to do it," he said. He brushed molted gray feathers from his face, from his arms. "Look at that," he said.

The sacks were alive with confused pigeons, two blobs rolling down the hill. You could see the birds struggling to take off, stupidly beating against the burlap. We ran after them, two drunks at a pigeon rodeo, each grabbing a sack.

We put the birds in the backseat of the car. I picked a downy feather from my father's ear.

"You still pissed?" he said.

"Don't make hollow threats."

"You think it was hollow?"

"I've heard it before."

"Feel like it was just yesterday I was driving around the woods with the Beauty Queen, trying to get my hand up her skirt."

My father laughed. The Beauty Queen was my mother. She'd been Miss Spanaway in 1954.

"Well," he said, gesturing broadly with a sweep of the bottle, "I did. Seven kids. One dead, one crazy. Four girls who don't want a damn thing to do with me. Then you. What the fuck's wrong with you, I wonder?"

"We going?"

The pigeons were insane, jumping around inside the sacks. A crazy burlap aviary. My father got out of the car, took the sacks, and spun the birds in circles. When he put them back in the seat, they were quiet.

"You're the only one left. You'll bury me," my father said. "You'll write my obituary."

Generally my father was what people call a paper killer. He drove to a firing range and clamped on ear protection and stood in a port lined with blue baffle shield and shot two-bit targets. Bull's-eyes, black silhouettes, now and then the joke target of a dictator's face in profile. At the end of an afternoon of shooting, he'd roll up and rubber band his targets, tacking the best to a wall in his den, like trophies. "You shoot against your old self," he'd told me. Of the boys, it was my crazy brother Miles who enjoyed guns. Jackie hated them. The first and only time he'd ever fired a gun, the barrel was in his mouth. Obviously, you don't need to be a sharpshooter to kill yourself. Even before Jackie, I'd never liked guns. My father sensed this hesitance, and took me out to the woods, trying to teach me to see things and then trying to get me to shoot them out of the trees. Squirrels, robins. The only time I'd actually fired a gun with him was at a gravel pit. He stood behind me and watched as I leveled his bolt-action .22 at a row of pop cans. He calmly gave me directions, but I quickly aimed high and pinched off a round, missing, then chambering another round and missing again, spent shells skittering at my feet in brassy flashes, until I dry-fired and knew the gun was empty. I was ten years old, and it was the first time I'd ever felt like I was not in control of myself. I'd been feeling the urge to turn around and shoot my father.

It was near dawn when we parked at the gravel pit. I hadn't been there in ten years and it was now abandoned, a maze of packed dirt roads, each ending in a cul-de-sac of bitten earth. I carried the pigeons and Dad carried the gun. The sky was just beginning to pale with a metallic dawn light outlining a dark fringe of trees. We sat down.

"Can't drink like I used to," Dad said.

I raised an eyebrow. "How'd you used to?"

"I didn't mean I don't drink like I used to," he said. "Just I can't." He coughed up a laugh, breathing in short, swift rasps. He lit a cigarette. "My lawyer call you?"

"He did."

"You gonna testify?"

I thought about it, briefly, as shapes in the gravel pit took on solidity. People were using it as a dump. Washing machines, the odd chair, boxes and lawnbags, bent and twisted gutters, a suitcase.

"I wouldn't let it go to trial," I said.

"You mean I don't have a chance?"

I imagined my father's life caught up in the snare of the law, the courts, in the web of family history, in all those things whose severest weapon is consistency, and I knew he would not fare well.

"I'd settle."

My father nodded. He pointed the shotgun at the gunnysack of pigeons.

"Better than skeet," he said.

"I'll release them."

"You don't want to shoot? You want, you can go first."

I looked at the gun, resting across my father's lap. I knew no magic inhered in the piece itself, that it was just a shotgun, but even though I could convince myself that the thing housed no resident bogey, I wouldn't touch it.

"I'll just do the birds," I said.

I carried both sacks about fifty yards away, intensely aware that my back was turned to my father. A spot at the base of my neck grew hot. My heart beat in a way that made me conscious of it. I untied the knot on the first sack and gently cradled a pigeon in my palm. I covered its eyes and looked at my father. He nodded. I spun the bird in circles, round and round, and then I set it down. It fell over. The next few moments were kind of vaudevillian. The pigeon flapped its wings, raising a cloud of dust, scooting sideways over the ground, pratfalling, and then it took flight, rising drunkenly in the air, executing a few goofy loops and turns. By instinct the pigeon appeared to know it was supposed to fly, but couldn't figure out the up and down of it. It smashed to the ground, leaden, then rose again. Before it could gain equilibrium and fly level, I heard the deep percussive blast of the shotgun, and the pigeon jerked back, propelled by the impact, and fell like a limp dishrag from the sky. Immediately I grabbed another bird. Its heart raced in my palm. Dad nodded. I spun it around and released it, watching as it rose so far and then exploded in a flakburst of gray feathers. Each time, for the moment I held the bird, I could feel its life, the heart and the breastbones and the soft cooing in its throat, but there really was no moment of decision on my part, no hesitation, as I released the bird. I tossed another into the air, watching it struggle wildly against falling, then rise erratically, lifting above the trees, and get blown out of the sky.

"Take a shot," my dad said.

"No thanks," I said.

He came to me, and we sat down again. He drank from the gin and passed the bottle.

"This used to be open country out here," he said. "But I think we're inside the city limits now. I think we're in the suburbs."

I took a drink, and said, "You know the christening dress? All of us were baptized in that. Mom was, and grandpa too."

"Yeah, so?"

"Where is it?"

"She'll get an annullment. Everything to nothing in the eyes—" I interrupted.

"But we'll never see it again, right?"

When he didn't answer, I said, "Let's head out."

"There's one more pigeon left."

I folded open the sack and let the bird go. It walked around, head bobbing, among the dead ones.

My father, on Thorazine, always became childlike. He walked in slanted, headlong, stumbling bursts that ended when he smacked into walls or collapsed in a heap on the carpet. He hid in closets, he broke his head open falling down stairs. We cleaned up after him, we mopped piss off the bathroom floor, we helped my mother wipe his muddied ass. At dinner, we wrapped a bedsheet around his neck and spoonfed him pureed carrots and canned spaghetti and pale green peas we mooshed with a fork. We fought over the chance to feed him, played airplane games with the zooming spoon. He babbled and sputtered and sometimes through the Thorazine fog the rudiments of language bubbled up. Once, while the nine of us sat at the table, silently eating our dinner, he began to mumble, and we all leaned forward to listen. "Fuck you," he said. "Fuck you. Fuck you. Fuck you." My mother pushed another spoonful of mashed potato in his mouth, and it burbled back out in a fuck you.

As the youngest I was never left alone with my father, never left to care for him by myself—except once, and briefly. Everyone was out and I remember the strangeness of being in the house alone with him. I asked him, did he want to watch TV? When he was crazy, the television ran constantly. I flipped the dial from sports to cartoons to network coverage of the last lunar mission, Apollo 17. Then he spoke—it was a miracle, like hearing a child's first words. He wanted me to go through the house and gather up all the sunglasses I could find. Despite his ongoing bouts of insanity, he was still my father, no crazier than the dads in the Old Testament, and I obeyed him. I thought it was a game. I tore through the house. "Thataboy," he shouted whenever I found a new pair of glasses. I gathered up Jackie's wire rims, a pair of aviators and blocky tortoise shells, the girls' red and yellow and green plastic Disney glasses. Ski goggles, protective eyeware. My father arranged them on the floor, shuffled them one way, then another way, and then he asked, "Who do you think we can call about these glasses?" I said I didn't think there was anyone. And he said, "Well, I guess we're sitting ducks then. I guess there's no hope. Isn't there anybody we can call?"

This memory came back to me at the open house. My father had put on his good suit and Sunday shoes but perversely decided not to wear his glasses. Immediately he looked lost. He stumbled around the house, filling shallow dishes with salted nuts, setting out a card table with potato chips and pretzels and pop. There were so many things missing from the house—things like family photos and favorite sympathy cards, things that had earned their places on the wall, on the fireplace mantel, simply by virtue of having always been there—that my father seemed spatially confused and kept rearranging his dishes of nuts, putting them down on the coffee table, then the end table, then setting them back in their original spots.

"Sit down," I said.

"I'm not supposed to be here," my father said. "Cynthia asked me to vacate for a while."

Cynthia, the agent, was openly miffed when she saw my father. She introduced prospective buyers to me, and then quickly moved on. I tagged along. She had a proprietary air as she showed the first few strangers through the house. She took a young, childless couple upstairs and showed them the master bedroom. She stood by the window and pointed to the view, the long sloping hill, the mountains in the west, offering this vista as a possibility for the future. We toured the kitchen, the living room. Then we all went downstairs, to the basement. Half of it was unfinished and the other half was paneled in knotty pine. While the Realtor talked about turning the basement into a rumpus room, I lifted the lid of an old Te-Amo cigarbox and found some pennies and pen caps, a few buttons, a harmonica and several hypodermics. When he was fifteen and sixteen, Jackie had been a junkie, and he'd shoot up in the basement. I'd find him downstairs, nodded off, a needle dangling from his arm. It felt like ages ago now, my childhood. I closed the box.

The most earnest and eager buyers showed up early, followed by a few dreamers who obviously couldn't make a reasonable offer. By afternoon, though, the tone of things changed. I was standing at the picture window when I saw Mrs. Wooley stroll up the walkway. She was wearing a short skirt and heels. She rang the doorbell, and I let her in.

"Bobby," she said. "I'm surprised to see you."

She was an intimate of my mother and had to have known, of course, that I'd left school. She had a daughter my age finishing up at Yale.

"Nice to see you Mrs. Wooley," I said.

"Call me Lois," she said. "I think you can do that now."

I offered her a drink. She looked at her watch and said, "No, thank you."

She bit her lip, and a little pink came off on her teeth.

"Last time I saw you," she said, "was at the funeral."

"You thinking of buying the house?"

"I was just in the neighborhood."

"Yeah, well, you always are. You live across the street. You're our neighbor."

"Lois, Lois," I heard my father say. He clasped her hand and smiled warmly. "It's been forever. How are you?" He looked down at his feet. "Things have been crazy."

"So I've heard," Mrs. Wooley said.

"Can I show you around the house?" he asked her.

Mrs. Kayhew tottered across the street and walked up the stone steps to our porch as if avoiding cracks. And shortly after, Mrs. Greyham followed, along with several other women from the neighborhood. My father greeted each of them with the same warm, somewhat chastened smile and then, like a docent, he led the entire group on a tour of our house. He was especially kind to Mrs. Kayhew. He took her arm in his and was guiding her up the stairs. Mrs. Kayhew turned her yellow face toward my father, holding it up at a precise angle, as if her blue eyes were pools of water she didn't want to spill.

The little group stood on the upstairs landing. All the bedroom doors were closed, and the thickly coated brown paint gave them a certain feel, as if they'd been sealed shut a long time ago.

My father nudged a crucifix with his foot. He'd knocked it off the wall the day he came home to find my mother gone. The brass Jesus had come un-nailed, and was wedged between two spikes in the bannister. Mrs. Greyham looked at the cross and then at my father. I waited to hear the lie he would tell.

"I knocked it off the wall," Dad said.

My dad hitched his trousers and bent down on one knee. He picked up the cross and the Jesus and held them, one in each hand, and then tried to fit them together.

He opened his bedroom door, and all the women stepped in. He showed them the deck and the half-bath and the big closet still filled with my mother's clothes. The big king bed still held the outline of my father in the wrinkled sheets, an intaglio of a head and legs and an arm stretching out toward the other pillow. He looked down at the impression, as if he might slip right back into bed, occupying the mold of himself.

My father offered to make a pot of tea.

"Tea?" I blurted out.

"That's okay," my dad said.

But none of these women had come to see the house, which was unexceptional; they'd come to see him. Now they were ready to leave.

When they left, I asked my father if he'd like to have a drink. The last light faded from the day and the streetlamps were flickering to life. My father seemed dispirited.

"I think I'll just sit," he said. He pointed to his chair in the living room and then followed his index finger. He sat down and removed his wingtips, his navy socks, and began massaging his feet.

"Boy, they're sore," he said, squeezing his toes.

He sat in the dark, very quietly, as if he'd discovered a still point.

"Any buyers?"

"Huh? Oh, maybe."

I went to the kitchen and fished my dad's last barbiturate from the garbage can. I rattled the amber bottle and popped the top and dry-swallowed the pill. I used to steal them out of his medicine cabinet all the time. The thing about barbiturates is they make you feel caressed or gently held, your skin humming all over with the touch of a thousand fingers. I sat at the dining table and took apart Miles's old reel, dabbing drops of Remington gun oil on the pawls, and then went outside and rigged up the fly rod, drawing the line through the guides. I stripped out twenty-five feet of line and began false casting. At first I was out of practice, throwing wide loops that dipped low on the backcast and piled up on the forecast, but with each stroke I made a minor adjustment and soon I could feel the rhythm, marking time. To Mrs. Wooley across the street I might have looked like a man sending semaphore to a distant ship. I worked the line until I was casting forty, fifty feet, and the back and forth motion felt substantial, bending the rod down to the butt. I took up a couple extra coils in my left hand and shot those forward. The line sailed smoothly through the guides and unfurled across the street.

Holding Miles's rod in my hand I thought of him, my living, wrecked brother. A few weeks after he jumped from the Aurora Bridge, I decided, one night, to walk out there. I'm terrified of heights, and I walked slowly out onto the bridge, step by step, my hand rubbing the dirty railing, until I'd made it midway onto the span. My legs weakened, my hands shook and burned with sweat. I had not yet looked down but I didn't need to; the fear rose toward me. I closed my eyes and felt the gritty wind suctioned by oncoming traffic. I heard the clack of tires over the concrete, the screech of a seagull. When I looked down, some three hundred feet, where the black water of Union Bay glinted with city lights, I couldn't move, I froze. My legs wouldn't work. I felt the fall in my stomach, an opening up and a hollowing out. I couldn't move forward up the bridge, or back where I'd come from. I couldn't let go of the rail. I might have been there for an hour, easy, when a woman, out walking her dog, came by. My fear of heights overcame my normal fear of speaking to strangers, and I told her I couldn't move. "I'm afraid," I said, pointing over the edge. She switched the leash to her other hand. "I thought I could cross," I explained. The woman took my hand. She talked us across, I know, because I remember the sound of her voice, but I have no idea what she said, and on the other side of the bridge I thanked her ridiculously, over and over, and the next day I rode the bus to pick up my truck.

My father came out. He was barefoot, but still wore the suit. He scratched the back of his hand, and looked over his shoulders at our house. I lifted the line off the street and started casting again.

"I'll never settle," he said.

"Your choice, I guess."

I kept casting, working the rod back and forth, the line flowing gently in watery curls, whispering over our heads.

"It's beautiful," my father said. "Like haiku."

"Let me give it a try," he said.

I let the line fall and stood behind him, closing his hand around the cork, then closing my hand over his.

Rick Moody

❅

The Mansion on the Hill

The Chicken Mask was sorrowful, Sis. The Chicken Mask was supposed to hustle business; it was supposed to invite the customer
to gorge him or herself within our establishment; it was supposed to be
endearing and funny; it was supposed to be an accurate representation
of the featured item on our menu. But, Sis, in a practical setting, in test
markets—like right out in front of the restaurant—the Chicken Mask
had a plaintive aspect, a blue quality (it was stifling, too, even in cold
weather), so that I'd be walking down Main, by the waterfront, after
you were gone, back and forth in front of Hot Bird (Bucket of Drum-
sticks, $2.99), wearing out my imitation basketball sneakers from Wal-
Mart, pudgy in my black jogging suit, lurching along in the sandwich
board, and the kids would hustle up to me, tugging on the wrists of
their harried, under-financed moms. The kids would get bored with
me almost immediately. They knew the routine. Their eyes would narrow, and all at once there were no secrets here in our town of service-
economy franchising: *I was the guy working nine to five in a Chicken
Mask*, even though I'd had a pretty good education in business administration, even though I was more or less presentable and well-spoken,
even though I came from a good family. I made light of it, Sis, I extem-
porized about Hot Bird, in remarks designed by virtue of my studies in
business tactics to drive whole families in for the new *low-fat roasters*, a
meal option that was steeper, in terms of price, but tasty nonetheless.
(And I ought to have known, because I ate from the menu every day.
Even the coleslaw.)

Here's what I'd say, in my Chicken Mask. Here was my pitch: *Feeling a little peckish? Try Hot Bird!* or *Don't be chicken, try Hot Bird!* The mothers would laugh their nervous adding-machine laughs (those laughs that are next door over from a sob), and they would lead the kids off. Twenty yards away, though, the boys and girls would still be staring disdainfully at me, gaping backward while I rubbed my hands raw in the cold, while I breathed the synthetic rubber interior of the Chicken Mask—that fragrance of rubber balls from gym classes lost, that bouquet of the gloves Mom used for the dishes, that perfume of simpler times—while I looked for my next shill. I lost almost ninety days to the demoralization of the Chicken Mask, to its grim, existential emptiness, until I couldn't take it anymore. Which happened to be the day when Alexandra McKinnon (remember her? from Sunday school?) turned the corner with her boy Zack—he has to be seven or eight now—oblivious while upon her daily rounds, oblivious and fresh from a Hallmark store. It was nearly Valentine's Day. They didn't know it was me in there, of course, inside the Chicken Mask. They didn't know I was *the chicken from the basement, the chicken of darkest nightmares*, or, more truthfully, they didn't know I was a guy with some pretty conflicted attitudes about things. That's how I managed to apprehend Zack, leaping out from the in-door of Cohen's Pharmacy, laying ahold of him a little too roughly, by the hem of his pillowy, orange ski jacket. Little Zack was laughing, at first, until, in a voice racked by loss, I worked my hard sell on him, declaiming stentoriously that *Death Comes to All*. That's exactly what I said, just as persuasively as I had once hawked *White-meat breasts, eight pieces, just $4.59!* Loud enough that he'd be sure to know what I meant. His look was interrogative, quizzical. So I repeated myself. *Death Comes to Everybody, Zachary.* My voice was urgent now. My eyes bulged from the eyeholes of my standard-issue Chicken Mask. I was even crying a little bit. Saline rivulets tracked down my neck. Zack was terrified.

What I got next certainly wasn't the kind of flirtatious attention I had always hoped for from his mom. Alex began drumming on me with balled fists. I guess she'd been standing off to the side of the action previously, believing that I was a reliable paid employee of Hot Bird. But now she was all over me, bruising me with wild swings, cursing, until she'd pulled the Chicken Mask from my head—half expecting, I'm sure, to find me scarred or hydrocephalic or otherwise disabled. Her denunciations let up a little once she was in possession of the facts. It was me, her old Sunday school pal, Andrew Wakefield. Not at the top of my game.

I don't really want to include here the kind of scene I made, once unmasked. Alex was exasperated with me, but gentle anyhow. I think she probably knew I was in the middle of a rough patch. People knew. The people leaning out of the storefronts probably knew. But, if things weren't already bad enough, I remembered right then—God, this is horrible—that Alex's mom had driven into Lake Sacandaga about five years before. Jumped the guardrail and plunged right off that bridge there. In December. In heavy snow. In a Ford Explorer. That was the end of her. *Listen, Alex*, I said, *I'm confused, I have problems and I don't know what's come over me and I hope you can understand, and I hope you'll let me make it up to you. I can't lose this job. Honest to God.* Fortunately, just then, Zack became interested in the Chicken Mask. He swiped the mask from his mom—she'd been holding it at arm's length, like a soiled rag—and he pulled it down over his head and started making simulated automatic-weapons noises in the directions of local passersby. This took the heat off. We had a laugh, Alex and I, and soon the three of us had repaired to Hot Bird itself (it closed four months later, like most of the businesses on that block) for coffee and biscuits and the chef's special spicy wings, which, because of my position, were on the house.

Alex was actually waving a spicy wing when she offered her life-altering opinion that I was too smart to be working for Hot Bird, especially if I was going to brutalize little kids with the creepy facts of the hereafter. What I should do, Alex said, was get into something positive instead. She happened to know a girl—it was her cousin, Glenda—who managed a business over in Albany, the Mansion on the Hill, a big area employer, and why didn't I call Glenda and use Alex's name, and maybe they would have something in accounting or valet parking or flower delivery, *yada yada yada*, you know, some job that had as little public contact as possible, something that paid better than minimum wage, because minimum wage, Alex said, wasn't enough for a guy of twenty-nine. After these remonstrances she actually hauled me over to the pay phone at Hot Bird (people are so generous sometimes), while my barely alert boss Antonio slumbered at the register with no idea what was going on, without a clue that he was about to lose his most conscientious chicken impersonator. All because I couldn't stop myself from talking about death.

Alex dialed up the Mansion on the Hill (while Zack, at the table, donned my mask all over again), penetrating deep into the switchboard by virtue of her relation to a Mansion on the Hill management-level employee, and was soon actually talking to her cousin: *Glenda, I got a friend here who's going through some rough stuff in his family, if you know what I mean, yeah, down on his luck in the job department too, but he's a nice bright guy anyhow. I pretty much wanted to smooch him throughout confirmation classes, and he went to . . . Hey, where did you go to school again? Went to SUNY and has a degree in business administration, knows a lot about product positioning or whatever, I don't know, new housing starts, yada yada yada, and I think you really ought to . . .*

Glenda's sigh was audible from several feet away, I swear, through the perfect medium of digital telecommunications, but you can't blame Glenda for that. People protect themselves from bad luck, right? Still, Alex wouldn't let her cousin refuse, wouldn't hear of it, *You absolutely gotta meet him, Glenda, he's a doll, he's a dream boat*, and Glenda gave in, and that's the end of this part of the story, about how I happened to end up working out on Wolf Road at the capital region's finest wedding- and party-planning business. Except that before the Hot Bird recedes into the mists of time, I should report to you that I swiped the Chicken Mask, Sis. They had three or four of them. You'd be surprised how easy it is to come by a Chicken Mask.

Politically, here's what was happening in the front office of my new employer: Denise Gulch, the Mansion on the Hill staff writer, had left her husband and her kids and her steady job, because of a wedding, because of the language of the vows—that soufflé of exaggerated language—vows which, for quality-control purposes, were being broadcast over a discreet speaker in the executive suite. Denise was so moved by a recitation of Paul Stookey's "Wedding Song" taking place during the course of the Neuhaus ceremony ("Whenever two or more of you / Are gathered in His name, / There is love, / There is love . . .") that she slipped into the Rip Van Winkle Room disguised as a late-comer. Immediately, in the electrifying atmosphere of matrimony, she began trying to seduce one of the ushers (Nicky Weir, a part-time Mansion employee who was acquainted with the groom). I figure this flirtation had been taking place for some time, but that's not what everyone told me. What I heard was that seconds after meeting each other—the bride hadn't even recessed yet—Denise and Nicky were secreted in a nearby broom closet, while the office phones bounced to voice mail, and were peeling back the layers of our Mansion dress code, until, at day's end, scantily clad and intoxicated by rhetoric and desire, they stole a limousine and left town without collecting severance. Denise was even fully vested in the pension plan.

All this could only happen at a place called the Mansion on the Hill, a place of fluffy endings: the right candidate for the job walks through the door at the eleventh hour, the check clears that didn't exist minutes before, government agencies agree to waive mountains of red tape, the sky clears, the snow ends, and stony women like Denise Gulch succumb to torrents of generosity, throwing half-dollars to children as they embark on new lives.

The real reason I got the job is that they were shorthanded, and because Alex's cousin, my new boss, was a little difficult. But things were starting to look up anyway. If Glenda's personal demeanor at the interview wasn't exactly warm (she took a personal call in the middle that lasted twenty-eight minutes, and later she asked me, while reapplying lip liner, if I wore cologne) at least she was willing to hire me—as long as I agreed to renounce any personal grooming habits that inclined in the direction of Old Spice, Hai Karate or CK1. I would have spit-polished her pumps just to have my own desk (on which I put a yellowed picture of you when you were a kid, holding up the bass that you caught fly-fishing and also a picture of the four of us: Mom and Dad and you and me) and a Rolodex and unlimited access to stamps, mailing bags and paper clips.

. . .

Let me take a moment to describe our core business at the Mansion on the Hill. We were in the business of helping people celebrate the best days of their lives. We were in the business of spreading joy, by any means necessary. We were in the business of paring away the calluses of woe and grief to reveal the bright light of commitment. We were in the business of producing flawless memories. We had seven auditoriums, or *marriage suites*, as we liked to call them, each with a slightly different flavor and decorating vocabulary. For example, there was the *Chestnut Suite*, the least expensive of our rental suites, which had lightweight aluminum folding chairs (with polyurethane padding) and a very basic altar table, which had the unfortunate pink and lavender floral wallpaper and which seated about 125 comfortably; then there was the *Hudson Suite*, which had some teak in it and a lot of paneling and a classic iron altar table and some rather large standing tables at the rear, and the reception area in Hudson was clothed all in vinyl, instead of the paper coverings that they used in Chestnut (the basic decorating scheme there in the Hudson Suite was meant to suggest the sea vessels that once sailed through our municipal port); then there was the *Rip Van Winkle Room*, with its abundance of draperies, its silk curtains, its matching maroon settings of inexpensive linen, and the *Adirondack Suite*, the *Ticonderoga Room*, the *Valentine Room* (a sort of giant powder puff), and of course the *Niagara Hall*, which was grand and reserved, with its separate kitchen and its enormous fireplace and white-gloved staff, for the sons and daughters of those Victorians of Saratoga County who came upstate for the summer during the racing season, the children of contemporary robber barons, the children whose noses were always straight and whose luck was always good.

We had our own on-site boutique for wedding gowns and tuxedo rentals and fittings—hell, we'd even clean and store your garments for you while you were away on your honeymoon—and we had a travel agency who subcontracted for us, as we also had wedding consultants, jewelers, videographers, still photographers (both the arty ones who specialized in photos of your toenail polish on the day of the wedding and the conventional photographers who barked directions at the assembled family far into the night), nannies, priests, ministers, shamans, polarity therapists, a really maniacal florist called Bruce, a wide array of deejays—guys and gals equipped to spin Christian-only selections, Tex-Mex, music from Hindi films and the occasional death-metal wedding medley—and we could get actual musicians, if you preferred. We'd even had Dick Roseman's combo, The Sons of Liberty, do a medley of "My Funny Valentine," "In-a-Gadda-Da-Vida," "I Will Always Love You" and "Smells Like Teen Spirit," without a rest between selections. (It was gratifying for me to watch the old folks shake it up to contemporary numbers.) We had a three-story, fifteen-hundred-slip parking facility on site, convenient access to I-87, I-90 and the Taconic, and a staff of 175 full- and part-time employees on twenty-four-hour call. We had everything from publicists to dicers of crudités to public orators (need a brush-up for that toast?)—all for the purpose of making your wedding the high watermark of your American life. We had done up to fifteen weddings in a single day (it was a Saturday in February 1991, during the Gulf War) and, since the Mansion on the Hill first threw open its doors for a gala double wedding (the Gifford twins, from Balston Spa, who married Shaun and Maurice Wickett) in June of 1987, we had performed, up to the time of my first day there, 1,963 weddings, many of them memorable, life-affirming, even spectacular ceremonies. We had never had an incidence of serious violence.

This was the raw data that Glenda gave me, anyway, Sis. The arrangement of the facts is my own, and in truth, the arrangement of facts constitutes the job I was engaged to perform at the Mansion on the Hill. Because Glenda Manzini (in 1990 she married Dave Manzini, a developer from Schenectady), couldn't really have hated her job any more than she did. Glenda Manzini, whose marriage (her second) was apparently not the most loving ever in upstate history (although she's not alone; I estimate an even thousand divorces resulting from the conjugal rites successfully consummated so far at my place of business), was a cynic, a skeptic, a woman of little faith when it came to the institution through which she made her living. She occasionally referred to the wedding party as *the cattle*; she occasionally referred to the brides as *the hookers* and to herself, manager of the Mansion on the Hill, as *the*

Madame, as in, *The Madame, Andrew, would like it if you would get the hell out of her office so that she can tabulate these receipts, or, Please tell the Hatfields and the McCoys that the Madame cannot untangle their differences for them, although the Madame does know the names of some first-rate couples counselors.* In the absence of an enthusiasm for our product line or for business writing in general, Glenda Manzini hired me to tackle some of her responsibilities for her. I gave the facts the best possible spin. Glenda, as you probably have guessed, was good with numbers. With the profits and losses. Glenda was good at additional charges. Glenda was good at doubling the price on a floral arrangement, for example, because the Vietnamese poppies absolutely had to be on the tables, because they were so . . . *je ne sais quoi.* Glenda was good at double-booking a particular suite and then auctioning the space to the higher bidder. Glenda was good at quoting a figure for a band and then adding instruments so that the price increased astronomically. One time she padded a quartet with two vocalists, an eight-piece horn section, an African drumming ensemble, a dijeridoo and a harmonium.

The other thing I should probably be up-front about is that Glenda Manzini was a total knockout. A bombshell. A vision of celestial loveliness. I hate to go on about it, but there was that single strand of Glenda's amber hair always falling over her eyes—no matter how many times she tried to secure it; there was her near constant attention to her makeup; there was her total command of business issues and her complete unsentimentality. Or maybe it was her stockings, always in black, with a really provocative seam following the aerodynamically sleek lines of her calf. Or maybe it was her barely concealed sadness. I'd never met anyone quite as uncomfortable as Glenda, but this didn't bother me at first. My life had changed since the Chicken Mask.

Meanwhile, it goes without saying that the Mansion on the Hill wasn't a mansion at all. It was a homely cinder-block edifice formerly occupied by the Colonie Athletic Club. A trucking operation used the space before that. And the Mansion wasn't on any hill, either, because geologically speaking we're in a valley here. We're part of some recent glacial scouring.

. . .

On my first day, Glenda made every effort to insure that my work environment would be as unpleasant as possible. I'd barely set down my extra-large coffee with two half-and-halfs and five sugars and my assortment of cream-filled donuts (I was hoping these would please my new teammates) when Glenda bodychecked me, tipped me over into my reclining desk chair, with several huge stacks of file material.

—And, listen up. In April we have an Orthodox Jewish ceremony taking place at 3:00 P.M. in Niagara while at the same time there are going to be some very faithful Islamic-Americans next door in Ticonderoga. I don't want these two groups to come in contact with one another at any time, understand? I don't want any kind of diplomatic incident. It's your job to figure out how to persuade one of these groups to be first out of the gate, at noon, and it's your job to make them think that they're really lucky to have the opportunity. And Andy? The el-Mohammed wedding, the Muslim wedding, needs prayer mats. See if you can get some from the discount stores. Don't waste a lot of money on this.

This is a good indication of Glenda's management style. Some other procedural tidbits: she frequently assigned a dozen rewrites on her correspondence. She had a violent dislike for semicolons. I was to double-space twice underneath the date on her letters, before typing the salutation, on pain of death. I was never, ever to use one of those cursive word-processing fonts. I was to bring her coffee first thing in the morning, without speaking to her until she had entirely finished a second cup and also a pair of ibuprofen tablets, preferably the elongated, easy-to-swallow variety. I was never to ask her about her weekend or her evening or anything else, including her holidays, unless she asked me first. If her door was closed, I was not to open it. And if I ever reversed the digits in a phone number when taking a message for her, I could count on my pink slip that very afternoon.

Right away, that first A.M., after this litany of scares, after Glenda retreated into her chronically underheated lair, there was a swell of sympathetic mumbles from my coworkers, who numbered, in the front office, about a dozen. They were offering condolences. They had seen the likes of me come and go. Glenda, however, who keenly appreciated the element of surprise as a way of insuring discipline, was not quite done. She reappeared suddenly by my desk—as if by secret entrance—with a half-dozen additional commands. I was to find a new sign for her private parking space, I was to find a new floral wholesaler for the next fiscal quarter, I was to *refill her prescription for birth-control pills.* This last request was spooky enough, but it wasn't the end of the discussion. From there Glenda starting getting personal:

—Oh, by the way, Andy? (she liked diminutives) What's all the family trouble, anyway? The stuff Alex was talking about when she called?

She picked up the photo of you, Sis, the one I had brought with me. The bass at the end of your fishing rod was so outsized that it seemed impossible that you could hold it up. You looked really happy. Glenda picked up the photo as though she hadn't already done her research, as if she had left something to chance. Which just didn't happen during her regime at the Mansion on the Hill.

—Dead sister, said I. And then, completing my betrayal of you, I filled out the narrative, so that anyone who wished could hear about it, and then we could move onto other subjects, like Worcester's really great semipro hockey team.

—Crashed her car. Actually, it was my car. Mercury Sable. Don't know why I said it was her car. It was mine. She was on her way to her rehearsal dinner. She had an accident.

Sis, have I mentioned that I have a lot of questions I've been meaning to ask? Have I asked, for example, why you were taking the windy country road along our side of the great river, when the four-lanes along the west side were faster, more direct and, in heavy rain, less dangerous? Have I asked why you were driving at all? Why I was not driving you to the rehearsal dinner instead? Have I asked why your car was in the shop for muffler repair on such an important day? Have I asked why you were late? Have I asked why you were lubricating your nerves *before* the dinner? Have I asked if four G&Ts, as you called them, before your own rehearsal dinner, were not maybe in excess of what was needed? Have I asked if there was a reason for you to be so tense on the eve of your wedding? Did you feel you had to go through with it? That there was no alternative? If so, why? If he was the wrong guy, why were you marrying him? Were there planning issues that were not properly addressed? Were there things between you two, as between all the betrothed, that we didn't know? Were there specific questions you wanted to ask, of which you were afraid? Have I given the text of my toast, Sis, as I had imagined it, beginning with a plangent evocation of the years before your birth, when I ruled our house like a tyrant, and how with earsplitting cries I resisted your infancy, until I learned to love the way your baby hair, your flaxen mop, fell into curls? Have I mentioned that it was especially satisfying to wind your hair around my stubby fingers as you lay sleeping? Have I made clear that I wrote out this toast and that it took me several weeks to get it how I wanted it and that I was in fact going over these words again when the call from Dad came announcing your death? Have I mentioned—and I'm sorry to be hurtful on this point—that Dad's drinking has gotten worse since you left this world? Have I mentioned that his allusions to the costly unfinished business of his life have become more frequent? Have I mentioned that Mom, already overtaxed with her own body count, with her dead parents and dead siblings, has gotten more and more frail? Have I mentioned that I have some news about Brice, your intended? That his tune has changed slightly since your memorial service? Have I mentioned that I was out at the crime scene the next day? The day after you died? Have I mentioned that in my dreams I am often at the crime scene now? Have I wondered aloud to you about that swerve of blacktop right there, knowing that others may lose their lives as you did? Can't we straighten out that road somehow? Isn't there one road crew that the governor, in his quest for jobs, jobs, jobs, can send down there to make this sort of thing unlikely? Have I perhaps clued you in about how I go there often now, to look for signs of further tragedy? Have I mentioned to you that in some countries DWI is punishable by death, and that when Antonio at Hot Bird first explained this dark irony to me, I imagined taking his throat in my hands and squeezing the air out of him once and for all? Sis, have I told you of driving aimlessly in the mountains, listening to talk radio, searching for the one bit of cheap, commercially interrupted persuasion that will let me put these memo-

ries of you back in the canister where you now at least partially reside
so that I can live out my dim, narrow life? Have I mentioned that I expect death around every turn, that every blue sky has a safe sailing out
of it, that every bus runs me over, that every low, mean syllable uttered
in my direction seems to intimate the violence of murder, that every
family seems like an opportunity for ruin and every marriage a ceremony into which calamity will fall and hearts will be broken and lives
destroyed and people branded by the mortifications of love? Is it all
right if I ask you all of this?

Still, in spite of these personal issues, I was probably a model employee for Glenda Manzini. For example, I managed to sort out the politics concerning the Jewish wedding and the Islamic wedding (both
slated for the first weekend of April), and I did so by appealing to certain aspects of light in our valley at the base of the Adirondacks. Certain kinds of light make for very appealing weddings here in our valley,
I told one of these families. In late winter, in the early morning, you begin to feel an excitement at the appearance of the sun. Yes, I managed
to solve that problem, and the next (the prayer mats)—because Kmart,
where America shops, had a special on bathmats that week, and I sent
Dorcas Gilbey over to buy six dozen to use for the Muslim families. I
solved these problems and then I solved others just as vexing. I had a
special interest in the snags that arose on Fridays after 5 P.M.—the
groom who on the day of the ceremony was trapped in a cabin east of
Lake George and who had to snowshoe three miles out to the nearest
telephone, or the father of the bride (it was the Lapsley wedding) who
wanted to arrive at the ceremony by hydrofoil. Brinksmanship, in the
world of nuptial planning, gave me a sense of well-being, and I tried to
bury you in the rear of my life, in the back of that closet where I'd hidden my secondhand golf clubs and my ski boots and my Chicken
Mask—never again to be seen by mortal man.

One of my front-office associates was a fine young woman by the
name of Linda Pietrzsyk, who tried to comfort me during the early
weeks of my job, after Glenda's periodic assaults. Don't ask how to
pronounce Linda's surname. In order to pronounce it properly, you

have to clear your throat aggressively. Linda Pietrzsyk didn't like her surname anymore than you or I, and she was apparently looking for a groom from whom she could borrow a better last name. That's what I found out after awhile. Many of the employees at the Mansion on the Hill had ulterior motives. This marital ferment, this loamy soil of romance, called to them somehow. When I'd been there a few months, I started to see other applicants go through the masticating action of an interview with Glenda Manzini. Glenda would be sure to ask, *Why do you want to work here?* and many of these qualified applicants had the same reply, *Because I think marriage is the most beautiful thing and I want to help make it possible for others.* Most of these applicants, if they were attractive and single and younger than Glenda, aggravated her thoroughly. They were shown the door. But occasionally a marital aspirant like Linda Pietrzsyk snuck through, in this case because Linda managed to conceal her throbbing, sentimental heart beneath a veneer of contemporary discontent.

We had Mondays and Tuesdays off, and one weekend a month. Most of our problem-solving fell on Saturdays, of course, but on that one Saturday off, Linda Pietrzsyk liked to bring friends to the Mansion on the Hill, to various celebrations. She liked to attend the weddings of strangers. This kind of entertainment wasn't discouraged by Glenda or by the owners of the Mansion, because everybody likes a party to be crowded. Any wedding that was too sparsely attended at the Mansion had a fine complement of *warm bodies,* as Glenda liked to call them, provided gratis. Sometimes we had to go to libraries or retirement centers to fill a quota, but we managed. These gate crashers were welcome to eat finger food at the reception and to drink champagne and other intoxicants (food and drink were billed to the client), but they had to make themselves scarce once the dining began in earnest. There was a window of opportunity here that was large enough for Linda and her friends.

She was tight with a spirited bunch of younger people. She was friends with kids who had outlandish wardrobes and styles of grooming, kids with pants that fit like bedsheets, kids with haircuts that were, at best, accidental. But Linda would dress them all up and make them presentable, and they would arrive in an ancient station wagon in order to crowd in at the back of a wedding. Where they stifled gasps of hilarity.

I don't know what Linda saw in me. I can't really imagine. I wore the same sweaters and flannel slacks week in and week out. I liked classical music, Sis. I liked historical simulation festivals. And as you probably haven't forgotten (having tried a couple of times to fix me up—with Jess Carney and Sally Moffitt), the more tense I am, the worse is the impression I make on the fairer sex. Nevertheless, Linda Pietrzsyk decided that I had to be a part of her elite crew of wedding crashers, and so for a while I learned by immersion of the great rainbow of expressions of fealty.

Remember that footage, so often shown on contemporary reality-based programming during the dead first half-hour of prime time, of the guy who vomited at his own wedding? I was at that wedding. You know when he says, *Aw, Honey, I'm really sorry*, and leans over and flash floods this amber stuff on her train? You know, the shock of disgust as it crosses her face? The look of horror in the eyes of the minister? I saw it all. No one who was there thought it was funny, though, except Linda's friends. That's the truth. I thought it was really sad. But I was sitting next to a fellow *actually named Cheese* (when I asked which kind of cheese, he seemed perplexed), and Cheese looked as though he had a hernia or something, he thought this was so funny. Elsewhere in the Chestnut Suite there was a grievous silence.

Linda Pietrzsyk also liked to catalogue moments of spontaneous erotic delight on the premises, and these were legendary at the Mansion on the Hill. Even Glenda, who took a dim view of gossiping about business most of the time, liked to hear who was doing it with whom where. There was an implicit hierarchy in such stories. *Tales of the couple to be married caught in the act on Mansion premises were considered obvious and therefore uninspiring.* Tales of the best man and matron of honor going at it (as in the Clarke, Rosenberg, Irving, Ng, Fujitsu, Walters, Shapiro or Spangler ceremonies) were better, but not great. Stories in which parents of the couple to be married were caught—in, say, the laundry room, with the dad still wearing his dress shoes—were good (Smith, Elsworth, Waskiewicz), but not as good as tales of the parents of the couple to be married trading spouses, of which we had one unconfirmed report (Hinkley) and of which no one could stop talking for a week. Likewise, any story in which the bride or the groom were caught *in flagrante* with someone other than the person they were marrying was considered astounding (if unfortunate). But we were after some even more unlikely tall tales: any threesome or larger grouping involving the couple to be married and someone from one of the other weddings scheduled that day, in which the third party was unknown until arriving at the Mansion on the Hill, and at which *a house pet was present*. Glenda said that if you spotted one of these tableaux you could have a month's worth of free groceries from the catering department. Linda Pietrzsyk also spoke longingly of the day when someone would arrive breathlessly in the office with a narrative of a full-fledged orgiastic reception in the Mansion on the Hill, the spontaneous, overwhelming erotic celebration of love and marriage by an entire suite full of Americans, tall and short, fat and thin, young and old.

In pursuit of these tales, with her friends Cheese, Chip, Mick, Stig, Mark and Blair, Linda Pietrzsyk would quietly appear at my side at a reception and give me the news—*Behind the bandstand, behind that scrim, groom reaching under his cousin's skirts.* We would sneak in for a look. But we never interrupted anyone. And we never made them feel ashamed.

You know how when you're getting to know a fellow employee, a fellow team member, you go through phases, through cycles of intimacy and insight and respect and doubt and disillusionment, where one impression gives way to another? (Do you know about this, Sis, and is this what happened between you and Brice, so that you felt like you personally had to have the four G&Ts on the way to the rehearsal dinner? Am I right in thinking you couldn't go on with the wedding and that this caused you to get all sloppy and to believe erroneously that you could operate heavy machinery?) Linda Pietrzsyk was a stylish, Skidmore-educated girl with ivory skin and an adorable bump in her nose; she was from an upper-middle-class family out on Long Island somewhere; her father's periodic drunkenness had not affected his ability to work;

her mother stayed married to him according to some mesmerism of devotion; her brothers had good posture and excelled in contact sports; in short, there were no big problems in Linda's case. Still, she pretended to be a desperate, marriage-obsessed kid, without a clear idea about what she wanted to do with her life or what the hell was going to happen next week. She was smarter than me—she could do the crossword puzzle in three minutes flat and she knew all about current events—but she was always talking about *catching a rich financier with a wild streak and extorting a retainer from him*, until I wanted to shake her. There's usually another layer underneath these things. In Linda's case it started to become clear at Patti Wackerman's wedding.

The reception area in the Ticonderoga Room—where walls slid back from the altar to reveal the tables and the dance floor—was decorated in branches of forsythia and wisteria and other flowering vines and shrubs. It was spring. Linda was standing against a piece of white wicker latticework that I had borrowed from the florist in town (in return for promotional considerations), and sprigs of flowering trees garlanded it, garlanded the spot where Linda was standing. Pale colors haloed her.

—Right behind this screen, she said, when I swept up beside her and tapped her playfully on the shoulder,—check it out. There's a couple falling in love once and for all. You can see it in their eyes.

I was sipping a Canadian spring water in a piece of company stemware. I reacted to Linda's news nonchalantly. I didn't think much of it. Yet I happened to notice that Linda's expression was conspiratorial, impish, as well as a little beatific. Linda often covered her mouth with her hand when she'd said something riotous, as if to conceal unsightly dental work (on the contrary, her teeth were perfect), as if she'd been treated badly one too many times, as if the immensity of joy were embarrassing to her somehow. As she spoke of the couple in question her hand fluttered up to her mouth. Her slender fingertips probed delicately at her upper lip. My thoughts came in torrents: *Where are Stig and Cheese and Blair? Why am I suddenly alone with this fellow employee? Is the couple Linda is speaking about part of the wedding party today? How many points will she get for the first sighting of their extramarital grappling?*

Since it was my policy to investigate any and all such phenomena, I glanced desultorily around the screen and, seeing nothing out of the ordinary, slipped further into the shadows where the margins of Ticonderoga led toward the central catering staging area. There was, of course, no such couple behind the screen, or rather Linda (who was soon beside me) and myself *were the couple* and we were mottled by insufficient light, dappled by it, by lavender-tinted spots hung that morning by the lighting designers, and by reflections of a mirrored *disco ball* that speckled the dance floor.

—I don't see anything, I said.

—Kiss me, Linda Pietrzsyk said. Her fingers closed lightly around the bulky part of my arm. There was an unfamiliar warmth in me. The band struck up some fast number. I think it was "It's Raining Men" or maybe it was that song entitled "We Are Family," which played so often at the Mansion on the Hill in the course of a weekend. Whichever, it was really loud. The horn players were getting into it. A trombonist yanked his slide back and forth.

—Excuse me? I said.

—Kiss me, Andrew, she said.—I want to kiss you.

Locating in myself a long-dormant impulsiveness, I reached down for Linda's bangs, and with my clumsy hands I tried to push back her blond and strawberry-blond curlicues, and then, with a hitch in my motion, in a stop-time sequence of jerks, I embraced her. Her eyes, like neon, were illumined.

—Why don't you tell me how you feel about me? Linda Pietrzsyk said. I was speechless, Sis. I didn't know what to say. And she went on. There was something about me, something warm and friendly about me. I wasn't fortified, she said; I wasn't cold, I was just a good guy who actually cared about other people *and you know how few of those there are*. (I think these were her words.) She wanted to spend more time with me, she wanted to get to know me better, she wanted to give the roulette wheel a decisive spin: She repeated all this twice in slightly different ways with different modifiers. It made me sweat. The only way I could think to get her to quit talking was to kiss her in earnest, my lips brushing by hers the way the sun passes around and through the interstices of falling leaves on an October afternoon. I hadn't kissed anyone in a long time. Her mouth tasted like cherry soda, like barbecue, like fresh hay, and because of these startling tastes, I retreated. To arm's length.

Sis, was I scared. What was this rank taste of wet campfire and bone fragments that I'd had in my mouth since we scattered you over the Hudson? Did I come through this set of coincidences, these quotidian interventions by God, to work in a place where everything seemed to be about *love*, only to find that I couldn't ever be a part of that grand word? How could I kiss anyone when I felt so awkward? What happened to me, what happened to all of us, to the texture of our lives, when you left us here?

I tried to ask Linda why she was doing what she was doing—behind the screen of wisteria and forsythia. I fumbled badly for these words. I believed she was trying to have a laugh on me. So she could go back and tell Cheese and Mick about it. So she could go gossip about me in the office, about what a jerk that Wakefield was. *Man, Andrew Wakefield thinks there's something worth hoping for in this world.* I thought she was joking, and I was through being the joke, being the Chicken Mask, being the harlequin.

—I'm not doing anything to you, Andrew, Linda said.—I'm expressing myself. It's supposed to be a good thing.

Reaching, she laid a palm flush against my face.

—I know you aren't . . .

—So what's the problem?

I was ambitious to reassure. If I could have stayed the hand that fluttered up to cover her mouth, so that she could laugh unreservedly, so that her laughter peeled out in the Ticonderoga Room . . . But I just wasn't up to it yet. I got out of there. I danced across the floor at the Wackerman wedding—I was a party of one—and the Wackermans and the Delgados and their kin probably thought I was singing along with "Desperado" by the Eagles (it was the anthem of the new Mr. and Mrs. Fritz Wackerman), but really I was talking to myself, *about work*, about how Mike Tombello's best man wanted to give his toast while doing flips on a trampoline, about how Jenny Parmenter wanted live goats bleating in the Mansion parking lot, as a fertility symbol, as she sped away, in her Rolls Corniche, to the Thousand Islands. Boy, I always hated the Eagles.

. . .

Okay, to get back to Glenda Manzini. Linda Pietrzsyk didn't write me
off after our failed embraces, but she sure gave me more room. She was
out the door at 5:01 for several weeks, without asking after me, without
a kind word for anyone, and I didn't blame her. But in the end who else
was there to talk to? To Marie O'Neill, the accountant? To Paul
Avakian, the human resources and insurance guy and petty-cash manager? To Rachel Levy, the head chef? Maybe it was more than this.
Maybe the bond that forms between people doesn't get unmade so easily. Maybe it leaves its mark for a long time. Soon Linda and I ate our
bagged lunches together again, trading varieties of puddings, often in
total silence; at least this was the habit until we found a new area of
common interest in our reservations about Glenda Manzini's management techniques. This happened to be when Glenda took a week off.
What a miracle. I'd been employed at the Mansion six months. The
staff was in a fine mood about Glenda's hiatus. There was a carnival atmosphere. Dorcas Gilbey had been stockpiling leftover ales for an office shindig featuring dancing and the recitation of really bad marital
vows we'd heard. Linda and I went along with the festivities, but we
were also formulating a strategy.

What we wanted to know was how Glenda became so unreservedly
cruel. We wanted the inside story on her personal life. We wanted the
skinny. How do you produce an individual like Glenda? What is the
mass-production technique? We waited until Tuesday, after the afternoon beer-tasting party. We were staying late, we claimed, in order to
separate out the green M&Ms for the marriage of U.V.M. tight end
Brad Doelp who had requested bowls of M&Ms at his reception, *ex-
cluding any and all green candies*. When our fellow employees were
gone, right at five, we broke into Glenda's office.

Sis, we really broke in. Glenda kept her office locked when she
wasn't in it. It was a matter of principle. I had to use my Discover card
on the lock. I punished that credit card. But we got the tumblers to
tumble, and once we were inside, we started poking around. First of
all, Glenda Manzini was a tidy person, which I can admire from an or-
ganizational point of view, but it was almost like her office was empty.

The pens and pencils were lined up. The in- and out-boxes were swept clean of any stray dust particle, any scrap of trash. There wasn't a rogue paper clip behind the desk or in the bottom of her spotless wastebasket. She kept her rubber bands banded together with rubber bands. The files in her filing cabinets were orderly, subdivided to avoid bowing, the old faxes were photocopied so that they wouldn't disintegrate. The photos on the walls (Mansion weddings past), were nondescript and pedestrian. There was nothing intimate about the decoration at all. I knew about most of this stuff from the moments when she ordered me into that cubicle to shout me down, but this was different. Now we were getting a sustained look at Glenda's personal effects.

Linda took particular delight in Glenda's cassette player (it was atop one of the black filing cabinets)—a cassette player that none of us had ever heard play, not even once. Linda admired the selection of recordings there. A complete set of cut-out budget series: *Greatest Hits of Baroque, Greatest Hits of Swing, Greatest Hits of Broadway, Greatest Hits of Disco* and so forth. Just as she was about to pronounce Glenda a rank philistine where music was concerned, Linda located there, in a shattered case, a copy of *Greatest Hits of the Blues.*

We devoured the green M&Ms while we were busy with our reconnaissance. And I kept reminding Linda not to get any of the green dye on anything. I repeatedly checked surfaces for fingerprints. I even overturned Linda's hands (it made me happy while doing it), to make sure they were free of emerald smudges. Because if Glenda found out we were in her office, we'd both be submitting applications at the Hot Bird of Troy. Nonetheless, Linda carelessly put down her handful of M&Ms, on top of a filing cabinet, to look over the track listings for *Greatest Hits of the Blues.* This budget anthology was released the year Linda was born, in 1974. Coincidentally, the year you too were born, Sis. I remember driving with you to the tunes of Lightnin' Hopkins or Howlin' Wolf. I remember your preference for the most bereaved of acoustic blues, the most ramshackle of musics. What better soundtrack for the Adirondacks? For our meandering drives in the mountains, into Corinth or around Lake Luzerne? What more lonesome sound for a state park the size of Rhode Island where wolves and bears still come to hunt? Linda cranked the greatest hits of heartbreak and we sat down on the carpeted floor to listen. I missed you.

I pulled open that bottom file drawer by chance. I wanted to rest my arm on something. There was a powerful allure in the moment. I wasn't going to kiss Linda, and probably her desperate effort to find somebody to liberate her from her foreshortened economic prospects and her unpronounceable surname wouldn't come to much, but she was a good friend. Maybe a better friend than I was admitting to myself. It was in this expansive mood that I opened the file drawer at the bottom of one stack (the *J* through *P* stack), otherwise empty, to find that it was full of a half-dozen, maybe even more, of those circular packages of *birth-control pills*, the color-coated pills, you know, those multihued pills and placebos that are a journey through the amorous calendars of women. All unused. Not a one of them even opened. Not a one of the white, yellow, brown or green pills liberated from its package.

—Must be chilly in Schenectady, Linda mumbled.

Was there another way to read the strange bottom drawer? Was there a way to look at it beyond or outside of my exhausting tendency to discover only facts that would prop up darker prognostications? The file drawer contained the pills, it contained a bottle of vodka, it contained a cache of family pictures and missives the likes of which were never displayed or mentioned or even alluded to by Glenda. Even I, for all my resentments, wasn't up to reading the letters. But what of these carefully arranged packages of photo snapshots of the Manzini family? (Glenda's son from her first marriage, in his early teens, in a torn and grass-stained football uniform, and mother and second husband and son in front of some bleachers, et cetera.) Was the drawer really what it seemed to be, a repository for mementos of love that Glenda had now hidden away, secreted, shunted off into mini-storage? What was the lesson of those secrets? Merely that concealed behind rage (and behind grief) is *the ambition to love?*

—Somebody's having an affair, Linda said. —The hubby is coming home late. He's fabricating late evenings at the office. He's taking some desktop meetings with his secretary. He's leaving Glenda alone with the kids. Why else be so cold?

—Or Glenda's carrying on, said I.

—Or she's polygamous, Linda said,—and this is a completely separate family she's keeping across town somewhere without telling anyone.

—Or this is the boy she gave up for adoption and this is the record of her meeting with his folks. And she never told Dave about it.

—Whichever it is, Linda said,—it's *bad*.

We turned our attention to the vodka. Sis, I know I've said that I don't touch the stuff anymore—because of your example—but Linda egged me on. We were listening to music of the delta, to its simple unadorned grief, and I felt that Muddy Waters's loss was my kind of loss, the kind you don't shake easily, the kind that comes back like a seasonal flu, and soon we were passing the bottle of vodka back and forth. Beautiful, sad Glenda Manzini understood the blues and I understood the blues and you understood them and Linda understood them and maybe everybody understood them—in spite of what ethno-musicologists sometimes tell us about the cultural singularity of that music. Linda started to dance a little, there in Glenda Manzini's office, swiveling absently, her arms like asps, snaking to and fro, her wrists adorned in black bangles. Linda had a spell on her, in Glenda's anaerobic and cryogenically frigid office. Linda plucked off her beige pumps and circled around Glenda's desk, as if casting out its manifold demons. I couldn't take my eyes off of her. She forgot who I was and drifted with the lamentations of Robert Johnson (hellhound on his trail), and I could have followed her there, where she cast off Long Island and Skidmore and became a naiad, a true resident of the Mansion on the Hill, that paradise, but when the song was over the eeriness of our communion was suddenly alarming. I was sneaking around my boss's office. I was drinking her vodka. All at once it was time to go home.

We began straightening everything we had moved—we were really responsible about it—and Linda gathered up the dozen or so green M&Ms she'd left on the filing cabinet—excepting the one she inadvertently fired out the back end of her fist, which skittered from a three-drawer file down a whole step to the surface of a two-drawer stack, before hopping and skipping over a cassette box, before free-falling behind the cabinets, where it came to rest, at last, six inches from the northeast corner of the office, beside a small coffee-stained patch of wall-to-wall. I returned the vodka to its drawer of shame, I tidied up the stacks of *Bride's* magazines, I locked Glenda's office door and I went back to being the employee of the month. (My framed picture hung over the water fountain between the rest rooms. I wore a bow tie. I smiled broadly and my teeth looked straight and my hair was combed. I couldn't be stopped.)

My ambition has always been to own my own small business. I like the flexibility of small-capitalization companies; I like small businesses at the moment at which they prepare to franchise. That's why I took the job at Hot Bird—I saw Hot Birds in every town in America, I saw Hot Birds as numerous as post offices or ATMs. I like small businesses at the moment at which they really define a market with respect to a certain need, when they begin to sell their products to the world. And my success as a team player at the Mansion on the Hill was the result of these ambitions. This is why I came to feel, after a time, that I could do Glenda Manzini's job myself. Since I'm a little young, it's obvious that I couldn't *replace* Glenda—I think her instincts were really great with respect to the service we were providing to the Capital Region—but I saw the Mansion on the Hill stretching its influence into population centers throughout the northeast. I mean, why wasn't there a Mansion on the Hill in Westchester? Down in Mamaroneck? Why wasn't there a Mansion on the Hill in the golden corridor of Boston suburbs? Why no Mainline Philly Mansion? Suffice to say, I saw myself, at some point in the future, having the same opportunity Glenda had. I saw myself cutting deals and whittling out discounts at other fine Mansion locations. I imagined making myself indispensable to a coalition of Mansion venture-capitalists and then I imagined using these associations to make a move into, say, the high-tech or bio-tech sectors of American industry.

The way I pursued this particular goal was that I started looking ahead at things like upcoming volume. I started using the graph features on my office software to make pie charts of ceremony densities, cost ratios and so forth, and I started wondering how we could pitch our service better, whether on the radio or in the press or through alternative marketing strategies (I came up with the strategy, for example, of getting various non-affiliated religions—small emergent spiritual movements—to consider us as a site for all their group wedding ceremonies). And as I started looking ahead, I started noticing who was coming through the doors in the next months. I became well versed in the social forces of our valley. I watched for when certain affluent families of the region might be needing our product. I would, if required, attempt cold-calling the attorney general of our state to persuade him of the splendor of the Niagara Hall when Diana, his daughter, finally gave the okey-dokey to her suitor, Ben.

I may well have succeeded in my plan for domination of the Mansion on the Hill brand, if it were not for the fact that as I was examining the volume projections for November (one Monday night), the ceremonies taking place in a mere three months, I noticed that Sarah Wilton of Corinth was marrying one Brice McCann in the Rip Van Winkle Room. Just before Thanksgiving. There were no particular notes or annotations to the name on the calendar, and thus Glenda wasn't focusing much on the ceremony. But something bothered me. That name.

Your Brice McCann, Sis. Your intended. Getting married almost a year to the day after your rehearsal-dinner-that-never-was. Getting married before even having completed his requisite year of grief, before we'd even made it through the anniversary with its floodwaters. Who knew how long he'd waited before beginning his seduction of Sarah Wilton? Was it even certain that he had waited until you were gone? Maybe he was faithless; maybe he was a two-timer. I had started reading Glenda's calendar to get ahead in business, Sis, but as soon as I learned of Brice, I became cavalier about work. My work suffered. My relations with other members of the staff suffered. I kept to myself. I went back to riding the bus to work instead of accepting rides. I stopped visiting fellow workers. I found myself whispering of plots and machinations; I found myself making connections between things that probably weren't connected and planning involved scenarios of revenge. I knew the day would come when he would be on the premises, when Brice would be settling various accounts, going over various numbers, signing off on the pâté selection and the set list of the R&B band, and I waited for him—to be certain of the truth.

Sis, you became engaged too quickly. There had been that other guy, Mark, and you had been engaged to him, too, and that arrangement fell apart kind of fast—I think you were engaged at Labor Day and broken up by M.L.K.'s birthday—and then, within weeks, there was this Brice. There's a point I want to make here. I'm trying to be gentle, but I have to get this across. Brice wore a beret. *The guy wore a beret.* He was supposedly a great cook, he would bandy about names of exotic mushrooms, but I never saw him boil an egg when I was visiting you. It was always you who did the cooking. It's true that certain males of the species, the kind who linger at the table after dinner waiting for their helpmeet to do the washing up, the kind who preside over carving of viands and otherwise disdain food-related chores, the kind who claim to be effective only at the preparation of breakfast, these guys are Pleistocene brutes who don't belong in the Information Age with its emerging markets and global economies. But, Sis, I think the other extreme is just as bad. The sensitive, New Age, beret-wearing guys who buy premium mustards and free-range chickens and grow their own basil and then let you cook while they're in the other room perusing magazines devoted to the artistic posings of Asian teenagers. Our family comes from upstate New York and we don't eat enough vegetables and our marriages are full of hardships and sorrows, Sis, and when I saw Brice coming down the corridor of the Mansion on the Hill, with his prematurely gray hair slicked back with the aid of some all-natural mousse, wearing a gray suede bomber jacket and cowboy boots into which were tucked the cuffs of his black designer jeans, carrying his personal digital assistant and his cell phone and the other accoutrements of his dwindling massage-therapy business, he was the enemy of my state. In his wake, I was happy to note, there was a sort of honeyed cologne. Patchouli, I'm guessing. It would definitely drive Glenda Manzini nuts.

We had a small conference room at the Mansion, just around the corner from Glenda's office. I had selected some of the furnishings there myself, from a discount furniture outlet at the mall. Brice and his fiancée, Sarah Wilton, would of course be repairing to this conference room with Glenda to do some pricing. I had the foresight, therefore, to jog into that space and turn on the speaker phone over by the coffee machine, and to place a planter of silk flowers in front of it and dial my own extension so that I could teleconference this conversation. I had a remote headset I liked to wear around, Sis, during inventorying and bill tabulation—it helped with the neck strain and tension headaches that I'm always suffering with—so I affixed this headset and went back to filing, down the hall, while the remote edition of Brice and Sarah's conference with Glenda was broadcast into my skull.

I figure my expression was ashen. I suppose that Dorcas Gilbey, when she flagged me down with some receipts that she had forgotten to file, was unused to my mechanistic expression and to my curt, unfriendly replies to her questions. I waved her off, clamping the headset tighter against my ear. Unfortunately, the signal broke up. It was muffled. I hurriedly returned to my desk and tried to get the forwarded call to transmit properly to my handset. I even tried to amplify it through the speaker-phone feature, to no avail. Brice had always affected a soft-spoken demeanor while he was busy extorting things from people like you, Sis. He was too quiet—the better to conceal his tactics. And thus, in order to hear him, I had to sneak around the corner from the conference room and eavesdrop in the old-fashioned way.

—We wanted to dialogue with you (Brice was explaining to Glenda), because we wanted to make sure that you were thinking creatively along the same lines we are. We want to make sure you're comfortable with our plans. As married people, as committed people, we want this ceremony to make others feel good about themselves, as we're feeling good about ourselves. We want to have an ecstatic celebration here, a healing celebration that will bind up the hurt any marriages in the room might be suffering. I know you know how the ecstasy of marriage occasions a grieving process for many persons, Mrs. Manzini. Sarah and I both feel this in our hearts, that celebrations often have grief as a part of their wonder, and we want to enact all these things, all these feelings, to bring them out where we can look at them, and then we want to purge them triumphantly. We want people to come out of this wedding feeling good about themselves, as we'll be feeling good about ourselves. We want to give our families a big collective hug, because we're all human and we all have feelings and we all have to grieve and yearn and we need rituals for this.

There was a long silence from Glenda Manzini.

Then she said:

—Can we cut to the chase?

One thing I always loved about the Mansion on the Hill was its emptiness, its vacancy. Sure, the Niagara Room, when filled with five-thousand-dollar gowns and heirloom tuxedos, when serenaded by Toots Wilcox's big band, was a great place, a sort of gold standard of reception halls, but as much as I always loved both the celebrations and the network of relationships and associations that went with our business at the Mansion, I always felt best in the *empty* halls of the Mansion on the Hill, cleansed of their accumulation of sentiment, utterly silent, patiently awaiting the possibility of matrimony. It was onto this clean slate that I had routinely projected my foolish hopes. But after Brice strutted through my place of employment, after his marriage began to overshadow every other, I found instead a different message inscribed on these walls: *Every death implies a guilty party.*

Or to put it another way, there was a network of sub-basements in the Mansion on the Hill through which each suite was connected to another. These tunnels were well-traveled by certain alcoholic janitorial guys whom I knew well enough. I'd had my reasons to adventure there before, but now I used every opportunity to pace these corridors. I still performed the parts of my job that would assure that I got paid and that I invested regularly in my 401K plan, but I felt more comfortable in the emptiness of the Mansion's suites and basements, thinking about how I was going to extract my recompense, while Brice and Sarah dithered over the cost of their justice of the peace and their photographer and their *Champlain Pentecostal Singers.*

I had told Linda Pietrzsyk about Brice's reappearance. I had told her about you, Sis. I had remarked about your fractures and your loss of blood and your hypothermia and the results of your post-mortem blood-alcohol test; I suppose that I'd begun to tell her all kinds of things, in outbursts of candor that were followed by equal and opposite remoteness. Linda saw me, over the course of those weeks, lurking, going from Ticonderoga to Rip Van Winkle to Chestnut, slipping in

and out of infernal sub-basements of conjecture that other people find
grimy and uncomfortable, when I should have been overseeing the unloading of floral arrangements at the loading dock or arranging for
Glenda's chiropractic appointments. Linda saw me lurking around,
asked what was wrong and told me that it would be better after the an-
niversary, after that day had come and gone, and I felt the discourses of
apology and subsequent gratitude forming epiglottally in me, but instead I told her to get lost, to leave the dead to bury the dead.

After a long excruciating interval, the day of Sarah Danforth
Wilton's marriage to Brice Paul McCann arrived. It was a day of chill
mists, Sis, and you had now been gone just over one year. I had passed
through the anniversary trembling, in front of the television, watching
the Home Shopping Network, impulsively pricing cubic zirconium
rings, as though one of these would have been the ring you might have
worn at your ceremony. You were a fine sister, but you changed your
mind all the time, and I had no idea if these things I'd attributed to you
in the last year were features of the *you* I once knew, or whether, in
death, you had become the property of your mourners, so that we
made of you a puppet.

On the anniversary, I watched a videotape of your bridal shower,
and Mom was there, and she looked really proud, and Dad drifted into
the center of the frame at one point, and mumbled a strange *harrumph*
that had to do with interloping at an assembly of such beautiful women
(I was allowed on the scene only to do the videotaping), and you were
very pleased as you opened your gifts. At one point you leaned over to
Mom, and stage-whispered—so that even I could hear—*that your car*
was a real lemon and that you had to take it to the shop and you didn't
have time and it was a total hassle and did she think that I would lend
you the Sable without giving you a hard time? My Sable, my car. Sure. If
I had it to do again, I would never have given you a hard time even once.

The vows at the Mansion on the Hill seemed to be the part of the
ceremony where most of the tinkering took place. I think if Glenda
had been able to find a way to charge a premium on vow alteration, we
could have found a really excellent revenue stream at the Mansion on
the Hill. If the sweet instant of commitment is so singular, why does it
seem to have so many different articulations? People used all sorts of

things in their vows. Conchita Bosworth used the songs of Dan Fogel-
berg when it came to the exchange of rings; a futon-store owner from
Queensbury, Reggie West, managed to work in material from a number
of sitcoms. After a while, you'd heard it all, the rhetoric of desire, the
incantation of commitment rendered as awkwardly as possible; you
heard the purple metaphors, the hackneyed lines, until it was all like legal language, as in any business transaction.

It was the language of Brice McCann's vows that brought this story
to its conclusion. I arrived at the wedding late. I took a cab across the
Hudson, from the hill in Troy where I lived in my convenience apartment. What trees there were in the system of pavement cloverleafs
where Route Seven met the interstate were bare, disconsolate. The
road was full of potholes. The lanes choked with old, shuddering
sedans. The parking valets at the Mansion, a group of pot-smoking
teens who seemed to enjoy creating a facsimile of politeness that involved both effrontery and subservience, opened the door of the cab
for me and greeted me according to their standard line, *Where's the
party?* The parking lot was full. We had seven weddings going on at
once. Everyone was working. Glenda was working, Linda was working. Dorcas was working. All my teammates were working, sprinting
from suite to suite, micro-managing. The whole of the Capital Region
must have been at the Mansion that Saturday to witness the blossoming
of families, Sis, or, in the case of Brice's wedding, to witness the way in
which a vow of faithfulness less than a year old, a promise of the future, can be traded in so quickly; how marriage is just a shrink-
wrapped sale item, mass-produced in bulk. You can pick one up
anywhere these days, at a mall, on layaway. If it doesn't fit, exchange it.

I walked the main hallway slowly, peeking in and out of the various
suites. In the Chestnut Suite it was the Polanskis, poor but generous—
their daughter Denise intended to have and to hold an Italian fellow,
A. L. DiPietro, also completely penniless, and the Polanskis were paying for the entire ceremony and rehearsal dinner and inviting the DiPi-
etros to stay with them for the week. They had brought their own floral
displays, personally assembled by the arthritic Mrs. Polanski. The
room had a dignified simplicity. Next, in the Hudson Suite, in keeping
with its naval flavor, cadet Bobby Moore and his high-school sweet-

heart Mandy Sutherland were tying the knot, at the pleasure of Bobby's dad, who had been a tugboat captain in New York Harbor; in the Adirondack Suite, two of the venerable old families of the Lake George region—the Millers (owners of the Lake George Cabins) and the Wentworths (they had the Quality Inn franchise) commingled their resort-dependent fates; in the Valentine Room, Sis, two women (named Sal and Martine, but that's all I should say about them, for reasons of privacy) were to be married by a renegade Episcopal minister called Jack Valance—they had sewn their own gowns to match the cadmium red decor of that interior; Ticonderoga had the wedding of Glen Dunbar and Louise Glazer, a marriage not memorable in any way at all, and in the Niagara Hall two of Saratoga's great eighteenth-century racing dynasties, the Vanderbilt and Pierrepont families, were about to settle long-standing differences. Love was everywhere in the air.

I walked through all these ceremonies, Sis, before I could bring myself to go over to the Rip Van Winkle Room. My steps were reluctant. My observations: the proportions of sniffling at each ceremony were about equal and the audiences were about equal and levels of whimsy and seriousness were about the same wherever you went. The emotions careened, high and low, across the whole spectrum of possible feelings. The music might be different from case to case—stately baroque anthems or klezmer rave-ups—but the intent was the same. By 3:00 P.M., I no longer knew what marriage meant, really, except that the celebration of it seemed built into every life I knew but my own.

The doors of the Rip Van Winkle Room were open, as distinct from the other suites, and I tiptoed through them and closed these great carved doors behind myself. I slipped into the bride's side. The light was dim, Sis. The light was deep in the ultraviolet spectrum, as when we used to go, as kids, to the exhibitions at the Hall of Science and Industry. There seemed to be some kind of mummery, some kind of expressive dance, taking place at the altar. The Champlain Pentecostal Singers were wailing eerily. As I searched the room for familiar faces, I noticed them everywhere. Just a couple of rows away Alex McKinnon and her boy Zack were squished into a row and were fidgeting desperately. Had they known Brice? Had they known you? Maybe they counted themselves close friends of Sarah Wilton. Zack actually turned and waved and seemed to mouth something to me, but I couldn't make it out. On the groom's side, I saw Linda Pietrzsyk, though she ought to have been working in the office, fielding calls, and she was surrounded by Cheese, Chip, Mick, Mark, Stig, Blair and a half-dozen other delinquents from her peer group. Like some collective organism of mirth and irony, they convulsed over the proceedings, over the scarlet tights and boas and dance belts of the modern dancers capering at the altar. A row beyond these Skidmore halfwits—though she never sat in at any ceremony—was Glenda Manzini herself, and she seemed to be sobbing uncontrollably, a handkerchief like a veil across her face. Where was her husband? And her boy? Then, to my amazement, Sis, when I looked back at the S.R.O. audience beyond the last aisle over on the groom's side, *I saw Mom and Dad.* What were they doing there? And how had they known? I had done everything to keep the wedding from them. I had hoarded these bad feelings. Dad's face was gray with remorse, as though he could have done something to stop the proceedings, and Mom held tight to his side, wearing dark glasses of a perfect opacity. At once, I got up from the row where I'd parked myself and climbed over the exasperated families seated next to me, jostling their knees. As I went, I became aware of Brice McCann's soft, insinuating voice ricocheting, in Dolby surround-sound, from one wall of the Rip Van Winkle Room to the next. The room was appropriately named, it seemed to me then. We were all sleepers who dreamed a reverie of marriage, not one of us had waked to see the bondage, the violence, the excess of its cabalistic prayers and rituals. Marriage was oneiric. Not one of us was willing to pronounce the truth of its dream language of slavery and submission and transmission of property, and Brice's vow, *to have and to hold Sarah Wilton, till death did them part, forsaking all others*, seemed to me like the pitch of a used-car dealer or insurance salesman, and these words rang out in the room, likewise Sarah's uncertain and breathy reply, and I rushed at the center aisle, pushing away cretinous guests and cherubic newborns toward my parents, to embrace them as these words fell, these words with their intimations of mortality, *to tell my parents I should never have let you drive that night, Sis. How could I have let you drive? How could I have been so stupid? My tires were bald—I couldn't afford better. My car was a deathtrap; and I was its proper driver, bent on my long, complicated program of failure, my program of futures abandoned, of half-baked ideas, of big plans that came to nought, of cheap talk and lies, of drinking binges, petty theft; my car was made for my own death, Sis, the inevitable and welcome end to the kind of shame and regret I had brought upon everyone close to me, you especially, who must have wept inwardly, in your bosom, when you felt compelled to ask me to read a poem on your special day, before you totaled my car, on that curve, running up over the bream, shrieking, flipping the vehicle, skidding thirty feet on the roof, hitting the granite outcropping there, plunging out of the seat (why no seat belt?), snapping your neck, ejecting through the windshield, catching part of yourself there, tumbling over the hood, breaking both legs, puncturing your lung, losing an eye, shattering your wrist, bleeding, coming to rest at last in a pile of mouldering leaves, where rain fell upon you, until, unconsciously, you died.*

Yet, as I called out to Mom and Dad, the McCann-Wilton wedding party suddenly scattered, the vows were through, the music was overwhelming, the bride and groom were married; there were Celtic pipes, and voices all in harmony—it was a dirge, it was a jig, it was a chant of religious ecstasy—and I couldn't tell what was wedding and what was funeral, whether there was an end to one and a beginning to the other, and there were shouts of joy and confetti in the air, and beating of breasts and the procession of pink-cheeked teenagers, two by two, all living the dream of American marriages with cars and children and small businesses and pension plans and social-security checks and grandchildren, and I couldn't get close to my parents in the throng; in fact, I couldn't be sure if it had been them standing there at all, in that fantastic crowd, that crowd of dreams, and I realized I was alone at Brice McCann's wedding, alone among people who would have been just as happy not to have me there, as I had often been alone, even in fondest company, even among those who cared for me. I should have stayed home and watched television.

This didn't stop me, though. I made my way to the reception. I shoveled down the chicken satay and shrimp with green curry, along with the proud families of Sarah Wilton and Brice McCann. Linda Pietrzsyk appeared by my side, as when we had kissed in the Ticonderoga Suite. She asked if I was feeling all right.

—Sure, I said.

—Don't you think I should drive you home?

—There's someone I want to talk to, I said. —Then I'd be happy to go.

And Linda asked:

—What's in the bag?

She was referring to my Wal-Mart shopping bag, Sis. I think the Wal-Mart policy which asserts that *employees are not to let a customer pass without asking if this customer needs help* is incredibly enlightened. I think the way to a devoted customer is through his or her dignity. In the shopping bag, I was carrying the wedding gift I had brought for Brice McCann and Sarah Wilton. I didn't know if I should reveal this gift to Linda, because I didn't know if she would understand, but I told her anyhow. *Is this what it's like to discover, all at once, that you are sharing your life?*

—Oh, that's some of my sister.

—Andrew, Linda said, and then she apparently didn't know how to continue. Her voice, in a pair of false starts, oscillated with worry. Her smile was grim. —Maybe this would be a good time to leave.

But I didn't leave, Sis. I brought out the most dangerous weapon in my arsenal, the pinnacle of my nefarious plans for this event, also stored in my Wal-Mart bag. The Chicken Mask. That's right, Sis. I had been saving it ever since my days at Hot Bird, and as Brice had yet to understand that I had crashed his wedding for a specific reason, I slipped this mask over my neatly parted hair, and over the collar of the wash-and-wear suit that I had bought that week for this occasion. I must say, in the mirrored reception area in the Rip Van Winkle Room, I was one elegant chicken. I immediately began to search the premises for the groom, and it was difficult to find him at first, since there were any number of like-minded beret-wearing motivational speakers slouching against pillars and counters. At last, though, I espied him preening in the middle of a small group of maidens, over by the electric fountain we had installed for the ceremony. He was laughing good-naturedly. When he first saw me, in the Chicken Mask, working my way toward him, I'm sure he saw me as an omen for his new union. *Terrific! We've got a chicken at the ceremony! Poultry is always reassuring at wedding time!* Linda was trailing me across the room. Trying to distract me. I had to be short with her. I told her to go find herself a husband.

I worked my way into McCann's limber and witty reception chatter and mimed a certain Chicken-style affability. Then, when one of those disagreeable conversational silences overtook the group, I ventured a question of your intended:

—So, Brice, how do you think your last fiancée, Eileen, would be re-acting to your first-class nuptial ceremony today? Would she have liked it?

There was a confused hush, as three or four of the secretarial beau-ties of his circle considered the best way to respond to this thorny question.

—Well, since she's passed away, I think she would probably be smil-ing down on us from above. I've felt her presence throughout the deci-sion to marry Sarah, and I think Eileen knows that I'll never forget her. That I'll always love her.

—Oh, is that right? I said,—because the funny thing is I happen to have her *with me here*, and . . .

Then I opened up the small box of you (you were in a Tiffany jew-elry box that I had spirited out of Mom's jewelry cache because I liked its pale teal shade: the color of rigor mortis as I imagined it), held it up toward Brice and then tossed some of it. I'm sure you know, Sis, that chips of bone tend to be heavier and therefore to fall more quickly to the ground, while the rest of the ashes make a sort of cloud when you throw them, when you cast them aloft. Under the circumstances, this cloud seemed to have a character, a personality. *Thus, you darted and feinted around Brice's head*, Sis, so that he began coughing and wiping the corners of his eyes, dusty with your remains. His consorts were hacking as well, among them Sarah Wilton, his troth. How had I missed her before? She was radiant like a woman whose prayers have been answered, who sees the promise of things to come, who sees uncertainties and contingencies diminished, and yet she was rushing away from me, astonished, as were the others. I realized I had caused a commotion. Still, I gave chase, Sis, and I overcame your Brice Mc-Cann, where he blockaded himself on the far side of a table full of spring rolls. Though I have never been a fighting guy, I gave him an elbow in the nose, as if I were a Chicken and this elbow my wing. I'm sure I mashed some cartilage. He got a little nosebleed. I think I may have broken the Mansion's unbroken streak of peaceful weddings.

At this point, of course, a pair of beefy Mansion employees (the Mc-Carthy brothers, Tom and Eric) arrived on the scene and pulled me off of Brice McCann. They also tore the Chicken Mask from me. And they never returned this piece of my property afterwards. At the moment of unmasking, Brice reacted with mock astonishment. But how could he have failed to guess? That I would wait for my chance, however many years it took?

—Andy?

I said nothing, Sis. Your ghost had been in the cloud that wreathed him; your ghost had swooped out of the little box that I'd held, and now, at last, you were released from your disconsolate march on the surface of the earth, your march of unfinished business, your march of fixed ideas and obsessions unslaked by death. I would be happy if you were at peace now, Sis, and I would be happy if I were at peace; I would be happy if the thunderclouds and lightning of Brice and Sarah's wedding would yield to some warm autumn day in which you had good weather for your flight up through the heavens.

Out in the foyer, where the guests from the Valentine Room were promenading in some of the finest threads I had ever seen, Tom McCarthy told me that Glenda Manzini wanted to see me in her office—before I was removed from the Mansion on the Hill permanently. We walked against the flow of the crowd beginning to empty from each of the suites. Our trudge was long. When I arrived at Glenda's refrigerated chamber, she did an unprecedented thing, Sis, she closed the door. I had never before inhabited that space alone with her. She didn't invite me to sit. Her voice was raised from the outset. Pinched between thumb and forefinger (the shade of her nail polish, a dark maroon, is known in beauty circles, I believe, as *Vamp*), as though it were an ounce of gold or a pellet of plutonium, she held a single green M&M.

—Can you explain this? she asked. —Can you tell me what this is?

—I think that's a green M&M, I said. —I think that's the traditional green color, as opposed to one of the new brighter shades they added in a recent campaign for market share.

—Andy, don't try to amuse me. What was this green M&M doing behind my filing cabinet?

—Well, I—

—I'm certain that I didn't leave a green M&M back there. I would never leave an M&M behind a filing cabinet. In fact, I would never allow a green M&M into this office in the first place.

—That was months ago.

—I've been holding on to it for months, Glenda said. —Do you think I'm stupid?

—On the contrary, I said.

—Do you think you can come in here and violate the privacy of my office?

—I think you're brilliant, I said. —And I think you're very sad. And I think you should surrender your job to someone who cares for the institution you're celebrating here.

Now that I had let go of you, Sis, now that I had begun to compose this narrative in which I relinquished the hem of your spectral bedsheet, I saw through the language of business, the rhetoric of hypocrisy. Why had she sent me out for those birth-control pills? Why did she make me schedule her chiropractic appointments? Because she could. *But what couldn't be controlled, what could never be controlled, was the outcome of devotion.* Glenda's expression, for the first time on record, was stunned. She launched into impassioned colloquy about how the Mansion on the Hill was supposed to be a *refuge*, and how, with my *antics*, as she called them, I had sullied the reputation of the Mansion and endangered its business plan, and how it was clear *that assaulting strangers while wearing a rubber mask is the kind of activity that proves you are an unstable person, and I just think, well, I don't see the point in discussing it with you anymore and I think you have some se-*

rious choices to make, Andy, if you want to be part of regular human society, and so forth, which is just plain bunk, as far as I'm concerned. It's not as if Brice McCann were a *stranger* to me.

I'm always the object of tirades by my supervisors, for overstepping my position, for lying, for wanting too much—this is one of the deep receivables on the balance sheet of my life—and yet at the last second Glenda Manzini didn't fire me. According to shrewd managerial strategy, she simply waved toward the door. With the Mansion crowded to capacity now, with volume creeping upward in the coming months, they would need someone with my skills. To validate the cars in the parking lot, for example. Mark my words, Sis, parking validation will soon be as big in the Northeast as it is in the West.

When the McCarthys flung me through the main doors, Linda Pietrzsyk was waiting. What unfathomable kindness. At the main entrance, on the way out, I passed through a gauntlet of rice-flingers. Bouquets drifted through the skies to the mademoiselles of the Capital. Garters fell into the hands of local bachelors. Then I was beyond all good news and seated in the passenger seat of Linda's battered Volkswagen. She was crying. We progressed slowly along back roads. I had been given chances and had squandered them. I had done my best to love, Sis. I had loved you, and you were gone. In Linda's car, at dusk, we sped along the very road where you took your final drive. Could Linda have known? Your true resting place is forested by white birches, they dot the length of that winding lane, the fingers of the dead reaching up through burdens of snow to impart much-needed instruction to the living. In intermittent afternoon light, in seizure-inducing light, unperturbed by the advances of merchandising, I composed a proposal.

Ethan Canin

✺

The Palace Thief

I tell this story not for my own honor, for there is little of that here, and not as a warning, for a man of my calling learns quickly that all warnings are in vain. Nor do I tell it in apology for St. Benedict's School, for St. Benedict's School needs no apologies. I tell it only to record certain foretellable incidents in the life of a well-known man, in the event that the brief candle of his days may sometime come under the scrutiny of another student of history. That is all. This is a story without surprises.

There are those, in fact, who say I should have known what would happen between St. Benedict's and me, and I suppose that they are right; but I loved that school. I gave service there to the minds of three generations of boys and always left upon them, if I was successful, the delicate imprint of their culture. I battled their indolence with discipline, their boorishness with philosophy and the arrogance of their stations with the history of great men before them. I taught the sons of nineteen senators. I taught a boy who, if not for the vengeful recriminations of the tabloids, would today have been President of the United States. That school was my life.

This is why, I suppose, I accepted the invitation sent to me by Mr. Sedgewick Bell at the end of last year, although I should have known better. I suppose I should have recalled what kind of boy he had been at St. Benedict's forty-two years before instead of posting my response so promptly in the mail and beginning that evening to prepare my test. He, of course, was the son of Senator Sedgewick Hyram Bell, the West Virginia demagogue who kept horses at his residence in Washington,

D.C., and had swung several southern states for Wendell Wilkie. The younger Sedgewick was a dull boy.

I first met him when I had been teaching history at St. Benedict's for only five years, in the autumn after his father had been delivered to office on the shoulders of southern patricians frightened by the unionization of steel and mines. Sedgewick appeared in my classroom in November of 1945, in a short-pants suit. It was midway through the fall term, that term in which I brought the boys forth from the philosophical idealism of the Greeks into the realm of commerce, military might and the law, which had given Julius Caesar his prerogative from Macedonia to Seville. My students, of course, were agitated. It is a sad distinction of that age group, the exuberance with which the boys abandon the moral endeavor of Plato and embrace the powerful, pragmatic hand of Augustus. The more sensitive ones had grown silent, and for several weeks our class discussions had been dominated by the martial instincts of the coarser boys. Of course I was sorry for this, but I was well aware of the import of what I taught at St. Benedict's. Our headmaster, Mr. Woodbridge, made us continually aware of the role our students would eventually play in the affairs of our country.

My classroom was in fact a tribute to the lofty ideals of man, which I hoped would inspire my boys, and at the same time to the fleeting nature of human accomplishment, which I hoped would temper their ambition with humility. It was a dual tactic, with which Mr. Woodbridge heartily agreed. Above the doorframe hung a tablet, made as a term project by Henry L. Stimson when he was a boy here, that I hoped would teach my students of the irony that history bestows upon ambition. In clay relief, it said:

> I am Shutruk-Nahhunte, King of Anshan and Susa,
> sovereign of the land of Elam.
> By the command of Inshushinak,
> I destroyed Sippar, took the stele of Naram-Sin,
> and brought it back to Elam,
> where I erected it as an offering to my god,
> Inshushinak.

> —Shutruk-Nahhunte, 1158 B.C.

I always noted this tablet to the boys on their first day in my classroom, partly to inform them of their predecessors at St. Benedict's, and partly to remind them of the great ambition and conquest that had been utterly forgotten centuries before they were born. Afterwards I had one of them recite, from the wall where it hung above my desk, Shelley's *Ozymandias*. It is critical for any man of import to understand his own insignificance before the sands of time, and this is what my classroom always showed my boys.

As young Sedgewick Bell stood in the doorway of that classroom his first day at St. Benedict's, however, it was apparent that such efforts would be lost on him. I could see that not only was he a dullard but a roustabout. The boys happened to be wearing the togas they had made from sheets and safety pins the day before, spreading their knees like magistrates in the wooden desk chairs, and I was taking them through the recitation of the emperors when Mr. Woodbridge entered alongside the stout, red-faced Sedgewick and introduced him to the class. I had taught for five years, as I have said, and I knew the frightened, desperate bravura of a new boy. Sedgewick Bell did not wear this look.

Rather, he wore one of disdain. The boys, fifteen in all, were instantly intimidated into sensing the foolishness of their improvised cloaks, and one of them, Clay Walter, the leader of the dullards—though far from a dullard himself—said, to mild laughter, "Where's your toga, kid?"

Sedgewick Bell answered, "Your mother must be wearing your pants today."

It took me a moment to regain the attention of the class, and when Sedgewick was seated I had him go to the board and copy out the Emperors. Of course, he did not know the names of any of them, and my boys had to call them out, repeatedly correcting his spelling as he wrote out in a sloppy hand:

> Augustus
> Tiberius
> Caligula
> Claudius
> Nero

Galba
Otho

all the while lifting and resettling the legs of his short pants in mockery of what his new classmates were wearing. "Young man," I said, "this is a serious class, and I expect that you will take it seriously."

"If it's such a serious class, then why're they all wearing dresses?" he responded, again to laughter, although by now Clay Walter had loosened the rope belt at his waist, and the boys around him were shifting uncomfortably in their togas.

From that first day, Sedgewick Bell became a boor and a bully, a damper to the illumination of the eager minds of my boys and a purveyor of the mean-spirited humor that is like kerosene in a school such as ours. What I asked of my boys that semester was simple, that they learn the facts I presented to them in an "Outline of Ancient Roman History," which I had whittled, through my years of teaching, to exactly four closely typed pages; yet Sedgewick Bell was unwilling to do so. He was a poor student, and on his first exam could not even tell me who it was that Mark Antony and Octavian had routed at Philippi, nor who Octavian later became, although an average wood beetle in the floor of my classroom could have done so with ease.

Furthermore, as soon as he arrived he began a stream of capers using spitballs, wads of gum and thumbtacks. Of course it was common for a new boy to engage his comrades thusly, but Sedgewick Bell then began to add the dangerous element of natural leadership—which was based on the physical strength of his features—to his otherwise puerile antics. He organized the boys. At exactly fifteen minutes to the hour, they would all drop their pencils at once or cough or slap closed their books so that writing at the blackboard my hands would jump in the air.

At a boys' school, of course, punishment is a cultivated art. Whenever one of these antics occurred I simply made a point of calling on Sedgewick Bell to answer a question. General laughter usually followed his stabs at answers, and although Sedgewick himself usually laughed along with everyone else, it did not require a great deal of insight to know that the tactic would work. The organized events began to occur less frequently.

In retrospect, however, perhaps my strategy was a mistake, for to convince a boy of his own stupidity is to shoot a poisonous arrow indeed. Perhaps Sedgewick Bell's life would have turned out more nobly if I had understood his motivations right away and treated him differently at the start. But such are the pointless speculations of a teacher. What was irrefutably true was that he was performing poorly on his quizzes, even if his behavior had improved somewhat, and therefore I called him to my office.

In those days, I lived in small quarters off the rear of the main hall, in what had been a slave's room when the grounds of St. Benedict's had been the estate of the philanthropist and horse breeder Cyrus Beck. Having been at school as long as I had, I no longer lived in the first-form dormitory that stood behind my room, but supervised it, so that I saw most of the boys only in matters of urgency. They came sheepishly before me.

With my bed folded into the wall, the room became my office, and shortly after supper one day that winter of his first-form year, Sedgewick Bell knocked and entered. Immediately he began to inspect the premises, casting his eyes, which had the patrician set of his father's, from the desk, to the shelves, to the bed folded into the wall.

"Sit down, boy."

"You're not married, are you, sir?"

"No, Sedgewick, I am not. However, we are here to talk about *you*."

"That's why you like puttin' us in togas, right?"

I had, frankly, never encountered a boy like him before, who at the age of thirteen would affront his schoolmaster without other boys in audience. He gazed at me flatly, his chin in his hand.

"Young man," I said, sensing his motivations with sudden clarity, "We are concerned about your performance here, and I have made an appointment to see your father."

In fact, I had made no appointment with Senator Bell, but at that moment I understood that I would have to. "What would you like me to tell the senator?" I said.

His gaze faltered. "I'm going to try harder, sir, from now on."

"Good, Sedgewick. Good."

Indeed, that week the boys reenacted the pivotal scenes from *Julius*

Caesar, and Sedgewick read his lines quite passably and contributed little that I could see to the occasional fits of giggles that circulated among the slower boys. The next week, I gave a quiz on the Triumvirate of Crassus, Pompey and Caesar, and he passed for the first time yet, with a C+.

Nonetheless, I had told him that I was going to speak with his father, and this is what I was determined to do. At the time, Senator Sedgewick Hyram Bell was appearing regularly in the newspapers and on the radio in his stand against Truman's plan for national health insurance, and I was loathe to call upon such a well-known man concerning the behavior of his son. On the radio his voice was a tobacco drawl that had won him populist appeal throughout West Virginia, although his policies alone would certainly not have done so. I was at the time in my late twenties, and although I was armed with scruples and an education, my hands trembled as I dialed his office. To my surprise, I was put through, and the senator, in the drawl I recognized instantly, agreed to meet me one afternoon the following week. The man already enjoyed national stature, of course, and although any other father would no doubt have made the journey to St. Benedict's himself, I admit that the prospect of seeing the man in his own office intrigued me. Thus I journeyed to the capital.

St. Benedict's lies in the bucolic, equine expanse of rural Virginia, nearer in spirit to the Carolinas than to Maryland, although the drive to Washington requires little more than an hour. The bus followed the misty, serpentine course of the Passamic, then entered the marshlands that are now the false-brick suburbs of Washington and at last left me downtown in the capital, where I proceeded the rest of the way on foot. I arrived at the Senate office building as the sun moved low against the bare-limbed cherries among the grounds. I was frightened but determined, and I reminded myself that Sedgewick Hyram Bell was a senator but also a father, and I was here on business that concerned his son. The office was as grand as a duke's.

I had not waited long in the anteroom when the man himself appeared, feisty as a game hen, bursting through a side door and clapping me on the shoulder as he urged me before him into his office. Of course I was a novice then in the world of politics and had not yet realized that such men are, above all, likable. He put me in a leather seat, offered a cigar, which I refused, and then with real or contrived wonder—perhaps he did something like this with all of his visitors—he proceeded to show me an antique sidearm that had been sent to him that morning by a constituent and that had once belonged, he said, to the coachman of Robert E. Lee. "You're a history buff," he said, "right?"

"Yes, sir."

"Then take it. It's yours."

"No, sir. I couldn't."

"Take the damn thing."

"All right, I will."

"Now, what brings you to this dreary little office?"

"Your son, sir."

"What the devil has he done now?"

"Very little, sir. We're concerned that he isn't learning the material."

"What material is that?"

"We're studying the Romans now, sir. We've left the Republic and entered the Empire."

"Ah," he said. "Be careful with that, by the way. It still fires."

"Your son seems not to be paying attention, sir."

He again offered me the box of cigars across the desk and then bit off the end of his own. "Tell me," he said, puffing the thing until it flamed suddenly, "What's the good of what you're teaching them boys?"

This was a question for which I was well prepared, fortunately, having recently written a short piece in *The St. Benedict's Crier* answering the same challenge put forth there by an anonymous boy. "When they read of the reign of Augustus Caesar," I said without hesitation, "when they learn that his rule was bolstered by commerce, a postal system and the arts, by the reformation of the senate and by the righting of an inequitable system of taxation, when they see the effect of scientific progress through the census and the enviable network of Roman roads, how these advances led mankind away from the brutish rivalries of potentates into the two centuries of *pax romana*, then they understand the importance of character and high ideals."

He puffed at his cigar. "Now, that's a horse who can talk," he said. "And you're telling me my son Sedgewick has his head in the clouds."

"It's my job, sir, to mold your son's character."

He thought for a moment, idly fingering a match. Then his look turned stern. "I'm sorry, young man," he said slowly, "but you will not mold him. I will mold him. You will merely teach him."

That was the end of my interview, and I was politely shown the door. I was bewildered, naturally, and found myself in the elevator before I could even take account of what had happened. Senator Bell was quite likable, as I have noted, but he had without doubt cut me, and as I made my way back to the bus station, the gun stowed deep in my briefcase, I considered what it must have been like to have been raised under such a tyrant. My heart warmed somewhat toward young Sedgewick.

Back at St. Benedict's, furthermore, I saw that my words had evidently had some effect on the boy, for in the weeks that followed he continued on his struggling, uphill course. He passed two more quizzes, receiving an A– on one of them. For his midterm project he produced an adequate papier-mâché rendering of Hadrian's Gate, and in class he was less disruptive to the group of do-nothings among whom he sat, if indeed he was not in fact attentive.

Such, of course, are the honeyed morsels of a teacher's existence, those students who come, under one's own direction, from darkness into the light, and I admit that I might have taken a special interest that term in Sedgewick Bell. If I gave him the benefit of the doubt on his quizzes when he straddled two grades, if I began to call on him in class only for those questions I had reason to believe he could answer, then I was merely trying to encourage the nascent curiosity of a boy who, to all appearances, was struggling gamely from beneath the formidable umbra of his father.

The fall term was by then drawing to a close, and the boys had begun the frenzy of preliminary quizzes for the annual Mister Julius Caesar competition. Here again, I suppose I was in my own way rooting for Sedgewick. Mister Julius Caesar is a St. Benedict's tradition, held in reverence among the boys, the kind of mythic ritual that is the currency of a school like ours. It is a contest, held in two phases. The first is a narrowing maneuver, by means of a dozen written quizzes, from which three boys from the first form emerge victorious. The second is a public tournament, in which these three take the stage before the assembled student body and answer questions about ancient Rome until one alone emerges triumphant, as had Caesar himself from among Crassus and Pompey. Parents and graduates fill out the audience. Out front of Mr. Woodbridge's office, a plaque attests to the Misters Julius Caesar of the previous half-century—a list that begins with John F. Dulles in 1901—and although the ritual might seem quaint to those who have not attended St. Benedict's, I can only say that, in a school like ours, one cannot overstate the importance of a public joust.

That year I had three obvious contenders: Clay Walter, who, as I intimated, was a somewhat gifted boy; Martin Blythe, a studious type; and Deepak Mehta, the son of a Bombay mathematician, who was dreadfully quiet but clearly my best student. It was Deepak, in fact, who on his own and entirely separate from the class had studied the disparate peoples, from the Carthaginians to the Egyptians, whom the Romans had conquered.

By the end of the narrowing quizzes, however, a surprising configuration had emerged: Sedgewick Bell had pulled himself to within a few points of third place in my class. This was when I made my first mistake. Although I should certainly have known better, I was impressed enough by his efforts that I broke one of the cardinal rules of teaching: I gave him an A on a quiz on which he had earned only a B, and in so doing, I leapfrogged him over Martin Blythe. On March 15th, when the three finalists took their seats on stage in front of the assembled population of the school, Sedgewick Bell was among them, and his father was among the audience.

The three boys had donned their togas for the event and were arranged around the dais on which a pewter platter held the green silk garland that, at the end of the morning, I would place upon the brow of the winner. As the interrogator, I stood front row, center, next to Mr. Woodbridge.

"Which language was spoken by the Sabines?"

"Oscan," answered Clay Walter without hesitation.

"Who composed the Second Triumvirate?"

"Mark Antony, Octavian and Marcus Aemilius Lepidus, sir," answered Deepak Mehta.

"Who was routed at Philippi?"

Sedgewick Bell's eyes showed no recognition. He lowered his head in his hands as though pushing himself to the limit of his intellect, and in the front row my heart dropped. Several boys in the audience began to twitter. Sedgewick's own leg began to shake inside his toga. When he looked up again I felt that it was I who had put him in this untenable position, I who had brought a tender bud too soon into the heat, and I wondered if he would ever forgive me; but then, without warning, he smiled slightly, folded his hands and said, "Brutus and Cassius."

"Good," I said, instinctively. Then I gathered my poise. "Who deposed Romulus Augustulus, the last Emperor of the Western Empire?"

"Odoacer," Clay Walter answered, then added, "in 476 A.D."

"Who introduced the professional army to Rome?"

"Gaius Marius, sir," answered Deepak Mehta, then himself added, "in 104 B.C."

When I asked Sedgewick his next question—Who was the leading Carthaginian General of the Second Punic War?—I felt some unease because the boys in the audience seemed to sense that I was favoring him with an easier examination. Nonetheless, his head sank into his hands, and he appeared once again to be straining the limits of his memory before he looked up and produced the obvious answer, "Hannibal."

I was delighted. Not only was he proving my gamble worthwhile but he was showing the twittering boys in the audience that, under fire, discipline produces accurate thought. By now they had quieted, and I had the sudden, heartening premonition that Sedgewick Bell was going to surprise us after all, that his tortoiselike deliberation would win him, by morning's end, the garland of laurel.

The next several rounds of questions proceeded much in the same manner as had the previous two. Deepak Mehta and Clay Walter answered without hesitation, and Sedgewick Bell did so only after a tedious and deliberate period of thought. What I realized, in fact, was that his style made for excellent theater. The parents, I could see, were impressed, and Mr. Woodbridge next to me, no doubt thinking about the next annual drive, was smiling broadly.

After a second-form boy had brought a glass of water to each of the contestants, I moved on to the next level of questions. These had been chosen for their difficulty, and on the first round Clay Walter fell out, not knowing the names of Augustus's children. He left the stage and moved back among his dimwitted pals in the audience. By the rule of clockwise progression the same question then went to Deepak Mehta, who answered it correctly, followed by the next one, which concerned King Jugurtha of Numidia. Then, because I had no choice, I had to ask Sedgewick Bell something difficult: "Which general had the support of the aristocrats in the civil war of 88 B.C.?"

To the side, I could see several parents pursing their lips and furrowing their brows, but Sedgewick Bell appeared to not even notice the greater difficulty of the query. Again he dropped his head into his hands. By now the audience expected his period of deliberation, and they sat quietly. One could hear the hum of the ventilation system and the dripping of the icicles outside. Sedgewick Bell cast his eyes downward, and it was at this moment that I realized he was cheating.

I had come to this job straight from my degree at Carleton College, at the age of twenty-one, having missed enlistment due to myopia, and carrying with me the hope that I could give to my boys the more important vision that my classical studies had given to me. I knew that they responded best to challenge. I knew that a teacher who coddled them at that age would only hold them back, would keep them in the bosoms of their mothers so long that they would remain weak-minded through preparatory school and inevitably then through college. The best of my own teachers had been tyrants. I well remembered this. Yet at that moment I felt an inexplicable pity for the boy. Was it simply the humiliation we had both suffered at the hands of his father? I peered through my glasses at the stage and knew at once that he had attached "The Outline of Ancient Roman History" to the inside of his toga.

I don't know how long I stood there, between the school assembled behind me and the two boys seated in front, but after a period of internal deliberation, during which time I could hear the rising murmurs of the audience, I decided that in the long run it was best for Sedgewick Bell to be caught. Oh, how the battle is lost for want of a horse! I leaned to Mr. Woodbridge next to me and whispered, "I believe Sedgewick Bell is cheating."

"Ignore it," he whispered back.

"What?"

Of course, I have great respect for what Mr. Woodbridge did for St. Benedict's in the years he was among us. A headmaster's world is a far more complex one than a teacher's, and it is historically inopportune to blame a life gone afoul on a single incident in childhood. However, I myself would have stood up for our principles had Mr. Woodbridge not at that point said, "Ignore it, Hundert, or look for another job."

Naturally, my headmaster's words startled me for a moment; but being familiar with the necessities of a boys' school, and having recently entertained my first thoughts about one day becoming a headmaster myself, I simply nodded when Sedgewick Bell produced the correct answer, Lucius Cornelius Sulla. Then I went on to the next question, which concerned Scipio Africanus Major. Deepak Mehta answered it correctly, and I turned once again to Sedgewick Bell.

In a position of moral leadership, of course, compromise begets only more compromise, and although I know this now from my own experience, at the time I did so only from my study of history. Perhaps that is why I again found an untenable compassion muddying my thoughts. What kind of desperation would lead a boy to cheat on a public stage? His father and mother were well back in the crowded theater, but when I glanced behind me my eye went instantly to them, as though they were indeed my own parents, out from Kansas City. "Who were the first emperors to reign over the divided Empire?" I asked Sedgewick Bell.

When one knows the magician's trick, the only wonder is in its obviousness, and as Sedgewick Bell lowered his head this time I clearly saw the nervous flutter of his gaze directed into the toga. Indeed I imagined him scanning the entire "Outline," from Augustus to Jovian, pasted inside the twill, before coming to the answer, which, pretending to ponder, he then spoke aloud: "Valentinian the First, and Valens."

Suddenly Senator Bell called out, "That's my boy!"

The crowd thundered, and I had the sudden, indefensible urge to steer the contest in young Sedgewick Bell's direction. In a few moments, however, from within the subsiding din, I heard the thin, accented voice of a woman speaking Deepak Mehta's name; and it was the presence of his mother, I suppose, that finally brought me to my senses. Deepak answered the next question correctly, about Diocletian, and then I turned to Sedgewick Bell and asked him, "Who was Hamilcar Barca?"

Of course, it was only Deepak who knew that this answer was not on the "Outline," because Hamilcar Barca was a Phoenician general eventually routed by the Romans; it was only Deepak, as I have noted, who had bothered to study the conquered peoples. He briefly widened his eyes at me—in recognition? in gratitude? in disapproval?—while, beside him, Sedgewick Bell again lowered his head into his hands. After a long pause, Sedgewick asked me to repeat the question.

I did so, and after another, long pause, he scratched his head. Finally, he said, "Jeez."

The boys in the audience laughed, but I turned and silenced them. Then I put the same question to Deepak Mehta, who answered it correctly, of course, and then received a round of applause that was polite but not sustained.

It was only as I mounted the stage to present Deepak with the garland of laurel, however, that I glanced at Mr. Woodbridge and realized that he too had wanted me to steer the contest toward Sedgewick Bell. At the same moment, I saw Senator Bell making his way toward the rear door of the hall. Young Sedgewick stood limply to the side of me, and I believe I had my first inkling then of the mighty forces that would twist the life of that boy. I could only imagine his thoughts as he stood there on stage while his mother, struggling to catch up with the senator, vanished through the fire door at the back. The next morning, our calligraphers would add Deepak Mehta's name to the plaque outside Mr. Woodbridge's office, and young Sedgewick Bell would begin his lifelong pursuit of missed glory.

Yet perhaps because of the disappointment I could see in Mr. Woodbridge's eyes, it somehow seemed that I was the one who had failed the boy, and as soon as the auditorium was empty I left for his room. There I found him seated on the bed, still in his toga, gazing out the small window to the lacrosse fields. I could see the sheets of my "Outline" pressed against the inside of his garment.

"Well, young man," I said, knocking on the doorframe, "that certainly was an interesting performance."

He turned around from the window and looked at me coldly. What he did next I have thought about many times over the years, the labyrinthine wiliness of it, and I can only attribute the precociousness of his maneuvering to the bitter education he must have received at home. As I stood before him in the doorway, Sedgewick Bell reached inside his cloak and one at a time lifted out the pages of my "Outline."

I stepped inside and closed the door. Every teacher knows a score of boys who do their best to be expelled; this is a cliché in a school like ours, but as soon as I closed the door to his room and he acknowledged the act with a feline smile, I knew that this was not Sedgewick Bell's intention at all.

"I knew you saw," he said.

"Yes, you are correct."

"How come you didn't say anything, eh, Mr. Hundert?"

"It's a complicated matter, Sedgewick."

"It's because my pop was there."

"It had nothing to do with your father."

"Sure, Mr. Hundert."

Frankly, I was at my wits' end, first from what Mr. Woodbridge had said to me in the theater and now from the audacity of the boy's accusation. I myself went to the window then and let my eyes wander over the campus so that they would not have to engage the dark, accusatory gaze of Sedgewick Bell. What transpires in an act of omission like the one I had committed? I do not blame Mr. Woodbridge, of course, any more than a soldier can blame his captain. What had happened was that instead of enforcing my own code of morals, I had allowed Sedgewick Bell to sweep me summarily into his. I did not know at the time what an act of corruption I had committed, although what is especially chilling to me is that I believe that Sedgewick Bell, even at the age of thirteen, did.

He knew also, of course, that I would not pursue the matter, although I spent the ensuing several days contemplating a disciplinary action. Each time I summoned my resolve to submit the boy's name to the honor committee, however, my conviction waned, for at these times I seemed to myself to be nothing more than one criminal turning in another. I fought this battle constantly, in my simple rooms, at the long, chipped table I governed in the dining hall and at the dusty chalkboard before my classes. I felt like an exhausted swimmer trying to climb a slippery wall out of the sea.

Furthermore, I was alone in my predicament, for among a boarding school faculty, which is as perilous as a medieval court, one does not publicly discuss a boy's misdeeds. This is true even if the boy is not the son of a senator. In fact, the only teacher I decided to trust with my situation was Charles Ellerby, our new Latin instructor and a kindred lover of antiquity. I had liked Charles Ellerby as soon as we had met because he was a moralist of no uncertain terms, and indeed when I confided in him about Sedgewick Bell's behavior and Mr. Woodbridge's response, he suggested that it was my duty to circumvent our headmaster and speak to Senator Bell again.

Less than a week after I had begun to marshall my resolve, however, the senator himself called *me*. He proffered a few moments of small talk, asked after the gun he had given me, and then said gruffly, "Young man, my son tells me the Hannibal Barca question was not on the list he had to know."

Now, indeed, I was shocked. Even from young Sedgewick Bell I had not expected this audacity. "How deeply the viper is a viper," I said, before I could help myself.

"Excuse me?"

"The Phoenician general was *Hamilcar* Barca, sir, not Hannibal."

The senator paused. "My son tells me you asked him a question that was not on the list, which the Oriental fellow knew the answer to in advance. He feels you've been unfair, is all."

"It's a complex situation, sir," I said. I marshalled my will again by imagining what Charles Ellerby would do in the situation. However, no sooner had I resolved to confront the senator than it became perfectly clear to me that I lacked the character to do so. I believe this had long been clear to Sedgewick Bell.

"I'm sure it is complex," Senator Bell said, "but I assure you, there are situations more complex. Now, I'm not asking you to correct anything this time, you understand. My son has told me a great deal about you, Mr. Hundert. If I were you, I'd remember that."

"Yes, sir," I said, although by then I realized he had hung up.

And thus young Sedgewick Bell and I began an uneasy compact that lasted out his days at St. Benedict's. He was a dismal student from that day forward, scratching at the very bottom of a class that was itself a far cry from the glorious, yesteryear classes of John Dulles and Henry Stimson. His quizzes were abominations, and his essays were pathetic digestions of those of the boys sitting next to him. He chatted amiably in study hall, smoked cigarettes in the third-form linen room, and when called upon in class could be counted on to blink and stutter as if called upon from sleep.

But perhaps the glory days of St. Benedict's had already begun their wane, for even then, well before the large problems that beset us, no action was taken against the boy. He became a symbol for Charles Ellerby and me, evidence of the first tendrils of moral rot that seemed to be twining among the posts and timbers of our school. Although we told nobody else of his secret, the boy's dimwitted recalcitrance soon succeeded in alienating all but the other students. His second- and third-form years passed as ingloriously as his first, and by the outset of his last with us he had grown to mythic infamy among the faculty members who had known the school in its days of glory.

He had grown physically larger as well, and now when I chanced upon him on the campus he held his ground against my disapproving stare with a dark one of his own. To complicate matters, he had cultivated, despite his boorish character, an impressive popularity among his schoolmates, and it was only through the subtle intervention of several of his teachers that he had failed on two occasions to win the presidency of the student body. His stride had become a strut. His favor among the other boys, of course, had its origin in the strength of his physical features, in the precocious evil of his manner, and in the bellowing timbre of his voice, but unfortunately such crudities are all the more impressive to a group of boys living out of sight of their parents.

That is not to say that the faculty of St. Benedict's had given up hope for Sedgewick Bell. Indeed, a teacher's career is punctuated with difficult students like him, and despite the odds one could not help but hope for his eventual rehabilitation. As did all the other teachers, I held out promise for Sedgewick Bell. In his fits of depravity and intellectual feebleness I continued to look for glimpses of discipline and progress.

By his fourth-form year, however, when I had become dean of seniors, it was clear that Sedgewick Bell would not change, at least not while he was at St. Benedict's. Even with his powerful station, he had not even managed to gain admission to the state university, and it was with a sense of failure then, finally, that I handed him his diploma in the spring of 1949, on an erected stage at the north end of the great field, on which he came forward, met my disapproving gaze with his own flat one and trundled off to sit among his friends.

It was with some surprise then that I learned in *The Richmond Gazette*, thirty-seven years later, of Sedgewick Bell's ascension to the chairmanship of EastAmerica Steel, at that time the second largest corporation in America. I chanced upon the news one morning in the winter of 1987, the year of my great problems with St. Benedict's, while reading the newspaper in the east-lighted breakfast room of the Assistant Headmaster's House. St. Benedict's, as everyone knows, had fallen upon difficult times by then, and an unseemly aspect of my job was that I had to maintain a lookout for possible donors to the school. Forthwith, I sent a letter to Sedgewick Bell.

Apart from the five or six years in which a classmate had written to *The Benedictine* of his whereabouts, I had heard almost nothing about the boy since the year of his graduation. This was unusual, of course, as St. Benedict's makes a point of keeping abreast of its graduates, and I can only assume that his absence in the yearly alumni notes was due to an act of will on his own part. One wonders how much of the boy remained in the man. It is indeed a rare vantage that a St. Benedict's teacher holds, to have known our statesmen, our policy-makers, and our captains of industry in their days of short pants and classroom pranks, and I admit that it was with some nostalgia that I composed the letter.

Since his graduation, of course, my career had proceeded with the steady ascension that the great schools have always afforded their dedicated teachers. Ten years after Sedgewick Bell's departure, I had moved from dean of seniors to dean of the upper school, and after a decade there to dean of academics, a post that some would consider a demotion but that I seized with reverence because it afforded me the chance to make inroads on the minds of a generation. At the time, of course, the country was in the throes of a violent, peristaltic rejection of tradition, and I felt a particular urgency to my mission of staying a course that had led a century of boys through the rise and fall of ancient civilizations.

In those days, our meetings of the faculty and trustees were rancorous affairs in which great pressure was exerted in attempts to alter the time-tested curriculum of the school. Planning a course was like going into battle, and hiring a new teacher was like crowning a king. Whenever one of our ranks retired or left for another school, the different factions fought tooth-and-nail to influence the appointment. I was the dean of academics, as I have noted, and these skirmishes naturally waged around my foxhole. For the lesser appointments I often feinted to gather leverage for the greater ones, whose campaigns I fought with abandon.

At one point especially, midway through that decade in which our country had lost its way, St. Benedict's arrived at a crossroads. The chair of humanities had retired, and a pitched battle over his replacement developed between Charles Ellerby and a candidate from outside. A meeting ensued in which my friend and this other man spoke to the assembled faculty and trustees, and though I will not go into detail, I will say that the outside candidate felt that, because of the advances in our society, history had become little more than a relic.

Oh, what dim-sighted times those were! The two camps sat on opposite sides of the chapel as speakers took the podium one after another to wage war. The controversy quickly became a forum concerning the relevance of the past. Teacher after teacher debated the import of what we in history had taught for generations, and assertion after assertion was met with boos and applause. Tempers blazed. One powerful member of the board had come to the meeting in blue jeans and a tie-dyed shirt, and after we had been arguing for several hours and all of us were exhausted he took the podium and challenged me personally, right then and there, to debate with him the merits of Roman history.

He was not an ineloquent man, and he chose to speak his plea first, so that by the time he had finished his attack against antiquity I sensed that my battle on behalf of Charles Ellerby, and of history itself, was near to lost. My heart was gravely burdened, for if we could not win our point here among teachers, then among whom indeed could we win it? The room was silent, and on the other side of the chapel our opponents were gathering nearer to one another in the pews.

When I rose to defend my calling, however, I also sensed that victory was not beyond my reach. I am not a particularly eloquent orator, but as I took my place at the chancel rail in the amber glow of the small rose window above us, I was braced by the sudden conviction that the great men of history had sent me forward to preserve their deeds. Charles Ellerby looked up at me biting his lip, and suddenly I remembered the answer I had written long ago in *The Crier*. Its words flowed as though unbidden from my tongue, and when I had finished I knew that we had won. It was my proudest moment at St. Benedict's.

Although the resultant split among the faculty was an egregious one, Charles Ellerby secured the appointment, and together we were able to do what I had always dreamed of doing: We redoubled our commitment to classical education. In times of upheaval, of course, adherence to tradition is all the more important, and perhaps this was why St. Benedict's was brought intact through that decade and the one that followed. Our fortunes lifted and dipped with the gentle rhythm to which I had long ago grown accustomed. Our boys won sporting events and prizes, endured minor scandals and occasional tragedies and then passed on to good colleges. Our endowment rose when the government was in the hands of Republicans, as did the caliber of our boys when it was in the hands of Democrats. Senator Bell declined from prominence, and within a few years I read that he had passed away. In time, I was made assistant headmaster. Indeed it was not until a few years ago that anything out of the ordinary happened at all, for it was then, in the late 1980s, that some ill-advised investments were made and our endowment suffered a decline.

Mr. Woodbridge had by this time reached the age of seventy-four, and although he was a vigorous man, one Sunday morning in May while the school waited for him in Chapel he died open-eyed in his bed. Immediately there occurred a Byzantine struggle for succession. There is nothing wrong with admitting that by then I myself coveted the job of Headmaster, for one does not remain four decades at a school without becoming deeply attached to its fate; but Mr. Woodbridge's death had come suddenly and I had not yet begun the preparations for my bid. I was, of course, no longer a young man. I suppose, in fact, that I lost my advantage here by underestimating my opponents who indeed were younger, as Caesar had done with Brutus and Cassius.

I should not have been surprised, then, when after several days of maneuvering, my principal rival turned out to be Charles Ellerby. For several years, I discovered, he had been conducting his own, internecine campaign for the position, and although I had always counted him as my ally and my friend, in the first meeting of the board he rose and spoke accusations against me. He said that I was too old, that I had failed to change with the times, that my method of pedagogy might have been relevant forty years ago but that it was not today. He stood and said that a headmaster needed vigor and that I did not have it. Although I watched him the entire time he spoke, he did not once look back at me.

I was wounded, of course, both professionally and in the hidden part of my heart in which I had always counted Charles Ellerby as a companion in my lifelong search for the magnificence of the past. When several of the older teachers booed him, I felt cheered. At this point I saw that I was not alone in my bid, merely behind, and so I left the meeting without coming to my own defense. Evening had come, and I walked to the dining commons in the company of allies.

How it is, when fighting for one's life, to eat among children! As the boys in their school blazers passed around the platters of fishsticks and the bowls of sliced bread, my heart was pierced with their guileless grace. How soon, I wondered, would they see the truth of the world? How long before they would understand that it was not dates and names that I had always meant to teach them? Not one of them seemed to notice what had descended like thunderheads above their faculty. Not one of them seemed unable to eat.

After dinner, I returned to the Assistant Headmaster's House in order to plot my course and confer with those I still considered allies, but before I could begin my preparations there was a knock at the door. Charles Ellerby stood there, red in the cheeks. "May I ask you some questions?" he said breathlessly.

"It is I who ought to ask them of you," was my answer.

He came in without being asked and took a seat at my table. "You've never been married, am I correct, Hundert?"

"Look, Ellerby, I've been at St. Benedict's since you were in prep school yourself."

"Yes, yes," he said, in an exaggeration of boredom. Of course, he knew as well as I that I had never married, nor started a family, because history itself had always been enough for me. He rubbed his head and appeared to be thinking. To this day, I wonder how he knew about what he said next, unless Sedgewick Bell had somehow told him the story of my visit to the senator. "Look," he said. "There's a rumor you keep a pistol in your desk drawer."

"Hogwash."

"Will you open it for me," he said, pointing there.

"No, I will not. I have been a dean here for twenty years."

"Are you telling me there is no pistol in this house?"

He then attempted to stare me down. He was a man with little character, however, and the bid withered. At that point, in fact, as his eyes fell in submission to my determined gaze, I believe the headmastership became mine. It is a largely unexplored element of history, of course, and one that has long fascinated me, that a great deal of political power and thus a great deal of the arc of nations arises not from intellectual advancements nor social imperatives but from the simple battle of wills among men at tables, such as had just occurred between Charles Ellerby and me.

Instead of opening the desk and brandishing the weapon, however, which of course meant nothing to me but no doubt would have seized the initiative from Ellerby, I denied to him its existence. Why, I do not know; for I was a teacher of history, and was not the firearm its greatest engine? Ellerby, on the other hand, was simply a gadfly to the passing morals of the time. He gathered his things and left my house.

That evening I took the pistol from my drawer. A margin of rust had appeared along the filigreed handle, and despite the ornate workmanship I saw clearly now that in its essence the weapon was ill-proportioned and blunt, the crude instrument of a violent, historically meager man. I had not even wanted it when the irascible demagogue Bell had foisted it upon me, and I had only taken it out of some vague sentiment that a pistol might eventually prove decisive. I suppose I had always imagined firing it someday in a moment of drama. Yet now, here it stood before me in a moment of torpor. I turned it over and cursed it.

That night I took it from the drawer again, hid it in the pocket of my overcoat and walked to the far end of the campus, where I crossed the marsh a good mile from my house, removed my shoes and stepped into the babbling shallows of the Passamic. *The die is cast*, I said, and I threw it twenty yards out into the water. The last impediment to my headmastership had been hurdled, and by the time I came ashore, walked back whistling to my front door, and changed for bed, I was ecstatic.

Yet that night I slept poorly, and in the morning when I rose and went to our faculty meeting, I felt that the mantle of my fortitude had slipped somehow from my shoulders. How hushed is demise! In the hall outside the faculty room, most of the teachers filed by without speaking to me, and once inside I became obsessed with the idea that I had missed this most basic lesson of the past, that conviction is the alpha and the omega of authority. Now I see that I was doomed the moment I threw that pistol in the water, for that is when I lost my conviction. It was as though Sedgewick Bell had risen, all these years later, to drag me down again. Indeed, once the meeting had begun, the older faculty members shrunk back from their previous support of my bid, and the younger ones encircled me as though I were a limping animal. There might as well have been a dagger among the cloaks. By four o'clock that afternoon, Charles Ellerby, a fellow antiquarian whose job I had once helped secure, had been named headmaster, and by the end of that month he had asked me to retire.

And so I was preparing to end my days at St. Benedict's when I received Sedgewick Bell's response to my letter. It was well-written, which I noted with pleasure, and contained no trace of rancor, which is what every teacher hopes to see in the maturation of his disagreeable students. In closing he asked me to call him at EastAmerica Steel, and I did so that afternoon. When I gave my name first to one secretary and then to a second, and after that, moments later, heard Sedgewick's artfully guileless greeting, I instantly recalled speaking to his father forty years before.

After small talk, including my condolences about his father, he told me that the reason he had returned my letter was that he had often dreamed of holding a rematch of Mister Julius Caesar, and that he was now willing to donate a large sum of money to St. Benedict's if I would agree to administer the event. Naturally, I assumed he was joking and passed off the idea with a comment about how funny it was, but Sedgewick Bell repeated the invitation. He wanted very much to be on stage again with Deepak Mehta and Clay Walter. I suppose I should not have been surprised, for it is precisely this sort of childhood slight that will drive a great figure. I told him that I was about to retire. He expressed sympathy but then suggested that the arrangement could be ideal, as now I would no doubt have time to prepare. Then he said that at this station in his life he could afford whatever he wanted materially—with all that this implied, of course, concerning his donation to the Annual Fund—but that more than anything else, he desired the chance to reclaim his intellectual honor. I suppose I was flattered.

Of course, he also offered a good sum of money to me personally. Although I had until then led a life in which finances were never more than a distant concern, I was keenly aware that my time in the school's houses and dining halls was coming to an end. On the one hand, it was not my burning aspiration to secure an endowment for the reign of Charles Ellerby; on the other hand, I needed the money, and I felt a deep loyalty to the school regarding the Annual Fund. That evening, I began to prepare my test.

As assistant headmaster, I had not taught my beloved Roman history in many years, so that poring through my reams of notes was like returning at last to my childhood home. I stopped here and there among the files. I reread the term paper of young Derek Bok on "The Search of Diogenes," and the scrawled one of James Watson on "Archimedes's Method." Among the art projects, I found John Updike's reproduction of the Obelisk of Cleopatra, and a charcoal drawing of the baths of Caracalla by the abstract expressionist Robert Motherwell, unfortunately torn in two and no longer worth anything.

I had always been a diligent notetaker, furthermore, and I believe that what I came up with was a surprisingly accurate reproduction of the subjects on which I had once quizzed Clay Walter, Deepak Mehta and Sedgewick Bell, nearly half a century before. It took me only two evenings to gather enough material for the task, although in order not to appear eager I waited several days before sending off another letter to Sedgewick Bell. He called me soon after.

It is indeed a surprise to one who toils for his own keep to see the formidable strokes with which our captains of industry demolish the tasks before them. The morning after talking to Sedgewick Bell I received calls from two of his secretaries, a social assistant and a woman at a New York travel agency, who confirmed the arrangements for late July, two months hence. The event was to take place on an island off the Outer Banks of Carolina that belonged to EastAmerica Steel, and I sent along a list from the St. Benedict's archives so that everyone in Sedgewick Bell's class would be invited.

I was not prepared, however, for the days of retirement that intervened. What little remained of that school year passed speedily in my preoccupation, and before I knew it the boys were taking their final exams. I tried not to think about my future. At the commencement exercises in June, a small section of the ceremony was spent in my honor, but it was presided over by Charles Ellerby and gave rise to a taste of copper in my throat. "And thus we bid adieu," he began, "to our beloved Mr. Hundert." He gazed out over the lectern, extended his arm in my direction, and proceeded to give a nostalgic rendering of my years at the school to the audience of jacketed businessmen, parasoled ladies, students in St. Benedict's blazers and children in church suits, who, like me, were squirming at the meretriciousness of the man.

Yet how quickly it was over! Awards were presented, "Hail Fair Benedict's" was sung, and as the birches began to lean their narrow shadows against the distant edge of the marsh, the seniors came forward to receive their diplomas. The mothers wept, the alumni stood misty-eyed, and the graduates threw their hats into the air. Afterward, everyone dispersed for the headmaster's reception.

I wish now that I had made an appearance there, for to have missed it, the very last one of my career, was a far more grievous blow to me than to Charles Ellerby. Furthermore, the handful of senior boys who over their tenure had been pierced by the bee-sting of history no doubt missed my presence or at least wondered at its lack. I spent the remnants of the afternoon in my house, and the evening walking out along the marsh, where the smell of woodsmoke from a farmer's bonfire and the distant sounds of the gathered celebrants filled me with the great, sad pride of teaching. My boys were passing once again into the world without me.

The next day, of course, parents began arriving to claim their children; jitney buses ferried students to airports and train stations; the groundsman went around pulling up lacrosse goals and baseball bleachers, hauling the long black sprinkler hoses behind his tractor into the fields. I spent most of that day and the next one sitting at the desk in my study, watching through the window as the school wound down like a clockspring toward the strange, bird-filled calm of that second afternoon of my retirement, when all the boys had left and I was alone, once again, in the eerie quiet of summer. I own few things besides my files and books; I packed them, and the next day the groundsman drove me into Woodmere.

There I found lodging in a splendid Victorian rooming house run by a descendant of Nat Turner who joked, when I told her that I was a newly retired teacher, about how the house had always welcomed escaped slaves. I was surprised at how heartily I laughed at this, which had the benefit of putting me instantly on good terms with the landlady. We negotiated a monthly rent, and I went upstairs to set about charting a new life for myself. I was seventy-one years old—yes, perhaps, too old to be headmaster—but I could still walk three miles before dinner and did so the first afternoon of my freedom. However, by evening my spirits had taken a beating.

Fortunately, there was the event to prepare for, as I fear that without it, those first days and nights would have been unbearable. I pored again and again over my old notes, extracting devilish questions from the material. But this only occupied a few hours of the day, and by late morning my eyes would grow weary. Objectively speaking, the start of that summer should have been no different from the start of any other; yet it was. Passing my reflection in the hallway mirror at the head of the stairs on my way down to dinner I would think to myself, *Is that you?* and on the way back up to my room, *What now?* I wrote letters to my brothers and sister, and to several of my former boys. The days crawled by. I introduced myself to the town librarian. I made the acquaintance of a retired railroad man who liked as much as I did to sit on the grand, screened porch of that house. I took the bus into Washington a few times to spend the day in museums.

But as the summer progressed, a certain dread began to form in my mind, which I tried through the diligence of walking, museum-going and reading, to ignore; that is, I began to fear that Sedgewick Bell had forgotten about the event. The thought would occur to me in the midst of the long path along the outskirts of town; and as I reached the Passamic, took my break and then started back again toward home, I would battle with my urge to contact the man. Several times I went to the telephone downstairs in the rooming house and twice I wrote out letters that I did not send. *Why would he go through all the trouble just to mock me?* I thought; but then I would recall the circumstances of his tenure at St. Benedict's and a darker gloom would descend upon me. I began to have second thoughts about events that had occurred half a century before: Should I have confronted him in the midst of the original contest? Should I never even have leapfrogged another boy to get him there? Should I have spoken up to the senator?

In early July, however, Sedgewick Bell's secretary finally did call, and I felt that I had been given a reprieve. She apologized for her tardiness, asked me more questions about my taste in food and lodging, and then informed me of the date, three weeks later, when a car would call to take me to the airport in Williamsburg. An EastAmerica jet would fly me from there to Charlotte, from whence I was to be picked up by helicopter.

Helicopter! Less than a month later I stood before the craft, which was painted head to tail in EastAmerica's green and gold insignia, polished to a shine, with a six-man passenger bay and red-white-and-blue sponsons over the wheels. One does not remain at St. Benedict's for five decades without gaining a certain familiarity with privilege, yet as it lifted me off the pad in Charlotte, hovered for a moment, then lowered its nose and turned eastward over the gentle hills and then the chopping slate of the sea channel, I felt a headiness that I had never known before; it was what Augustus Caesar must have felt millennia ago, carried head-high on a litter past the Tiber. I clutched my notes to my chest. Indeed I wondered what my life might have been like if I had felt this just once in my youth. The rotors buzzed like a beehive. On the island I was shown to a suite of rooms in a high corner of the lodge, with windows and balconies overlooking the sea.

For a conference on the future of childhood education or the plight of America's elderly, of course, you could not get one-tenth of these men to attend, but for a privileged romp on a private island it had merely been a matter of making the arrangements. I stood at the window of my room and watched the helicopter ferry back and forth across the channel, disgorging on the island a *Who's Who* of America's largest corporations, universities and organs of policy.

Oh, but what it was to see the boys! After a time, I made my way back out to the airstrip, and whenever the craft touched down on the landing platform and one or another of my old students ducked out, clutching his suit lapel as he ran clear of the snapping rotors, I was struck anew with how great a privilege my profession had been.

That evening all of us ate together in the lodge, and the boys toasted me and took turns coming to my table, where several times one or another of them had to remind me to continue eating my food. Sedgewick Bell ambled over and with a charming air of modesty showed me the flashcards of Roman history that he'd been keeping in his desk at EastAmerica. Then, shedding his modesty, he went to the podium and produced a long and raucous toast referring to any number of pranks and misdeeds at St. Benedict's that I had never even heard of but that the chorus of boys greeted with stamps and whistles. At a quarter to nine, they all dropped their forks onto the floor, and I fear that tears came to my eyes.

The most poignant part of all, however, was how plainly the faces of the men still showed the eager expressiveness of the first-form boys of forty years ago. Martin Blythe had lost half his leg as an officer in Korea, and now, among his classmates, he tried to hide his lurching stride, but he wore the same knitted brow that he used to wear in my classroom; Deepak Mehta, who had become a professor of Asian history, walked with a slight stoop, yet he still turned his eyes downward when spoken to; Clay Walter seemed to have fared physically better than his mates, bouncing about in the Italian suit and alligator shoes of the advertising industry, yet he was still drawn immediately to the other do-nothings from his class.

But of course it was Sedgewick Bell who commanded everyone's attention. He had grown stout across the middle and bald over the crown of his head, and I saw in his ear, although it was artfully concealed, the flesh-colored bulb of a hearing aid; yet he walked among the men like a prophet. Their faces grew animated when he approached, and at the tables I could see them competing for his attention. He patted one on the back, whispered in the ear of another, gripped hands and grasped shoulders and kissed the wives on the lips. His walk was firm and imbued not with the seriousness of his post, it seemed to me, but with the ease of it, so that his stride among the tables was jocular. He was the host and clearly in his element. His laugh was voluble.

I went to sleep early that evening so that the boys could enjoy themselves downstairs in the saloon, and as I lay in bed I listened to their songs and revelry. It had not escaped my attention, of course, that they no doubt spent some time mocking me, but this is what one grows to expect in my post, and indeed it was part of the reason I left them alone. Although I was tempted to walk down and listen from outside the theater, I did not.

The next day was spent walking the island's serpentine spread of coves and beaches, playing tennis on the grass court, and paddling in wooden boats on the small inland lake behind the lodge. How quickly one grows accustomed to luxury! Men and women lounged on the decks and beaches and patios, sunning like seals, gorging themselves on the largess of their host.

As for me, I barely had a moment to myself, for the boys took turns at my entertainment. I walked with Deepak Mehta along the beach and succeeded in getting him to tell me the tale of his rise through academia to a post at Columbia University. Evidently his rise had taken a toll, for although he looked healthy enough to me he told me that he had recently had a small heart attack. It was not the type of thing one talked about with a student, however, so I let this revelation pass without comment. Later, Clay Walter brought me onto the tennis court and tried to teach me to hit a ball, an activity that drew a crowd of boisterous guests to the stands. They roared at Clay's theatrical antics and cheered and stomped their feet whenever I sent one back across the net. In the afternoon, Martin Blythe took me out in a rowboat.

St. Benedict's, of course, has always had a more profound effect than most schools on the lives of its students, yet nonetheless it was strange that once in the center of the pond, where he had rowed us with his lurching stroke, Martin Blythe set down the oars in their locks and told me he had something he'd always meant to ask me.

"Yes," I said.

He brushed back his hair with his hand. "*I* was supposed to be the one up there with Deepak and Clay, wasn't I, sir?"

"Don't tell me you're still thinking about that."

"It's just that I've sometimes wondered what happened."

"Yes, you should have been," I said.

Oh, how little we understand of men if we think that their childhood slights are forgotten! He smiled. He did not press the subject further, and while I myself debated the merits of explaining why I had passed him over for Sedgewick Bell four decades before, he pivoted the boat around and brought us back to shore. The confirmation of his suspicions was enough to satisfy him, it seemed, so I said nothing more. He had been an Air Force major in our country's endeavors on the Korean peninsula, yet as he pulled the boat onto the beach I had the clear feeling of having saved him from some torment.

Indeed, that evening when the guests had gathered in the lodge's small theater, and Deepak Mehta, Clay Walter and Sedgewick Bell had taken their seats for the reenactment of Mister Julius Caesar, I noticed an ease in Martin Blythe's face that I believe I had never seen in it before. His brow was not knit, and he had crossed his legs so that above one sock we could clearly see the painted wooden calf.

It was then that I noticed that the boys who had paid the most attention to me that day were in fact the ones sitting before me on the stage. How dreadful a thought this was—that they had indulged me to gain advantage—but I put it from my mind and stepped to the microphone. I had spent the late afternoon reviewing my notes, and the first rounds of questions were called from memory.

The crowd did not fail to notice the feat. There were whistles and stomps when I named fifteen of the first sixteen emperors in order and asked Clay Walter to produce the one I had left out. There was applause when I spoke Caesar's words, *"Il iacta alea esto,"* and then, continuing in carefully pronounced Latin, asked Sedgewick Bell to recall the circumstances of their utterance. He had told me that afternoon of the months he had spent preparing, and as I was asking the question, he smiled. The boys had not worn togas, of course—although I personally feel they might have—yet the situation was familiar enough that I felt a rush of unease as Sedgewick Bell's smile then waned and he hesitated several moments before answering. But this time, all these years later, he looked straight out into the audience and spoke his answers with the air of a scholar.

It was not long before Clay Walter had dropped out, of course, but then, as it had before, the contest proceeded neck-and-neck between Sedgewick Bell and Deepak Mehta. I asked Sedgewick Bell about Caesar's battles at Pharsalus and Thapsus, about the shift of power to Constantinople and about the war between the patricians and the plebeians; I asked Deepak Mehta about the Punic Wars, the conquest of Italy and the fall of the republic. Deepak, of course, had an advantage, for certainly he had studied this material at university, but I must say that the straightforward determination of Sedgewick Bell had begun to win my heart. I recalled the bashful manner in which he had shown me his flashcards at dinner the night before, and as I stood now before the microphone I seemed to be in the throes of an affection for him that had long been underwraps.

"What year were the Romans routed at Lake Trasimene?" I asked him.

He paused. "217 B.C., I believe."

"Which general later became Scipio Africanus Major?"

"Publius Cornelius Scipio, sir," Deepak Mehta answered softly.

It does not happen as often as one might think that an unintelligent boy becomes an intelligent man, for in my own experience the love of thought is rooted in an age long before adolescence; yet Sedgewick Bell now seemed to have done just that. His answers were spoken with the composed demeanor of a scholar. There is no one I like more, of course, than the man who is moved by the mere fact of history, and as I contemplated the next question to him I wondered if I had indeed exaggerated the indolence of his boyhood. Was it true, perhaps, that he had simply not come into his element yet while at St. Benedict's? He peered intently at me from the stage, his elbows on his knees. I decided to ask him a difficult question. "Chairman Bell," I said, "which tribes invaded Rome in 102 B.C.?"

His eyes went blank and he curled his shoulders in his suit. Although he was by then one of the most powerful men in America, and although moments before that I had been rejoicing in his discipline, suddenly I saw him on that stage once again as a frightened boy. How powerful is memory! And once again, I feared that it was I who had betrayed him. He brought his hand to his head to think.

"Take your time, sir," I offered.

There were murmurs in the audience. He distractedly touched the side of his head. A man's character is his fate, says Heraclitus, and at that moment, as he brushed his hand down over his temple, I realized that the flesh-colored device in his ear was not a hearing aid but a transmitter through which he was receiving the answers to my questions. Nausea rose in me. Of course I had no proof, but was it not exactly what I should have expected? He touched his head once again and appeared to be deep in thought, and I knew it as certainly as if he had shown me. "The Teutons," he said, haltingly, "and—I'll take a stab here—the Cimbri?"

I looked for a long time at him. Did he know at that point what I was thinking? I cannot say, but after I had paused as long as I could bear to in front of that crowd, I cleared my throat and granted that he was right. Applause erupted. He shook it off with a wave of his hand. I knew that it was my duty to speak up. I knew it was my duty as a teacher to bring him clear of the moral dereliction in which I myself had been his partner, yet at the same time I felt myself adrift in the tide of my own vacillation and failure. The boy had somehow got hold of me again. He tried to quiet the applause with a wave of his hand, but this gesture only caused the clapping to increase, and I am afraid to say that it was merely the sound of a throng of boisterous men that finally prevented me from making my stand. Quite suddenly I was aware that this was not the situation I had known at St. Benedict's School. We were guests now of a significant man on his splendid estate, and to expose him would be a serious act indeed. I turned and quieted the crowd.

From the chair next to Sedgewick Bell, Deepak Mehta merely looked at me, his eyes dark and resigned. Perhaps he too had just realized, or perhaps in fact he had long known, but in any case I simply asked him the next question; after he answered it, I could do nothing but put another before Sedgewick Bell. Then Deepak again, then Sedgewick, and again to Deepak, and it was only then, on the third round after I had discovered the ploy, that an idea came to me. When I returned to Sedgewick Bell I asked him, "Who was Shutruk-Nahhunte?"

A few boys in the crowd began to laugh, and when Sedgewick Bell took his time thinking about the answer, more in the audience joined in. Whoever was the mercenary professor talking in his ear, it was clear to me that he would not know the answer to this one, for if he had not gone to St. Benedict's School he would never have heard of Shutruk-Nahhunte; and in a few moments, sure enough, I saw Sedgewick Bell begin to grow uncomfortable. He lifted his pant leg and scratched at his sock. The laughter increased, and then I heard the wives, who had obviously never lived in a predatory pack, trying to stifle their husbands.

"Come on, Bell!" someone shouted, "Look at the damn door!" Laughter erupted again.

How can it be that for a moment my heart bled for him? He, too, tried to laugh, but only halfheartedly. He shifted in his seat, shook his arms loose in his suit, looked uncomprehendingly out at the snickering crowd, then braced his chin and said, "Well, I guess if Deepak knows the answer to this one, then it's *his* ball game."

Deepak's response was nearly lost in the boisterous stamps and whistles that followed, for I am sure that every boy but Sedgewick recalled Henry Stimson's tablet above the door of my classroom. Yet what was strange was that I felt disappointment. As Deepak Mehta smiled, spoke the answer, and stood from his chair, I watched confusion and then a flicker of panic cross the face of Sedgewick Bell. He stood haltingly. How clear it was to me then that the corruption in his character had always arisen from fear, and I could not help remembering that as his teacher I had once tried to convince him of his stupidity. I cursed that day. But then in a moment he summoned a smile, called me up to the stage, and crossed theatrically to congratulate the victor.

How can I describe the scene that took place next? I suppose I was naïve to think that this was the end of the evening—or even the point of it—for after Sedgewick Bell had brought forth a trophy for Deepak Mehta, and then one for me as well, an entirely different cast came across his features. He strode once again to the podium and asked for the attention of the guests. He tapped sharply on the microphone. Then he leaned his head forward, and in a voice that I recognized from long ago on the radio, a voice in whose deft leaps from boom to whisper I heard the willow-tree drawl of his father, he launched into an address about the problems of our country. He had the orator's gift of dropping his volume at the moment when a less gifted man would have raised it. *We have opened our doors to all the world*, he said, his voice thundering, then pausing, then plunging nearly to a murmur, *and now the world has stripped us bare*. He gestured with his hands. The men in the audience, first laughing, now turned serious. *We have given away too much for too long*, he said. *We have handed our fiscal leadership to men who don't care about the taxpayers of our country, and our moral course to those who no longer understand our role in history.* Although he gestured to me there, I could not return his gaze. *We have abandoned the moral education of our families.* Scattered applause drifted up from his classmates, and here, of course, I almost spoke. *We have left our country adrift on dangerous seas.* Now the applause was more hearty. Then he quieted his voice again, dropped his head as though in supplication and announced that he was running for the United States Senate.

Why was I surprised? I should not have been, for since childhood the boy had stood so near to the mantle of power that its shadow must have been as familiar to him as his boyhood home. Virtue had no place in the palaces he had known. I was ashamed when I realized he had contrived the entire rematch of Mister Julius Caesar for no reason other than to gather his classmates for donations, yet still I chastened myself for not realizing his ambition before. In his oratory, in his physical presence, in his conviction, he had always possessed the gifts of a leader, and now he was using them. I should have expected this from the first day he stood in his short-pants suit in the doorway of my classroom and silenced my students. He already wielded a potent role in the affairs of our country; he enjoyed the presumption of his family name; he was blindly ignorant of history and therefore did not fear his role in it. Of course it was exactly the culmination I should long ago have seen. The crowd stood cheering.

As soon as the clapping abated a curtain was lifted behind him, and a band struck up "Dixie." Waiters appeared at the side doors, a dance platform was unfolded in the orchestra pit, and Sedgewick Bell jumped down from the stage into the crowd of his friends. They clamored around him. He patted shoulders, kissed wives, whispered and laughed and nodded his head. I saw checkbooks come out. The waiters carried champagne on trays at their shoulders, and at the edge of the dance floor the women set down their purses and stepped into the arms of their husbands. When I saw this I ducked out a side door and returned to the lodge, for the abandon with which the guests were dancing was an unbearable counterpart to the truth I knew. One can imagine my feelings. I heard the din late into the night.

Needless to say, I resolved to avoid Sedgewick Bell for the remainder of my stay. How my mind raced that night through humanity's endless history of injustice, depravity and betrayal! I could not sleep, and several times I rose and went to the window to listen to the revelry. Standing at the glass I felt like the spurned sovereign in the castle tower, looking down from his balcony onto the procession of the false potentate.

Yet, sure enough, my conviction soon began to wane. No sooner had I resolved to avoid my host than I began to doubt the veracity of my secret knowledge about him. Other thoughts came to me. How, in fact, had I been so sure of what he'd done? What proof had I at all? Amid the distant celebrations of the night, my conclusion began to seem far-fetched, and by the quiet of the morning I was muddled. I did not go to breakfast. As boy after boy stopped by my rooms to wish me well, I assiduously avoided commenting on either Sedgewick Bell's performance or on his announcement for the Senate. On the beach that day I endeavored to walk by myself, for by then I trusted neither my judgment of the incident nor my discretion with the boys. I spent the afternoon alone in a cove across the island.

I did not speak to Sedgewick Bell that entire day. I managed to avoid him, in fact, until the next evening, by which time all but a few of the guests had left, when he came to bid farewell as I stood on the tarmac awaiting the helicopter for the mainland. He walked out and motioned for me to stand back from the platform, but I pretended not to hear him and kept my eyes up to the sky. Suddenly, the shining craft swooped in from beyond the wave break, churning the channel into a boil, pulled up in a hover and then touched down on its flag-colored sponsons before us. The wind and noise could have thrown a man to the ground, and Sedgewick Bell seemed to pull at me like a magnet, but I did not retreat. It was he, finally, who ran out to me. He gripped his lapels, ducked his head and offered me his hand. I took it tentatively, the rotors whipping our jacket-sleeves. I had been expecting this moment and had decided the night before what I was going to say. I leaned toward him. "How long have you been hard of hearing?" I asked.

His smile dropped. I cannot imagine what I had become in the mind of that boy. "Very good, Hundert," he said. "Very good. I thought you might have known."

My vindication was sweet, although now I see that it meant little. By then I was on the ladder of the helicopter, but he pulled me toward him again and looked darkly into my eyes. "And I see that *you* have not changed either," he said.

Well, had I? As the craft lifted off and turned westward toward the bank of clouds that hid the distant shoreline, I analyzed the situation with some care. The wooden turrets of the lodge grew smaller and then were lost in the trees, and I found it easier to think then, for everything on that island had been imbued with the sheer power of the man. I relaxed a bit in my seat. One could say that in this case I indeed had acted properly, for is it not the glory of our legal system that acquitting a guilty man is less heinous than convicting an innocent one? At the time of the contest, I certainly had no proof of Sedgewick Bell's behavior.

Yet back in Woodmere, as I have intimated, I found myself with a great deal of time on my hands, and it was not long before the incident began to replay itself in my mind. Following the wooded trail toward the river or sitting in the breeze at dusk on the porch, I began to see that a different ending would have better served us all. Conviction had failed me again. I was well aware of the foolish consolation of my thoughts, yet I vividly imagined what I should have done. I heard myself speaking up; I saw my resolute steps to his chair on the stage, then the insidious, flesh-colored device in my palm, held up to the crowd; I heard him stammering.

As if to mock my inaction, however, stories of his electoral effort soon began to appear in the papers. It was a year of spite and rancor in our country's politics, and the race in West Virginia was less a campaign than a brawl between gladiators. The incumbent was as versed in treachery as Sedgewick Bell, and over my morning tea I followed their battles. Sedgewick Bell called him "a liar when he speaks and a crook when he acts," and he called Sedgewick Bell worse. A fistfight erupted when their campaigns crossed at an airport.

I was revolted by the spectacle, but of course I was also intrigued, and I cannot deny that although I was rooting for the incumbent, a part of me was also cheered at each bit of news chronicling Sedgewick Bell's assault on his lead. Oh, why was this so? Are we all, at base, creatures without virtue? Is fervor the only thing we follow?

Needless to say, that fall had been a difficult one in my life, especially those afternoons when the St. Benedict's bus roared by the guesthouse in Woodmere taking the boys to track meets, and perhaps the Senate race was nothing more than a healthy distraction for me. Indeed I needed distractions. To witness the turning of the leaves and to smell the apples in their barrels without hearing the sound of a hundred boys in the fields, after all, was almost more than I could bear. My walks had grown longer, and several times I had crossed the river and ventured to the far end of the marsh, from where in the distance I could make out the blurred figures of St. Benedict's. I knew this was not good for me, and perhaps that is why, in late October of that year when I read that Sedgewick Bell would be making a campaign stop at a coal-miners' union hall near the Virginia border, I decided to go hear him speak.

Perhaps by then the boy had become an obsession for me—I will admit this, for I am as aware as anyone that time is but the thinnest bandage for our wounds—but on the other hand, the race had grown quite close and would have been of natural interest to anyone. Sedgewick Bell had drawn himself up from an underdog to a challenger. Now it was clear that the election hinged on the votes of labor, and Sedgewick Bell, though he was the son of aristocrats and the chairman of a formidable corporation, began to cast himself as a champion of the working man. From newspaper reports I gleaned that he was helped along by the power of his voice and bearing, and I could easily imagine these men turning to him. I well knew the charisma of the boy.

The day arrived, and I packed a lunch and made the trip. As the bus wound west along the river valley, I envisioned the scene ahead and wondered whether Sedgewick Bell would at this point care to see me. Certainly I represented some sort of truth to him about himself, yet at the same time I also seemed to have become a part of the very delusion that he had foisted on those around him. How far my boys would always stride upon the world's stage, yet how dearly I would always hope to change them! The bus arrived early, and I went inside the union hall to wait.

Shortly before noon the miners began to come in. I don't know what I had expected, but I was surprised to see them looking as though they had indeed just come out of the mines. They wore hard hats, their faces were stained with dust, and their gloves and tool belts hung at their waists. For some reason I had worn my St. Benedict's blazer, which I now removed. Reporters began to filter in as well, and by the time the noon whistle blew, the crowd was overflowing from the hall.

As the whistle subsided I heard the *thump-thump* of his helicopter, and through the door in a moment I saw the twisters of dust as it hovered into view from above. How clever was the man I had known as a boy! The craft had been repainted the colors of military camouflage but he had left the sponsons the red-white-and-blue of their previous incarnation. He jumped from the side door when the craft was still a foot above the ground, entered the hall at a jog and was greeted with an explosion of applause. His aides lined the stairs to the high platform on which the microphone stood under a banner and a flag, and as he crossed the crowd toward them the miners jostled to be near him, knocking their knuckles against his hard hat, reaching for his hands and his shoulders, cheering like Romans at a chariot race.

I do not need to report on his eloquence, for I have dwelled enough upon it. When he reached the staircase and ascended to the podium, stopping first at the landing to wave and then at the top to salute the flag above him, jubilation swept among the throng. I knew then that he had succeeded in his efforts, that these miners counted him somehow as their own, so that when he actually spoke and they interrupted him with cheers it was no more unexpected than the promises he made then to carry their interests with him to the Senate. He was masterful. I found my own arm upraised.

Certainly there were five hundred men in that hall, but there was only one with a St. Benedict's blazer over his shoulder and no hard hat on his head, so of course I should not have been surprised when within a few minutes one of his aides appeared beside me and told me that the candidate had asked for me at the podium. At that moment I saw Sedgewick Bell's glance pause for a moment on my face. There was a flicker of a smile on his lips, but then he looked away.

Is there no battle other than the personal one? Was Sedgewick Bell at that point willing to risk the future of his political ideas for whatever childhood demon I still remained to him? The next time he turned toward me, he gestured down at the floor, and in a moment the aide had pulled my arm and was escorting me toward the platform. The crowd opened as we passed, and the miners in their ignorance and jubilation were reaching to shake my hand. This was indeed a heady feeling. I climbed the steps and stood beside Sedgewick Bell at the smaller microphone. How it was to stand above the mass of men like that! He raised his hand and they cheered; he lowered it and they fell silent.

"There is a man here today who has been immeasurably important in my life," he whispered into his microphone.

There was applause, and a few of the men whistled. "Thank you," I said into my own. I could see the blue underbrims of five hundred hard hats turned up toward me. My heart was nearly bursting.

"My history teacher," he said, as the crowd began to cheer again. Flashbulbs popped and I moved instinctively toward the front of the platform. "Mr. Hundert," he boomed, "from forty-five years ago at Richmond Central High School."

It took me a moment to realize what he had said. By then he too was clapping and at the same time lowering his head in what must have appeared to the men below to be respect for me. The blood engorged my veins. "Just a minute," I said, stepping back to my own microphone. "I taught you at St. Benedict's School in Tallywood, Virginia. Here is the blazer."

Of course, it makes no difference in the course of history that as I tried to hold up the coat, Sedgewick Bell moved swiftly across the podium, took it from my grip and raised my arm high in his own and that this pose, of all things, sent the miners into jubilation; it makes no difference that by the time I spoke, he had gestured with this hand so that one of his aides had already shut off my microphone. For one does not alter history without conviction. It is enough to know that I *did* speak, and certainly a consolation that Sedgewick Bell realized, finally, that I would.

He won that election not in small part because he managed to convince those miners that he was one of them. They were ignorant people, and I cannot blame them for taking to the shrewdly populist rhetoric of the man. I saved the picture that appeared the following morning in the *Gazette*: Senator Bell radiating all the populist magnetism of his father, holding high the arm of an old man who has on his face the remnants of a proud and foolish smile.

I still live in Woodmere, and I have found a route that I take now and then to the single high hill from which I can see the St. Benedict's steeple across the Passamic. I take two walks every day and have grown used to this life. I have even come to like it. I am reading of the ancient Japanese civilizations now, which I had somehow neglected before, and every so often one of my boys visits me.

One afternoon recently, Deepak Mehta did so, and we shared some brandy. This was in the fall of last year. He was still the quiet boy he had always been, and not long after he had taken a seat on my couch I had to turn on the television to ease for him the burden of conversation. As it happened, the Senate Judiciary Committee was holding its famous hearings then, and the two of us sat there watching, nodding our heads or chuckling whenever the camera showed Sedgewick Bell sitting alongside the chairman. I had poured the brandy liberally, and whenever Sedgewick Bell leaned into the microphone and asked a question of the witness, Deepak would mimic his affected southern drawl. Naturally, I could not exactly encourage this behavior, but I did nothing to stop it. When he finished his drink I poured him another. This, of course, is perhaps the greatest pleasure of a teacher's life, to have a drink one day with a man he has known as a boy.

Nonetheless, I only wish we could have talked more than we actually did. But I am afraid that there must always be a reticence between a teacher and his student. Deepak had had another small heart attack, he told me, but I felt it would have been improper of me to inquire more. I tried to bring myself to broach the subject of Sedgewick Bell's history, but here again I was aware that a teacher does not discuss one boy with another. Certainly Deepak must have known about Sedgewick

Bell as well, but probably out of his own set of St. Benedict's morals he did not bring it up with me. We watched Sedgewick Bell question the witness and then whisper into the ear of the chairman. Neither of us was surprised at his ascendance, I believe, because both of us were students of history. Yet we did not discuss this either. Still, I wanted desperately for him to ask me something more, and perhaps this was why I kept refilling his glass. I wanted him to ask, "How is it to be alone, sir, at this age," or perhaps to say, "You have made a difference in my life, Mr. Hundert." But of course these were not things Deepak Mehta would ever say. A man's character is his character. Nonetheless it was startling, every now and then when I looked over at the sunlight falling across his bowed head, to see that Deepak Mehta, the quietest of my boys, was now an old man.

Issue 128, 1993

Contributors

✣

Agha Shahid Ali (1949–2001) wrote several volumes of poetry, including *The Country Without a Post Office* and *Rooms Are Never Finished*.

A. R. Ammons (1926–2001) received the National Book Award in 1973 for *Collected Poems* and in 1993 for *Garbage*.

J. G. Ballard is the author of several novels and story collections, including *Empire of the Sun*. His most recent book is *The Day of Creation: A Novel*.

T. Coraghessan Boyle is the author of several novels and story collections, including *Greasy Lake*. His most recent book is *Drop City*.

William S. Burroughs (1914–1997) wrote many novels, including *Junkie* and *Naked Lunch*.

Ethan Canin is the author of several novels and story volumes, including *The Palace Thief*. His most recent book is *Carry Me Across the Water*.

Jim Carroll is the author of several volumes of poetry, as well as a memoir, *The Basketball Diaries*. His most recent book is *Void of Course: Poems 1994–97*.

Raymond Carver (1938–1988) wrote many volumes of poetry and stories, including *Will You Please Be Quiet, Please?* and *Where I'm Calling From*.

Billy Collins, a former U.S. Poet Laureate, is the author of several volumes of poetry, including *Picnic, Lightning*. His most recent book is *Nine Horses: Poems*.

Charles D'Ambrosio is the author of *The Point,* a collection of stories.

Lydia Davis is the author of several novels and story collections, including *Break It Down*. Her most recent book is *Samuel Johnson Is Indignant: Stories*.

Junot Díaz is the author of *Drown,* a collection of stories.

Stuart Dybek is the author of several volumes of poetry and stories, including *The Coast of Chicago*. His most recent book is *I Sailed with Magellan*.

Albert Goldbarth received the National Book Critics Circle Award in 2002 for *Saving Lives: Poems*. His most recent book is *Pieces of Payne*.

Lucy Grealy (1963–2002) wrote several books, including a memoir, *Autobiography of a Face*.

Paul Hoover, coeditor of *New American Writing*, is the author of a novel and several volumes of poetry, including *Somebody Talks a Lot*. His most recent book is *Winter (Mirror)*.

Karl Iagnemma received The Paris Review Discovery Prize in 2002 for "On the Nature of Human Romantic Interaction," the title piece from his debut collection of stories.

Denis Johnson is the author of several novels and story collections, including *Jesus' Son*. His most recent work is *Shoppers: Two Plays*.

Edward P. Jones is the author of *Lost in the City*, a story collection. His most recent book is the novel *The Known World*.

X. J. Kennedy, a former poetry editor of *The Paris Review*, is the author of many volumes of poetry, including *Nude Descending a Staircase*. His most recent work is *Talking Like the Rain: A Read-to-Me Book of Poems*.

Suji Kwock Kim is the author of *Notes from the Divided Country*, a collection of poems.

Jamaica Kincaid is the author of several novels and essay collections, including *Annie John*. Her most recent book is *Mr. Potter*.

Philip Larkin (1922–1985) wrote several collections of poetry, including *The North Ship* and *High Windows*.

James Lasdun received the Sundance Film Festival's best dramatic feature and best screenplay awards in 1997 for *Sunday*. His most recent book is *Walking and Eating in Tuscany and Umbria*.

Yiyun Li received the Plimpton Prize for New Writers in 2003 for "Immortality."

William Maxwell (1908–2000), a former editor at *The New Yorker*, received the National Book Critics Circle Award in 1995 for his collected stories, *All the Days and Nights*.

Heather McHugh has written several volumes of poetry and essays, including *Broken English: Poetry and Partiality*. Her most recent book is *Eyeshot*.

Rick Moody is the author of several novels and story collections, including *The Ice Storm*. His most recent book is *The Black Veil: A Memoir with Digressions*.

Alice Munro received the National Book Critics Circle Award in 1998 for *The Love of a Good Woman*. Her most recent book is *Hateship, Friendship, Courtship, Loveship, Marriage: Stories*.

V. S. Naipaul received the Nobel Prize for Literature in 2001 for such novels as *A House for Mr Biswas* and *A Bend in the River*. His most recent book is *Literary Occasions*.

Joyce Carol Oates received the National Book Award in 1970 for *them*. Her most recent book is *Rape: A Love Story*.

Sharon Olds received the National Book Award in 2002 for *The Unswept Room*. Her other poetry collections include *The Dead and the Living*.

Carl Phillips is the author of several volumes of poetry, including *From the Devotions*. His most recent book is *Coin of the Realm: Essays on the Art and Life of Poetry*.

Robert Pinsky, a former U.S. Poet Laureate, is the author of many volumes of poetry and essays, including *The Figured Wheel*. His most recent book is *Jersey Rain*.

V. P'yetsukh is the author of several story collections, including *Me and So On*. **Mark Halperin** is the author of several books of poems, including *Time as Distance*. **Dinara Georgeoliani** is an assistant professor of Russian at Central Washington University.

Richard Powers is the author of several novels, including *Galatea 2.2*. His most recent book is *The Time of Our Singing*.

Lawrence Raab is the author of several volumes of poetry, including *What We Don't Know About Each Other*. His most recent book is *Visible Signs: New and Selected Poems*.

Philip Roth received the Pulitzer Prize in 1997 for *American Pastoral*. His most recent book is *The Dying Animal*.

Ira Sadoff is the author of *Uncoupling*, a novel, and several volumes of poetry. His most recent work is *Barter: Poems*.

Helen Schulman is the author of several novels and story collections, including *The Revisionist*. Her most recent work is *P.S.: A Novel*.

Vijay Seshadri received the Bernard F. Conners Award for Poetry in 1995 for "Lifeline." His most recent book is *The Long Meadow*.

Ben Sonnenberg, founder and former publisher of *Grand Street*, is the author of *Lost Property: Memoirs and Confessions of a Bad Boy*.

Patricia Storace, a former poetry editor of *The Paris Review*, is the author of *Heredity*, a book of poems. Her most recent book is *Sugar Cane: A Caribbean Rapunzel*.

Deborah Warren is the author of *The Size of Happiness*, a book of poems.

Richard Wilbur, a former U.S. Poet Laureate, received the Pulitzer Prize in 1957 for *Things of This World* and in 1989 for *New and Collected Poems*. His most recent book is a translation of Moliere's *Tartuffe*.

C. K. Williams received the Pulitzer Prize in 2000 for *Repair*, a volume of poetry. His most recent book is *The Singing: Poems*.

Joy Williams is the author of several novels and story collections, including *The Quick and the Dead*. Her most recent book is *Ill Nature*, a volume of essays.

Acknowledgments

✵

✠

Join Us for the Next Fifty Years:
SUBSCRIBE to *The Paris Review*